SEARCH FOR SANSARI

RED REALMS BOOK 2

WARWICK EDEN

Copyright © 2022 Warwick Eden

The right of Warwick Eden to be identified as the author of this work has been asserted in accordance with the Copyright, Designs and Patents Act 1998.

All rights reserved. No part of this publication may be reproduced or used in any manner without the prior written permission of the copyright owner, except for the use of brief quotations in a book review.

This book is a work of fiction. Any resemblance to actual persons, living or dead, or actual events is purely coincidental.

ISBN: 9798847378635

Cover artwork by www.daniellefine.com

www.warwickeden.com

For Ian,
The alpha of all betas ;)

Warwick Eden is an ex-engineer with a weakness for cheese and wine, nineties music, and a slightly unhealthy obsession with trains.

Currently working in the IT industry and understandably frustrated by current AI capabilities of the *real* world, Warwick finds writing novels the only means of bringing to life these ambitions and ideas.

The author currently lives in London with partner, Jessie, and daughter, Lily.

PROLOGUE

213 YEARS AGO

RED PALACE, AGERON

*T*he convoluted corridors of the ancient quarters were Draeger's favourite haunt, out of all the places the sprawling Red Palace had to offer a boy. A labyrinth of passageways beneath the foundations of the palace, they branched and spread out like a vast network of arteries, past the palace grounds, tunnelling under neighbouring villages and reaching deep into the bowels of the Red Mountain itself. With low ceilings and dark panelled walls, every corridor looked very much like the next one: lined with endless doors —some nondescript, others ornate—and almost always locked shut. Devoid of windows, these passageways gave no indication as to where he was in relation to the palace grounds above.

Draeger wound the string of wool around his hand as he skipped forward, his footsteps muffled by the richly carpeted floor. In his other hand, he held a toy—a figure of an Ageronian soldier complete with red cloak and sword—a recent gift from Father. The claustrophobic tangle of passageways didn't bother him, and his eyes adapted easily to the

RED PALACE, AGERON

scant light offered by the wall sconces, enabling him to view his surroundings as if it were bright as day. It was only in the dark that Draeger felt truly at ease, where his strange basilisk eyes served him best and he didn't feel his unusual looks as keenly noticed by others.

Draeger pulled the string taut, winding it faster and faster round his hand. He knew his way out from memory of course, but this was his way of checking, for there would be no way out if he made a mistake. The ancient quarters were so vast and unmapped that even the servants dared not venture this far in lest they got lost themselves. There would be no one to call out to for help if he got lost here.

Finally, he emerged from the tunnels and out onto the courtyard, squinting in the golden sunlight. He tore gleefully through the palace gardens, the twin suns warm on his back and the soft breeze cool on his cheeks. From the gardens Draeger ran on, waving his toy soldier this way and that, through the plant-lined walkways shaded by vines and laden with fruit, until at long last he reached the royal quarters. Here, amidst the tall pines and silver palms that towered over its formal planting, he slowed down, remembering being told off for making too much noise the last time and disturbing Father's consorts.

The royal quarters were a series of self-contained apartments arranged along a terrace that ran on all four sides of a rectangular courtyard filled with formal planting. A majestic pergola overrun with climbing jasmine covered the terrace surrounding it and overlooking this terrace were the royal apartments with their elegant tiled roofs and pillars of marble. These residences and the lush, densely planted courtyard were reserved solely for the Emperor's consorts.

Draeger strolled along the terrace, enjoying the cool of the stone slabs beneath his bare feet, and stopped to listen to the

PROLOGUE

musical warble of birds in the trees. A warm breeze carried the faint scent of jasmine in the air, along with the soft voices of women speaking. He presumed the voices to be one of Father's wives and perhaps her handmaid.

"Please, don't...," a woman pleaded.

Draeger turned towards her voice. It came from behind the door of Lady Cassia. It was ajar, no more than a finger's breadth, and a baby's cry drifted out.

Lady Cassia's newborn...

Draeger stepped back, ready to retrace his steps. Only last week, they had rebuked him for disturbing the then heavily pregnant Lady Cassia. And now prince Titus, born only a few days ago, had arrived. Draeger knew Father was keen to see him, for Lady Cassia was Father's current favourite and Chancellor Rasmus had mentioned to him that Father would cut short his trip to Vasa to return home if the baby came early.

I wonder if Father's here already? wondered Draeger, and decided to take a peek before stealing away.

He dropped to his knees and crept forward silently, nudging the door open a little more with the top of his head. He peered in cautiously, careful to stay out of sight.

Father was not in the room. Lady Cassia, however, was lying on her bed, pale and no doubt weakened by the strains of the recent birth. Another woman stood over her, holding baby Titus. She had her back towards Draeger, but from her blonde locks and the curve of her pregnant belly, he recognised her as Lady Alin, another of Father's consorts.

"Please, my lady," begged Lady Cassia weakly. Her baby mewled like a helpless kitten in Lady Alin's arms.

"Don't you see Lady Cassia," said Lady Alin as she walked over to the baby's cot, still cradling the child in her arms, "the predicament you've placed yourself in?" She moved a pillow aside and sat at the foot of Lady Cassia's bed. Then she placed the baby on her lap and tucked its swaddle back into place. The baby stopped crying and began to make soft gurgling noises instead. "There," cooed Lady Alin softly as the babe looked into her glacial blue eyes. "I'm not so bad after all, am I?" She stroked the child's face lightly with the tips of her fingers.

Lady Cassia looked at her uncertainly. "Please, Lady Alin," she started again, pleadingly. "We are but sisters in the same household."

"Sisters?" snapped Alin icily. "The audacity to think that! I am the daughter of Aleksander, Emperor of House Ellagrin. A *highborn*, unlike the rest of you whores." She picked up the pillow and examined it with a casual air.

Lady Cassia started crying and shaking. "Please, my lady," she whimpered. "Titus will not stand in line for the throne, no matter what Ageron says. I will make sure of that. You have my word. I *promise* it. Please…"

Lady Alin looked up and studied Lady Cassia's face carefully.

"B… besides," ventured Lady Cassia, "it is not my Titus that will be heir to the throne. It is the sorceress' child you want, is it not?"

Lady Alin glared at her. "Simple minds," she said with disdain. "You have such simple minds, you peasant crud. One must be systematic. Methodical. Ageron's eldest son will get his turn, but now is not the time. Now is the time to clear the rest of the path first."

She lifted the pillow and placed it over the baby's face.

Lady Cassia reached out, shaking uncontrollably, her watery eyes wide with fear. "Nooo, please *no*…," she begged weakly, but her cries rapidly diminished into feeble sobs as she cowered under Lady Alin's stare.

"It will be alright, Lady Cassia." Lady Alin pressed the

PROLOGUE

pillow down hard. The baby squirmed and moved but gave barely a struggle. "I will take care of you, as always." The muffled cries of the infant soon stopped, as did all slight movements from underneath the pillow.

Draeger dropped his toy soldier with a clatter.

In an instant, Lady Alin whirled around. Her eyes bore down on him, freezing him to the spot.

"Come in Draeger," she snapped.

Draeger got to his feet reluctantly. His legs felt like lead.

Lady Alin got up and walked towards the cot to place the limp body of the baby in it, as if nothing was amiss and it was the most natural thing to do. Lady Cassia looked blankly at the bundle. Her eyes were glazed over and her face streaked with tears. She whimpered quietly, like a lost child herself.

Draeger suddenly felt very frightened.

"Come here, child," ordered Lady Alin.

Reluctantly, Draeger entered. The force of Lady Alin's voice seemed to have stripped him of what little remaining free will he possessed.

Lady Alin sat down at Lady Cassia's dressing table and beckoned him nearer. "Let me see you, Draeger," she said pleasantly and bade him stand in front of her. Her cold blue eyes looked at him. They were arctic blue and reminded Draeger of the glaciers of Foss in Ellagrin—alluring but chilling to the bone. He glanced away and looked down at his feet uncertainly.

"Draeger my sweet, did you see anything?" Lady Alin's words tumbled out easily but Draeger could sense she was staring intently at him as she said them.

Draeger shook his head and turned the other way. He avoided looking at the cot. A sickly feeling churned in his stomach.

"You look pale," Lady Alin continued, smiling at him.

RED PALACE, AGERON

"Come, let me cut you some fruit." She picked up the knife beside Lady Cassia's elegant fruit basket and, locking him in between her arms, reached for a bloodfruit and began peeling it.

The jewels in the hilt glinted as her blade slit through the fruit easily, letting its crimson juices drip. Caged in by both her arms, Draeger could feel her pregnant belly brush lightly against his back as she continued to make cuts into the fruit, lacerating its flesh and causing even more deep-red juices to trickle down her hands. Lady Alin leaned over, so her lips were almost brushing his ears. "So, my young lord," she whispered, handing Draeger a piece of bloodfruit, "what do you think we should do next?"

Draeger looked up. He could see Lady Cassia shaking again, her eyes transfixed on him. They were blank with terror.

Lady Alin put the rest of the fruit down on the table and rested her hand on Draeger's shoulder. Sticky with juice, the sickly sweet fragrance of the fruit wafted up his nostrils. In her other hand, she still held the knife. This she lifted slowly, its bejewelled hilt holding Draeger transfixed like a snake charmer's pipe. Gradually, she brought it closer, all the time at level with his neck. Nearer and nearer until it disappeared from the periphery of his vision.

Lady Cassia's eyes widened.

"There you are."

At the sound of the voice behind, Draeger whirled round.

Lady Alin lowered her arms as he turned and ran to his mother, the sorceress Yinha.

"My lady," greeted Lady Alin coldly as she rose from her seat.

The sorceress nodded as she swept into the chamber, her dark robes flowing around her like molten tar. She stopped at the foot of Lady Cassia's bed and looked at her. Her eyes, pitch-black like Draeger's, resembled endless voids as they stared impassively at Lady Cassia and then at the cot.

Lady Alin shifted uneasily.

"Draeger," said the sorceress without looking at her son, "Vasili has been looking for you. You are late for your lesson. Why don't you go find him now?"

Draeger nodded, relieved, and headed for the door.

The sorceress Yinha turned her attention to Lady Cassia again. "My deepest condolences, Lady Cassia," she said quietly and shifted her gaze towards Lady Alin.

The two women faced each other squarely: one closed and composed, the other defiant and dangerous.

"What shall we do next indeed," murmured sorceress Yinha. Her voice was deceptively soft, but before Lady Alin could reply, she continued, this time with a steely edge to it. "I will tell you what will happen next, my dear Lady Alin." From within the folds of her robe, she produced a gold bracelet with the engravings of love symbols.

Lady Alin give a little gasp and tried to snatch it from Lady Yinha but as soon as her hand neared, the bracelet swirled into oblivion beneath the sorceress' robe, leaving her hand to grasp at empty air.

"Yes," the sorceress told her with icy curtesy, "from now on, you will not so much as *touch* my son." Her eyes bore into the fair queen, unearthly and sharp as obsidian. "In fact, you will protect him and you will make it your prime concern to ensure no harm—not even a scratch—comes to him." She looked at Queen Alin's belly and gave a chilling smile. "For should you even harm a hair on my son's head, I shall expose your little secret to all. Ageronians, as you know, are unforgiving royalists. I would hazard a guess that they would deem a revelation such as this treasonous and undoubtedly punishable by death. Death, which I hasten to add, not only restricted to yourself."

Lady Alin's lips trembled and for a moment, anger flashed in her eyes. But she remained silent.

A small whimper escaped Lady Cassia. The woman had retrieved her baby and was clutching the dead infant to her breast, rocking it gently. She had long ceased crying and her eyes, blank and unseeing, had a half-crazed look about them.

Lady Alin shot a furtive look at Lady Yinha, then at the knife, still slick with traces of bloodfruit on it. Slowly, she picked it up and cleaned the blade with her sleeve. Then she held it out to Lady Cassia.

Sorceress Yinha's gaze bore into Alin at the audacious move. Her eyes were hard and black. Then she looked at Lady Cassia once more and said, "Perhaps this is the only merciful way out."

With that, the sorceress turned to leave the chamber without looking back.

And as the last of her swirling robes drifted out of the room, Lady Cassia took one more look at the lifeless bundle at her breast, reached for the knife and put it to her wrist as Lady Alin sat patiently to watch her.

PRESENT DAY

RED PALACE,
PLANET AMORGOS, AGERON SYSTEM

The view of the palace gardens below had begun to recede into darkness, the outline of the central courtyard with its ancient pergola illuminated only in places where the rays of the setting suns lingered. From where he stood in the northwest tower, Lord Draeger looked out across the darkening vista of crimson and black, gazing at the dimming shapes of the gardens he knew so well. In his mind's eye, he saw not the sparse stunted shrubs in the courtyard but lush silver palms swaying softly in the breeze and leafy vines hanging from the pergola, glinting in golden sunshine. Closing his eyes for a moment, he could almost smell the heady sweetness of jasmine in the air.

That pergola used to be covered with it...

Draeger looked at the gardens again, a stark difference to the image still vividly entrenched in his memories. *How the climate has changed over the last hundred years.* Now arid and desolate, only a few hardy barbthorn bushes remained, belligerent-looking survivors where once hundreds of lush and exotic plants flourished.

PLANET AMORGOS, AGERON SYSTEM

Belligerence.

Draeger frowned. That was certainly the prevailing feeling of the hour. But then, the Red Palace was always a dangerous place to be, even in the relatively carefree days of his childhood. Now, with Emperor Akseli under house arrest and facing charges of conspiring with the Ellagrins to invade Ageron, there was no doubt as to this undercurrent of belligerence and hostility within the Palace.

"My lord," Chancellor Rasmus spoke up. "Queen Alin has asked once more. To see him."

"*No*," replied Draeger firmly. "The Emperor is not to have contact with anyone, *especially* the Queen Mother." With the Senate still debating whether to impeach Akseli, the Queen Mother, with her ties to certain members of the Senate from days of old, was, in his estimation, far more dangerous than Akseli himself. No, Akseli was not to have contact with anyone until Draeger himself was clear what had to be done next.

The Chancellor nodded in response but added: "My lord, Emperor Akseli cannot languish in house arrest forever, you know. The Senate needs to decide if he is to stand trial or not."

Draeger gave an irritated grunt. "I have no doubt Akseli and the Queen Mother will try to get the trial dismissed."

"Indeed," affirmed the Chancellor. "Both mother and son would want to avoid a trial at all costs. If found guilty of treason, Emperor Akseli will face execution."

Draeger turned to face the Chancellor. His strange dark eyes beheld the old man's cool, grey ones. "And if the impeachment trial goes ahead, have we sufficient evidence against my brother?" he asked.

"Yes," answered the Chancellor. "From those who carried out his orders at Lagentia to the fake rebels ordered to start

PRESENT DAY

those riots all over the Realm to distract and disperse our army. We have sufficient evidence of Emperor Akseli's plans and intentions, my lord."

"And what line of defence do you think Akseli will take?" asked Draeger. "That he tried to reopen the Lagentian Gateway for the good of the Realm? To evacuate the people?"

Rasmus rubbed his chin thoughtfully. "No. We know that argument will not hold. There were no plans to organise an evacuation, not even one for the capital planet, never mind the others in the Realm. Not to mention that the act of endangering the life of the last Nehisi to reopen the Gateway, which is tantamount to murder. No, in all likelihood, he will say that you set this up to frame him and to seize the throne for yourself."

"Yes," agreed Draeger, "and I have no doubt the Queen Mother will get her supporters lined up to attest to that. Lord Reku for one…"

"Indeed," said Rasmus. "We will need to tread carefully with the Senate. Some of these old Praetors are loyal to the Queen Mother and, thusly, the Emperor."

"You know," Draeger said slowly, "I should ensure Akseli hangs for treason." He eyed Rasmus knowingly and continued, "This has always been the way…"

Chancellor Rasmus sighed. Throughout history, the struggle for power within House Ageron was always fraught with fratricide. Brother against brother, vying for the throne. *Although more often than not, it was consort against consort, trying to influence the emperor,* the Chancellor noted grimly. *And frequently disposing of the competition by murder rather than via legal methods, too.* He shook his head. *It is usually the mothers who will stop at nothing to ensure the future of their own offspring.*

"Yet," continued Draeger, reigning him from his thoughts,

PLANET AMORGOS, AGERON SYSTEM

"he is my half-brother and we have both done well to survive after all this time."

The old Chancellor nodded. "I would say the odds were much better in your father's time," he said. "Emperor Ageron III was one out of a hundred and twenty-five potential heirs, whereas you and Akseli had over two hundred siblings—"

"None of whom survived," noted Draeger drily and not without seriousness. "And if I should die after ascending the throne..."

"Well, in that case, you might want to start planning for an heir," the Chancellor said with a twinkle in his eye, "lest any of Akseli's bastards decide to claim it."

Draeger shook his head vigorously at the thought, inviting a brief and circumspect glance from the Chancellor. "Oh no, no, no," he said firmly. "I have enough on my plate as it stands without the added complication of siring heirs. Still," he continued, "I am not that insecure as to let something as paltry as a surviving sibling threaten my position. If you remember, I was quite happy to let him be Emperor—"

"Until he opened our doors to invasion," reminded the Chancellor.

"Until that," agreed Draeger grimly. The severity of Akseli's actions was not lost on him. "But if we choose not to put him on trial, which in all likelihood will result in his execution, where does that leave me in terms of options?"

"Not a lot, I'm afraid, my lord," replied Chancellor Rasmus. "Imprisonment? Indefinite house arrest? Banishment? These are no guarantee against him returning to overthrow you or worse."

Draeger looked at him gravely. "So you're saying trial is the only option then..."

Rasmus bowed his head. He didn't answer but the answer was plain to see.

PRESENT DAY

"Trial it is then," said Draeger, making his mind up. "We will push the Senate to call for it."

Rasmus nodded. "Yes, my lord."

"Now what about the Exodus?" said Draeger, changing the subject.

Before the failed invasion, the Exodus—the century-old programme to resettle their people in Ellagrin—had been their solution to evacuate the billions of Ageronians from their dying planetary system. With ties to House Ellagrin now severed, there was nowhere to resettle Ageronians and the Exodus programme had ground to a halt. Equally worrying was the uncertainty of settlement treaties that had been agreed in the past. By galactic law, these had to be honoured but if Elena was capable of conspiring with Akseli to invade Ageron, who was to say what she would do with those treaties?

Draeger cursed softly, almost to himself. *Why by Dyaeus, Elena... What possessed you to collude with Akseli?* He thought of the decades they had spent working together behind the scenes—her, Lady Elena, sister to Emperor Niklas of House Ellagrin and he as Supreme Commander of House Ageron under his father, Emperor Ageron III. After the War, they had engineered a truce between their Houses and when it transpired that Ageron's binary suns were failing at an accelerated rate, they had negotiated the first settlement treaties (for agreed vast sums of *ore* to House Ellagrin) in order to resettle evacuated Ageronians in Ellagrin.

That was the start of the Exodus, recalled Draeger, *the colossal task of pooling together our empire's resources to build thousands of spacecarriers with which our people would make their journey, in longsleep, to designated settlements in the Ellagrin system.*

But Elena had betrayed him. Murdered her only brother, Niklas, and sided with Draeger's brother, Akseli, instead. The

PLANET AMORGOS, AGERON SYSTEM

two of them had struck a bargain behind Draeger's back. Akseli had kidnapped Tors and used her to open the Lagentian Gateway in order to let the Ellagrin army in to take over its capital planet, Amorgos. With Draeger's armies spread thinly across the Realm, putting out 'rebellion uprisings' staged by Akseli, the plan had been to wrestle military control from Draeger, consequently enabling Akseli to wield real and total power over Ageron. In return, with Ageron's military support, Elena would take Niklas' place and rule Ellagrin without contest from the Ellagrin Doges, who would never condone a female in power.

But the invasion failed. They failed.

Draeger sighed. *Perhaps, had they succeeded,* he noted with irony, *we would have had a solution at least where Ageronians would have somewhere to evacuate to.*

"What will happen to our people already on their way to Ellagrin—those aboard the *Delphinium*, the *Almirante*, the *Carinthia*?" Draeger wondered aloud. "The settlement treaties for those... will Elena renege on them? Decades from now when those people finally reach Ellagrin and find that it no longer welcomes them, what then?" He frowned. Things were a mess and to make matters worse, the constant barrage of natural disasters due to the dying suns seemed to do nothing but focus the spotlight on their ever-decreasing set of options.

"We must persevere with the alternatives we have in front of us," the Chancellor replied. "Don't forget, our emissaries to the Tilkoen system should return soon. The Tilkoens will help us."

Yes, the Tilkoens. Draeger turned to stare out the window once more. *Technologists, inventors, the original creators of Gate technology. It was Ageron II who approached them with the idea of building the Gateways, to make Bridged Travel possible.* "It only

PRESENT DAY

seems like yesterday that we sent our emissaries out," Draeger murmured. "Has it been a century already?"

The Chancellor nodded. "It has, my lord. Time flies..."

"Indeed," agreed Draeger. He moved away from the window as the last crimson rays of the setting suns disappeared, plunging the view of the outside into total darkness. "Fifty years to get there, and fifty to come back. If our emissaries return with agreement from the Tilkoens to take us in, then we shall have the all-clear for the Exodus programme to resettle our people in Tilkoen instead of Ellagrin." He frowned. "But at the rate our suns are declining, time may well be running out."

His thoughts shifted to their other remaining option—the one foremost in his mind every day since the day she left with Marcus, Pihla and Niko to search for the Sansari Gate.

Tors...

"Which leaves us the last option," he said. He grimaced. "We should have sent more than the three of them with her. For protection."

The Chancellor shook his head. "You know that wouldn't have been prudent, my lord. Any more would make it difficult for them to move them in and out of the Ether. A larger group would also attract unwanted attention, and every additional person multiplies their risk of exposure." The old Chancellor looked at him and nodded. "You were right to choose those specific individuals to go with her. We can only be sure with those who have no ties with the Senate and consequently, no hidden loyalties to the Emperor."

Draeger conceded. "Let us hope they find Sansari soon," he said pensively.

Tors, Marcus, Niko and Pihla...

Tasked to look for the Sansari Gate, the opposite endpoint to our Arnemetiaen Gate here in Ageron. Draeger felt great unease. *A*

PLANET AMORGOS, AGERON SYSTEM

mammoth mission for a group so small. They had taken with them the spare beacon, the *only* beacon, left by the Tilkoens during Ageron II's reign, to carry along with them on their journey through the Ether, all the way from the Arnemetiaen Gate here in Ageron to the Sansari Gate in Tilkoen. This was necessary in order for the beacon to 'learn' the route and establish the link between the two endpoints once installed at Sansari. In the same manner the first Gateways were set up, Tors and the team would repeat this same process once more. *Once reactivated, both Gates will connect to form the Arnemetiaen Gateway, linking Ageron to Tilkoen. Just like the old days, except crucially this time, it will be to allow our people to escape Ageron before its destruction.* But would it work? Would the technology at Sansari have changed after all these centuries? Would the Gate itself even be there? And if so, was it still operable? And then there was the ultimate question: *would the Tilkoen High Council allow a few billion Ageronians into their planetary system?*

He wondered where Tors and the other were at that moment. Were they still in the Ether? Had they exited somewhere to rest or replenish supplies?

"Where do you think they are now?" he wondered aloud. "Would they have emerged through some of the old known endpoints?"

"Possibly," speculated the Chancellor. "They will most likely track the same paths the Nehisi took long ago, and stumbling upon old endpoints perhaps, if the currents of the Ether haven't shifted too much over the past six centuries."

"But the Ether does not remain static," Draeger pointed out.

"That may be," agreed the Chancellor, "but we know there are spots where its currents tend to remain more or less constant. There is a chance they may well exit the Ether into some of these well-known endpoints for food and rest during their search for Sansari—Kaldr or Brekka in Ellagrin, perhaps even Yoon."

"However, Sansari itself…" Draeger looked grim. "Historical records say it was pure luck the first Nehisi stumbled upon it, for that part of the Ether where its endpoint exists is particularly chaotic." He looked at Rasmus with concern. "It took us another twenty years to find Namsos in Ellagrin. The Ether is transient, its currents ever changing, which means they could locate Sansari in a year or in twenty. There is no guarantee…"

"That is true," said Chancellor Rasmus gravely, "but the Nehisi have always detected these natural endpoints by instinct and I have no doubt Tors' instincts will guide her to it. She *will* find Sansari."

Draeger remained silent. *Let us hope so,* he said to himself, thinking of her. *The Ether is the one place I can't reach you. Where I cannot help or protect you...*

"On a slightly separate note, my lord," said Rasmus, wresting him from his thoughts, "I have arranged for us to fly to Alandia tonight. You need to show your face at the *Comitium*."

"Why?"

"We need to garner support for Akseli's impeachment trial," explained Chancellor Rasmus. "Even with the overwhelming evidence against him, we shouldn't take anything for granted."

The Comitium was the hub of administration for all of Ageron, where the Praetors, civil officers and diplomats met, mingled and worked tirelessly to govern the Realm.

This is where you need to exert your diplomatic skills, Rasmus thought, glancing at Lord Draeger. *When it is likely the Emperor will be found guilty and stripped of his role, it is even more important you are seen to be in the heart of running the empire...*

PLANET AMORGOS, AGERON SYSTEM

"You should pay more attention to the politics, my lord," advised the Chancellor gravely. "It is not always the sword that kills a man."

"I understand that," acknowledged Draeger.

Despite that, fancied the Chancellor, it seemed Draeger's thoughts were elsewhere. Far away.

As far away as the Ether perhaps, he thought.

PART I

THE SEARCH

TORS

ETHER

Tors awoke to a gentle tap on her shoulder. It was Marcus. He stretched stiffly and gestured, asking if she was all right. She nodded and sat up, bleary with fatigue.

It was dim in the Ether but ahead, she could see Niko resting, propped up against his backpack and morosely flicking his switchblade in and out. Near him, lay Pihla, still napping, arms around her sword like a babe cuddling a toy. Like nomads, they had been journeying for what seemed like an eternity through the gloomy planes of the Ether and Tors was aware of the toll their relentless trek was having on the group.

Niko especially, finds it torturous to breathe in this environment. The Ether was viscous, heavy and almost fluid which made breathing in it, for the unaccustomed, an experience uncomfortably close to drowning. A handful of times she had to cleave an exit out of it in order for them to replenish supplies and for a welcomed chance to rest and breathe naturally. This Tors did only when necessary and with caution. She grimaced, recalling their last exit which nearly ended in disaster. In her haste to exit the Ether, they had almost stepped out onto the lava plane of a molten planet. Tors chastised herself. *Another reason why one should use naturally occurring endpoints instead of cleaving a temporary exit yourself.* However, natural endpoints were few and far between, and for months now since the day they started their quest, they had not seen a single natural endpoint as yet, never mind the one they had set out to find.

Tors' instincts told her that they were much, much farther from the Ageron system than any of the others could possibly imagine. As they journeyed through the Ether, she had sensed the unfamiliar worlds beyond, worlds so distant their existence were likely outside their galaxy.

She stood up and wrapped her cloak around her. The strange winds of the Ether had begun to pick up again. There were no seasons here. No day, no night. Only the curious ebb and flow of the inter-dimensional winds that flowed through the perpetual gloom.

Tors gestured for the rest to pack up and move on. Over the past few weeks, they had established amongst themselves common hand signals in order to communicate with each other. It was a useful practice for the Ether carried no sound. Now, Tors signalled for them to move quickly. From experience, she knew the silent winds would pick up in strength soon, making it difficult to walk and crucially, she had felt the tug of a natural endpoint not far off which could mean a convenient exit out of the Ether and the avoidance of facing its strong winds with nowhere to shelter.

An hour passed as they trekked on. The group strained against the buffeting winds, pressing forward, following Tors' lead. Then at last, in the distance ahead, Tors spotted the faint glimmer she was after.

Pihla, sharp as always, noticed it too. She nudged Niko who had been keeping his head down to avoid the headlong winds. He looked up and saw the endpoint shining like a window in a dark room, revealing the bright outside. It grew larger and larger as they approached and soon the group ran eagerly towards it, peering curiously at the opening.

This is the first time they've seen a natural endpoint in the Ether, grinned Tors as her companions crowded around the irregularly-shaped opening. It was fairly small, no more than four feet high and roughly elliptical in shape. Soft, rippling shades of blue and green light filtered through, casting hauntingly beautiful light shapes upon their fascinated faces. Marcus' expression was the most incredulous of them all. He had the endearing wide-eyed look of a schoolboy.

Tors laughed and peered through the portal herself to observe the source of his bewilderment. On the other side, in the green-blue expanse, was a school of brightly-coloured fish. Like a coruscating stream of jewels, they hurtled towards him at great speed.

Marcus ducked.

Tors let out a silent chortle. *They always forget. A natural endpoint is like a one-way mirror.*

The shoal changed tack at the last second and flicked away, gradually disappearing into the murky distance. Then, Pihla stepped forward tentatively and stuck her arm through the portal. She withdrew it almost immediately, startled, and examined her hand. It was dry to the touch.

No elements from the worlds may pass through...

Mother's words echoed in Tors' mind as she looked on, entertained by the looks on their faces. It reminded her of her first forays into the Ether with her mother. Her thoughts then turned, a little uncertainly, to the yet unborn child in her belly.

Soon, I will be a mother myself, she realised. The prospect of motherhood seemed as daunting as their mission. *What could I teach you apart from coaxing the Ether and finding your way within it?* She realised with dread that she had absolutely no idea. *What could I teach you indeed? How to steal? To maim with maximum efficiency? To kill? What kind of mother would that make me?*

By now, the winds had escalated to a full-blown gale and a sudden gust threatened to blow her off her feet. Marcus grabbed her arm to steady her. At any other time, Tors would have rebuffed the gesture but her reflexes nowadays were slower due to her changing body and she seemed to tire more easily, so she was glad for his help.

She peered through the opening to see if it was safe for them to pass through. It was definitely a body of water on the other side. A lake or the sea perhaps. She checked again, shifting a little to the side to let Marcus have a look as well. On the other end of the portal, the water's surface was visible to them, gleaming like an undulating mirror, and no more than ten feet above from where they were. *We can swim to the surface. It is possible.*

Marcus touched her elbow to get her attention. She could tell he was thinking the same thing. She nodded in response to his querying look, agreeing it was probably safe to try this exit. At any rate, with the winds as strong as they were, staying inside the Ether was no longer viable.

Turning to the others, Marcus gestured for them to affix their osmostrips to their noses and get ready.

Going first, he stepped through the portal. Tors moved into position behind him.

He registered a brief look of surprise as he entered the water and then swivelled to face her, his hand outstretched. She grasped it and together, they swam towards the surface. The water was pleasantly cool, almost warm. Tors beckoned the others to follow.

Moments later, they all emerged at the surface.

Marcus, head bobbing above water, was already scanning

their surroundings. He pointed at what appeared to be land a few hundred yards ahead and they all swam towards it. Soon, they clambered onto shore, dripping wet.

"Let's hope this stop is better than the previous ones," coughed Niko, fishing his waterproof pack out of the water and detaching his osmostrip. He looked up at the sky and breathed deeply, visibly glad to be out of the Ether. "At least I don't see any flying beasts trying to eat us this time," he said with a grin.

Tors recalled that particular stop a month ago and chuckled. It had looked idyllic and peaceful enough, until a couple of flying reptilians the size of urbangliders swooped by and decided they were dinner. She flicked off the last few drops of water that hadn't slid off her lubricote cloak and looked around. The air was cool but not cold, and laden with the briny smells of the sea. Overhead, the vivid blue sky was clean and clear, marred only by the occasional seafaring bird crying out in the distance.

"Do you think this is Sansari?" Niko asked.

"No," said Marcus, shaking his head. "Unlikely, as where we came in from, there was no trace of the mechanical parts of a gate. Besides this endpoint's underwater."

"I think we're somewhere within the Ellagrin system," said Tors. She couldn't explain it but it just felt so.

"Sure feels like it, climate-wise at least," said Pihla. "I agree this can't be Sansari. Tilkoens are technologists and ardent machinists. If this were Sansari, we'd be in the middle of an ultra-modern city."

Marcus nodded in agreement.

Tors placed her backpack beside her and looked around. They appeared to be sitting atop a skerry, formed from clusters of rounded granite boulders, all as smooth and undulant as the sea around them. Nestled nearby were a few more islets, all either a hop or quick swim apart, with no apparent dwellings or signs of habitation. Vegetation was sparse apart from the odd scrubby bush between the pink and grey rocks, and every islet seemed pocked with small natural pools that were constantly replenished by the lapping waves of the sea.

She stood up and looked across the sea, one hand above her brow, shielding her eyes from the glare of the sun. Something or rather some things, shiny and glinting, caught her eye. Stretching into the horizon, past the islets was the endless expanse of ocean and scattered across it, thousands upon thousands of hemispherical pods, round as the boulders themselves, scintillating in the bright sunlight. "Over there!" Tors pointed, squinting. "What *are* they?"

Pihla stood up to have a look. "Sea-pods, I believe," she replied.

"Sea...what?" Tors asked.

"Sea-pods," repeated Pihla. "Farms," she explained. "Those shiny pods are algae-based hydroponic farms. I know this because I used to work on one in Ilia." She sat back down on the rocks and said, looking at all of them, "Well, one thing's for sure, this planet's inhabited alright."

Marcus nodded, squinting at the horizon. "We should be on our guard as we don't know where we are yet. I propose we look around, replenish our supplies and then—"

He stopped short when a splash startled him.

Tors whirled round just in time to glimpse a pair of legs disappear underwater. Moments later, a small head emerged, followed by the lithe body of a young girl, no older than six or seven. She pulled herself up onto the rocks and sat across from them, staring intently. Her hair was pale as buttermilk and her cheeks were flushed from the nip of the ocean. The child wore no clothes save a pair of briefs to shield her modesty.

"Whoaaa!" Niko exclaimed, jumping to his feet. "Where did she come from?"

Marcus surveyed their surroundings, puzzled. "I don't see where…"

The child grinned mischievously and pointed between the rocks. There, sunken and cleverly camouflaged, was a natural groove between the boulders, just wide and deep enough for a grown person to walk through unseen from above.

"A sunken path between the rocks," noted Tors. The path wound round the curvature of the rocks, but where it led to, none of them could tell as both path and rock merged into one the further the eye went.

"Interesting," said Marcus. He looked at the girl but she seemed content with just staring and made no attempt to speak or engage with any of them.

Tors stood up and tried to approach her but the child started from her perch, making clear that she would take off if anyone came near. "Fine, fine," Tors said, backing off and held out her hands in a placating gesture. She sat back down on the rocks opposite the child, then looked towards Marcus who did nothing except shrug and smile back at her. "Well, this is all very nice," said Tors, tapping her fingers impatiently, "… suppose we just sit here and look at each other, shall we?"

"Patience," murmured Marcus good-naturedly. "Give her a moment." Then much to Tors' annoyance, he leant back onto the rocks to lie in the sun. She gave a disapproving tutt in reply.

A few minutes passed before Marcus sat back up and reached for his backpack. He fished out a packet of biscuits, unwrapped it and took a piece out. He proceeded to examine the biscuit closely, turning it this way and that before taking a bite out of it. "Mmmm," he mumbled, and took another bite. "Would you like one?" he asked Tors innocently.

Tors eyed him with dour indulgence. She had learnt from past experience, not to rise to the bait when Marcus was in one of his toying moods. "Sure," she replied and took it from him.

"Delicious isn't it?" added Marcus, dipping his hand into the packet once more without taking his eyes off her. His lips curled into a suggestive grin. "You know, there's more where that came from—"

Pihla gave a snort and rolled her eyes at the two of them.

"Well," continued Marcus unperturbed, "may I tempt you with another, Tors?"

Tors waved him off brusquely.

"Oh," said Marcus a little dejectedly. He looked at the biscuit, pondered a bit, and then held it out to the little girl instead. At first she ignored his outstretched hand, pretending not to notice the biscuit in it, so Marcus popped the rest into his mouth and licked his fingers with relish after.

The child's face fell instantly.

Suppressing a grin, Marcus reached into the packet and took out another biscuit. He held it out to her again.

This time she reached to grab it from his hand. Sniffing it tentatively at first, she proceeded to nibble it and finally when she had gobbled the rest up, she stretched out her hand for more.

"More?" teased Marcus. "Well then, you'll have to show us where you live first."

The child nodded eagerly. Grinning, she leapt down from her rock onto the sunken path and beckoned them to follow.

"Patience. I told you," said Marcus grinning. He gave Tors a nudge. "Now we know she understands Standard Lang."

"Or Biscuit," quipped Tors before grudgingly acknowledging his triumphant tactic with smile.

They followed the child down the path as she led them

between the boulders, pausing every so often to badger Marcus for yet another biscuit.

"You seem to have a way with her," said Tors as the girl dangled the last morsel in front of her, in glee, before popping it ostentatiously into her mouth.

Marcus slowed down to walk beside Tors and gazed at her with those beguiling brown eyes of his. There was a hint of mirth behind them. "It only works on younglings and animals," he said with a heavy sigh, "but sadly, nothing else."

Tors rolled her eyes.

* * *

THE SUN WARMED the tops of their heads as they walked on and overhead, the sky was alive with the calls of seabirds. It was a beautiful day and apart from a few sections ankle-deep in water, where the waves had deposited the sea, the footpath was mostly dry and flat, making for a pleasant walk.

Tors guessed they were headed further and further inland. *Still, these islands cannot be all that large—I can still hear and smell the sea around us.* The sea was no longer visible but they could still make out the faint roar of the waves beyond the boulders and the salty scent of ocean spray hung in the air like a persistent mist.

"Where do you think she's taking us?" Niko asked as they walked.

Marcus shrugged. "To where she lives I guess. There must be a settlement somewhere nearby where we can get supplies."

Niko cast him an uncertain look. "Do you think they're friendly? What if they're cannibals?"

"*Fool!*" Pihla said, elbowing him sharply. "Does she look like a cannibal to you? More likely she's Ellagrin."

"You think we're on an Ellagrin planet?"

Marcus turned around to shush them. "I suggest you keep your thoughts to yourself. We shall find out soon enough."

It was another hour's walk before the girl stopped at a junction. In front, intersected two other paths.

"Ooof!" went Niko, walking right into the back of Pihla. A quick *Ow!* followed as she elbowed him in retaliation. "We're finally stopping?" he asked, rubbing his midriff. "Why are we stopping?"

The girl looked at them and then pointed up the path on the right.

Tors and Marcus exchanged a quick glance.

A man was walking up the path towards them. He was tall, blonde and unmistakably Ellagrin.

AN ENCOUNTER

And here we go...

Tors fervently hoped he wouldn't ask too many questions. After all, none of them looked Ageronian and could, she hoped, pass for inhabitants of Ellagrin. Pihla, tan and brawny, was unmistakably Tilkoen in appearance but unlike Ageronians, Tilkoens had played no part in recent hostilities and had no political enmity with Ellagrins. Granted, Tilkoens in Ellagrin were few and far between, but allowing for the generation of Tilkoens marooned here and unable to return to the Tilkoen system since the fall of the Gateways, Pihla's presence could be easily explained. Niko, with his slight build, was clearly human which was nothing out of the ordinary as humans were spread all over the known galaxy. Herself—she hoped no one could tell. After all, there had been no Nehisi for centuries. And finally, looking at Marcus, she hoped he was fair-haired enough to pass as an Ellagrin half-breed.

She wondered if Ellagrins still hated Ageronians. *It has been after all, not counting the recent invasion attempt, over two centuries since we mingled with their population. What would they do to us if they found out?* She looked at the approaching man and wondered if it was her childhood fear of Ellagrins that was clouding her judgement and making her nervous. The man didn't look menacing. In fact, he looked almost friendly.

"Enok!" he called out and waved as he approached. The child bounded up the path towards him and reached out to touch his face in greeting.

"You've been out a long time, Enok," said the man. "I was coming to get you." He took her hand in his and together they walked up to Tors and the others. "What have you brought back with you this time?" he asked, looking at them good-naturedly. His eyes, the colour of the ocean, crinkled humorously and like Ellagrins in general, he was tall, broad-shouldered and blonde.

The girl made a few hand signs, grinning at him. He smiled and then said, "Greetings! I am Hakon and this is my daughter Enok." Enok looked up and smiled at the mention of her name and her father gave her chin an affectionate tug. "You folks visiting Vijker?"

Marcus answered for them. "Greetings," he replied. "I am Marcus and these are my companions: Tors, Pihla and Niko. Our skiff unfortunately sank not far from here and we were wondering if there was somewhere we could rest and replenish our supplies before we continued on our way?"

Hakon nodded and smoothed his hand over Enok's tangled hair. "Yes, the ocean can look deceptively tame if you're not used to the seasonal currents," he said. "It is well you were not hurt when your ship sank." Then nodding towards the path from which he came, he said, "Please, this way." and led the way.

. . .

The path they took was rockier than the one before. Carved into the same grey-pink granite which now towered over their heads, it took them further inland, winding this way and that. Underfoot, sharp, protruding rocks jutted from the ground, forcing the group to walk round or where not possible, clamber over them. Several times Marcus grabbed Tors' arm to stop her from slipping onto the sharp, jagged protrusions.

"So your ship sank off the coast not far from here, you say?" asked Hakon as they picked their way through the jagged path. Marcus nodded. "That's strange," replied Hakon. "We didn't see any smoke and none of the sensors reported any breaches to the pod perimeters."

Tors tensed at the comment but Marcus gave a laid-back shrug. "We were quite far out when we crashed," he said casually, meeting Hakon's sea-blue eyes with ease.

"Well, I'm glad no pods seem to have been damaged," said Hakon, clearly more concerned about his pods than their ship. "The monsoons are going to be upon us and I don't want to have to be out in the open sea replacing pods any time soon. We have one final harvest before the season ends and then, Enok and I shall be very glad to have some well deserved rest."

"Indeed," agreed Marcus as Tors breathed out in silent relief. Once again, Marcus' remarkable knack for fitting in had gotten them through what could have been a tricky situation.

Soon, the path widened into a fair-sized street, also cut into rock itself and flanked on both sides by natural boulders towering at least ten feet over them. They had arrived at a small village of some sort. Here, all dwellings were carved into the rock, leaving only scrub and boulders above visible to the eye. *Which explains why we couldn't see any signs of habitation,* realised Tors.

"Ah! We are here," announced Hakon, beaming. He extended his arm in a sweeping gesture. "Welcome to our little town of Vijker, home to the best smoked *scomber* in all of Ellagrin!"

VIJKER WAS an Ellagrin town nothing like what Tors imagined.

No soldiers here, she noted with relief as Hakon led them through throngs of its inhabitants, past neat little dwellings and shops carved out of rock. Ahead, cramped market stalls hugged the pavements and narrow side alleys ran off the main street where they walked.

Tors took in her surroundings with interest. Vijker with its apparent lack of technological influences possessed a rather old-world feel and compared with the crimson cities of Ageron, seemed almost quaint in appearance. The salty air rang with the cacophony of saws and hammers as they walked past blacksmiths and carpenters, hard at work in their workshops. The small town was bursting with people everywhere. Farmers and fishermen, carting harvest and haul, jostling their way through the tight streets with their laden hovertugs, merchants haggling furiously outside their establishments, and people bustling about, buying fish, fruit and vegetables from stalls, all within these walls of rock.

The sea must be just beyond these walls, thought Tors for she could hear the soft lapping of waves beyond, high above her head. Marcus too, appeared to arrive at a similar conclusion. "I can hear the sea," he said, "and I think we're slightly below sea level."

Hakon led them down a turning off the main street and into a small close. Here, a handful of houses nestled in a semi circle, all excavated from the same piece of rock. Each had a wooden front door, painted in a bright colour. As they neared, Enok ran ahead to open the one with the orange door. She leant against it to keep it open and beckoned them excitedly. Hakon smiled. "I think she wants to show you our home," he said.

Their cottage was compact and they had to duck to enter in order to keep from banging their heads against the lintel. Inside was sparse but comfortable, consisting of a main living area that served as a basic kitchen, dining and sitting room. Along the smooth, curved walls were three further doors—one slightly ajar, leading to what looked like the toilet and the other two, Tors presumed, for sleeping or storage. The floors were bare stone, covered with knotted rugs to denote different living areas and like the floors, the walls were of polished stone, grey with embedded streaks of pink, just like the rest of the skerry. A small stove provided the means to cook and heat the place, although judging by what they'd seen so far, the surrounding sea appeared to keep temperatures fairly constant and mild enough not to require a lit fire.

"Please…" urged Hakon, offering them a seat on a cushioned bench and disturbing an elderly *auk* in the process. It gave an indignant screech, flapped its short wings and jumped off. The bird waddled comically in front of them before Enok picked it up and tucked it under her arm. She grinned at them and made a small hand sign.

"That's Majki our pet," translated Hakon. He smiled at his daughter. "There aren't many options for pets here in Vijker," he said. "Only seabirds and geckos." He walked over to the the stove and above it, unhooked a small slab of white meat which he began to cut into thin slices. "Most of us here are either farmers or fishermen," he said as he added fresh leaves to the sliced meat, a sprinkling of seeds and a few hunks of bread torn from a larger loaf.

"Enok, bring the amarinthe," he instructed and brought the platter of food to their guests.

Enok dropped Majki carelessly and ran to pour the amarinthe from a jug into small brightly-painted glasses. These she placed in an enamel tray and carried over to them, handing out a glass each. Once done, she placed the tray aside and sat on the floor, chin cupped in her hands, her bright blue eyes looking at them as intently as she did earlier by the rocks.

As the food was passed from one person to the next, the party tucked in ravenously. After months subsisting on dried fare in the Ether, they were all glad to be eating fresh food again.

"This is delicious!" Tors exclaimed, ravenously devouring the slices of pale flesh. They were tender yet firm and had a subtle hint of smokiness in them.

"Smoked scomber," said Hakon. "They are very abundant here and you may have seen them in our waters, those brightly-coloured shoals. They're the fastest swimmers on the planet."

Marcus nodded, flashing Tors a grin. "Yeah," he said. "I think we encountered some earlier."

Enok pressed her palms together and made a wriggling sign. "Yes, fish," affirmed her father. He signed back at her and she scooped Majki up in her arms and went to play outside. Hakon looked after her fondly.

"My wife died a few years ago," he said. "Enok's our only child."

"I'm sorry to hear that," answered Marcus, looking at Enok playing outside. "She seems very happy though."

Hakon nodded. "Enok thankfully, has always been an easy child." He topped up Marcus' glass and continued. "She was barely two at the time. My wife and I were erecting the pods out at sea when the storm hit us. That day, I lost our boat and her mother…"

Outside Enok was teasing Majki with a sliver of fish in her hand.

"She used to talk all the time," said Hakon, "but after that day, she never spoke a single word again." He shrugged. "Still, here it is not a problem for us. We're a tight community. Everyone understands and Enok has all she needs around her." He paused to bring some more bread to the table and then looked out onto the street. Enok had disappeared off to play elsewhere. "We are simple people here," he said, "but our food, whilst simple, is of the highest quality. " He smiled proudly. "Vijker may be a farming outpost but here, we produce and consume the best vegetables and grains in all of planet Kaldr." He looked at Pihla and indicated towards the outside of the house. "Did you know those pods at sea are Tilkoen? My father brought them back with him and to this day, they are still used out there."

"Impressive," said Pihla.

"Tilkoen technology," Hakon said. "It's a class on its own I can tell you." He smiled at Pihla. "We don't see many Tilkoens this far out in Ellagrin, not since the Gateways fell."

Pihla nodded. "Yes," she replied, "As a child, I got separated when the Gateways fell. I have not seen Tilkoen or my mother since."

Hakon took another sip of amarinthe. "We here, thankfully, are too far from the capital to have felt much of the war at the time," he said. "And because of that too, we remained mostly unaffected by the economic consequences after." Then he stood up. "Right," he said," let's get you somewhere to rest; you must be tired." He threw open the two doors leading off the living room. As Tors had guessed, they were sleeping quarters.

"I'm afraid our home is quite small," said Hakon apologetically. He nodded towards Tors and Pihla. "Perhaps you two could share Enok's room here tonight. Enok will sleep with me and the men can sleep out here in the living room."

"You are very kind but we wouldn't want to intrude—" started Marcus but Hakon shook his head vigorously.

"No, no, it's no trouble," he said kindly. "Besides, there are no guesthouses here in Vijker. " He grinned. "Only smokehouses... for fish."

He ducked into the first room and emerged with a bundle of bedding and a child's toy in his arms. These he tossed into the second room which Tors guessed was his. "There!" he said, and lobbed another bundle of bedding into the first room. "Now you are set for the night."

Just then, Enok ran back into the house. Tors suppressed a chuckle as the little girl shot her father a less-than-impressed look at his bed-making skills. Then, to her surprise the little girl grabbed the toy and clambered up her lap.

"Oh!" exclaimed Tors as the child settled in the hollow between her thighs, docile as a lamb.

"Looks like you have a way with younglings too," Marcus remarked. He had a twinkle in his eye.

Hakon smiled and signed to Enok. She signed back and went back to playing with her toy. Hakon turned to Tors. "She says she likes you because you don't talk much," he said with a laugh.

Tors laughed back as Enok, ignoring them all, settled comfortably in her lap.

"Tonight you can sleep here and here," said Hakon pointing at his rather haphazardly placed bedding and blankets in the bedroom and in the living area.

"Thank you," replied Tors gratefully. Enok nestled sleepily against her chest and she found herself absently stroking the child's hair. She glanced across the room only to see Marcus looking at her with a funny smile on his face.

Hakon cleared his throat to get everyone's attention. "Tomorrow," he announced, "I will take you to see Alber, our mayor."

"Your mayor?" asked Marcus.

"Yes," Hakon replied. He gave an apologetic shrug. "I'm a simple man and I don't care for details of who you are and where you're from. As far as I'm concerned, that is your business and yours alone. However, our mayor Alber does want to know these things, so I have to take you to see him."

"Alber…" repeated Marcus.

Hakon nodded. "Yes, Mayor Alber. He'll want to know about visitors to Vijker so I'd better take you to see him or I'll never hear the end of it." He handed Marcus and Niko a blanket each. "And then after that," he said, bursting into a smile again, "you can help Enok and me harvest our crops to earn your keep."

Marcus nodded agreeably. "That we certainly can," he said with a broad smile. "That we certainly can."

ALBER

VIJKER,

PLANET KALDR, ELLAGRIN SYSTEM

*T*he early shafts of sunlight fingered their way through the slits of the shutters, gilding the walls with their aurous touch.

Pihla awoke, snug beneath her blanket and rubbed her eyes. At first her unfamiliar surroundings confused her. The room was low and rounded, and with its smooth stone walls and low ceiling, felt more like a cave dwelling than a house. She sat up and glanced sleepily at the futon next to her where two sleeping forms curled. A small fuzzy head of hair nestled in the crook of Tors' arm stirred slightly. Then she remembered. *The little one crept in here last night and made a bee line for Tors.* Pihla breathed in deeply and sighed. It was good to be able to just breathe normally. *We are in Ellagrin,* she reminded herself, *not in the Ether...*

Tors awoke at Pihla's stirring and lifted her head to look at her. "Morning," she whispered a little croakily. Gently, she edged her arm out from under Enok so as not to wake her. Then, tucking the duvet over the little girl, she slid out from under the futon to put her shoes on.

Both women smiled at each other in greeting as they got up. Outside, beyond the shuttered windows, cries of seabirds in the air heralded the new day. It had been the first time in a long while where she had had a good night's sleep and Pihla's body, rested and refreshed, was thankful for it. Quietly, the two women left the room to enter the kitchen, closing the door softly behind them.

"Good morning," greeted Marcus. He was sitting at the table, steaming cup in hand, looking just as restored as they felt. Behind him, bent over the stove, was Hakon stirring some porridge in a cast iron pot. He greeted them with a smile and set the pot on the table with a flourish. "Did you sleep well?" he asked and brought out fresh bread, some honey and a bowl of treacly red berries for the porridge.

"Yes, thank you," replied Pihla and sat down. Hakon handed her a cup of strong black *kofi* which she gratefully accepted. Next, he ladled some porridge into her bowl and indicated at the honey and fruits to go with it.

"Please…" he gestured graciously and then sat down to join them. Snores from Niko still asleep in the couch nearby, floated over in soft rumbling swells.

"This is delicious!" exclaimed Pihla tucking in. The porridge, hot and sweetened with honey, was rich and creamy and the red berries, sprinkled in, provided bursts of tartness against the richness of the meal.

Hakon beamed, clearly pleased with how his breakfast was received.

"So what's the plan for today?" asked Marcus.

Hakon looked up from his porridge. "Yes, yes, today," he said. "After this, I shall bring you to see Alber, our mayor."

Pihla groaned. "Do we have to? I'd much rather go and see your pods."

Hakon opened his hands in a helpless gesture. "I'm afraid I

have to. Alber is our mayor and he is rather particular about any outsiders. You see, we don't get visitors that often. So…"

He doesn't seem too happy at the prospect of seeing Alber either, thought Pihla. She gave a quick glance at Marcus to check.

"Well, Alber sounds like the typical bureaucrat," said Marcus, obligingly. "We'll come along if we have to, as long as we don't stay long."

Hakon smiled back, relieved. "I'm glad you understand," he said and then brightened up. "After that, we can go see the pods."

Marcus nodded.

"That is," added Hakon, "…as soon as your friend wakes up." He glanced towards Niko with an amused grin. "He seems very tired."

"I can fix that," answered Pihla. She walked over to Niko, bundled snugly in his thick swath of blankets, and gave him a big, fat kick.

A SHORT WHILE LATER, with Niko fully awake and breakfasted, they set off for mayor Alber's house. The mayor lived in the other end of the town on one of the nicer streets, in a house as wide and as generously proportioned as he was.

The front door was wide open when they arrived with people coming and going. "Welcome," Alber beamed, bidding them enter.

Like all the other houses in Vijker, Alber's was carved out of the natural rock but unlike Hakon's and most of the town, his was by far larger and grander than the rest.

His lounge alone is as large as Hakon's house, noted Pihla looking around. Large as that might be, it was being packed to the rafters with stacks of boxes, with ever more being brought in by a stream of big, strong men. But despite the clutter, it was a fine home with granite walls polished smooth and painted over in a soft shade of buttermilk. *Rather lavish for a farming village mayor,* observed Pihla looking at the gleaming floor tiles with its whorls of golden patterns.

"You'll have to excuse the mess," Alber beamed apologetically. "We've run out of space at the warehouse and these need to go indoors somewhere in case the rains come."

Pihla looked at the men hurrying to and fro, stacking their boxes in mayor Alber's living room and ducking out again to retrieve the next lot. They were a tall, muscular lot that didn't talk much. A faint whiff of the sea wafted over from within the boxes.

"Smoked fish," said Alber, clicking his fingers impatiently at the men to hurry them along. He even jabbed at one or two of them. One of the men flinched but dared not look at Alber.

Pihla looked at Alber's rotund form jiggling up and down in impatience. *What a round, little dictator,* she observed with distaste.

"These are from my smokehouse down the road," said Alber proudly, his flabby jowls quivering. "Made with fish from my fisheries, although I myself don't do the fishing anymore." He patted his big belly by way of explanation, "Too old and too fat! Heh! Heh!"

Alber motioned for a servant to bring in some chairs and gestured for them to sit down.

"Sit! Sit!" he said and they all sat amongst the growing stacks of boxes. Alber himself sat his hefty rump on a stool which creaked and wobbled intermittently whilst he kept one eye on them and the other on the stream of workers coming in and out of the house.

"So Hakon tells me you arrived here yesterday," he said, beaming. His eyes latched interestedly first at Pihla, then at Tors. She noticed his wide smile lessened as his gaze moved on from the ladies to the men. "Pray tell me where you're from and what can we at Vijker do to make you welcome?"

Spoken like a true bureaucrat. Pihla shifted a little uncomfortably in her chair but Marcus who didn't appear to mind answered.

"We're on our way to my uncle's at Dalr when our ship sank off the coast," he said. "We were hoping to rest up, replenish our supplies and then make our way to the nearest city."

Good call Dalr, thought Pihla. *Picking the largest planet in all of Ellagrin should give us sufficient scope to lie about just about anywhere we're heading.*

"Ah! Dalr," nodded Alber vigorously. "I sell quite a lot of my smoked scomber all over the capital planet! Some of the finest delicatessens at Namsos stock my smoked scomber!"

"Well, we shall make a note to try them when we get there," said Marcus, smiling agreeably.

Alber beamed even wider, his jowls aquiver. "Yes do that," he said, "but first you must try some of them here. *Fresh!*" He wobbled excitedly. "I say, why don't you stop over tonight for dinner eh? My little woman will cook for us and you will sample some of the finest cooking from this region! I *guarantee* you that!"

Hakon began to protest but Alber waved him off. "No, no, I *insist,*" he said. "After all, these are our guests."

Hakon looked a trifle uncomfortable but Alber would have none of it.

"Bring your little one along too," he said. His eyes bore down eagerly at Hakon. "We shall have a *feast*, yes? And I won't talk business, I promise!"

Hakon managed a reluctant nod.

"Good! Good!" exclaimed mayor Alber thumping him enthusiastically on the back as he rose to see them out. "I shall see you all later then!" He waddled to the door with them. "So where are you all off to now, eh?"

"I'm taking them to the pods," said Hakon.

"Ah, the pods," said Alber nodding. "Absolute hassle to maintain, those. Heh!" He looked at Hakon and his eyes gleamed. "So when are you going to sell me yours, young man? You don't want the cost of upkeep hanging round your neck heh!" He turned to Tors and the others and added, "Apart from me, Hakon here is the only other person in Vijker who owns his own agro-pods"—he smiled oleaginously—"and I've been trying for years to convince him to sell them to me."

"They were my father's," explained Hakon. "Everyone else here leases theirs from Alber."

Alber nodded enthusiastically. "Much less hassle for them I'd say. They have it so *easy* — just concentrating on growing their crops. I maintain the pods for everyone, apart from Hakon that is. Repairs, servicing, everything! I cover all that and it's cheaper for everyone. Economies of scale and all that you see! So you'll think about it, Hakon?"

Hakon shrugged. "Perhaps," he said noncommittally as he made his exit.

Alber grasped his arm as he walked past. "*Think* about it," he pressed but Hakon said nothing further and pushed past. "Don't forget, I'll see you here at seven tonight!" Alber called out as he waved them off.

HARVESTING

"*S*top over and my little woman will cook you something," repeated Niko, grinning at Pihla as they made their way through the path towards the sea. "I *do* like the sound of that, don't you?"

Tors chuckled as Pihla shot him a withering look. They had just dropped Enok off at her school and were making their way to the pods. "So is this what you do everyday?" she asked Hakon.

He nodded. "It is," he replied smilingly, "although I usually drop Enok at her school a little earlier than this."

It wasn't long before the familiar salty smells of the sea filled the air and overhead, in the still pink-streaked morning sky, calls from seabirds signalled their arrival at the seafront. Hakon's mood seemed to lift as the expanse of the ocean with its sparkling domes in the distance greeted them.

"Aahh…" He breathed in deeply. "The life of an Ellagrin farmer! Farm, eat, sleep, and repeat." His eyes shone blue-green like the sea. "It is a good life," he said contentedly, "and one richer by far than any city folk may think."

Tors looked at their surrounding landscape and found herself agreeing. That statement, as genuine and straightforward as Hakon himself, certainly had appeal to it.

He led them to the waterfront. Here, three sea scooters, which he referred to as skimmers, bobbed lazily by the edge of the shore. Tors and Pihla exchanged amused glances. Water sports were practically unheard of in the Realm so the prospect of skimming over the ocean on these was about to drive all of them, in particular the menfolk of their group, into ecstatic overdrive.

"I only have three," Hakon said, "so you're going to have to share." He waved Marcus and Tors towards the first skimmer. "I'll show you how to operate it," he said as Marcus climbed on and helped Tors behind him, in tandem.

"No stunts please," said Tors a little sternly, noting that Marcus had not stopped grinning like a fool since he first set eyes on the skimmer.

"PIHLAAAAAA!" shouted Niko as his skimmer swerved to an abrupt stop in front of Pihla, causing a mini tidal wave to sweep over her, drenching her from head to toe. To his credit, he did manage to get it to stop before running her to the ground. Wobbling precariously on the pedals, Niko stood up, puffed out his chest and sported his most vainglorious pose to date.

Pihla flicked the water off her clothes. "Fool!" she said, pursing her lips in disapproval.

Niko nodded at the backseat of his skimmer. "Wanna ride?" he asked, waggling an eyebrow at her, but she ignored his offer and sauntered coolly past him.

And hopped aboard Hakon's craft instead.

. . .

Suitably briefed, the three skimmers headed out to sea with Hakon, and Pihla in tandem, leading the way. With the sun warming their backs and the salt spray cooling their faces, it was going to be a glorious day.

"Wooo hooooo!" Niko sped past in exhilaration.

In the distance, the pods gleamed like shiny blobs of mercury. Hakon banked left and headed for them.

"Having fun yet?" yelled Marcus grinning at Tors holding on behind as he sped up to keep up with Hakon. His tousled fair hair gleamed, seemingly set alight by the golden morning light.

Tors smiled back and trailed her hand in the water, drawing gilded lines behind them. Above, as the seabirds called out, she felt her heart answer them in chorus and breathed in, exhilarated and happy.

The life of an Ellagrin! Is this what freedom feels like?

The three skimmers sped on, making trails along the glittering sea. A few minutes later, as they approached the pods, Hakon signalled for them to slow down.

As they neared, Tors could make out each perfect sphere, bobbing half-submerged in the calm sea. Up close, each pod was a transparent bubble, made from a lightweight glassy material coated with a reflective film, which gave it its mercurial sheen. Along its circumference, just above the surface of the water, a thin translucent platform ran all the way around the sphere.

Hakon signalled for them to circle round the pod and as they did so, he reached out to pull their skimmers in towards the pod.

Now Tors understood why the bow of each skimmer was shaped in a concave manner—it matched the upper curve of the pod. The moment the skimmer touched the pod, its engines stopped and the vehicle fitted itself neatly against the side, remaining attached as if anchored to the pod somehow.

Pihla bent to look closer. "Nice," she said, trying to figure out the mechanism.

"Affinity suction," said Hakon. "That's why they don't float off."

"Ah," said Pihla, nodding.

"Come," said Hakon, leaping onto the thin platform, "let me show you the inside."

THE POD WAS ENCLOSED with a single panel left open, presumably for entry as well as ventilation. Hakon led them through the opening and into the pod.

Inside, radiating from its centre like spokes of a wheel, were slim paths made of the same lightweight material as the platform outside. Above, at head-height, hung wire mesh covered in vines, their convoluted branches filling every square inch of space in the pod. The space inside was roughly the size of a small room but with the burgeoning plants taking up most of the space and the five of them crowded round, it felt a little claustrophobic.

"Come, come," beckoned Hakon, "come have a closer look. There's more space than you think and these platforms are sturdier than they look. This will take all our weight and some."

Stepping gingerly, they followed him along one of the paths.

Tors peered through the platform into the depths below. There, submerged in the water like the beard of Dyaeus himself, floated a mass of wispy roots swaying gently in the current. From these rose thicker canes which spread up and out, eventually branching again and again into the tangle of vines hanging off the wire mesh above. She gazed at the trailing vines and their emerald green leaves thinking how pretty it all looked.

Then quite unexpectedly something moved.

Tors jumped back, startled.

Marcus grabbed her to stop her from falling into the water. "What is it?" he asked, looking around warily.

Tors pointed at the moving vines.

"Are you sure these are *plants*?" Marcus called out, concerned. The vines coiled and curled. Constantly. Twisting and writhing like serpents.

"What do you mean?" Hakon looked at them quizzically.

"It's just that we've come across something like this before," Pihla said, " except they weren't plants…"

Hakon laughed. "Assuredly, these are plants," he answered.

Tentatively Tors reached out and touched the twirling vines, noting each one ended with a star-shaped spread of five smaller tendrils all covered in tiny fibres. "Oh! They're sticky," she exclaimed, rubbing her fingers against her thumb.

"Yes," Hakon said, "it helps them grasp the fruit."

"He's right!" said Pihla, pointing excitedly. "*Look!*"

Tors looked. The vine curled itself around the small round, nut-brown fruit before twisting and pulling it off, before dropping it into the water below.

"Trees that pick their own fruit?" Pihla sounded as incredulous as the rest of them. The vines were constantly moving, twirling languidly in and out, and around each other. And some did indeed pulled off fruit in the process!

Hakon looked at them with an amused smile on his face. "Yes, that's exactly what it is. They are picking the fruit and what's more, they only pick the ripe ones."

"But how? Are they *aware?*" asked Niko. There was a trace of fear in his voice.

Tors glanced at him. *He's thinking of the LON...*

Hakon laughed. "No, it's a plant I told you. What you see is merely a response to a stimulus."

"A stimulus?" repeated Niko.

Hakon nodded. "These are *sagarnuts*," he explained, bending down to scoop a few of them bobbing on the surface, "engineered to thrive in high-salt environments and produce a chemical compound when ripe." He chuckled. "The same chemical compound herbivorous cutters emit so that the plant will think the ripe fruit is the insect itself."

"So it's trying to rid itself of its ripened fruit because it thinks the fruit's an *insect?*" asked Pihla.

Hakon nodded. "Exactly."

"Hmm clever!" said Pihla.

"And now all we have to do is collect the floating fruit off the water," said Hakon scooping the sagarnuts bobbing on the surface with a small handnet and transferring them to the cloth bag slung across his shoulder.

"Don't you have machinery to pick these?" asked Pihla.

Hakon smiled at her. "Spoken like a true Tilkoen," he said. "Sorry, we're only good at crafting plants, not machines."

Pihla grinned in reply.

"What do these taste like?" Niko asked, examining the fruit interestedly.

"Nutty I guess," replied Hakon, "but we don't eat them like that. These are used for medicine." He scooped another one up deftly.

"Medicine?"

"Yes," said Hakon. "Don't you recognise them?"

Niko shook his head.

"*Sagcycline, Sagbiotika?* Your common antibiotics, the ones you get from the pharm. They all come from sagarnuts."

"Ah," nodded Niko, pretending to recognise the names. Then Hakon handed each of them a shoulder bag like his.

"Now that you know what to do, you can each start with a pod and work your way through the first sector," he said, shepherding them out of the pod. "I'll be nearby so if you need help, just wave."

THE MORNING PASSED QUICKLY as each team went from one pod to the next collecting sagarnuts and then emptying their shoulder bags, full of the fruit, into large floating nets Hakon had secured behind each skimmer. It wasn't long before each they started comparing the number of sagarnuts bobbing in their nets and things began to get competitive.

Hakon had gone ahead to check on the next sector, leaving Pihla to share Niko's skimmer whilst Marcus and Tors kept theirs.

To speed things up, Tors and Marcus had begun by harvesting a pod each, with Marcus dropping Tors off at one pod before himself speeding to the next one on the skimmer, and then whizzing back to collect Tors and her load.

However, with Pihla surprisingly quick on her feet and Niko speeding recklessly from pod to pod, it wasn't long before Marcus decided that his strategy was taking too long and announced that he would be leaving Tors to drive the skimmer whilst he swam from one pod to the next. "You use the skimmer," he said, eyeing Niko and Pihla with competitive zeal. "I'll collect the nuts and leave them on the platform for you to pickup. Then, I'll swim to the next pod. *Don't* wait for me."

Tors gave a chuckle. They would cover more pods that way. It was a good plan.

"Eat my dust Marcuuuus!" yelled Niko as he swept past them with a provoking splash.

"You mean spray, fool!" corrected Pihla and waved tauntingly from the backseat.

Tors gestured defiantly at them as Marcus hauled himself up the platform to help her load her haul into the nets. He shook the water off his back like a dog, making her squeal as the droplets rained all over her. There was a moment's pause when their eyes locked and he bent towards her.

"I, uh, left the load just over ther—," was all she managed to get out before Marcus kissed her full on the lips. She blinked with surprise but he moved closer. *Funny, I never noticed the flecks of gold in those brown eyes...*

"I don't think…," she started and then stopped. She didn't know what to think for she had stopped thinking. In fact, her mind was rather blank that moment, staring at those flecks of gold in his eyes.

"I really don't—" she ventured one last time, before Marcus reached forward and pulled her gently in to kiss her.

DINNER

The streets of Vijker were almost deserted by the time they made their way to mayor Alber's house that evening. The market stalls had been stored away and a cheerful glow coming from the uncurtained windows of people's homes now illuminated the darkened streets.

Tors walked down the middle of the street flanked by Pihla on one side and Hakon on the other. Hakon had little Enok perched on his shoulders whilst Marcus and Niko were content to follow behind on the leisurely walk to the mayor's house. It was a mild night and the air fresh with the familiar tang of salt and sea.

Hakon was telling the girls something about the village baker's wife and some wayward *scomber* which made Tors laugh out loud. It was a hearty laugh and one Marcus had not heard coming from her before. He also couldn't help staring at her. She had never looked more beautiful than tonight, her dark hair hanging loose about her shoulders and the carefreeness in her stride. It had been a good day at sea tending to the pods and one, dared he hope, that brought them closer. *Perhaps I may have my chance yet...*

He glanced sideways at Niko who was dragging his feet, head cast downwards. *And whilst my chances with Tors may be going the right way, his with Pihla may be going the opposite direction.* "Why so glum?" he asked, giving Niko a friendly pat on the back.

Niko gave a despondent shrug. "I pissed her off earlier, whilst helping her gather the sagarnuts," he said.

"Really?" said Marcus. They had stopped walking and were now standing in front of the mayor's house. In front, Hakon lifted Enok from his shoulders to stand her on the ground beside him. "For helping her?" continued Marcus, surprised.

Niko nodded. "Yeah," he said, his voice low as someone opened the door and Hakon and the girls entered ahead of them. "We saw you and Tors," continued Niko, "and well, I said I could kiss her like that too. You know, just to even things out between us teams."

Marcus chortled and shook his head as they entered the house. One never really knew what went on between those two. Niko of course, had been trying to get past the bestmates stage with Pihla for years, but with Pihla, Marcus had no idea. She'd always held her cards close to her chest. Still, he had to hand it to Niko—he was persistent for sure, even if his methods were unorthodox.

Mayor Alber was already in his lavish dining room when they were shown in, seated at the table next to a portly woman, much shorter than he but just as round. They were talking animatedly and laughing whilst servants stood in the background holding flagons of amarinthe and platters of entrees.

"Ah! Our guests have arrived," exclaimed Alber waving them over. "Come! Come! Sit! Sit!" His face was already flushed from drinking and he beckoned them over enthusiastically. "May I present you my wife, Fjalla," said Alber.

"Enchanted," replied Marcus kissing her outstretched hand.

Fjalla beamed like the full moon.

"Ahh! Little Enok!" exclaimed Alber bending forward. "Come! Come say hello to Uncle Alber!"

Enok withdrew behind Tors and tightened her hold on Tors' hand. Alber tried to cajole her some more before eventually giving up and sitting back down.

"So, did you go harvesting at the pods earlier today?" he asked as his servant went round to fill their glasses.

"Yes, we did," replied Marcus. "It was most enjoyable."

"You were all very quick too," grinned Hakon. "I might hire you for the year end's harvest if you decide to stopover at Vijker again then."

"Ah! Here we are! Heh heh!" announced Alber as the servants began to bring in the food. He beamed at them as it was placed on the table.

First to be set down in pride of place at the centre was a platter of seafood including slices of smoked scomber. Next, plates of meaty succulents, hot-baked breads and buttered root vegetables were brought in. Marcus noted the food was heavily spiced and decadently rich, a stark contrast to Hakon's simple, clean cooking.

"Please! Please! Eat! *Eat*!" Alber urged them enthusiastically as the food kept coming, platter after platter.

"So how do you find the food?" he asked between mouthfuls.

"Delicious!" said Niko.

"Excellent isn't it?" Alber continued animatedly. "What did

I tell you? Fjalla's cooking is the best on this side of Kaldr, is it not?"

"It's certainly the best I've ever eaten in a long time," replied Marcus truthfully and gave a little bow at Fjalla to acknowledge her fine cooking skills. "My compliments to the chef!"

Fjalla blushed like a ripe peach.

"Fjalla is from the city. Trom, in fact—the gourmet capital of Kaldr," continued Alber. "Which is why her cooking has such ah… *sophistication*." Alber looked proudly at his beaming wife. Fjalla said nothing but smiled so widely Marcus thought her cheeks must have hurt.

She beams like the moon, and is silent as one. Although that hardly mattered for Alber talked enough for the two of them. "Of course, our food here is of the highest quality," continued Alber. "Vijker is a well-known farming town and here, we grow the best vegetables and grains in all of planet Kaldr."

Marcus nodded. "Indeed," he said. "We saw the pods this morning. Your use of genomics in agro-pharming is impressive."

"We are pretty good at this, heh heh!" Alber's smile widened and it dawned on Marcus how Alber's neat little teeth resembled a string of pearls in his mouth. "Despite us being so far away from the capital planet, our techniques are very much the latest in all of Ellagrin and we have continued to experiment and improve these further ourselves," he said. He leant forward and rubbed his hands with glee. "In fact, we have something I'd like you to sample," he said. "An exciting new fruit which Fjalla and I have been cultivating in our prototype nurseries!" He signalled to one of his servants. "Mona! Bring us some of the *new* fruit!"

Mona disappeared into the kitchen and returned with a small plate of purple berries.

"Ah! Try it! Try it!" urged Alber, popping one greedily into his mouth. "Tell me, what do you think."

They each took some. Little Enok reached out to take one too, but Alber waggled his fat finger at her. "Only for adults little Enok," he said with a smile, purple juice dribbling over his lower lip.

Enok withdrew with a pout and contented herself with more bread.

Marcus took a bite. The berries were good. *Very* good in fact. He glanced at Tors sitting next to him. "Mmmmm!" he said and she nodded in agreement. It was unlike any berry he'd tasted before—sweet like molasses but zingy on the palate and left you wanting more. Marcus popped several more into his mouth, savouring its irresistibly perfumed concoction. *This tastes just like honeybread from my childhood,* he thought feeling intensely happy, *…and candy corn, caramel bon bons and sugar lions all put together. This fruit is AMAZING!*

He looked around the table contentedly. Alber was telling a joke and sending the rest of them into fits of laughter. Fjalla was bobbing up and down giggling and Niko was laughing so hard tears streamed down his face. Elated, Marcus reached out and grasped Tors' hand. He felt its warmth and that warmth seemed to spread through his body like wildfire. He gazed at her, drinking in her beauty. She flashed him a tentative smile and then leant over to plant a soft kiss on his lips. Marcus felt so happy he could burst.

"So…" began Alber, eyeing Pihla a trifle lustily, "So, you are Tilkoen? Heh heh!"

Pihla nodded and leant back into her chair, her arms thrown carelessly behind her head.

That woman's clearly had a bit too much amarinthe, mused Marcus. He looked at Tors who seemed equally lightheaded and put his arm around her shoulders protectively. She made no move to protest, instead met his gaze and settled further into his embrace, affectionate and vulnerable. *If I drown in this sea of emerald, so be it,* thought Marcus, euphoric.

"So what do you think of our pod technology eh?" asked Alber, smiling at Pihla. "Lightweight, compact and durable! Did you know, the ones you see have been in operation for centuries? Heh! They look just as shiny and as new as the day my father first bought them." He reached forward and offered Pihla some more of the 'happy' fruit. "Tilkoen technology," continued Alber, munching energetically, "is a class on its own. Nothing else like it *heh?*" He studied Pihla with his bright beady eyes "Shame we don't see many Tilkoens here anymore, not since the War. I'm afraid Tilkoens generally don't trust us anymore. Shame..." He shook his head sadly.

Yes, shame... what a great pity, sniffed Marcus thinking about all the times Pihla had helped them with all their engineering emergencies. He removed his arm from Tors' shoulder to blow his nose. It was true, what Alber said. *Yes,* thought Marcus agreeing wholeheartedly, *we could all do with more Tilkoens. They are such a great people!*

Alber filled Marcus's glass and went on. "It was a long time ago, during the Age of Prosperity, when the Gateways were still in use,"—he nodded at Niko—"Some of you may not even have heard of these but I remember we had all sorts of people travel through here in those days."

Marcus nodded wholeheartedly. *Those were the days...Sigh! Bring back those glory days!* He took a few more berries and quaffed down some more amarinthe in commiseration.

"My father, Ysgarh rest his soul," sniffed Alber emotionally, "used to take our produce to Namsos and distribute them all over the galaxy using the Gateways." Alber wiped away a tear and blew on his bulbous nose. "He would take our smoked scomber to Ageron via the Lagentian Gateway and once or twice from there, he'd venture into Tilkoen using the other Gateway… the uh, the uh, I cannot recall its name."

"The Arnemetiaen Gateway?" offered Pihla helpfully.

Alber nodded, "Heh! *Yes*! That's the one! The Gateway that connected Ageron to the Tilkoen city of Sansari." He indicated towards the outside of the house, in the direction of the sea. "Did you know our pods are Tilkoen?"

Pihla giggled. "Yes, I think you did mention that before," she said.

Alber put his hand against his chest in reverence. "Father brought those back with him from Sansari and to this day, our livelihoods depend on them."

"They are impressive," Pihla agreed, "although I noticed you don't have much in way of automation when it comes to harvesting."

"Ah, *automation*," said Alber nodding vigorously. "I'm afraid that's the stark difference between our two cultures. Ellagrin biotech expertise may be second to none, but I'm afraid technology as a whole, is not our strong point. We are farmers, not machinists." Fjalla nodded, agreeing with her husband and bade the servant Mona bring some more fruit and amarinthe.

"Tell me," said Alber, suddenly turning towards Marcus, "where are you from originally?" His beady eyes appeared to narrow considerably.

And here come the questions… thought Marcus headily, but before he could answer, Pihla cut in.

"Sansari originally," she answered slurring a little. "But when the gates fell…"

Marcus shot her a wary look. *The amarinthe has loosened her tongue.*

But fortunately, Pihla, sloshed, left the sentence unfinished.

Alber nodded gravely. "Yes, yes, most tragic," he said melodramatically, hand on his chest in grief. "I too, lost contact with some of my extended family when that happened." He shook his head disconsolately. "So many ties cut, families separated. War is a terrible thing! Tell me, do you have family here on Ellagrin?"

"No," replied Pihla welling up, "sadly I'm the only one left here."

That's right, thought Marcus, picking up on her sorrow. *After your father died, you had no family left in Ageron. That was why you asked me if there was a place on the Carinthia, to take you to the Ellagrin system so that you could eventually make your way to the Tilkoen system from there. Oh Pihla...*

"Well, at least you're okay," said Alber. He consoled her with a couple of heavy thumps on her back although by now, Pihla seemed too woozy to notice. Then he turned back to face Marcus. "Hakon tells me you crashed off the coast, not far from our pods." He swivelled round to ask Hakon. "Which sector was that you said?"

"Sector three I think," Hakon answered. Marcus thought he looked a trifle uncomfortable. "Near the bloodfruit and hoop beans."

"That's strange," replied Alber not taking his eyes off Marcus. "There was no report of any smoke and none of the sensors reported any breaches to the pod perimeters…"

Marcus sipped his amarinthe to give himself a moment. *The man is getting suspicious,* he told himself, trying to clear his head. He glanced around the room. The servants had disappeared.

A faint wash of uneasiness suddenly swept over him. *It would be just as well if we went on our way sharpish,* thought Marcus. *Too many questions are being asked and not enough satisfactory answers for them...* He signalled at Niko, who looked as if he had eaten something that hadn't quite agreed with him, but as they rose to leave, Marcus noticed Hakon's eyes trained on the doorway.

The room had gotten quiet all of a sudden.

Where the servants had waited moments before, now a row of tall, formidable men stood silently by the door. Marcus recognised one or two of them. They were the same workers that had been shifting the crates earlier that day. He turned to yank Tors up by the arm but like Pihla, she was in too much of an inebriated state to move.

The berries! thought Marcus, suddenly feeling sick. *The berries...*

He stood on his feet, swaying slightly, as one by one, Alber's men filed into the room. The first one pushed him back into his chair, keeping him there. Alber nodded at Hakon who rose reluctantly to shut the door behind them.

The silence became deafening.

Alber leant forward in his seat. He didn't look as jolly or as drunk as he did a minute ago. "Hakon tells me you didn't come here by ship," he said, his black beady eyes suddenly sharp and enquiring. He looked up at Hakon.

"Enok said you emerged from down below," Hakon said, his eyes avoiding Marcus'. "From the sea..." He stopped as Alber rose ponderously to his feet.

"I have lived here since the Age of Prosperity," he said, his voice trembling with emotion, "and as a child, I used to play by the rocks like Enok, and once, a very long time ago, a bunch of outworlders came from below, just where she found you." He cast his gaze around the table and continued, his voice now contemptuous, "They were Nehisi, my father told me—the *scourge* of the developing worlds and the source of inequality amongst the Houses of our galaxy. Conspirators to our enemy, the Ageronians, and the reason for the decline of our great empire." He glared at them and rubbed his chin thoughtfully. "But the thing is," he said, his voice vastly lowered in volume, "we were told they no longer exist—we eradicated them all."

Then his voice turned deadly serious. "There is no skiff and there is no spaceship" he stated. "You haven't come from the sea or the stars, and you haven't come from nearby islands either. It is as if you've just appeared out of thin air…"

He turned to look at Marcus, his beady little eyes hard and vicious like two black beetles. "There is no Gate in this archipelago," he said slowly, "yet here you are…"

His eyes settled on Tors leaning weakly in her seat.

PART II

AGERON

THE COMITIUM

ALANDIA CITY,
PLANET AMORGOS, AGERON SYSTEM

When Lord Draeger alighted from his urbanglider to set foot upon the modernistic steps of the *Comitium*, Ageron's central governing office, he was met by two Praetors—Lords Conor and Metavius. They were old friends and possibly the only two members of the entire Senate he considered as such.

"My lord," greeted Lord Metavius, the older of the two men. Tall and broad, with a mountainous chest and a coarse peppered beard, the Praetor exuded the same commanding presence Draeger remembered throughout his father's reign.

He was one of Lord Marius' senators when Father appointed him Praetor of Olicana, recalled Draeger, *making him one of the youngest planetary governors in living history, much to Lord Marius' displeasure.* Draeger clasped Metavius' hand and shook it heartily. "Good to see you again Metavius," he said. "I see senate life has not aged you as much as it has with Conor."

Lord Metavius let out an involuntary snort and chuckle.

"Not as much as thwarting an invasion, my lord," said Lord Conor as he stepped forward to give Draeger a handshake and

PLANET AMORGOS, AGERON SYSTEM

slap on the back. Lean and athletic, with a clean-shaven face and fierce brown eyes, Lord Conor was closer in age to Draeger than the redoubtable Lord Metavius. Their careers too, seemed to have mirrored each other's, with both Conor and Draeger rising up their respective ranks at roughly about the same time over the years—Conor, within the administrative world of the Senate and Draeger, through the ranks of the military.

"The next chapter of events may well be even more eventful than the failed invasion," Draeger replied drily and directed a knowing look at both men before activating his vizard to obscure his face. Then, together, they all walked up the silver steps to enter the Comitium.

The Comitium, standing tall in the middle of Alandia's prestigious central district, was a slender, twelve-sided building clad in onyx, its prismatic outline gleaming like a thoroughly sleek and modern piece of jewellery. Inside, twelve conjoined tower blocks, arranged in circular fashion, made up the building's main shaft, giving it its overall twelve-sided shape.

Twelve sides to represent the twelve planets of Ageron. Draeger stood in the middle of the atrium and looked at the twelve towers surrounding them, each comprising floor after floor of offices, meeting rooms and debating chambers. The building was teeming with hundreds of bustling civil servants, all industriously going about with the administrative business of running the empire.

"This way," said Lord Conor and led them into one of the service stairwells at the side. After several flights of stairs, they emerged at the fifth floor and onto a corridor used by service staff.

Lord Conor gave a wry grin and put his finger to his lips before opening a small plain-looking door.

They entered quietly and Draeger let out a soft grunt of surprise when he recognised where they were. This was the back of the Comitium's main assembly hall, often referred to as the Ecclesia.

The Ecclesia was a cavernous semi-circular space surrounded by ascending rows of seating, much like a concert hall. Even at full attendance, as was usual on a normal day like this, the last ten rows all round the back were rarely filled. Secure in the relative dimness of his surroundings, Draeger deactivated his vizard as Lord Conor led them to the farthest section of this unlit backend of the chamber, away from the occupied rows in front, where they could sit and observe proceedings with little risk of being noticed or heard.

As they tiptoed in, Lord Metavius nudged Draeger and nodded towards the far corner. There in the dimness, sat the grey, lanky figure of the Chancellor. "The old wolf," grinned Lord Metavius, "is already watching events like a hawk." Noiselessly, they made their way towards Chancellor Rasmus to sit with him.

"Chancellor," acknowledged Draeger as Chancellor Rasmus gave him a discreet nod in lieu of a bow.

"I've taken the liberty of asking Senator Mamercus to raise the issue of the emperor's impeachment," whispered the Chancellor. "To test the waters so to speak. We shall get a general feel for what the Senate thinks of all this before we formally table the article of impeachment." Draeger nodded as they sat down to watch the debate in the gallery below.

"We will need a majority vote from the Senate to impeach the emperor," murmured Lord Metavius. "You won't believe the amount of debate this question of whether to impeach him or not has been generating within the Senate. Those loyal to the Queen Mother such as Lord Reku, have been particularly vocal."

PLANET AMORGOS, AGERON SYSTEM

"Yes, but the Queen Mother has no political claim and therefore no say in all of this," said Lord Conor.

"Nevertheless, her influence extends beyond the royal circles and into the Senate," countered Lord Metavius. "If we don't get enough Praetors voting for impeachment, we will have a problem on our hands..."

Lord Draeger nodded gravely. Metavius was right. The motion for Akseli's impeachment would be voted on by the entire Senate, comprising twelve Praetors—each governor of one of Ageron's twelve planets, and the hundred or so senators that served beneath them. The decision made by each Praetor would be hugely influential for the senators were likely to follow in the way of the Praetors they served.

He glanced at Metavius and Conor, and thought about the power held by the Praetors. Like governors of Old Earth, Praetors served as Chief Justices, but on a planetary scale, and were responsible for matters of government including the administration of their respective planets, health and welfare.

But not the military, Draeger reminded himself. Praetors had no control over the military unless like Lord Reku, they held the title of Legatus as well. But aside from the odd special case, Ageron's generals (the Legati), their centurions and legions all answered to *him*, the Supreme Commander and not the Senate.

"To get the Senate to vote for impeachment may well require some... *persuasion*," Draeger said drily. "Will you make sure the Senate knows that the generals are also keen to see a trial, in order that the full measure of justice can be applied?"

Lord Conor nodded with a bemused smile. "Will do," he said. "I'm sure that will certainly help focus minds,"

"Once impeached, the date for the Emperor's trial will be set," said Chancellor Rasmus. "The trial is where the real work begins. Don't forget, we will need a two-thirds majority vote from the Senate in order to depose the emperor."

Lord Metavius pointed his chin in the direction of the central gallery where Senator Mamercus had begun to speak. "Well, let's see what appetite the Senate has for a trial in the first place, shall we?"

* * *

"MEMBERS OF THE SENATE," began the senator, "we must discuss the question of Emperor Akseli's impeachment—"

Voices rose as Praetors and senators alike asserted their varying opinions on the matter. Lord Reku stood up, his portly form looking even more dense and rotund in his richly-brocaded outfit, and proceeded to wave down Senator Mamercus.

"We have bigger issues to deal with than a trial!" he bellowed, looking round the gallery to gather support. "With the recent destruction from heatstorms in Olicana and Ilia, is all this talk of impeachment even *necessary*?"

"And now they reveal themselves," muttered Lord Conor leaning forward, "*Now* we see who's in favour of impeachment and who's not."

"Pah! Reku is all hot air and no substance," said Metavius. "He may be the Queen Mother's ally but he has no clout."

"He has his legions though," said Draeger quietly. "Don't forget, my father made him Legatus."

"That may be," murmured Chancellor Rasmus, " but it is not Reku that I wonder about…" He directed his gaze slowly towards another elderly figure in the gallery below—Lord Marius, Praetor of Ceos.

"Marius?" queried Metavius, surprised. "But Marius hasn't even once said a word against the motion for impeachment."

PLANET AMORGOS, AGERON SYSTEM

"And *that's* what worries me," said the Chancellor. "Lord Marius and the Queen Mother were close once…"

Draeger nodded. "There were whispers of a scandal. I was a boy then but I think Father banished Marius all the way to Ceos."

"Your father I believe, made him *Praetor* for Ceos," corrected Chancellor Rasmus. He flashed Draeger a knowing look and added, "…at Queen Alin's insistence."

"Hmmm," said Draeger. "That's a little shortsighted. These days, it would appear that position has become a boon rather than a burden."

"Yes," admitted the Chancellor with some regret. "I failed to see it then but it would seem that that move has turned out in Lord Marius' favour after all."

Draeger nodded gravely. Ceos may have been one of the backwater planets with little natural resource compared to other planets in Ageron, but to Lord Marius' good fortune, it happened to have a large population. Most of whom joined the army for there was little else to do. *Which makes Marius' legions one of the largest in the Realm,* noted Draeger, *so much so that Father bestowed upon him the additional title of Legatus in order to oversee them.* Lord Marius therefore became one of the two Praetors who were also Legati, setting him aside from other Praetors who served as mere administrators, and giving him direct control over the armies in planet Ceos.

"But Lord Marius has so far toed the line all these years," said Draeger. "His legions have served me without question and he has never once interfered with my decisions as far as the military has been concerned, even though by law, they are his."

"That may be," said the Chancellor. "Nevertheless, we should tread carefully with this one. Queen Alin has many supporters, not all in plain sight." He paused to listen as Lord Patrin, Praetor of Segontia, came forward to speak next.

"If our emperor is innocent, then a trial will prove it," said Lord Patrin. "Too long has the empire been mired in scandal. Government must be without reproach. We must show our people that we do not tolerate corruption and certainly not treason. A fair trial I say, in order for all to decide. After all, how can we all move forward if we have all this hanging over our heads?"

"Hear, hear," murmured Lord Metavius as Lord Patrin's speech seemed to bring to a close the outbursts in the gallery.

"Well *that's* one way to get on the Queen Mother's good side," said Lord Conor with a chuckle.

"Patrin brings calm and logic to the table," said Chancellor Rasmus. "He is impartial and the Senate respects him."

"Many of the Praetors will listen to Patrin," agreed Lord Metavius. He glanced at the Chancellor, encouraged. "It will be a landslide vote if Patrin decides that it is right that the Emperor should go to trial—"

He stopped short as Lord Reku's indignant voice punctured through the calm. "But what good is impeachment under present circumstances?" Lord Reku challenged. "What is a trial even going to achieve? My lords, Ageron is facing imminent destruction and we are arguing about a stupid trial! By Dyaeus, at the rate the binary suns are failing, our entire planetary system will be uninhabitable soon!"

"Hear! Hear!" shouted another senator. "Impeachment is the least of our worries at the moment. Climate change is accelerating across our entire planetary system—we thought we had a century or two but now, it's looking closer to fifty years at best. The entire Ageronian system could be uninhabitable by then!"

"Indeed, indeed," agreed Lord Reku. "And recent hostilities

PLANET AMORGOS, AGERON SYSTEM

from House Ellagrin has meant the Exodus programme is no longer viable. If we can no longer evacuate our people to the Ellagrin system, then where will we go? Where *can* we go?"

"Absolutely!" fretted Lord Velius. "And why are we even continuing with the Exodus? What are we building all these ships for? What options do we have left?"

Draeger glowered, the lines on his face deepening with every word uttered on the floor and the growing undercurrent of panic in the voices that carried them. *They are right. With House Ellagrin now our enemy, we have nowhere to evacuate our people to.* For a fleeting moment, he even considered the possibility of resuming negotiations with Elena. *Would repairing relations with an empire that just tried to invade you be possible? Or prudent?*

"My lords," Lord Patrin spoke up, loudly and firmly, "we cannot and should not stop building our spacecarriers. We still have options. Our emissaries to the Tilkoen system have yet to return. Indeed, they are expected some time this decade and there is no foreseeable reason why the Tilkoens will not take us in. We shall know then if we can send our Exodus ships to Tilkoen instead of Ellagrin going forward." He raised his hand to still a few objecting voices. "And don't forget, my lords, the expedition into the Ether to search for Sansari is currently underway, giving us the other option of evacuation into Tilkoen via the Arnemetiaen Gateway. Finally, if all else fails, perhaps even a diplomatic arrangement with House Ellagrin could be explored. All this is still on the cards—"

"All this is just *talk!*" declaimed Lord Augusta. "Talk and nothing more! Last week's heatstorms have obliterated two more equatorial cities on Bellun! We need a *solution!*"

"And we *will* get one," countered Lord Patrin, "but only if we continue to pursue the plans we've set in motion—"

More voices rose to join in the resulting commotion.

Chancellor Rasmus shook his head, concerned. "The Senate is becoming fractious in the face of these mounting disasters…"

"…and Queen Alin will use this weakness and lack of direction to dismiss Akseli's trial," said Lord Metavius, finishing the sentence for him. His bushy brows furrowed.

"We will prevent that," said Lord Conor, determinedly. He turned to Lord Draeger, "So, my lord, shall we start the impeachment process?"

"Yes," Draeger said. He had seen enough and now was a good time as any.

"Very well. We will start proceedings," said Lord Conor. He looked critically at Lord Reku who had sat down, seemingly pleased at the panicked frenzy he had helped whip up. "What is with Reku anyway?" he said. "I bet the Queen Mother has something on him. He panders to her like a dog."

"I'm sure she has," agreed Lord Metavius. "She favoured him in the early years of Emperor Ageron's reign. Even helped influence his progression up the Senate too if I remember rightly."

Chancellor Rasmus gave a snort. "Queen Alin is a seasoned manipulator but even she cannot influence all of the Senate," he said. "And those like Lord Patrin are far too straight-laced for her to get her talons on."

"Indeed," agreed Draeger, "as is with you, Chancellor." As they all rose to exit the chamber, he gave the old man a glance, the corner of his lips twitching with amusement. "You old wolf," he said, "how is it she's never had one on you? Have you no secrets, Rasmus?"

The old man cackled with mirth. "I simply have no weaknesses to exploit, my lord," he said. But as Draeger walked down the stairs to leave the building, the old Chancellor reminded himself: *Ah but I do hold a secret. One entrusted to me by your late mother, Lady Yinha. A secret which has kept you safe from the Queen Mother all these years...*

Then he looked at the man, poised to be Emperor of Ageron, despite his total and utter reluctance, and wished him a safe journey home.

LIANNE

COMITIUM,
ALANDIA CITY, AGERON

Lianne paused outside the meeting room to cast a quick glance at her own reflection on the glass door.

When did I become so old and grey? she asked herself as she tucked a stray strand of hair back into the braid coiled round at the nape of her neck like a rope of tarnished silver. She examined her face briefly and lifted her chin, observing with despair, the creases that hung around the base of her jaw and neck like unwanted necklaces. Then, with a resigned sigh, she pushed the door to enter.

He was sat at the meeting table, clad as always, in grey, poring over some documents. It had been just a few months shy of a decade since she saw him last.

Too long, thought Lianne to herself, *and yet he has not changed one bit. I on the other hand...*

"You look well," she said, then closed the door behind her and hobbled towards him.

Chancellor Rasmus lifted his gaze to look at her.

He is not pleased to see me, she thought, pained at the look he gave her. Nevertheless, she approached the table and pulled out one of the chairs. *My knees will not last if I talk standing up.* She gave a sigh of relief as she settled into its cushioned base and turned to face him.

"What are you doing here?" The Chancellor's sharp, grey eyes searched hers as he posed the question. It was not meant to be unkind but Lianne detected an undercurrent of impatience in it.

"I heard you and the Supreme Commander arrived here at the Comitium yesterday," she replied.

Rasmus pursed his lips in annoyance. "You know we cannot be seen together Lianne," he said, ignoring her words. "It is not safe. I've told you before. If it's an emergency, send me the signal and we will meet at one of the usual places." He stood up and walked across to the window. "Have you no secrets, Rasmus," he muttered, repeating yesterday's passing comment by Lord Draeger under his breath and finishing off with an acerbic sigh.

Despite his years, Chancellor Rasmus exuded a certain distinguished countenance about him and with his eyes of flint and hair to match, could still pass off as a handsome man. To any passer-by that might have chanced to see the two of them together, Lianne might have looked like an older relative who had come to visit.

Looking at the sprightly Chancellor, Lianne suddenly felt the weight of all her hundred and ninety-one years upon her. "But I wanted to see you—" she began, getting up from her chair stiffly. *Does my presence shame you so?*

The Chancellor gave a sigh and turned round to look at her. "What is it Lianne? Are you short of funds? How is the interpreter role at Lord Reku's office going? Are you happy there? If not, you can always change your job."

Lianne bit her lip. "I do not need any *ore* from you and the work I do for Lord Reku is not the problem." She shuffled towards him and took his hand in hers. "Please, I want to do more to help. So much has been happening here on Amorgos. Why are they talking of impeaching the emperor? Is it true what they say—that he let the Ellagrins invade us?"

"Yes, our emperor is going to be impeached for aiding and abetting the invasion."

"But how? The Lagentian Gate has been closed for centuries. And people have been saying there is no evidence of any Nehisi who could have opened it to the Ellagrins." Lianne looked at Chancellor Rasmus. "Is the Supreme Commander seizing power? Are you siding him on this?"

The Chancellor wrenched his hands loose from hers. "Is this the drivel that has been circulating in our civil service?" There was anger and frustration in his voice. "The emperor is to stand trial for treason and you people think the Supreme Commander is seizing power?"

Lianne flinched. "This is what some people are saying, that's all. I am merely relaying the public's view of this to you." She searched his face. "You've always been a loyal supporter of our emperor. Why would he help the Ellagrins invade us?"

The Chancellor frowned at her, his expression troubled. "I have always been a faithful servant to House Ageron. All these years I have served Ageron and I still do so with its interest and sanctity at the centre of everything I do. You have to believe me, Lianne, when I say that it was the emperor himself who had attempted to seize power, and not the other way around."

"But Lord Draeger is the one who is rumoured to have liaisons with the Ellagrin empress, not Emperor Akseli," said Lianne. *This is what everyone knows and consequently you cannot blame what everyone makes of this.*

"There are things you do not know about, Lianne. Things you do not understand—"

ALANDIA CITY, AGERON

"Then *make* me understand," pressed Lianne. "Let me work here at the Comitium alongside you. I can do so much more than be some Praetor's interpreter. Give me a role here so I may serve the Realm. I want to be someone of consequence, Rasmus. I want to make a *difference*." She looked at him earnestly, her eyes large and zealous. *Let me work alongside you. Help you, even in my little inconsequential ways. Let me be with you...*

The Chancellor studied her time-worn face.

Lianne looked away, ashamed of her wrinkles and her withered looks. *I look old enough to be your mother. Is this why you hide me away so? Am I that vile to you?* She searched his eyes for an answer but saw none.

Then he touched her face lightly and said, "I promise you I shall think about it."

Lianne nodded. *At the very least, he has not denied me outright.* She looked on as he strode towards the door to leave the room. *Even after all these years, does he not trust me to be near him without letting on our secret? And yet despite these wasted years, I still love him. But does he love me I wonder? Has he ever loved me?*

Lianne wondered.

QUEEN ALIN

RED PALACE, AGERON

Queen Alin paced up and down the polished, ebony floors of Lord Draeger's solar. She was nervous, a state she was not accustomed to being in for a long time. However this time the stakes were far higher. Akseli's fate hung in the balance and she would need all the diplomatic skills she had honed through the years to save him.

"Queen Mother," greeted Lord Draeger. His tall, hawkish figure carved a dark and formidable outline at the door.

Queen Alin whirled around, startled. She had not heard him approach. She gathered herself together and faced him. "My lord," she acknowledged stiffly as Lord Draeger swept in.

The room was gloomy, barely illuminated by the two lit sconces in the corner, but Alin knew full well that Draeger's eyes, suited to the dark, had no problems seeing in surroundings much dimmer than this. He gestured for her to take a seat before taking one himself. "You requested to see me, Queen Mother," he said, his voice quiet and a touch wary.

She hesitated a moment and then replied, "I hear the

article of impeachment has been discussed and the Senate is to hold a vote on it soon."

"Yes." His reply was curt.

This does not bode well...

"My lord," she began, "there must be an alternative to impeachment. Impeachment would only serve to break the unity of the Realm and the publicity of it will not do us any favours in quelling the disquiet that grows amongst our people. You see that don't you?"

Draeger said nothing. However, something in his silence lent Alin the courage to go on.

"Akseli has done wrong, I know. But he is young and brash, misguided by a skewed sense of what power is." Alin steeled herself to look into Draeger's strange eyes, but she saw little of what she sought in them to give her comfort or confidence. Like endless voids, they were black as pitch and devoid of human emotion. She flinched, repulsed. *He is just like his witch mother...*

Nevertheless she pressed on. "He is your brother, my lord. A trial is as good as a hanging." Her throat felt dry as she uttered those words. *If Akseli stands trial, in all likelihood he will be found guilty. And if guilty, he will be executed.*

"Akseli opened the Lagentian Gateway and let the Ellagrins in to invade us," stated Draeger. "That is an act of treason."

Alin flushed. "He was not thinking clearly," she said. "The dire state of the Realm, the Rebellion, the settlement treaties with Ellagrin...," she opened her hands in a gesture of powerlessness, "he was trying, in his own way, to find a solution."

Draeger remained aloof and silent.

Alin shifted uncomfortably in her seat. "The private portal," she continued a little hesitantly. "It has been sealed..." Apart from the Lagentian Gate which was destroyed in the failed invasion, the private portal was their only link to the Ellagrin system light years away. *The only way I can reach Elena, and I **must** speak with her.*

"Yes," replied Draeger flatly. "It has been sealed. For obvious reasons."

Alin's eyes narrowed. Yes. No doubt he would have ordered that small, physical gateway to be sealed shut. *After all, who would want to keep communications open with the enemy.* The Queen Mother bit her lip. "If it were opened again," she ventured, "if I could speak with Lady Elena… *Empress* Elena, perhaps we could salvage the settlement treaties and negotiate a way forward with future ones for the Exodus." She glanced at Draeger. *This abomination may not value Akseli's life but the people of Ageron mean something to him and with relations between Houses Ageron and Ellagrin severed since the failed invasion, he will be concerned for those in the Exodus programme already on route to Ellagrin. He will want to know if Elena will still honour the resettlement treaties for them.*

Alin pondered further. *Ah, but not only that.* Her eyes gleamed at the realisation. *Going forward, he will need to resettle his people in Ellagrin as there is no guarantee word from Tilkoen will come back in time for the Exodus to evacuate the people to Tilkoen. Even less probable still, is if the Nehisi woman and her expedition team find Sansari in time to re-establish the gateway to Tilkoen.* Her pulse quickened as the opportunities these current constraints presented her began to unravel. *He needs Elena to resettle his people in Ellagrin and she in turn needs him in order to consolidate her position as empress. No doubt Ellagrin will be in need of funds after the failed invasion, funds that could come from Ageron in exchange for further settlement treaties. Funds that will no doubt help strengthen Elena's position as the new ruler of Ellagrin.* Her eyes glittered. *And if the relationship between these two were rekindled, even if Elena can't persuade him to drop the trial, renewed relations with House Ellagrin will give Akseli leverage —it will be harder to criticise House Ellagrin and its conspiracy with him if House Ageron were dependent on Ellagrin.*

And if all else fails, thought Alin to herself, *Draeger and Elena's relationship will cast doubt on the invasion itself. We could say the Gate was never opened and Draeger planned this to seize the throne.* Alin drew a deep breath. Whilst there was no clear-cut solution to getting Akseli out of his predicament, there were certainly a few options worth exploring. *I can at least work with these odds...*

She willed herself to push on. "I know my niece well, Lord Draeger, as if she were my own daughter. Perhaps even better than her own mother ever did, *Ysgarh* keep my sister's soul. Let us not be hasty with Akseli's fate. Keep him under house arrest if you wish and let us focus our efforts on pressing matters first. The fate of our people in transit to Ellagrin—the Carinthia and before that, Almirante, Taurus, the Delphinium and many, many more—are at great risk at the moment. And I can help."

Frowning, Lord Draeger stood up and walked to the window.

For a brief moment, Queen Alin saw in her mind's eye, the young Draeger looking out at the courtyard all those centuries ago. *Even then he was rational, methodical and with the same unnatural detachment to all things as his mother, the sorceress Yinha.* Her mouth thinned to a bitter, resentful line as she recalled the ill-fated day he stumbled onto her and Lady Cassia. *I should have killed you when I had the chance. But then I never did—your mother saw to that.* After the sorceress left, she had stayed on in the chamber to make sure Lady Cassia was well and truly dead. Emperor Ageron was devastated of course, for Lady Cassia was his favourite but it wasn't long before Alin herself gave birth to Akseli and with the presence of a new baby in the royal household, whatever traces of sentimentality Ageron may have had for the memory of Lady Cassia and her infant quickly evaporated. How protective Alin had felt for her own flesh and blood even then.

Unlike the sorceress and her kind.

Queen Alin shuddered at the thought. Lady Yinha's 'kind' was a strange, matriarchal race who resided in the cloud-covered mountains of the far-flung planet of Yoon. The Yoons were a strange race indeed, thought to be many things—scryers, soothsayers, mentalists, philosophers—descriptions none could agree upon. It was said Lady Yinha was the thirteenth daughter of the Empress Dowager of House Yoon, ruler of the Yoon people and according to historical accounts, Lady Yinha had been given to Emperor Ageron II (Ageron III's father) to foster as his own a mere three days after she was born, with the agreement that she was to be betrothed to the yet-unborn Ageron III at the time.

How did they know Ageron III would come to be born a year hence? Queen Alin grew cold. *And how did they know, out of all one hundred and twenty-five sons, that it would be he that would ascend the throne?*

Queen Alin looked at Draeger. She could guess what he was thinking. *He's weighing the risks up.* Her heart raced. *Why would Draeger risk his position by sparing Akseli? What could he possibly gain in doing so, except allow my son time to gather support and overthrow him once more?* Power struggles amongst princes rarely ended happily. After all, of all two hundred of Ageron's sons, only Draeger and Akseli had survived. Where the other consorts had not played a hand in the untimely deaths of the others, *she,* Alin, had made sure the rest were whittled out.

If not for your mother holding onto my secret as insurance, I would have snuffed you out too, she thought bitterly. *Instead, I had to keep you alive, if only for my sake and Akseli's. Still, your mother could not save herself...*

Lord Draeger turned to face her. He seemed to have made his mind up.

Quickly, before it is too late! Queen Alin plucked up courage to throw in her final card. "Lord Draeger," she said quickly, "Elena will honour those treaties. You think she will not speak with you but if you will just reopen the private portal, I can talk to her. Persuade her. Spare Akseli from trial and I will get her to not only honour existing treaties but agree to new ones. I *guarantee* it."

"Guarantee it?" Draeger sounded unconvinced.

Queen Alin nodded. "Why wouldn't she? After all, she is with child..."

Draeger looked at her.

"*Yours*," said Alin. She held her breath after that and watched his face closely. *Will it work? Have I done enough?*

And then she knew then that she had hit the mark for Draeger said nothing. Instead, he turned and walked out of the room like a man caught in a trance.

THE QUEEN MOTHER CONTEMPLATES

PLANET OLICANA, AGERON

The morning dawned bright but blustery, sending a few clouds racing across the otherwise clear sky. From her bedroom window, Queen Alin watched the twin suns rise, glowing red orbs ascending the heavens like two waning pearls. *The dying suns...*

She had decamped to her residence on the planet Olicana for a few days' respite from the searing heat in Amorgos and to gather her thoughts after her meeting with Lord Draeger at the Red Palace. The Queen sat at her table tapping her fingers meditatively when Anneliese, her handmaid entered with her usual breakfast of dry toast and a black *kofi* .

"You seem distracted, my lady," said Anneliese.

Queen Alin smiled. She liked Anneliese for she was a sharp young thing. *Quick-witted and ambitious too…*

"I am contemplating, my dear Anneliese," she murmured, looking out the window. She observed a young hawk in the distance chasing a darting *kakawu*, it gilded feathers glinting in the sunlight like a beacon, handicapping its ability to outrun its predator even further. Kakawu were nocturnal, coming out only at night to hunt small insects. It was therefore unusual to see one flying about in the daytime.

The hawk must have lured it from its nest, thought Queen Alin to herself. It was not unheard of. Instances where hawks resorted to disrupting tactics in lean times to force the kakawu to leave the safety of their nests and take to the air at a time when they would normally be asleep. *All creatures can be influenced despite their inherent nature,* thought the Queen Mother as the hawk's talons closed in on its target.

"Contemplating my lady?" Anneliese lifted the pot of kofi and proceeded to pour the steaming liquid into a dainty cup.

"Indeed, my young Anneliese," answered Queen Alin indulgently. "Contemplating." She bit into her toast and munched it distractedly. Dry toast was all she ever allowed herself at breakfast. The Queen Mother's tastes in this regard were much less indulgent, severe even, compared with most royals, but today, her mind was far away from the rituals of breakfast and toast.

How by Ysgarh can we avoid Akseli being impeached? she asked herself. Her meeting with Lord Draeger had not filled her with confidence. The chances of Draeger calling off the impeachment was slim. There simply wasn't sufficient incentive for him to do so. *But how do I persuade the Senate to vote against impeachment?*

She ruminated further. Her handful of old allies within the Senate would not be enough to sway a vote against impeachment for Akseli. Two Praetors, at best three, out of the twelve were loyal to Akseli. The hundred or so senators that served the twelve would generally vote in line with their respective Praetors. Several here and there, perhaps, could be persuaded to support Akseli but overall, not enough for a majority vote. She grimaced. *There **has** to be a way to influence the Senate to vote against impeachment. I have to at least try.*

"Tell me Anneliese, do you have family?" she asked, taking a sip of her kofi.

"No, my lady," answered Anneliese.

"None at all?"

"No, my lady. I'm an orphan my lady."

"Ah I see. And have you a man in your life perhaps?"

Anneliese blushed a little. "No, my lady. None at the moment."

"None at all?" murmured Queen Alin idly. "I find that hard to believe, a girl as pretty as you."

"I have no time, my lady," Anneliese replied. There was a briefest of pauses and then she added, "Besides, there seem to be only useless louts or boors to choose from these days."

"I dare say you're right Anneliese," replied Queen Alin. She eyed her handmaid with an appraising look. "Perhaps you aren't looking in the right circles, my dear Anneliese." Queen Alin gave a sigh and went back to nursing her cup of kofi. "Perhaps Olicana is far too provincial compared with our capital planet Amorgos *where the action is*, as you young people say."

"Olicana is pleasant enough, my lady," replied Anneliese agreeably.

"Getting what one wants requires some form of planning, you know," said Queen Alin, her eyes following Anneliese as the girl tidied up the breakfast things, "even though sometimes, the plan itself isn't quite clear."

"I'm sure you are right my lady," replied Anneliese.

"One should cast one's options far and wide, Anneliese," continued the Queen Mother. Her eyes gleamed in a steely blue as she seemed to come to a decision. "Like seeds," she said with a hint of determination, "…in order to reap the rewards of the few that succeed."

"Yes, my lady," answered Anneliese dutifully as she tidied

up around the Queen. "Is there anything else you require my lady?"

"Yes there is, Anneliese," answered Queen Alin. "I need my things packed today. I leave tonight, for Amorgos."

Anneliese looked surprised. "Back to the capital planet so soon, my lady?"

"Yes," answered Queen Alin, "I think I shall visit a friend or two there."

"Yes, my lady," answered Anneliese. "I shall start packing right away."

The Queen arose to leave. It troubled her that she had no clear solution in sight. Akseli's situation remained a perilous one and she knew she had to persuade the Senate somehow. *Like the hawk, I must find a way to shake the kakawu. Induce it to change its mind.*

She looked on as Anneliese picked up the tray and started piling in the breakfast service. *And like a good little farmer, I must scatter my seeds far and wide in hope that some will flourish and yield a way forward through all this.* "Oh, and Anneliese?"

"Yes my lady?"

"Pack your things as well. You are coming with me."

"Yes my lady," answered Anneliese meekly.

LORD PATRIN

ALANDIA CITY, AGERON

*L*ady Ursule arose from her garden daybed and ambled cumbrously through the grove of low, sculptural trees towards the marble table and chairs where Queen Alin stood waiting. Shafts of light trickled through the dark, waxy leaves overhead, casting patches of crimson onto the chalky-white mosaic path that she followed.

The air in the courtyard was still and stifling for in a sense, it was no longer an outdoor courtyard. Overhead, a transparent dome had been erected to seal it from the harsh heatstorms outside. Amorgos, like most other planets had been experiencing harsher, more turbulent weather and Lady Ursule's villa, like many other residences of the wealthy and powerful, had had to have modifications such as protective coverings to shield against the unpredictable storms of late.

"My dear Lady Ursule," greeted Queen Alin as Lady Ursule approached.

"My dear Queen Alin, how nice of you to drop by." Lady Ursule leant forward as the two ladies exchanged kisses. Alin noted her bump extended far beyond her already protuberant breasts.

"You look well," said Queen Alin genially. "And how are Lord Patrin and yourself keeping these days?"

"As well as can be, my dear Queen Alin," replied Lady Ursule. "Patrin is buried in work these days, what with all these climate emergencies cropping up. I hardly see him, my lady. The man is married to his work."

"Ah, how admirable," murmured Queen Alin. "I can see why the entire Senate looks up to Lord Patrin. Your husband is entirely devoted to the empire and of course, to you, my dear. It is most noble. Most noble indeed."

Lady Ursule blushed a little. "You are too kind, Queen Mother. Yes, Patrin is one of the rare few who have no blemish to his record, I'm proud to say. No corrupt dealings, no mistresses, no vices. If only more of the Senate were like him, we'd have far less dissension amongst our people and distrust in our government." She stopped and glanced hesitantly at Queen Alin. "Of course, that's entirely the humble opinion of a wife, you understand…"

"Of course, of course," smiled Queen Alin. "Tell me, how far along are you, my dear?"

Lady Ursule caressed her bump. "The baby is due next month so not long now," she said. She gestured for Queen Alin to take a seat and plumped herself down on one of the chairs herself. It was filled with so many cushions it seemed to be on the verge of overflowing with them.

The maid approached to pour the tea. Lifting the pot gingerly, the girl proceeded to pour the hot liquid from a height as was customary. But this she did clumsily, misjudging the arc of the pouring liquid and spilling much of it onto the table instead.

"Dimwit!" snapped Lady Ursule, flicking the girl away the tea with her napkin. "Go and get a cloth to wipe this up!"

As the maid hurried away, Lady Ursule sighed exasperatedly. "It is so difficult to get decent help these days my lady." She shook her head vexedly. "And what with the imminent arrival of a baby too."

Queen Alin patted her hand and smiled understandingly. "It must be terribly difficult for you Lady Ursule, with a babe on the way, in these uncertain times."

"Indeed, Queen Alin, indeed," assented Lady Ursule, much troubled. "I have been looking for maids but so far, all the girls that come to me have been sadly inadequate." She looked at Queen Alin desperately. "And there's not much to choose from either. Many have fled to the outer planets for fear of the heatstorms that have become increasingly frequent these past few months. Patrin tells me there are no plans to build shielding domes over the most residential neighbourhoods. That is why they have all left." Lady Ursule sighed. "You would think many would be begging to work here simply for the privilege of living in the villa, but sadly even those seem to have left. I am loathe to leave Amorgos for Segontia as Patrin needs to be here for work and when I go into labour, I will want him close. It is most dire, Queen Alin, most dire." Lady Ursule wiped her brow delicately with her handkerchief.

"There, there my dear," comforted Queen Alin. "As it happens I have brought with me my most excellent Anneliese. She is young but extremely capable. Indeed she sees to my every need and comfort without my having to instruct her." She paused a moment and then continued, "In fact, Anneliese is looking to base herself here in Amorgos. Why don't you take her?"

Lady Ursule was taken aback. "But my dear Queen Alin,"

she protested, "I cannot be taking your servant in your time of need!"

"Ah but I insist," said Queen Alin smiling sympathetically. "I am an old lady and at my age, my daily requirements are few. I have other handmaids that will be able to take care of my simple needs."

"But I don't want to inconvenience you, my dear Queen Alin," murmured lady Ursule. There was scant resistance in her tone.

"Nonsense," said Queen Alin firmly, "I insist." She looked into Lady Ursule's eyes which now shone with gratitude and relief. "Anneliese is a competent young girl and I have no doubt she will learn to nurse the babe too when the time comes." Queen Alin took Lady Ursule's hand in hers. "Then it's settled, my dear. I shall leave Anneliese here when I return to the Red Palace later tonight."

"What's settled?" a voice called out from behind. Lord Patrin, Lady Ursule's husband strode into the courtyard.

"Lord Patrin," Queen Alin murmured politely.

"Queen Alin, welcome." Lord Patrin bowed before turning to give his wife a quick peck on the cheek. He towered over their seated forms, his tall figure and angular face exuding an air of authority and rectitude which somehow Queen Alin found grating.

"Queen Alin has been most kind to us, as ever, my lord," said Lady Ursule smilingly.

"Oh?" murmured Lord Patrin politely.

His wife nodded. "Indeed," she said. "Queen Alin has offered me her best handmaid to help in our household. At last, I can get rid of that useless Tullia. I can't tell you what a relief this has been to me, my lord."

Lord Patrin rubbed his wife's back affectionately. "You are

most kind, my dear Queen Alin. We are touched by your generosity."

Queen Alin waved her hand graciously. "These are troubled times, my dear Lord Patrin," she said. "We must do all we can to help each other…"

"Indeed, indeed, " came the reply. "Tell me, what brings you back here to Amorgos, my lady? Weather patterns are worsening here. I would imagine your residence at Olicana would be far more comfortable than Amorgos."

Queen Alin sighed. "Indeed Lord Patrin. However I am here to try and see the emperor." She opened her palms in a gesture of helplessness. "A mother's bond…," she said sadly. "I pray for the fortitude to carry on fighting this terrible injustice that shackles my son."

"My poor Queen Alin," said Lady Ursule, clearly moved by the old woman's plight. "Is the emperor still under house arrest?"

Queen Alin nodded sadly. "He is, dear Lady Ursule and the Supreme Commander refuses to let me see him."

"Oh, how terrible it must be for you," said Lady Ursule. She looked pleadingly at her husband, "Is there *anything* we could do to help, my lord?"

The Queen Mother cut in. "I am sure that if there was anything that could have been done, my dear Lord Patrin would have already done it by now," she said.

"Queen Alin is correct," replied Lord Patrin looking kindly at his extremely pregnant wife. "Emperor Akseli is currently under house arrest until the Senate decides whether to impeach him for his involvement in the failed Ellagrin invasion. Until then, the Senate will oversee urgent matters of our Realm. With the dying suns escalating natural disasters on the innermost planets, we have much to contend with at the moment."

Queen Alin nodded, murmuring, "Lord Patrin is as wise as he is kind." She ventured a smile and continued, "But with the dire circumstances surrounding our Realm at the moment, surely it would benefit all to focus on these issues and drop the call for impeachment, don't you think, my lord?"

Lord Patrin gave her a measured look. "You know we can't do that, my lady," he said flatly. "The accusations against the emperor are too serious to be overlooked. They have to be addressed and the only way to do that is to progress with the impeachment process." He straightened up and continued, "As Praetors, it is our duty to remain impartial. I am sure the facts will speak for themselves if Emperor Akseli goes to trial to clear his name."

Queen Alin was briefly silent as she took in Lord Patrin's words, effectively a refusal to persuade the rest of the Senate to drop the impeachment. *He thinks himself impartial and righteous, the pompous ass,* she thought embittered. *Well, we shall see about that...*

"I will make sure Emperor Akseli is given a fair chance to air his side of the story," said Lord Patrin.

The Queen Mother shook her head disconsolately. "My son will hang if he goes to trial," she spoke, her voice hard. "Akseli will not be given a fair hearing." With that, she rose to depart, leaving Lord Patrin standing and Lady Ursule looking on helplessly.

LORD MARIUS

Fianchetto: Chess term. Development of a bishop by moving it one square to a long diagonal. An opening move whose philosophy is to delay the direct occupation of the centre with the plan of undermining and destroying the opponent's central outpost.

Lord Marius moved his pawn forward and stroked his chin thoughtfully, making the bristle of his greying beard rasp crisply. Queen Alin sat across him staring at the chessboard, her thin lips curled into the smallest hint of a smile. She moved her bishop by a mere step and leant back. A flicker of triumph gleamed in her eyes.

"Ah, *fianchetto*," Lord Marius sighed with resignation. "I should have seen that coming." He glanced at her with grudging admiration. Beneath the creases of age, Queen Alin's eyes still shone with the keen artic-blue he remembered from his days of youth. *The blue of steel.* She was attractive once, he recalled. *She still is,* came his thoughts unbidden. But Lord Marius was no fool. He knew the Queen Mother well and what she was capable of, beneath that charming patina.

"Are you still playing chess with people's lives?" he murmured. They were in his private residence in the outskirts of Alandia, Marius' base where he decamped to whenever duty to the empire brought him to the capital. Today, the servants had been sent away to give him and his visitor complete privacy.

Queen Alin looked up from the game and surveyed the room. It was a very masculine room in her opinion, with no trace of what Marius would have termed 'womanly touches'. The walls were of panelled wood, a rarity in the Realm and beyond priceless these days. However Lord Marius' tastes were not ostentatious in the slightest. In fact, Queen Alin thought them rather restrained. *Restrained but very, very expensive.*

"My son's life hangs in the balance, Lord Marius," she replied. "It is not a game to me."

Lord Marius nodded and looked at her.

She felt him pause as he considered her remark. Marius was an old fox and a deft hand at political games. One did not become Praetor and Legatus as well without skill and a whole lot of court secrets at their disposal. Through the years, Queen Alin had seen him rise up the ranks from court official to Praetor of Ceos and then conferred the military rank of Legatus by her late husband Emperor Ageron III, a title which effectively meant the armies under his praetorian region of power, although seconded to the Supreme Commander, belonged to Ceos and therefore to him. In all of Ageron, only two Praetors held the title of Legatus and Lord Marius was one of them.

But then it was I who helped you gain that title, recalled Queen Alin, looking at him. *I who convinced Ageron all those years ago. Without military control, you would be but a glorified administrator like all the other Praetors. For that, you owe me.*

"So, are you planning to have Akseli avoid impeachment and him reinstated at the throne?" Always a few steps ahead, Marius cut to the chase.

Queen Alin nodded, snapping to business. "Akseli is the rightful heir to the throne," she said. "Ageron himself named him emperor. " She gazed levelly at Lord Marius. " I have no doubt there will be many that will not stand by and allow this... *coup* by the Supreme Commander to happen."

Lord Marius raised an eyebrow. "Perhaps," he said, "but if you remember, Lord Draeger turned down the throne in the first place. In favour of Akseli. Why then would he turn around and accuse Akseli of treason if there were no truth in that? And for what purpose?" He eyed Queen Alin knowingly and added, "You do realise that there is no way the Senate are going to just ignore what has happened and just forget about the subject of impeachment."

Queen Alin bit her lip. "Yes, but if we can persuade enough members of the Senate to vote against impeachment—"

Lord Marius cut in. "You won't have enough votes," he said, shaking his head. "Unless you can get the likes of Chancellor Rasmus or Lord Patrin to influence the other Praetors."

"I've already tried Patrin," remarked Queen Alin sourly. "The pompous ass refuses to get down from his high chair and insists the only way to get to the truth is by trial."

"And the Chancellor?" asked Lord Marius.

Queen Alin gave him a frosty glare.

Lord Marius let out a chuckle. "What has the old wolf got against you, Alin?" He shot her a curious glance. "I never did understand why you didn't rid of him when he was younger. There were certainly... opportunities, especially after Lady Yinha's tragic death."

Believe me I would have done so if I could, but he still holds my secret. An image of a golden bracelet burned in her mind's eye.

However her face remained closed. "We have an understanding, he and I," she said coldly, leaving it at that.

"Whichever way you view it," Lord Marius said, "Lord Draeger controls the armies and whoever controls the military controls the Senate. You know that."

"Yes," admitted Alin, "but some of the Praetors—yourself, Lord Reku—you are also Legati. Your praetorian regions are large and both combined, make up at least half of Draeger's legions."

"So what if they do?" asked Marius. "There is no rationale for me to call upon my armies directly. I am not a soldier and even if I were, I cannot possibly justify the cost of a civil war nor wager the odds of winning one against Lord Draeger. On what grounds would I threaten the Senate to refuse impeachment? They will never go along with this, no matter how you spin it."

Lord Marius shook his head and patted Alin's hand. "I understand that Akseli's life is at stake but in all likelihood, you won't be able to get the Senate to abandon the call for impeachment. The Praetors may be loyal to House Ageron but that unfortunately does not translate to loyalty towards the emperor himself. They're not easily swayed and most will listen to that uptight, upright Patrin. And don't forget the Chancellor. You've never been able to get rid of Rasmus and you know the Praetors accede to him. They will be far less likely to take your side with him around."

Queen Alin remained in sullen silence.

Lord Marius continued. "Members of the Senate like stability, especially when it comes to the stability of their own pockets. And as loyal protector of House Ageron, Chancellor Rasmus is as steady as they come. I'm afraid even your charms my lady, will not sway his kind."

Queen Alin gave him a cool look. "Let me worry about

Rasmus," she told him, withdrawing her hand from his. "I shall find a way forward with that little problem. It is high time I rid myself of that thorn in my side. All I ask from you, for now, is that you vote against impeachment and gather as many senators as you can to follow suit."

"Very well, my lady," assented Lord Marius.

Alin studied him with an open, merciless appraisal. "And when the time comes," she said, her voice tremulous, "...when Draeger is sufficiently weakened, can I count on your help? In return, you shall have Rasmus' seat before his blood has cooled. *That*, I can promise you."

Lord Marius considered a moment. "Very well," he said. His eyes flickered with a keen light. "Very well."

LORD REKU

It was dusk by the time Queen Alin had completed her business with Lord Marius, but the Queen Mother was not yet done. Her next stop after seeing herself out from his residence was not her quarters at the Red Palace but the swanky home of Lord Reku. As with her visit to Lord Marius, she made her way there with the utmost discretion. It had been a long day and by the time she reached Lord Reku's, it was under the cover of darkness and long after sundown.

Queen Alin drew her cloak around her tightly as she regarded the ostentatious entrance of Lord Reku's villa. The night air was chilly but so dry each breath felt like an abrasive intake of frigid, fine sand. She shivered. *What was it that they said in the news streams? Atmosphere erosion due to the failing binary suns, which contributed to the accelerated loss of moisture in the air.*

She hurried on, the chirring of *wetabugs* in their night-time chorus filling the air as she swiftly made her way past the gilded front doors, around the corner and to the side where a small innocuous door was left open for her arrival.

"My lady…" Reku's manservant bowed and held out his hand to take her cloak. "This way," he murmured and led her down the corridor.

The entire building was eerily quiet and very much empty. She was led to the back of the villa and into a small, intimate walled garden. A fire pit stood crackling cheerfully in the centre and soft twinkling lights along the stone walls illuminated the exquisite flowering climbers that covered much of it. On closer inspection, Queen Alin noticed that the 'blossoms' were in fact panicle clusters of white needle-thin thorns.

"My lady, Lord Reku is expecting you," said the servant indicating towards Lord Reku and withdrew discreetly.

"Welcome to my humble abode, my dear lady," Lord Reku beamed. His pampered, rotund form bobbled and quivered like mounds of jelly as he waddled towards Queen Alin.

"Lord Reku," she said returning his greeting and holding out her hand. *By Ysgarh, let's hope he doesn't eat himself into the grave before he can be of use to me,* she thought to herself.

Lord Reku took her hand and bent to kiss it noisily.

Queen Alin managed a smile despite the fleeting image of a slobbering pig that crossed her mind. "You look well, Lord Reku," she said graciously as she sat down on the cushioned bench before the fire, grateful for the warmth. "How are things?" she enquired.

"So, so my lady, although I have to say things could be better," replied Lord Reku. He offered her a glass of amarinthe and proceeded to slurp his before his rump even touched the bench.

"How so?" inquired Queen Alin politely.

Lord Reku cast his fleshy arms about him agitatedly. "This!" he said, shaking his head. "All *this*! At the rate our weather is behaving, I shall have to leave all this behind! They say it will only be a matter of time before the heatstorms hit us like they did in Anavio. My garden! My beautiful villa!" He looked at Queen Alin, his pot belly bobbing up and down in exasperation. "And no one will buy this! This beautiful jewel of a masterpiece! Can you imagine? Fashioned to the utmost detail, after the Castra de Sicilia of Old Earth and no one will buy it! Not even those Caggi traders and *they* offered Lord Maxim twice the value of this villa for his old fort!" Lord Reku shook his head, aggrieved.

"It is most distressing indeed," murmured Queen Alin sympathetically, "but I suppose an old fort provides better shelter from our heatstorms than a villa. Still, are you not looking to move regardless? This villa, as well built as it is, is no fort."

"Indeed," agreed Lord Reku. His flabby torso wobbled dejectedly.

"And you will be returning to Othon I presume? It will be less hot there at least."

Lord Reku nodded. "Yes, I will have to return, my lady. I am their Praetor and there are plans to evacuate more citizens from Trimon to Othon as things worsen, something which I shall have to oversee."

"Indeed," agreed Queen Alin.

"So, my lady," said Lord Reku pouring himself another glass of amarinthe, "what is it that brings you here in such secrecy?"

Queen Alin looked disconsolate. "My Lord Reku," she began, "my son languishes under house arrest like a prisoner awaiting the gallows."

Lord Reku nodded, commiserating. "I have been trying to dissuade the Senate from impeachment, my lady."

The Queen nodded. "Yes, I heard, and for that I am deeply grateful, Lord Reku," she said. "This blatant abuse of power by

Lord Draeger... my late husband Ageron himself named Akseli ruler of the Realm, the rightful heir to House Ageron, and yet..."

"There, there," consoled Lord Reku, placing a sweaty palm on her hand, "do not upset yourself, my lady. We mustn't give up."

Queen Alin sighed and fixed her gaze upon him. "Sadly, the Senate these days are filled with many who are self-serving and biased. I look to you Lord Reku, to help rectify the views of the naive and spread word of the injustice our emperor currently endures."

Lord Reku wilted slightly under the intensity of her piercing eyes. "But of course, my lady," he said. "I will do everything in my power to dissuade the other Praetors from supporting the impeachment. You have my word, my lady."

Queen Alin regarded him for a brief moment. Then, seemingly satisfied with his sincerity, she lifted her glass and sipped her drink delicately. "I wonder how your sister is," she contemplated aloud. "Of course it would have been two hundred years since you last had contact with her and your brother-in-law." The Queen Mother looked up wistfully at the stars above. "Do you ever wonder what's happened to family and loved ones after the Gateways were destroyed?"

Lord Reku leant back. "Ah," he sighed shaking his head, "... the War." He gave a sigh. "Ria's children must be grown up by now and how many more she would have had since, I can only guess. But Ria was always the more forward thinking of us two, so perhaps it was for the best that she had chosen to live in Sansari rather than in Ageron when the Arnemetiaen Gateway fell. Ria and her love for Tilkoen modernity, their shiny machines and gadgets. She would have been stifled with our love for tradition here."

"Quite so, quite so," Queen Alin nodded, agreeing. "And

her Tilkoen husband? He was an entertaining one, was he not?"

Lord Reku smiled at the memory. "Ah! *Ram*! Yes, and a good drinking partner," he said, chuckling.

"Rather ambitious too," added the Queen.

"Oh yes! *Very*!" agreed Lord Reku. "Even in the early days, before the fall of the Gateways, Ram was well on his way to being elected one of the High Twelve. I expect he must be a member of the Tilkoen High Council by now."

"Yes," said Queen Alin. "I have no doubt he will have done well for himself." She then gave him a look that made him sit up. "I hope he remembers *us*, Lord Reku, and our *pact*..."

"I am sure my brother-in-law has not forgotten, my lady," he said quietly. "In fact, I believe it was his actions that enabled the Ellagrins to destroy the beacon at Sansari in the War all those years ago. Fear not, if there ever is any danger of the Arnemetiaen Gateway being reactivated again, he will know what to do."

Queen Alin looked at him, satisfied. "Then I am at ease, Lord Reku. I am at ease...," she said. *We cannot afford to have the Arnemetiaen Gateway reopened to allow Ageronians to evacuate to Tilkoen. House Ageron will cease to rely on Ellagrin if that happens. Besides, the last thing we need is for the Arnemetiaen Gateway to be resurrected once again, making Lord Draeger a hero.* She breathed out venomously at the thought. *How I wish I had killed you when I had the chance.*

She rose wearily to bid Lord Reku farewell, her disquietude unassuaged despite her conversations with both Praetors today. As Lord Marius had mentioned earlier, there was little chance of getting the Senate to abandon the call for impeachment but she had done her best to maximise Akseli's chances of getting out of this alive. For now.

My two bishops, she noted, reflecting on how her two allies resembled her bishops in the chess game earlier. *Fianchetto indeed...*

THE COMITIUM

Queen Alin could hear the commotion outside even before she reached the entrance of the Ecclesia. Her throat constricted. *Please don't let it be what I think it is,* she said to herself as she struggled through the throng of senators entering the Comitium's main debating chamber.

Oh how she hated the Comitium, with its atmosphere of assiduousness and the self-importance of its denizens, scuttling here and there like the insignificant insects they were.

I should have had someone here as my eyes and ears all this time, to keep abreast of goings on here at the Senate, she said to herself ruefully. *A little shortsighted of me but too late now.* She exhaled vexedly as the tall figure of the Chancellor striding towards her came into view.

The old man approached her and Queen Alin met his keen flint eyes with discomfort. "Chancellor Rasmus," she greeted, "I was hoping to get a moment of your time." Alin squirmed inwardly at her situation. She certainly did not relish having to pander to the Chancellor of all people.

"What can I do for you, my lady?" asked the Chancellor perfunctorily.

"I was hoping to discuss the… article of impeachment with yourself," said Queen Alin. Her voice was deliberately low as she sought to keep their exchange as private as was possible in the midst of all the people passing by.

The Chancellor guided her to one side. "I'm afraid there is nothing to discuss that isn't being discussed at Senate, my lady," he said flatly.

"The emperor is but a victim of a power struggle between two brothers," hissed Queen Alin. "You *know* it, Rasmus. This plan to impeach Akseli is but an outright attempt by Draeger to depose him. You *cannot* let this happen!" Her arctic blue eyes pierced into his like shards of ice. "If you do, I will make sure you regret every single day for the remainder of your sad lonely life, old man! And as for Lord Draeger, I will use every favour, every connection, every leverage I have and I will *bring him down*, do you hear me?"

The Chancellor straightened up and met her gaze unflinchingly. "I suggest you *back off*, my lady and stop meddling," he said quietly. "In case you've forgotten your agreement with the late Lady Yinha? Make no mistake, I will reveal your secret to the world if you so much as initiate anything against the Supreme Commander. And then, we shall see what becomes of your favours, connections and leverage in the Senate."

Queen Alin seethed in silence.

"Besides," continued the Chancellor, "it's too late anyway." He nodded towards the last of the senators going into the Ecclesia. "The vote for impeachment is about to be cast as we speak. We shall know if the Senate decides to impeach or not."

A pang of dismay hit Queen Alin. *When did they decide this?*

"You can join me in the chamber as the Senate casts its

votes," said the Chancellor simply. He held out his arm in a gesture directing Queen Alin towards the Ecclesia. Dumbstruck, she followed the Chancellor and took a place at the back with him and other observing members of the audience.

* * *

THE ENTIRE PROCESS took no more than an hour to conclude. The article of impeachment which had been discussed and debated at length over the past few weeks was read out to all in its summarised version as a formality. Then members of the Senate were invited to cast their votes. And soon, it was over and Lord Patrin stepped into the central gallery to read the results out loud for all to hear.

"The ayes to the right: seventy three," Lord Patrin's voice rang loud and clear, "the noes to the left: sixty-eight. The ayes have it. The ayes have it."

Queen Alin paled. *Akseli's impeached.*

She turned and exited the chamber quickly, resisting the impulse to run and instead, held her head high as she strode out the door. Thankfully Chancellor Rasmus did not follow.

The vote had gone the way Marius had predicted and deep down Queen Alin knew it would, too. However, that did nothing to allay her fears of what was to come next—a trial and then the final vote from the Senate, of which a two-thirds result would be enough to convict Akseli.

The corridor ahead seemed to lead to a different section of the building, one that looked unfamiliar. Queen Alin stopped abruptly, confused. By right, she would have reached the double doors leading into the foyer by now. However, it seemed, in her haste to leave, she had taken a wrong turn.

"Confounded place," she muttered to herself and turned

around to retrace her steps… only to bump into an elderly woman holding an armful of files.

"Oh!" she exclaimed as the stack of papers fluttered to the ground.

Queen Alin let out a sigh of exasperation as she contemplated stepping over the kneeling woman and her mound of papers to find her exit. Instead, she stopped to help the woman pick up the rest of her fallen papers.

"Thank you," said the woman. Her eyes widened a little as she noticed Queen Alin's rich robes. "M..my lady," she stammered.

Queen Alin merely nodded and regarded her with scorn. *Probably one of the secretaries working here*, she guessed, *and nearing retiring age from the looks of it*. However the woman's characteristics—deeply tan, with a broad face, angular jawline and slightly stocky, almost dumpy build—made her pause a moment. *Tilkoen*, she realised, recognising the typical Tilkoen features the woman possessed. The woman struggled to get back up and Queen Alin, refraining from rolling her eyes, extended her arm to help her up. *Old and arthritic too,* she observed as the woman stumbled to stand back up, her coiled braid of ashen hair loosening onto her shoulders in the process.

"You are too kind, my lady," she said, straining at the effort of getting back on her feet and keeping the stack of files securely in her arms at the same time.

"Do you work here?" asked Queen Alin, eyeing her disparagingly.

"Yes, my lady," answered the woman, breathlessly. "For Lord Reku," she added. "I'm an interpreter, although I am in actual fact, seeking ah… further challenges within the Comitium."

Queen Alin regarded her for a brief moment. "How

commendable," she said, "...to seek further challenges." She studied the woman for a moment and then said: "Lord Reku as it happens, is an old friend of mine. As a matter of fact, I'm actually looking for an... assistant. To be based here at the Comitium." She eyed the woman again and asked, "What is your name, my dear?"

The woman beamed, not believing her good fortune. "Lianne, my lady," she answered eagerly. "My name is Lianne."

PART III

THE SEARCH

TOP OF THE WORLD

Several days had passed but Tors still slept fitfully, unable to block out the memories even within the safety of the Ether cocooning her in its dark embrace. When her dreams took her, scenes of the ambush reared unbidden, lurid and chaotic.

At first, she had not been able to tear an opening into the Ether for them to escape. *Those berries...*

Alber had spiked them with the berries and she could barely stand up never mind cleave an opening into the Ether. *If I had been quicker to get us into the Ether, we could have avoided all that bloodshed...and she'd be alive.*

Tors moved restlessly in her sleep as her mind replayed the events again and again in a torturous loop. Alber's men had closed in on them and Marcus had shoved her aside, out of their reach. Tors saw him draw his blade as the men moved in on the two of them.

"Look out!" she had shouted, reaching for her gladius. Despite her grogginess, she joined Marcus who was ringed by three of them. Together, they fended their attackers off with their swords, their blades a blur of glinting metal, the result of their movements or due to her drugged state, she couldn't tell.

Next, Pihla had leapt across the table and dispensed with her challenger by smashing a heavy flagon into his face. She went on to help Niko. He was on his knees, tussling with one man whilst trying to dislodge another from his back. Tors had run to help them but her way was obstructed by another before she was even halfway across the room.

He hefted his sword and advanced. Her vision was blurry at best and she was seeing double. Not knowing which version of her opponent to strike, she had closed her eyes as she often did at sword practice, and let her instincts take over. It worked and when her blade found its place beneath his sternum, she twisted.

Behind her, the doors to the back garden flew open and more of Alber's men poured in. They had to get out now and the Ether offered the only viable way of escape. But the aftereffects of the berries were a problem—she couldn't focus enough to create an opening.

Tors looked around frantically and her eyes paused at the table. The jug!

She scrambled towards it and then emptied the jug of iced water over her head. The cold jolted her senses back into action and her vision cleared a little. She remembered Enok huddled in a corner opposite looking on fearfully.

Nothing happened at first. Then after what seemed like an eternity, a faint shimmer materialised in front of her, followed by a sliver of a shadow, gradually widening into the familiar darkness.

Quickly... quickly...

It was so, so hard to focus.

Finally, she managed to coerce the opening into a size large enough to fit through.

"The *Nehisiiii*! She's escaping!" Fjalla's shrill voice pierced through the commotion.

In an instant, Tors felt all attention focussed on her.

Alber, seeing Hakon nearest to Tors and his other men otherwise occupied, pushed him to move in. "Get her!" he screamed but Hakon hesitated. So Alber reached out to grab Enok instead.

"No!" Hakon cried out as Enok struggled helplessly in Alber's grip.

"Then stop *her*," urged Alber, his black beady eyes trained on Tors.

Reluctantly, Hakon withdrew his dagger and advanced towards her.

"Boss!" yelled Pihla spotting the opening into the Ether. "Time to *go*!"

Marcus cut loose and bounded towards them as Niko wrenched the final man off him and clambered over.

"NO!" screamed Alber. His gelatinous bulk bristled menacingly. Still grasping Enok like a small rag doll, he gestured wildly to his men to stop them.

Tors started towards Enok to try and free her from Alber but Marcus stopped her. "We have to go," he said firmly.

"But—" Tors protested but Marcus held onto her tightly.

"We *can't*," he said, not letting go.

Alber advanced at them, this time his arm raised holding his sword. "I cannot let you leave," he said, his eyes vicious and bloodthirsty. "And if you so much as take one step into the Ether, this little one dies," he continued, shaking Enok like a small sack of sagarnuts.

Tors struggled to free herself from Marcus' grip but he pushed her into the Ether.

"Nooo....!" she screamed as she tumbled through.

In that same instant, Hakon lunged at Alber, tussling him

to the ground. They fell. Alber's sword swung wildly and slashed a bright red line across Enok's pale neck. The little girl collapsed into a heap, followed by Alber beside her.

By the time Niko and Pihla had leapt into the Ether, all Tors could see through the disappearing gap was Hakon crawling over Alber to his daughter's side.

They died. Needlessly. Because I was too slow...

Now, within her dreams, nightmare would take over from memory.

Tors found herself looking down at her belly, swelled in girth and protruding massively in the front. Strangely, she could see through her tunic, through the flesh and into the womb. There lay the foetus, curled up in a ball.

Tors whimpered. This was the scene that haunted her over and over again. The part where the foetus would turn and stare back at her.

Such old eyes...

They looked familiar.

My baby...

But it was wrinkled and hairless.

The Oracle!

Except its eyes were not pink and watery like the Oracle's. Instead, they were dark as pitch.

They are Draeger's eyes.

And then the eyes would lighten and brighten until they became Enok's eyes.

No, no. Not Enok!

Then it would open its mouth to speak, except no voice would come out. But Tors knew it was screaming. She felt it screaming. It was a soundless scream. Just as Enok's screams would have been.

* * *

Tors opened her eyes with a jolt. Her head swam and her temples throbbed. In front of her, Marcus' face seemed to shimmer and shake.

You okay? he mouthed. He looked worried. She shivered and he pulled her to him, rubbing all over her arms vigorously to warm her up. It was cold in the Ether. She had not eaten since the day before and was still weak from the fighting. They all were.

We have to exit the Ether soon, she thought to herself, *to tend to our injuries and to stock up on food at the very least.* There had been a faint tug. Even in her sleep she had felt it. They were in a part of the Ether that felt entirely unfamiliar to her but that couldn't be helped now. At Kaldr, they had no choice but to leave when the attack occurred. It was impossible to retrace their steps within the Ether and all she could hope for was that they eventually find their way to the Sansari endpoint somehow.

Marcus helped her get up. She staggered to her feet, leaning against him, the weight of her body pressing heavily on his for support. She felt him wince a little.

He had been injured too.

She glanced at his bandage. Thankfully the gash on his side was no longer weeping blood.

The Ether suspends the festering of wounds, even promotes its healing. Mother used to say a day in the Ether worked better than a course of bio-rejuvenation. But now they needed sustenance, not the Ether, and she had to get them out quickly before her own strength ran out.

They gathered their things and pushed onwards, Marcus supporting her and Pihla helping Niko limp along. The crosswinds of the Ether whipped and nipped at them like angry phantasms, wrenching at their cloaks in eerie silence and threatening to push them over in sharp sudden gusts. As they went on, it picked up in strength and ferocity, so much so that at one point, they were forced to huddle together in order to avoid being blown off their feet. The Ether, devoid of objects, offered nothing that could be used as shelter or stops against its buffeting currents. Marcus held her tight as they all crouched down low to expose as little as possible of themselves to the strong gusts.

I mustn't lose consciousness, Tors thought desperately as she clung to Marcus. The last blast of wind had nearly blown her small frame off the ground and would have taken her with it had he not held her. The world around her seemed to be swirling and whirling round her like a carousel spun out of control. Tors closed her eyes to steady herself.

Breathe, she told herself, remembering her training. *Calm yourself...*

Something pulled at her. *That's not the wind.*

Tors opened her eyes and looked for it. Ahead, small, faint but unmistakeable, was a faint glimmer of light.

An endpoint!

Tors, too tired to signal, merely pointed at it. The others saw it too and headed for it. Marcus, half supporting, half lifting her, helped her towards it. Finally, they stumbled gratefully out through the opening.

THE WINDS STOPPED the moment they stepped through and the sight that greeted them was glorious. It was calm, sunny and bright, and all Tors could see was an expanse of gleaming azure.

"I'm standing *on top of the world!*" exclaimed Niko. He stood up, arms outstretched and reached for the sky.

The rest of them remained sitting, exhausted, and were

content to admire their surroundings from their seated positions.

They were on a mountain top, so high the vivid blue sky above seemed to be within touching distance and far below, so far they looked like model miniatures, were more snow-covered mountain ranges. Further down still, valleys with rivers like thin blue veins could be seen.

Tors looked back at the endpoint they had just come through. It was not just a natural endpoint but appeared to have been a Gate at some point in the past. Much smaller than any of the Gates they had previously seen, it was unpowered and abandoned but the machinery surrounding it was unmistakably man-made. It was clearly a constructed Gate.

Tors looked at it admiringly. Its elegant, silvery arc of solenite gleamed untarnished in the sunlight, startlingly beautiful against the breathtaking backdrop of pure blue. However, unlike the other Gates she'd seen before, there was nothing else around it—no station building, no transportation links, and no signs of life.

Which Gate is this and why would anyone construct one in the middle of nowhere?

The others began to stand up to look across the horizon. Tors stood up stiffly to join them but no sooner had she taken her first step, she felt light headed again.

Something's wrong.

Directly ahead Niko crumpled to the ground.

Then Pihla.

Tors glanced at Marcus, her heart thumping hollowly against her chest. He was standing looking at her, his back facing the cliff edge. The sky seemed to swirl behind him.

The air, she realised in horror. *The air's too thin.*

"No oxygen…" gasped Marcus as he fell backwards. Tors couldn't see any ground behind him where he fell.

"Marcus!" She felt her legs give way and then her sight began to darken.

A figure shimmered in the distance; a shepherd perhaps. If only she had the strength to call out for help. She remembered trying to lift her arm as her vision dimmed to slits.

"He-lp…" she called out desperately and blacked out.

THE MOUNTAINS OF YOON

As she stirred in her sleep somewhere between slumber and wakefulness, Tors dreamt of the Villa Castra and of Draeger. They were training, sparring in the courtyard and snow was falling around them mutedly in soft, feathery clusters. A few flakes settled lightly on her face and trembled delicately at the tip of her nose each time she breathed.

The fight was in full flow and with each blow and parry, seemed to increase with speed. Faster and faster they parried, each move and countermove more rapid than the last, eventually becoming a blur of motion until only the falling snow and the warm clouds of their breath hung at a standstill.

Tors spun around as Draeger lifted his sword to strike. She raised her blade up above her head to intercept the blow. But instead of bringing his sword downward, he cast it aside and bent to kiss her. First on the forehead, then lightly on her eyelids making her close them both, before moving down her neck. As his lips grazed her collar bone, she held his head on both sides in attempt to stop him. He did not heed her protest, instead dipped further to kiss her breasts. Tors let out a gasp, clutched his head, and looked down. But his hair was not ebony as she had expected. In fact it was almost blonde.

Blonde like Marcus...

Tors awoke with a start, aching and disorientated. Affixed to her nose and enveloping the nostrils was a breathing mask of some sort. It emitted a constant wheeze and she could feel the slight tickle of air as traces of it escaped past the tip of her nose. *Not snowflakes then,* she realised, slightly abashed at where her thoughts were headed a few moments ago. *I was dreaming.*

She was lying on a bed, covered with blankets of fur, in a small low-ceilinged room. Despite its modest proportions, the room was tranquil and airy and a simple unadorned window revealed the cloudless sky outside in a perfect square of vivid cerulean.

There was someone at the far end of the room.

Tors struggled to lift her head to get a better look but her efforts made her vision blur again.

"Aeh, aeh, not so fast," came a voice from the same direction, followed by the soft rustle of the person approaching her bed. Gentle hands supported her as she struggled to get up.

Tors blinked in attempt to clear her vision. Those hands, old and wiry, helped lift her upper body so she could sit upright. Once propped against the bedhead, Tors leant back with a sigh. Before her, slightly obscured by her oxygen mask, was an old woman dressed in a simple robe, the colour of butter. She lifted the mask from Tors' face and offered her a handleless cup containing a warm drink.

"Tea," she said.

Tors accepted it gratefully. She sipped the warm beverage and at the same time, studied the woman up close.

She had a shaven head and her robe, draped to leave her

right arm and shoulder bare, revealed a brown, sinewy arm spotted with age and covered with skin stretched so taut and thin it looked like parchment. But it was her facial features that startled Tors the most. The woman's nose, barely there, was long and thin—a subtle elongated ridge starting between the eyebrows and ending in a small rise just above the cupid's bow. There, on either side of the bridge, were the smallest of nostrils, tiny apertures really, barely slits and hardly visible to the eye. Her eyes, deep set beneath a well-developed forehead, were basilisk and almost lidless—like two dark pebbles, the colour of midnight, infinite and unfathomable.

Eyes like Draeger...

"Here, let me get the cup for you, sister, " said the old woman, gently taking Tors' drained cup.

"Where am I?" asked Tors. She felt weak but the tea, slightly astringent, seemed to revive her.

"You are in Akasa, the royal monastery of Yoon," replied the woman, "and I am Sister Soo-Yeon."

Yoon, thought Tors, *...we must have come through the Huang-shan Gate.* "I am Tors," she replied, introducing herself, "from the Red Realm."

Sister Soo-Yeon looked blankly at her.

Ah, remembered Tors. *They wouldn't know the Red Realm as such.* "I meant Ageron," she said, using Ageron's original name. It was only after the War when the decline of Ageron's binary suns began that the empire began to be known as the Red Realm. However, as Chancellor Rasmus had explained, by that time the Yoons had already withdrawn from the rest of civilisation.

Sister Soo-Yeon nodded, registering some recognition of the name and smiled, creasing her ancient face even further. Ironically, it seemed to make her look childlike, almost cherubic, despite the ridges and ravages of age. "In that case," Sister Soo-Yeon pointed out, "you are far from home."

Tors nodded. *The planet Yoon is on the far fringes of the known galaxy—past Ageron, past the Ellagrin system and certainly past the Tilkoen system. We are very far from home indeed.* "We!" said Tors, suddenly remembering. "The others... where are they?"

Sister Soo-Yeon patted her hand reassuringly. "They are all safe," she said. "Even the one that fell down the cliff partway."

Oh thank Dyaeus. Marcus survived the fall.

"You were lucky the shepherd found you in time," continued Sister Soo-Yeon. "You were at one of the highest points of the Huangshan Mountains where the air is extremely thin." She looked at Tors with kindly eyes and said candidly, "Very lucky indeed. You would all have expired from the lack of oxygen in minutes."

Tors touched her belly instinctively. *I should be more careful*, she reminded herself. She looked at the Sister. "May I see my friends?" she asked.

"Of course," answered Sister Soo-Yeon and helped Tors out of bed. "They are in the refectory, eating. They will be glad to see you."

* * *

Following Sister Soo-Yeon, Tors emerged from the room and on to a long balconied corridor, bathed in dazzling sunlight. The air was crisp and the low balcony provided unobstructed views across the valleys and mountains beyond. Finely dusted with snow, its simple metal rod railings, encrusted with ice crystals, sparkled in the sun. Tors paused to take in the splendour of her surroundings.

The monastery of Akasa was perched on a mountain.

Above, there was only sky, gleaming pure and unblemished. Below, and all around as far as the eye could see, were the fabled Huangshan Mountains, glistening majestically in pure, brilliant white. On the right and directly below Akasa, nestled under the protected curve of the mountain, was a village comprising about twenty to thirty small dwellings, all huddled closely trying to fit within the tiny ledge they shared. Those at the edge perched precariously, half on stilts, jutting out and clinging to the side of the mountain like discs of bracket fungi. There were more dwellings further up the mountain and Tors could see steep paths cut into the rock face, winding their way up, connecting the dwellings and then looping back towards the monastery. The left side of the mountain by contrast, was far less crowded. Here, the mountain landscape flowed, unobstructed, into wide, undulating slopes where glissades and ski trails criss-crossed its vast white landscape like shiny threads glazed in ice.

"This way," said Sister Soo-Yeon softly, pulling Tors' attention away from the magnificent vista and back to matters at hand. She led the way down the corridor, past several more dormitories and down a spiral stone staircase. From there, they walked through sheltered cloisters where several groups of women, all dressed in similar robes, sporting smooth, shaven heads, passed by. The women bowed in greeting as they passed each other, as did Sister Soo-Yeon in return. Every single Yoon had minuscule noses and deep-set eyes the colour of midnight.

"This is the refectory," announced Sister Soo-Yeon, opening the door. "Your friends will be pleased to see you…"

Inside, at a long table flanked on both sides by simple wooden benches, sat Marcus, Pihla and Niko. Two other Yoons sat with them. The two ladies bowed their heads to greet Sister Soo-Yeon and Tors.

"Sister Hyun and Sister Chun-Hei," introduced Sister Soo-Yeon, bowing genially. Sister Hyun, slightly younger in appearance than sister Soo-Yeon, beckoned Tors over. Like Sister Soo-Yeon, she was of slight build and with an imperturbable countenance.

Tors took her place on the bench between Sister Hyun and Pihla. Across them, next to the slightly chubby Sister Chun-Hei, sat Marcus sporting a bandage round his head.

"By Dyaeus, I'm so glad you're finally back in the land of the living!" said Pihla, giving Tors a solid hug.

"Me too," replied Tors, relieved to see them all. Sister Hyun placed a steaming cup of tea in front of her and invited her to help herself to the food on the table.

"We thought we'd let you sleep in," joked Niko as he helped himself to what looked like a blue fig. Bright crimson juice trickled down to his hand and elbow as he bit into it with relish.

"Nah...don't listen to him," said Pihla. "We've just woken up ourselves about an hour ago."

"Apparently it was a close call for all of us," Marcus spoke up gruffly as he looked at her. "We didn't realise it at the time, but we were on high altitude. Higher than we ever imagined."

Niko nodded. "They said a shepherd found us."

"...and it was sheer luck he appeared when he did," continued Marcus. "We wouldn't be alive if he hadn't dragged us down here in time." He handed Tors a chunk of bread slathered with butter. "Eat," he said. "It's good."

"Everything is buttered here, even the tea," said Pihla as she slurped hers heartily.

Niko downed his contentedly. "Butter tea," he purred, "second best drink in the galaxy, after amarinthe."

"Here, here," agreed Pihla raising her cup to clink his.

Tors looked at Marcus' bandage. "I saw you fall down the

ravine," she said recalling the last moments before losing consciousness.

Marcus grinned. "It was nothing," he said, "only a few metres—I was saved by a ledge."

"He has a minor concussion," Pihla chipped in, "which sadly has not led to any improvement in his leadership qualities." She turned to Marcus. "So, boss, what do we do next?"

Marcus shot a quick sideways glance at Tors. "We rest first," he said. "Then we go back and check the Gate out... see if its beacon and power ports are still serviceable."

Tors raised a quizzical eyebrow.

"We have been talking with the nuns," Marcus continued. "The Gate we came through earlier is the Huangshan Gate all right—the Yoon end of the Leodis Gateway which connects to our Leodis Gate in Ageron. But apparently no one has touched or even gone near it for centuries."

"Are you trying to see if the Huangshan Gate can be opened?"asked Tors.

Marcus nodded. "No harm in checking to see if it's still operational," he said.

"I'm afraid there will be no attempt to reopen the Huangshan Gate," interrupted Sister Soo-Yeon politely. Her voice was gentle but firm. "For centuries, we Yoons have withdrawn from the rest of the galaxy. We no longer wish to reconnect with the other Houses. Besides, it won't be possible. The beacon on our end is no more—it was destroyed shortly after the War began, when the last of our people returned home."

There was a brief silence as her words sank in.

"I see," said Marcus at last, clearly disappointed.

Sister Soo-Yeon bowed. "Now," she continued with a smile, "you are most welcome to stay here as long as you wish and Sister Chun-Hei has volunteered to show you around Akasa and the village below if you feel rested enough."

Tors looked at her and the other two nuns as Marcus and the others thanked them. The women seemed completely relaxed and open, and yet something niggled.

And then it occurred to her what it was. As the sisters left them to finish up in the refectory, she realised that not one of them had asked them what they were doing here. Unlike Hakon and the other Ellagrins, none of the nuns seemed curious in the slightest.

So why haven't they asked us who and why we are here?

* * *

LATER THAT AFTERNOON, they were shown around the monastery. Akasa was deceptively large, comprising various levels, nooks and crannies, all cleverly carved out of the honey-coloured stone of the mountain. Facing east, its dormitory balconies jutted out precariously, looking out onto the mountains beyond and directly below, was a sheer drop of several thousand feet to the base of the mountain where the village stood. Two spiral staircases, one on each end, led to the level below the dormitories where the main sprawl of the monastery lay—a refectory with warming house, a kitchen and an oratory, all linked via several sheltered cloisters.

"This is the main cloister," explained sister Chun-Hei as they walked through what was arguably the longest and most ornate cloister of all. "If you ever lose your bearings, always start from here and find your way from this passageway."

"So what's on that end over there?" asked Marcus, pointing at a pair of large heavy doors at the opposite end. Arched and solid, they were ornately carved with black iron fastings on its hinges and panels.

"Beyond those doors is the Inner Palace," said sister Chun-Hei. "That's where the Empress lives."

"Empress?" repeated Tors.

Sister Chun-Hei nodded.

The Empress Yoon, thought Tors. *The last Empress to be seen by the Ageronians would have been Lady Yinha's mother, about two hundred years ago, just before the Yoons went into seclusion. Would she still be alive and reigning behind those doors, I wonder?*

"Do people get to see her," asked Pihla, "your Empress?"

"Only if summoned," replied Sister Chun-Hei. "Occasionally her Reverence comes out to grace us with her presence. However more often than not, we are summoned in to see her, although the last time this happened was a few years ago."

Sister Chun-Hei glanced at their surprised looks and nodded understandingly. "Empress Yoon has her own attendants who live in the Inner Palace with her. We don't enter unless called and they never leave the confines of the residence."

"Never?" repeated Niko, incredulous.

"Never," replied Sister Chun-Hei straight-faced.

Next, Sister Chun-Hei led them down the cloister and past the main hall where the sisters gathered for their daily *pujas*. The air was filled with melodious chanting as voices, beautiful and hypnotic, floated through amplified by the hall's vaulted ceilings.

"Ah…" murmured sister Chun-Hei, letting the canorous voices wash over her, "the Contemplation of Emptiness—never fails to lift the spirits!" Then she turned to face them and beamed, "Now who wants to go *skating*?"

ON THE SLOPES OF HEAVEN

Pihla tightened the laces of her skates with a sharp tug and made haste to catch up with the rest in front.

"Whoo hooo!" yelled Niko, tearing down the glissade in pure abandon. They were skating along slidderies—silvery paths that criss-crossed the mountain slopes—with Sister Chun-Hei who had taken them there after showing them around the monastery.

Niko skated round and halted abruptly next to Pihla just before the start of the next sliddery, spraying ice and snow at her. "What are you looking at?" he asked. He seemed to have gotten bolder with her lately, especially when she had let slip that she had never skated before.

"What are *you* looking at?" Pihla retorted, feeling a little defensive at his side glances at her. She had no doubt she looked a little out of place with her tanned muscular arms and her skates and furs.

Niko drew a deep breath and cast his arms wide. "This amazing view of course," he beamed.

Pihla had to agree. "We are truly on the slopes of heaven," she said, taking in the spectacular landscape around them. From their vantage point, the mountain seemed to stretch on forever with miles and miles of uninterrupted slopes covered with snow, and spread across them were the faint lines of the slidderies, similar to the ones they had been skating on, glinting brightly in the sun. The slidderies acted as roads for the locals, weaving their way through the village and spreading out across the slopes like gleaming snail trails. Skating trails, as Sister Chun-Hei had explained to her earlier, treated with some form of crystalline substance to keep them smooth and unblemished by snow.

Further up the mountain, sister Chun-Hei was careering dangerously down towards them.

"Lively one isn't she?" chuckled Niko as the buxom nun zigzagged down the winding sliddery at top speed. "I was going to skate up there," said Niko, "but she wouldn't let me."

"Hmmph," came Pihla's reply.

They both looked on as Sister Chun-Hei approached at frightening speed. Tucked low, her skates struck smoothly against the ice gaining momentum as she slid downhill, her generous outline giving the impression of a hurtling cannonball.

"She wouldn't let you skate up there because the air's too thin up there," explained Pihla as the nun whizzed past them in a gusty blur.

"But she's doing it," said Niko.

"The sir's too thin for us, but not them," explained Pihla. "Look at their slim noses," she said. "Have you noticed how tiny their nostrils are?"

"Ah, is that it?" said Niko. "It's a nose thing then, is it?"

"It's all to do with their breathing," Pihla continued, as they both witnessed Sister Chun-Hei flying recklessly off the ski jump ahead. "Their physiology appears to have evolved over time to adapt to the cold and high altitude."

"I can certainly see that," said Niko, looking on enviously as Sister Chun-Hei, clad in her light silken tunic, whizzed past, completely impervious to the cold. It was a sharp contrast to their bulky outfits weighed down in heavy furs. He turned to Pihla with an impish grin. "Did you know that the Yoons are a matriarchal society?" he said. "I just found that out today."

Pihla shrugged. "So?"

"So. that means here, the females run the entire place, that's what," said Niko. "Sister told me. Property, land inheritance—all passed from mother to daughter. Lineage is traced through the mother and the mother is the head of the family. Everything here is ruled by women. *Women*! Imagine that!"

Pihla raised an eyebrow at him. "You sound almost shocked," she said unamused.

"I *am*!" Niko replied, impassioned. "I mean the order of nuns in the monastery—*that* I can understand, but the *entire* society of an entire *planet*?"

"Why not?" snapped Pihla. "You think a society can't be run by women?"

"Weeell…,"said Niko, aware he was getting into risky territory but going for it anyway, "No. Not really. I mean, think about it—most empires in our galaxy: Ageron, Ellagrin, Tilkoen, by Dyaeus even the Asgharians are patriarchal. All I'm saying is it's very rare for a society to be ruled by women, not men."

Pihla's eyes flashed. "Is that so?" she said, anger bubbling up in her voice. "Well, maybe that's what's fundamentally wrong with everything. Did that ever occur to you? So far, our galaxy has had one mad emperor commit genocide on the only tribe that could save us, our very own emperor has colluded with the enemy to invade us, and we've witnessed an emperor fool enough to get murdered by his own sister. And what's the common denominator amongst these? All from empires ruled by *men*." She shot him an angry glare and then skated off in a huff.

"Ooooh, did I interrupt something?" Marcus appeared at Niko's side, breath ragged from the exertion of trying to keep up with sister Chun-Hei on the lower slopes.

Niko said nothing but looked after Pihla, crestfallen.

Marcus slapped him encouragingly on the back. "Well, whatever you've said to wind her up this time, I'm sure it can't be that bad. She'll come round."

But Niko gave a ponderous shake of his head. "No," he replied despondently. "I've blown it. I've truly blown it this time…" He skated off with his head down and hands tucked into his furs.

"What's the matter with them?" piped Tors, halting abruptly next to Marcus. They both stared at Niko disappearing in one direction and Pihla skating off in another.

"A difference in aspirations, perhaps," answered Marcus. He looked thoughtfully into the distance and then asked, "How are you doing so far?"

Tors shrugged. "I'm alright," she said. "Rested enough I guess."

"Good." He nodded and gazed at her. A gentle breeze had picked up and teased out a few locks of her hair from beneath her woollen cap. Amidst the surrounding whiteness her tresses appeared so black they seemed almost blue.

Tors flicked a few strands absently away from her lips and cheeks. "Do you think we should leave this place soon?" she asked looking into the distance.

"Perhaps," answered Marcus, not taking his eyes off her. "But we can stay here a bit if you need—to rest up a little."

"It's so peaceful here…" sighed Tors. Her eyes shone like bright emeralds, reflecting the brilliance of the snow.

"It is… breathtaking," agreed Marcus, not looking at the scenery.

"It's so beautiful," breathed Tors. "So beautiful I can almost believe it never happened." Her eyes clouded at the memory. She turned to him, catching him unawares. Marcus felt a constriction in his throat at the haunted look on her face. "I got a child killed, Marcus. I killed little Enok!"

Marcus held her arms and grasped her firmly. "We got a child killed but we didn't kill her," he said. "Alber did and he would have killed us all if you didn't get us out."

Tors buried her head in his chest.

"Look, you cannot blame yourself for what happened," said Marcus. "If anything, I am to blame. *Me*, not you. *Me*. For not realising the berries were spiked. For not protecting us." He swallowed thickly. "It will not be the first time someone has died on account of my decisions or actions… in the past and now in this quest. But we can only do our best based on what we know at the time and no more." He lifted her chin gently and looked into her eyes. "That is all *anyone*—the empire, our people, even Dyaeus himself—can ask of us."

Tors nodded sadly.

"We can stay here a little longer if you like," ventured Marcus. "Maybe even request an audience with the Empress Yoon."

Tors looked at him and Marcus felt the heat rising on his cheeks under her gaze. "Are you not curious to see the Empress Yoon?" he asked, hastily moving the subject on. "You know, they say she's as old as the mountains…" He tried to sound as natural as possible.

She looked at him, her eyes seemed to intensify as her expression lightened. "Chancellor Rasmus did say that Lady

Yinha's mother, meaning Lord Draeger's grandmother, was empress of Yoon at the time of Emperor Ageron III's reign. We know Lady Yinha was born approximately four centuries ago so if the Yoons' lifespans are roughly the same as Ageronians, I'm guessing the current Empress would be at least over four centuries old. Or quite possibly dead."

"So perhaps one of Lady Yinha's sisters if the latter case?"

Tors shrugged. "Probably."

"Then we should see her. Maybe she doesn't share the previous Empress' views on isolating from the rest of civilisation. Maybe we could ask her if there is any way to reopen the Huangshan Gate? They may not have destroyed it even though they said they did."

"Yes," said Tors, "but you heard Sister Soo-Yeon—we might be waiting years before we get to see the Empress."

"Not a bad thing waiting a bit here," Marcus said gently, glancing at her belly. She was slender but the beginnings of a bump were becoming visible. She hadn't said anything and he hadn't asked, but he had a feeling she knew that he knew.

Tors looked at him unsteadily. "Marcus…," she began and faltered.

He tucked her windblown hair behind her ear. "I'll take care of you," he said gently. "You could have the baby here safely and we could take care of it. I don't need to know anything else."

"But Sansari. Our expedition…"

Marcus hesitated a moment. "It will be a few decades yet before the suns begin their spiral of decay," he said, trying to sound hopeful. "We have time, don't we?"

Tors looked into his eyes. For a brief moment, she wavered. Then, she shook her head. "No, we can't," she said finally. "We both know time is of the essence to evacuate our people. We don't know how long it'll take to find Sansari and this time the Ether feels… different." She looked worried. "I don't know, but I can't seem to detect anything out there. It feels like I'm trying to see my way through a churning cyclone." She looked at him, concerned. "Searching for Sansari—it may take us months or it may take years. We must continue so that we can return to Ageron as soon as possible."

Marcus flinched at the last sentence. "Perhaps your loyalty to House Ageron holds too strong a sway on you," he said. There was a touch of bitterness in his voice.

Tors looked at him. "That's not what I meant Marcus," she said, "and I have no wish to remain in Ageron once our expedition is done."

He knew from her voice that that was true and he softened.

"We have paid the price of failure once already in Kaldr," she said bitterly. "And neither you nor I can afford the price of failure several billion times over—the lives of so, so many. *Too* many. We *cannot* afford to be too late…"

Reluctantly, Marcus had to agree. "With Ellagrin now the enemy, we don't even have the option of the Exodus anymore," he said. "I shall tell the others. We'll leave tomorrow." He looked at her tenderly. At that moment, framed against the white of the snow, her lips roseate and her cheeks flushed from the crisp air, Marcus stood transfixed, unable to tear his eyes away from the woman standing in front of him. *Perhaps this is as good as it's ever going to get,* he realised with a twinge of sadness, *and all I can ever hope to have of you. But for now at least, I get to be with you each day whilst this mission continues.* He strengthened his resolve. *That would have to be enough.*

* * *

"Rrrright! Who wants to race back to the monastery?" shouted Niko barging in from behind. "I'll race you!"

Marcus laughed. "And I accept!"

"As do I," grinned Tors.

Pihla coasted by and skidded to a stop. "What are we doing?" she asked, looking at them.

"We're going to race back to the monastery," Tors said.

"Haha!" said Pihla, "Count me in!"

Niko shot her a cheeky glance. "Then may the best *man* win!" he said and she shot him an icy glare. "Ready… Steady… GO!"

And they were off!

"Cheat!" Marcus bellowed, scrambling on his feet at Niko's snap signal.

They sped off towards the village as fast as they could, spraying ice behind them as they went.

As they entered the village, they veered away from each other, to take what each thought were shorter, quicker routes back to the monastery; Niko turned right and headed for the market square whereas Pihla and Tors sped between the low houses round the quieter residential streets where the assumption was that there would be less traffic to contend with. Marcus chose a slightly different route, preferring to go around the periphery of the village, presumably to then cut across at a later stage.

Arms swinging furiously, their skates clattered against the smooth, hard slidderies, echoing down the silvered streets. Pihla and Tors shot past the residences and soon found themselves back on the high street in minutes. A few yards ahead of them was Marcus, who had come in from the periphery of the village. He was a fast skater, his strokes smooth and powerful, but Tors was equally swift, her strides though smaller, were executed far more economically and thus more effective. Head tucked low and arms to the side, she gradually outpaced Pihla and gained up on Marcus.

"Watch ouuuuut!"came a yell from behind as Niko pushed past an inattentive villager, barely avoiding knocking him over. "Sorry!" he called out as he swerved, spraying ice and snow at another passer-by.

Pihla turned to see him behind her, sliding and slipping, trying to gain on her. With an angry growl, she stroked her skates with all her might. A novice at skating, nevertheless her powerful quadriceps propelled her forward, a little wobbly but enough to keep her well ahead of Niko. Panting heavily and dripping with sweat, he struggled to keep up.

On they raced, through the village, the cold wind slamming in their faces and the sharp blades of their skates whistling and clacking furiously until clearing the final approach, they reached the steps of Akasa.

* * *

WHEN THEY EVENTUALLY PUSHED THROUGH the heavy gates of the monastery, they were breathless and laughing with exhilaration.

"Oh by Dyaeus, my lungs are bursting!" howled Niko.

Tors, flushed with the excitement of their race, could only manage a vigorous nod in agreement.

"By Dyaeus, I'm going to miss this place," panted Pihla.

Marcus nodded. "It will be hard to say goodbye to a place as beautiful as this," he agreed, "but leave, we must." He looked round at all of them and added, "Tomorrow."

Niko eyed him soberly through his windswept hair. "Well," he said with a sigh, "I suppose we'd better continue with our mission." He nudged Pihla. "And I'd better break the news to those two old biddies here," he said. "You know they'll be so heartbroken to see me go, they probably won't survive the heartache…"

Pihla rolled her eyes in disgust and headed for the door to go in. But scarcely had she touched it, it flew wide open.

Sister Soo-Yeon stood at the doorway, looking a little flustered. "I have been looking *everywhere* for you," she said breathlessly. "You have been summoned, " she continued wide-eyed, "by our *Empress*."

EMPRESS YOON

⦅❀⦆

*D*espite the fact that an audience with the Empress was an occurrence of the utmost rarity, the heavy doors to the Inner Palace that so intrigued them earlier, were opened without ostentation or ceremony. From the folds of her robe, Sister Soo-Yeon had produced a large iron key to unlock the door and then led them down another open-air passageway on the other side, past the fragrant jasmine that hung from its ornate iron awnings, to another set of solid doors at the end.

"This is where I leave you," she said, bowing. She extended her hand towards a thin red cord hanging beside the door and pulled it. As a faint chime sounded from beyond the doors, she withdrew respectfully, retracing her steps back from where they had come.

"Should we knock?" asked Niko, peering at the closed doors.

Pihla elbowed him. *"Fool,"* she chastised. "The sister has already sounded the bell which means there'll be someone to let us in soon. Can you not just *wait*?"

But before Niko could reply, the doors opened noiselessly inwards. They were unmanned.

The gloom of the Inner Palace was punctuated at intervals by lit sconces along both sides of its entrance—a wide passageway stretching at least twenty metres ahead into the gloom. Its ceiling was shrouded in thick darkness and Tors could only surmise its immense height from the echoes of their footsteps floating up to the rafters.

How is this possible? she wondered. *This place appears much more expansive from the inside!*

Positioned along the way beneath the light of the sconces were statues of creatures in all manner of the exotic and extraordinary. Carved out of jade and onyx, encrusted with jewels, these whimsical creatures of stone winked in the flickering light, seemingly alive in the darkened recesses of the passage.

The group walked on following the dimly lit trail, their footsteps echoing eerily into the thick, soupy darkness. On and on they went until finally the passageway opened up into a wide circular hall. Here, light was not supplied by sconces or lamps, but streamed in from the open sky above. They looked around in wonder at the open-aired auditorium. By now, sunset had come and gone, and the smooth mirrored floor silvered by the moon above was all that illuminated the space.

* * *

Tors sensed her even before she glimpsed her.

In the centre of the circle sat the Empress—a small figure within the large expanse of the hall. Her presence, dense and concentrated, seemed to flow around them like a swirling mist. She motioned for them to come closer.

Niko walked up first, followed by Pihla, then Marcus and

finally Tors. They stood in front of the Empress Yoon, heads bowed in reverence.

The Empress spoke slowly, as if just awakened from slumber: "Welcome travellers…" Her voice was ancient, throaty and carried with it the weight of centuries past.

* * *

NIKO WAS first to look up at her when she spoke. He felt the hair on the back of his head stand.

The Empress was very old. Stretching out a shrivelled and leathery hand, she beckoned him closer. To Niko's surprise, he found himself approaching the Empress despite his reluctance, his legs seemingly moving with a mind of their own. Then he sat down at the foot of her throne as if it were the most natural thing in the world to do. From that seating position, he found himself looking upon her the same way he used to look upon his Nana's face when she told her bedtime stories. Try as he might, he was unable to look away and he sensed too, that the others were also sat at the foot of her throne, equally transfixed.

I see you, the Empress greeted him. She spoke directly to his mind.

Niko nodded in reply, too surprised to vocalise his answer.

You have come far traveller, the Empress continued. Her mental voice was melodic, lilting and had the smooth timbre of one much, much younger. *For two hundred years, we have not had visitors. Why are you here and what is it you seek?*

Niko tried in his mind, rather cumbersomely, to explain that they were looking for the Sansari Gate. However to his alarm he found his thoughts and feelings for Pihla surfacing instead. Embarrassed, he fought to shut them out but failed.

The more he tried to suppress his thoughts of her, the more they surfaced.

Ah, came the response, followed by a sentiment of amusement. *Both admirable quests,* came the approving reply, *but not without difficulty...* The Empress then presented a vision to him.

He was standing on the roof of some tall building and could feel the turmoil and confusion of war around him. He flinched for the vision enveloped him entirely, filling his eyes and ears with the ongoing chaos and commotion as if he himself were there. A few shells hit the ground close by, shaking the deck and scattering smoke and debris everywhere. He looked up to see Pihla facing him. She was hanging precariously at the open door of an urbanglider about to lift off, her tawny hair in her face, buffeted around by the turbulence. She smiled at him. He tried to reach for her, to grab her hand, but the aircraft was pulling away. She was yelling something to him. The pounding of the air strikes drowned what little hope he had of hearing her words, but as it took off, she blew him a kiss and mouthed 'goodbye'. His hands grasped thin air as she lifted away. And then the image was gone.

Noooo! Niko felt a tightness in his throat at the thought of losing Pihla. And then another thought: *A second war? We're fighting a second war?* He felt afraid at the prospect—*I'm only human and humans are too weak to survive a war between the tougher races.*

Take heart, said the Empress gently. Her voice seemed to dip into a whisper: *We were once human too you know. A long, long time ago...* Then she smiled, which was strange, for her face had not moved and yet in his mind he could see her smiling. *And now look at us—for even the weakest can prevail.*

Niko jolted backwards, his gaze released from the

Empress, uncertain of what he had just witnessed. Unbeknownst to him, at the same time, the others too saw visions from the Empress but different ones. Visions specific and personal to them.

* * *

FOR PIHLA, the Empress presented her with two images. The first was that of a man, a Tilkoen and ruggedly handsome in the roguish way she was partial to. He held out his hand to her and as he did so she had sensed a choice, or rather an offer. With his outstretched hand came the offer of her old life, its familiarity and its uncomplicatedness. *Freedom from the burden of duty.* But Pihla hesitated.

A choice indeed, interjected the Empress but without waiting for an answer, presented her with the second image.

This time, Pihla was standing with the High Council of House Tilkoen. *How do I know this?* she wondered bemusedly. *I've never even seen the Tilkoen High Council before.* She looked around at the rest of the members standing beside her. The High Twelve, they were called—members of the High Council, House Tilkoen's ruling elite. They were all standing in a line next to her. She counted them and realised she had counted eleven. Twelve in all if she included herself. Her eyes widened. *I'm one of the High Twelve?*

They were in the centre of an immense auditorium. Members of the Council, a thousand strong, all sat surrounding them. The High Twelve led this thousand-strong Council, representative leaders of House Tilkoen. Pihla scanned them—a sea of Tilkoen faces looking back at her. All save one. She recognised him immediately.

Niko.

***

MARCUS SAW himself staring across a vast plain. It was dawn, just at the beginning of sunrise and the golden fingers of the sun were sweeping across the hushed rippling sheaves of grain. In his arms he carried a small bundle wrapped in a soft linen blanket. It wriggled slightly and gurgled.

A baby.

Directly ahead, a dark elliptical opening stood surreally in mid-air, a jarring dense, oval of black against the idyllic backdrop of whispering fields.

An opening into the Ether.

The opening exuded a feeling of familiarity. Of home.

Ageron.

He knew home was waiting for him if he stepped into it. He also knew that that opening was not going to stay open forever. As he watched, it began to shrink. Smaller and smaller. *Soon it will be too small to go through.*

But Marcus remained steadfast, cradling the child in his arms, rocking it gently until at long last the opening disappeared altogether, leaving him with a churning mix of emotions. Of contentment and regret at the same time.

***

I SEE YOU, the Empress said to Tors. *Nehisi...*

Your Imperial Highness, greeted Tors.

Ah! Delight rippled from the Empress. *At last, one who speaks!* The Empress paused and Tors felt her presence float around her, not probing, rather observing her, as if one were walking in the garden studying its flowers. *Where have you come from, Nehisi?*

The planetary system of Ageron, your Highness, replied Tors.

Ageron... A fleeting image of recollection. *It has been a long time.* The Empress paused again. *And Emperor Ageron III?*

He is succeeded by his son, Lord Draeger.

Draeger... A tinge of melancholy. *Yinha's son...* Fondness. Love.

Do you know him, Your Highness?

No. Not yet. But Yinha... A sigh.

She was your daughter...

Yes... Another sigh. *She was but a newborn then. We gave her to Lady Arnemetiae, my closest friend and wife to Emperor Ageron II. To be raised as his ward and to be betrothed to their son, Ageron III, the one destined to be born in the upcoming year of Hiems. My Yinha...* Love. Duty. Anguish.

Tors felt the emotions wash over her like an ocean wave. Then it receded.

The flow of time, mused the Empress. *Like the sea it returns again and again. Same but different.* Another sigh. *Like echoes. Draeger, we shall finally meet. Soon...*

Tors was astonished. The Empress was indeed old and if she was Draeger's grandmother, that would make her about eight centuries old, twice the age of the average Ageronian or Ellagrin for that matter.

Older, corrected the Empress. *I am, as someone here mentioned the other day, as old as the mountains.* Amusement. *It has been a long, long time.* She turned her focus on Tors and smiled, *and we have not had babies for a long while.* Her smile was warm and inviting, like the sun on one's face. *She is beautiful, Nehisi...*

She? Tors felt her belly. *It's a girl. A girl!*

But it is not time to rest yet Nehisi...

I know...

The chain of events have yet to play out. Many choices. Many possibilities. But soon these will begin to fall away and leave us with but a handful of options. But will they be the right ones? Consternation. Despair. Hope.

Tors felt the Empress' emotions flow over her like cascading waves.

Whatever happens Nehisi, the billions of lives in Ageron must be saved. You must not fail...

Tors' chest tightened. *The Sansari Gate,* she said worriedly, *I have tried to find it. To retrace its location from old steps—from Arnemetiae and into the Ether—but it is no longer where it used to be. I cannot feel it, I cannot find it.*

The Empress acknowledged her consternation. *Nothing stays the same in the Ether,* she said. *You know that.* She paused for a moment, deep in thought. Then a nod at the recollection. *Yes, the currents of the Ether flow strong there. More so than anywhere else. Chaotic. It would have moved.*

Then how will I find it? Tors felt the familiar knot twist in her insides, the same worry that had plagued her all these months—that perhaps the location of the Sansari endpoint would forever be beyond her abilities. *If the Sansari endpoint randomly moves, then I may never find it.* The knot in her stomach twisted some more.

Not random, answered the Empress. *Like a float loose on the sea, it is there. There is a way...*

There is a way? Tors' heart leapt. The Empress knows. She knows a way! *How? How will I find it?*

The Empress paused again. This time she leant forward. With her wizened fingers, she held Tors' face lightly in her hands. They reminded her of the desiccated husk of a mantis.

Tors looked at her beseechingly. *I am afraid I may not find Sansari in time. Will you help me? So many lives depend upon this.*

The Empress' eyes searched hers. *Ah, but for you that is not the main reason, is it Nehisi?*

No, Tors admitted.

The Empress read her heart. *You wish to be free of... an attachment.* The Empress paused briefly, as if scenting a rose for its fragrance notes. *From... him?*

I made him a promise—to save his people.

Yes. The Empress sighed. *You made him a promise...*

And when I deliver that promise, I shall be absolved from that debt... and from him too. Please, will you help me?

I shall, the Empress replied, *but on one condition. An exchange. An agreement but with me this time. In exchange for the location of Sansari.*

Tors looked at her.

I will show you the way to Sansari, but in return, you must bring him to me.

Him?

The Empress nodded. *Draeger. I must see him. My Yinha's son.*

Tors felt the intensity of the Empress' gaze upon her.

When you have found Sansari and returned to Ageron, you must bring him here. To me. Will you do that, Nehisi?

Yes.

There was a brief pause. *Promise me that,* said the Empress.

I promise.

Good. Then the Empress leant forward and touched her forehead lightly against Tors'. There was a flash of recognition. An imprint. The innate knowledge of that particular area of the Ether as the Empress transferred the knowledge over to Tors. Now, it sat in her mind, an in-built vision of that part of the Ether.

Sansari... I understand. Tors' eyes widened. *So this is how the currents change and return.* The natural rhythms of the Ether—

its ebb and flow—as indeterminate as it was, became as clear and present to Tors as watching the waves in the ocean in front of her.

The Empress chuckled amused. *We have perfected the art of imparting sight of the Ether as it changes, as it moves with time and dimension. The beauty of looking inwards is the consequent ability to expand out.* The Empress leant forward again and once more they touched foreheads lightly. *And now the imprint to find your way back here to fulfil your promise to me.* Tors felt the warmth of her smile on her. *Remember your promise Nehisi. Bring Draeger to me. He must prepare. I will tell him.*

Prepare? For what?

War.

War?

A sigh. *Like currents of the Ether, war will return. War amongst the Houses. And therein, when the chain of events have played out and your task is done, his will begin.*

I don't understand...

But the Empress had already withdrawn.

* * *

THE VISIONS FADED AWAY and the four of them found themselves sitting at the foot of the throne. The Empress lifted her hand slowly in a gesture of dismissal and they retraced their steps silently back to the doors of the Inner Palace to the exit.

Tors glanced at the others and wondered what they had experienced. Something told her the Empress had shared different things with each of them. Niko looked a little apprehensive but hopeful, whereas Pihla was frowning, deep in thought. Then she looked at Marcus who had a far-off look on his face and seemed troubled.

There is much ahead of us to overcome, she thought to herself uneasily.

They returned to Sister Soo-Yeon at the refectory and by sunrise the next day, the group stepped through the Yoon Gate once more and entered the Ether.

PART IV

POWER PLAYS

EVACUATION

DECEDO-FIVE, PLANET TRIMON, AGERON

Heatstorms destroy ENTIRE CONTINENT of Bellun!

*S*creamed the latest headline on the projected news ticker encircling the cavernous community hall of Decedo-Five, Trimon's main evacuhub. As evacuees waited in their lines, the news ticker cheerfully spewed headline after headline of news and social media comments from across the Realm for their benefit.

The next headline flashed across the hall, chasing the first one:

Entire continents wiped out and we are funding an impeachment? Where are our priorities?

This one was clearly a social media headline, and no prizes for guessing who it probably originated from. Draeger glanced away to look at the crowd instead. If the headline rankled him, he certainly made sure it didn't show on his face. He and Chancellor Rasmus were surveying the latest evacua-

PLANET TRIMON, AGERON

tion in progress on Trimon, third planet from the twin suns after Anavio and Bellun with Lord Velius, Praetor of Trimon, supposedly in charge of the entire operation.

So very in charge that I have to have my Reds here to see that the job gets done in time, scoffed Draeger inwardly as he stood between Chancellor Rasmus and the oleaginous Lord Velius on stage overlooking the soldiers moving the masses along. Conditions inside the hall were becoming stifling as temperatures outside climbed. With the next heatstorm forecast to hit the area in a few hours' time, it was imperative this lot were evacuated on time.

"...and from here, it is but a short walk through the boarding bridges and into the hypershuttles," said Lord Velius, eagerly trying to demonstrate his handle on the entire operation. But Draeger had had enough of his handling. They were running late as it was. He raised his hand to halt the Praetor's babbling and scowled at the first news stream ticker still chasing round the hall, flashing spiritedly for all to see.

"Heatstorms destroy entire continent of Bellun," read out Lord Velius, much to the annoyance of Draeger. The Supreme Commander glowered. Unlike Trimon, Bellun had been bombarded by the latest solar flare which incinerated its entire continent, Aprica. What the headline didn't state was the fact that Aprica was no longer inhabited, for Bellun's citizens had already been evacuated to the outer planets before the storms struck.

"What kind of fool blares out all these fabrications in the run up to his trial?" he fumed, turning to the Chancellor.

"The emperor is capitalising on the latest climate disasters to mislead the masses and appeal to their emotions," replied Chancellor Rasmus., "probably with the view of his upcoming trial in mind, I would guess."

"And what of Bellun's Praetor, Lord Augusta?" voiced

Draeger glaring at the headline frustratedly. "Why hasn't he said something? At least to correct this very public misconception!"

"He has, my lord," replied Chancellor Rasmus, "but Augusta is old and weak. His statements are far less attention-grabbing than Akseli's and often fail to feature in the headlines." He looked on distastefully, first at the clueless Lord Velius and then at the sensationalistic ticker headline. Unfortunately, the news was obviously being read by all the people here, judging from the ripple of raised heads whenever a headline whizzed round the hall. The old Chancellor continued, "With impeachment passed and trial preparations underway, Emperor Akseli has taken the opportunity outside house arrest to reach out to the populace via the media channels." As if on cue, the news ticker proceeded to spew the next few headlines ranging from ludicrous to outright seditious:

NO MORE TIME OR FUNDS WASTED ON THIS IMPEACHMENT SCAM!

A STRAIGHT-OUT CONSPIRACY TO TAKE OVER THE THRONE BY MY BROTHER! FAKE NEWS ORCHESTRATED BY DERANGED DRAEGER!

"He is twisting the facts and stating outright lies," fumed Draeger. "Akseli's the one spreading fake news!" He clenched his fists in fury.

"Akseli is fighting back," said Chancellor Rasmus quietly, "perhaps not in the courtroom yet, but certainly out in this media circus."

Draeger drew a deep breath and reigned in his anger. "He is hitting back by insinuating that *I* orchestrated this, that *I'm* framing him because *I* want the throne." He looked on at the next headline that flashed past:

PLANET TRIMON, AGERON

WHAT ABOUT PREVIOUS LIAISONS OUR DERANGED DRAEGER HAS HAD WITH LADY ELENA, SISTER TO ELLAGRIN'S EMPEROR? WHY ISN'T THE COMMITTEE LOOKING INTO THAT??

Lord Draeger looked at the Chancellor, exasperated. "Is there *any* of this drivel he is spewing that we can use against him?"

The Chancellor shook his head. "Unfortunately not. And we cannot block critics by virtue of freedom of speech, my lord."

"Oooh, the Lady *Elena*," piped up Lord Velius, his eyes following the ticker headline. He steepled his long tapered fingers and rippled them against each other with rapt interest. "Weren't you involved in some sort of, ahem... *diplomatic overture* with her before, Lord Draeger?"

Lord Draeger looked at him coldly. "Those diplomatic talks obviously failed when Akseli conspired with her to let her people invade us."

"Of course, of course," said Lord Velius, nodding vigorously. His eyes shifted from side to side with gossipy salacity.

"All this, of course, has no bearing on our evacuation efforts," said Lord Draeger stiffly. "My brother's actions will be decided at trial. In the meantime, we have more urgent matters to attend to."

The men halted their exchange as an announcement to 'Commence embarkation' rang out loud and clear. The lines of evacuees began to shuffle forward slowly.

"Ah! They've opened the ship at last," said Lord Velius, beaming self-importantly as if the entire effort had been due to him alone.

Lord Draeger looked past him and directed his gaze at the far end of the queues where the Reds had been mobilised and were efficiently funnelling queues of people into the boarding bridges. These led to the hypershuttles parked outside, ready to evacuate them to one of the outer planets of the Realm. "And which settlement is this one headed for?" he asked.

"Quelo Three in Othon, northern hemisphere," answered Lord Velius with an air of officiousness. A young family walked past and he flashed an exaggerated smile at them before bending down to pat their young son on the head. The child looked up at him. There were tears in his eyes. The mother placed a reassuring hand on her son's shoulder before nudging him gently to stay in the queue. She gave Lord Velius an uncertain look and asked, "What is Quelo like, my lord?" But before Lord Velius could answer, her husband cut in: "I hear settlements like Quelo are very basic. Many of them are in the middle of nowhere with the nearest city hundreds of miles away." His eyes passed over the three of them, searching for answers. "Is this true, my lords?"

Lord Velius shook his head. "No, no, no, of course not," he said flashing a reassuring smile. "Every settlement is self-sufficient in terms of amenities, housing, health facilities, the like. You and your family will be well catered for, don't worry. "

"But what are we going to do for a living?" asked the woman. "Will there be jobs for us there? Will we be housed near our neighbours? Our friends?" She looked around at several other families around them and her eyes welled. "This was our neighbourhood, our life, our home. And you are making us leave all this behind."

"Well, you can't stay here in Trimon much longer anyway. We have severe water shortages and our reservoirs have dried up" said Lord Velius rather insensitively. "Besides, with sea levels rising, most coastal cities like this one will be gone in a year."

The woman let out a sob and buried her head in her husband's shoulder.

PLANET TRIMON, AGERON

"Well, this isn't good enough!" her husband said. His eyes were red too. "You cannot just remove people from their homes like this! Without giving us a choice! And to leave everything behind—our home, our friends, our livelihoods, our *entire* lives! It's not fair. It's not right!" He shook his fists at Lord Velius angrily and then gave Draeger a furtive glance before walking on quickly. Another family behind them walked past, casting bitter looks as well. One man even muttered, "You're supposed to save us, not punish us."

"Now look here," huffed Lord Velius, "what do you think we are doing right now?" But the line had moved along again. Antagonised, he strode after the man, trying to refute the his points. "We are trying to get you out before the next heatstorm destroys the city and this is the gratitude we get...?"

Chancellor Rasmus looked on after the trotting Lord Velius and sighed. "People aren't happy we don't evacuate them fast enough," he said, "and when we do, they aren't happy to leave either." He gave Draeger a concerned look. "Protests by ordinary people are becoming more frequent too, my lord."

Draeger nodded, his lips drawn tight. "They want the empire to do something about these natural disasters, which we can't. The suns are dying and planetary scattering is accelerating. Evacuating our people to the outer planets is but a short term solution. If we do not address the Exodus issue soon, there may not be enough goodwill to run Akseli's trial impartially." The Supreme Commander's brows furrowed as the palpable weight upon his shoulders wore him down.

The Chancellor nodded in silent empathy. His gaze followed the moving lines of people slowly making their way into the boarding bridges, and then back on the news ticker, still rendering its unending supply of headlines:

EVACUATION

> ONCE AGAIN, DERANGED DRAEGER IS USING THIS IMPEACHMENT TRIAL AS AN EXCUSE TO DISTRACT US FROM CLIMATE DISASTER. FROM THE EXODUS. THE ENEMY IS CORRUPTION WITHIN THE SENATE! THE ENEMY IS DRAEGER!

The Chancellor nudged Draeger gently. "I think we have seen enough for one day, don't you?" he said.

Draeger gave a brief nod in reply.

As they made their way to the doors to leave the hall, a slight tremor shook the side of the building. A rustling sound enveloping the hall followed. The Chancellor stiffened.

"The heatstorm's arrived early," Draeger said grimly and gestured hurriedly at his soldiers to move the evacuees into the boarding bridges. *Most of these civilians do not have any antithermal clothing to protect themselves against the heated gusts. We need to get them out of here before the storm destroys this flimsy shelter.*

His Reds calmly hurried the people on. Within minutes, most had gone through the doors on the other end of the hall and into the adjoining boarding bridges. Draeger nodded approvingly. *We might just get them all into the shuttles before the storm's full-blown.*

By now, the enveloping rustle had crescendoed as winds outside whipped up in strength, hurling dry sand at the building, until all that could be heard was the constant deafening swish of white noise.

"We should go now, my lord!" yelled Chancellor Rasmus and tugged Draeger's sleeve to get his attention. "The evacuation is complete!" he said, pointing at the last few evacuees ducking through the doors. They only just made it in time for that very moment, the main entrance to Decedo-Five flew open, pushed apart by the severe gusts.

The last few Reds ran for the boarding bridges themselves.

Draeger waved off two closest to him who had hesitated, having spotted him and the Chancellor still standing at the stage, and ordered them to evacuate with him. The storm howled with fury and the thin roof of the community hall began to shake and shudder. As they ran out the doors and into Draeger's hyperglider, the wall paint of the building began to peel off, charring and curling in the heat.

As their aircraft took off, Draeger turned to have one last look at the diminishing hall that was Decedo-Five before the dust from the storm swallowed it up. He thought of those in other areas who had yet to endure the ferocity of these heatstorms and of the hurricanes, flash floods and rising sea levels to come. And then, like the evacuees that had just escaped, the many who will be displaced but only to delay the inevitable for a few decades. He considered the Realm's stark circumstances—the climate disasters, their limited options for escape, his gamble on finding Sansari.

What if all our options do not come through in time or at all? He felt as trapped as his people. *Perhaps resuming diplomatic relations with House Ellagrin has its merits. We have to have somewhere for my people to go. At the very least, assurances from Ellagrin on existing settlement treaties so that those on route to Ellagrin will be taken care of.*

Draeger weighed his options uncomfortably. The thought of contacting Elena filled him with a sense of foreboding. *What about previous liaisons our Deranged Draeger has had with Lady Elena?* He flushed at the recollection of Akseli's earlier headline and realised, perversely, that the sensationalist comment no longer sounded as wildly fallacious as it had before.

ELENA

SUMMER PALACE
PLANET SKANSGARDEN, ELLAGRIN

*E*lena cast a critical eye at her reflection as she rearranged the draping of her dress. It was deep blue silk, the lustrous colour of sapphire, and flowed effortlessly over her curves. Apart from her burgeoning bump, barely noticeable beneath the draping, she was not displeased with how she looked.

The gown, accentuated by a high, tapered collar that widened provocatively at the décolletage, showed off her breasts which had become fuller and more voluptuous of late. Elena gave a satisfied nod; she had achieved the look she was after.

The demure whore. Who would've thought that possible. From her own assessments of Lord Vigyo, Elena understood that it was female attractiveness that the Doge understood, not facts nor logic nor discussion. Her lips drew into a thin line. She had her work cut out for her today.

"What do you think, Varg?" she asked.

As usual, Varg, Elena's ever present bodyguard remained

silent. All she got from him this time was a subtle nod of the head—of acknowledgement or of approval, it wasn't clear.

"Your Majesty..." The dulcet tones of Lady Berit's voice arrested her attention. "Lord Vigyo has arrived."

"He has, has he?" replied Elena languidly.

Lady Berit permitted herself a tiny flicker of a smile. "Are we keeping this one waiting as well?" she asked.

Elena pondered a moment, then shook her head. "Not this time," she said. "I have to go over some finances with Tadeusz after this before next week's Administrative Council meeting."

"Ah, the Council meeting," nodded Lady Berit, putting two and two together. "Lord Vigyo I'm sure will be amenable to supporting whatever you intend to be tabling there next week." She gave Elena a knowing smile. "He's not too bad looking either, Your Majesty..."

Elena let out a sardonic laugh. "I wouldn't go *that* far, Lady Berit but yes, Lord Vigyo being younger than the other decrepit old fools would certainly make him one of the slightly more palatable suitors we've had so far."

Lady Berit smiled. "I'm sure he'll be... effective in helping you influence the other Doges, Your Majesty."

"*Doubly* effective, Lady Berit," said Elena drily. "Both Lord Vigyo and his father Odo are Doges."

"Very good, Your Majesty," replied Lady Berit, "but you are aware that Lord Vigyo is most likely here to ask you the question." Lady Berit gave a delicate cough before continuing, "... the question of marriage."

"I am well aware of that, Lady Berit," snapped Elena.

"Apologies, Your Majesty," said Lady Berit, "I did not mean—"

Elena dismissed her apology with a wave. "It's alright, Lady Berit," she said, her lips pursed and bitter. Lord Vigyo had been but one of the many, many Doges trying to court her since Niklas died. "This is just one of the things I have had to bear with since the passing of Niklas. Ysgarh help us if our Doges should have to endure a *woman* ruling them!"

Lady Berit nodded sympathetically. "Not that I agree with any of this, but Ellagrin has always been a patriarchal society and the Doges especially have always been men."

"And *obviously* one cannot have a *woman* rule the empire!" added Elena, incensed. "That would be unheard of!" She gave a snort of disgust.

"But if you marry someone like Lord Vigyo," suggested Lady Berit, "who could be, ah… *compliant* to your… *ideas* perhaps?"

Elena's mouth grew hard.

"If he asks today," asked Lady Berit, curious, "will you marry him?"

Elena turned to look at her lady-in-waiting, her cobalt eyes flared as she pondered her answer. *No!* she screamed inwardly, fury and frustration threatening to boil over. ***No. Never!*** *And I shall cut the balls off every single Doge before I have to marry any of them in order to rule by proxy!*

Outwardly, she gave Lady Berit a noncommittal smile in reply.

Elena was well aware that her hold on the throne was a tenuous one. *For now, I rule as Niklas' sister.* Subconsciously her hand moved to caress her bump. *As Queen Regent,* she corrected herself, *to the next emperor of Ellagrin.* Her brows furrowed. *But for how long?* Her hope was that when the baby finally came, the pressure on her to marry would lessen, leaving her to rule as Regent and when the child was old enough, as advisor to him on matters of the empire.

But will they leave me alone until then? For now, she had hoped to keep her suitors guessing, to delay things until the baby was born. However, her position was a precarious one and whilst the Doges who came calling, came as suitors, the others who didn't were undoubtedly usurpers. That worried her. She touched her bump tenderly. *I have to keep you safe somehow,* she thought.

"Your Majesty...?" ventured Lady Berit, wresting Elena from her thoughts. "Lord Vigyo?"

Elena reigned in her worries, patted her coiled hair in place and sat herself down on the chaise, carefully draping her gown over it. "Varg," she said, looking at the silent giant of a man, "I'll need you to wait out of sight, like with the others." Varg gave a brief nod and lumbered out. "Send him in Lady Berit," Elena said.

* * *

A FEW MOMENTS LATER, the soft rustle of Lady Berit's skirt heralded the arrival of Lord Vigyo. Elena also caught the faint but sharp intake of breath as the Doge saw her. She smiled inwardly. *The power of first impressions,* she noted, fully aware of her carefully orchestrated presence to the Doge. Elena knew her power over men such as Lord Vigyo but she was painfully aware of the balancing act she would have to pull off today.

"Empress Elena," greeted Lord Vigyo, bowing low.

Elena held out her hand to him as Lady Berit closed the doors quietly on her way out. "Lord Vigyo, do have a seat," Elena murmured languidly and indicated at the settee nearby. Lord Vigyo's eyes lingered over her curves as he sat down to face her. "How are you, Lord Vigyo and how is your father?"

"My father is well, thank you Your Majesty," replied Lord Vigyo. Elena noted that his eyes had settled to just above her bosom but hadn't yet reached her gaze. "He is still very much active in the Administrative Council, as you may have well seen, Your Majesty."

"Indeed," murmured Elena. "In fact, I believe we exchanged a few words at the Blomst Summit a few weeks ago. A most charming man, I must say…"

Lord Vigyo gave a feeble laugh, his gaze finally flipped upwards to meet Elena's eyes. "Politics and partying," he said lightly, "that's my father alright." Then he became serious. "However today is neither about government nor games," he said. "I have come to discuss matters of importance with yourself, Your Majesty."

"And what would that be?" asked Elena, smiling sweetly. She rose from her seat to pour some amarinthe into two glasses.

"It has come to my attention," began Lord Vigyo, "that quite a few of my fellow Doges have, ah, approached Your Majesty in the last few months… That is to say, to, ah —"

"*Drink?*" interrupted Elena innocently. She handed him a glass of the ruby red liquid.

Lord Vigyo blinked mid-sentence, accepted it and took a big gulp. "What I mean to say," he continued, "is… I would like to formally ask for your hand in marriage." He drew a deep breath and looked at her.

Elena looked downwards, pretending to be surprised. "Why Lord Vigyo," she said coyly, "This is so soon… We barely know each other."

Lord Vigyo cleared his throat. "Now, now, Elena," he said, "I would hardly say that's the case. This is after all, not my first visit of a personal capacity. And as for barely knowing each other"—his eyes narrowed—"I should think our ah… liaisons over the past few months is proof enough of our ah, *relationship*."

"Come now, Lord Vigyo," said Elena with a disarming

smile, "you know I cannot make my mind up just yet." She sighed heavily. "Too much weighs on my mind still—Niklas's death, his failed invasion of Ageron. The financial losses of that alone, not to mention half our military wiped out..." She shook her head. "We have much to do to rebuild Ellagrin before I can think of my own happiness." She eyed him cautiously, adding, "*Our* happiness...which reminds me: I'd like to put forward the proposal for a new survey to assess the assets of all members of our Council in next week's Administration meeting—"

But Lord Vigyo cut her short. "Now look here," he said, standing up. He was a tall man, despite all the preening and posturing he was renown for. And heavyset. At that moment, he showed a side of belligerence which Elena had not expected. "Don't think I don't know what you are playing at!" he said, shaking his finger angrily at her. "You and I know that I am your best bet. The others are either covetous vultures or so old they're halfway in the grave." He reached out and grabbed her wrist, holding it tight. "And maybe," he said, smiling thinly at her, "*maybe*, if you play your part well, we shall even get your survey passed at Council."

Elena twisted her hand to extricate herself from his hold. Her cobalt eyes flashed with fury as she backed away from him and got to her feet to face him squarely.

"You cannot prolong this forever you know," Lord Vigyo continued. "You must choose or they will come for you." He towered threateningly over her. "Or worse, your *child*."

His last words chilled her heart. "How dare you!" screamed Elena and swung her glass at him. It shattered as it struck his face and left a thin line of red where the delicate glass cut across the cheek. "Get *out*!" she said dangerously. "Get out! Get out! Get out!"

At that very instant, the door to the adjoining room flew

ELENA

open as Varg charged through. Without a word, two strong arms, thick as trees reached out to lift Lord Vigyo bodily off the floor.

"What the—!" yelled Lord Vigyo as Varg hauled him out of the room. Elena could hear scuffling as the Doge was dragged down the corridor before unceremoniously thrown out of her private quarters.

Lady Berit ran in, alerted by the commotion. "Are you all right, Your Majesty?" she asked concerned.

But Elena ignored her and turned to run.

"Your Majesty—"

She ran down the corridors of the Summer Palace, Lady Berit's voice ringing behind her, until at last she reached the Sun Room. She stumbled in as its biometric locks opened to let her through.

In the middle of the marbled-floor and glass-domed ceiling of the Sun Room stood the antique French armoire.

The private portal.

The miniature version of the commercial Gateways, built by Ageron III which connected the Red Palace in Ageron to the Summer Palace here on Ellagrin.

Elena hesitated for a moment, then taking a deep breath, headed away from it and walked towards her writing desk. Reaching underneath it, she felt for the secret button and pressed it. A small hidden drawer slid open revealing a small pill-shaped device, the size of her palm.

The beacon.

Elena took it and walked up to the armoire. Here, another hidden clasp revealed the receptacle for the beacon.

Lord Vigyo's words had shaken her to the core. *I will not let them kill me or my baby.* Furiously, she wiped her tears away. *I need support from Ageron if I am to stay in power. I need to talk to*

Draeger. A flash of uncertainty. *But will he talk to me after all that has happened?*

But nothing, not even deplorable actions like that, had ever stopped Elena nor compelled her to deviate from her course. Gingerly, she placed the beacon inside its receptacle and opened the door of the armoire.

Nothing. No whirring sounds. No bright white tunnel. No gateway.

He would have deactivated the beacon on his side after the Lagentian invasion. It will only work if both ends are activated.

Elena took the beacon out and reinserted it once more. *Try again.*

But it remained inactive.

Elena sat down heavily on the floor and leaned back against the armoire. The Sun Room which until now had been her private sanctuary suddenly felt empty, desolate.

What do I do? she asked herself at a loss. For the first time in a long, long time, she had no answer.

DRAEGER

COMITIUM
PLANET AMORGOS, AGERON

Draeger felt a little ill at ease sitting in the forefront of the Ecclesia, the Comitium's main debating hall. It was an environment as alien to him as the battlefield was to the majority of these genteel senators. However, as Chancellor Rasmus pointed out, his presence here at the Comitium was more crucial than ever in light of Akseli's approaching trial.

You need to be seen to be taking charge of matters, the Chancellor had reminded him, *not least because you will have to take the helm if Akseli is found guilty. And let's not forget, Akseli will be making an appearance at the Comitium today, causing havoc if he can, so you need to be present to clamp down on any subversive comments or acts of his.*

Across the bench, staring impertinently through him, sat Akseli, flanked on either side by two burly bodyguards, his personal forcefield shield raised and shimmering like a bubble of haze around him.

As if anyone would try to take him out here, thought Draeger contemptuously. *He thinks the Ecclesia is an Asgharian brawling-*

den. But then, discussions at the Ecclesia today certainly seemed headed the way of a brawl.

"There needs to be an overall plan to address this accelerating climate change, my lords," began Lord Augusta, taking to the floor and addressing the Senate from there. The rheumy-eyed senator's voice trembled as he struggled to be heard all the way to the back benches.

"All coastal cities in your jurisdiction have been evacuated, Lord Augusta. What more do you *urgently* need now?" bellowed Lord Reku from the benches.

"I'll have you know that Bellun has the highest rate of heatstorms, hurricanes and floods, compared to even Anavio!" came Lord Augusta's indignant reply. "And yet, the central aid we have received so far has been next to nothing! Why last week millions of *ore* were spent financing the evacuation of Trimon's residents instead! *Why* Trimon and not Bellun? Bellun is second closest to the suns. Trimon is third. Why then are we being ignored despite us suffering these warming effects more acutely? Our central cities are still inhabited and exposed to solar flares and heatstorms. My lords, I have millions still living in the northern hemisphere and I need the funds, *urgent* funds, to install heat-domes over our houses and our farms!"

There was an uproar from the benches at the mention of funds.

"We must be practical," said Lord Velius. "Bellun is a gone-case! We don't have infinite resources to waste on heat-domes and such when we know your entire planet will cease to be habitable in under fifty years. Evacuation yes, heat-domes and climate control measures—most certainly *not*!"

"You would say that, what with your planet getting the lion's share of funds at the moment!" yelled Lord Augusta, dyspeptic. He shook his fists angrily at Lord Velius and doddered back to his bench to sit down and continue his tirade from there.

"Trimon is getting help now because it's had to wait so long for *your* Bellun to evacuate," said Lord Velius. "We could have received much needed assistance earlier to tackle rising temperatures if it weren't for Bellun! As it is, our crops are no longer viable—"

"Your crops would not have survived anyway," cut in Lord Albertus. "Planetary climate change is irreversible. That and acute water shortage—"

"Well, you would say that," grumbled Lord Augusta from his seat, "the capital planet Amorgos gets an additional slice of central funds for 'administration' no matter what, doesn't it?"

"Now look here—" protested Lord Albertus before Lord Patrin stepped in.

"My lords," he said gesturing placatingly at the senators. "Let us keep this civil. We have a joint problem to address—"

"Joint problem*sss*," corrected Lord Albertus grumpily.

Lord Patrin took a moment to let everyone simmer down. "There are some joint problems," he said calmly. "The beginnings of planetary scatterings due to our failing suns are starting to cause us problems, particularly in the inner planets —Anavio, Bellun, Trimon—who are feeling its effects already."

A murmur of agreement rippled through the benches.

Lord Patrin continued. "For the first time ever, we are experiencing climate change at unprecedented scale and speed. Rising sea levels, hurricanes and heatstorms have seen entire cities wiped out and the ever increasing temperatures mean our crops are no longer viable in many areas."

"Hear, hear," agreed Lord Marius. "Food prices have shot up too, markedly so across the Realm."

Lord Augusta nodded, agreeing. "The outer planets are being stripped of resources too, due to the population increase from evacuees." He added, "We also can't grow enough or quickly enough to feed the influx of people."

"...which is the problem we should start looking at," said Lord Patrin, "instead of throwing ore at measures in the inner planets that are temporary at best."

"How dare you label my problems temporary?" Lord Augusta piped up angrily. Then Akseli spoke up.

"I'm sure the people of Bellun will *not* appreciate life and death issues being labelled as such, Lord Patrin," he chastised, his voice ringing loud and clear.

Draeger's eyes narrowed. Akseli always had a way of displaying his authority in any form of public oratory. And twisting facts.

"The current process of evacuation is *disgraceful*," continued Akseli, not giving Lord Patrin the chance to respond. "To be treated worse than cattle! Throw them far and forget about them!"

"Hear! Hear!" agreed Lord Augusta. He threw his arms in the air. "And food. What are my citizens going to do for food? We can no longer grow crops in most places."

Lord Patrin assented. "Before, shortfalls in food production have not been a problem for us with the additional imports available from Ellagrin. However since the invasion, all this has stopped and the Ellagrins have diverted any residual long-distance consignments to other star systems. We must think of alternative measures to tackle this burgeoning problem."

"Well, we can't just start finding crops that will cope with hotter climates—we're not Ellagrins! We don't have their know-how! And I need not point out that Bellun is not the only planet with this problem. If we can't import food or obtain tougher strains to grow, what do you suggest we do?"

Someone from the back heckled, "Get our Supreme

Commander to talk to House Ellagrin! He's done it before, why not again?"

Akseli smiled in response and several senators nearby shot sideways glances in Draeger's direction.

Draeger fought to keep his composure and as he felt an unfamiliar heat rise up his neck. Once again, Chancellor Rasmus' words of warning rang in his ear: *Be vigilant! He will twist the facts.*

"Let us leave House Ellagrin out of this discussion, my lords," said Akseli with a benevolent gesture. "After all," he continued wryly, "they allegedly instigated an offensive against us."

"*Especially* because of that," spoke up Draeger eyeing his brother with venom.

"As to the basis or indeed the reliability of that accusation, we have yet to determine. At trial, of course," added Akseli, slyly. "But for now, as you can see, we have matters far more urgent to resolve." He stood up to face the members of the Comitium. "Remind me, *why* are we wasting time and resources on this impeachment?"

There was a murmur of assent from the chamber, notably from the likes of Lord Reku, Draeger observed.

"*Why* are we pushing ahead with a witch hunt when we can be building ships to get our people out?" continued Akseli revving up the Senate. Draeger could feel the heat rising up his cheeks.

These fools.

"*Why?*" shouted Akseli raising his arms. "When we can be constructing better settlements in our outer planets and feeding our displaced?"

A cheer rose up from the back benches.

Encouraged, Akseli raised his voice and whipped them into a fervour, "We should be shoring up our defences! We should be thinking about *payback* to the Ellagrins! We should be invading *them* instead!" He opened his arms out to an overwhelming deluge of cheers and clapping, much to Draeger's chagrin.

Draeger stood up abruptly. The shouts and cheers went down a notch as he did so but not enough as Akseli raised his arms to whip up their response further. Furious, Draeger strode out the chamber.

As the doors of the Ecclesia closed behind him, Akseli roared: *"Let's make Ageron great again!"*

* * *

THAT EVENING, in the sanctuary of the Red Palace, Draeger found himself in the depths of the ancient quarters, standing in front of a nondescript door, one of many in the labyrinth of corridors within the underground maze.

The private portal.

He had inserted the beacon into the hidden receptacle without even thinking about it. Taking a deep breath, he opened the door.

The familiar artificial light of the gateway tunnel washed over him, light, bright and sterile.

The Gateway's active, he realised, vaguely surprised. He hadn't expected the gateway to reconnect, not without reactivating it on both ends.

Which means Elena must have restored the beacon on her end too...

He wondered for a moment what to do next. Then like a man caught in a trance and with Akseli's taunts and the Senate's cheers still ringing in his ears, he walked through the private portal once again and into the Summer Palace at Ellagrin.

REUNION

SUMMER PALACE,
PLANET SKANSGARDEN, ELLAGRIN

The room was just as he had remembered it. Constructed almost entirely of glass, its slender frames, gilded and ornamented with lapis lazuli, stretched upwards all the way to the domed ceiling above. It was daytime here in Ellagrin and the Sun Room, awash with daylight, seemed to glow with a golden luminescence of its own.

Draeger stepped out of the private portal and softly closed the door of the old armoire behind him.

She was sitting at her writing desk as was her usual manner, her blonde tresses loose around her shoulders, gleaming where they caught the light. The room and its contents were unchanged from the last time he was there: the gilded chairs, occasional table, chaise and of course, the French armoire he had just exited.

Draeger moved noiselessly towards Elena. She had not detected his arrival but his movement caught her eye and she looked up in surprise, dropping her pen with a clatter.

"Empress," he greeted, bowing low.

"Lord Draeger," faltered Elena. She regained her composure quickly and added, "It has been a while..."

"Indeed, Empress," replied Draeger. He regarded her a moment. Elena was an exquisite beauty—pale, elegant and slender—although this time, her curves were a little more accentuated and the beginnings of a bump in her belly were becoming noticeable. Queen Alin's words rang in his ears. The child is *yours,* she had told him.

"You look well," he continued, wondering if Elena would bring this up.

"As well as can be, I suppose," she replied. There was a hint of reproach in her voice.

Why? he wondered. "I was not the one who initiated the... hostilities, Elena," he reminded her quietly.

"No," Elena conceded, "but you left me..." A flicker of resentment flashed in her cobalt eyes for an instant.

Ah...

Then she recanted. "I am sorry," she said. "It was my fault. I should never have gone down that road."

Draeger responded with an almost imperceptible nod in acknowledgement. There was almost too much to disentangle and besides, he couldn't think of what to say in response anyway.

Elena flashed him a smile. "So how are things in Ageron these days?" she asked brightly.

"Challenging," replied Draeger, glad of the change of subject. He reflected a moment and then added, "It is almost as if we've come full circle in terms of our two Houses..."

"How so?" Elena asked innocently.

"The twin suns are failing at an accelerated rate and planetary scatterings have begun," Draeger said, not missing the irony that he would rather talk about Ageron's plight than whatever it was that hung between them. "The Senate is behaving like a headless chicken in the face of an issue we have known about for over a century now, since the beginning of the Exodus programme." He clenched his jaw in annoyance at the recollection of the day's meeting at the Comitium earlier. *If I am not careful, a mad man will lead the fools in our Senate.*

Elena gave him a faint smile. "I am guessing the Senate are panicking over the future of the Exodus," she said, "and the uncertainty of where to evacuate people to."

Draeger nodded grimly but did not elaborate further. Elena saw all things in terms of a balance sheet and it would not be in his interest to point out the obvious deficit in Ageron's time of need. *At any rate, she'll work it out herself.* He also did not offer any news regarding Akseli. "And how are you finding your role as empress?" he asked, changing the subject.

Elena's look hardened. "Vexing," she replied bluntly. "The Doges whinge and fuss like newborn chicks, their mouths wide open expecting me to feed and furnish them as Niklas did."

The failed invasion would have hurt their coffers...

Her eyes narrowed. "And being ruled by a woman appears to be a novel experience for many in the Doge Council."

"That has never stopped you before, empress," Draeger pointed out.

Elena nodded. "Indeed," she agreed, "but then I've never had an *entire* council of Doges try to either marry or usurp me before." She laughed easily enough at her own comment but Draeger could have sworn he detected a haunted look in her eyes for a second.

"So," she ventured, "is Akseli…?"

"Impeached," answered Draeger.

"Ah," replied Elena. "Well, at least that's one thing less to worry about, I suppose," she said.

If only you knew... Draeger told himself grimly.

She paused briefly. "I only agreed to it to escape Niklas," she said. "You know that don't you?" She turned to look at him. "I *had* to do what I did, don't you see?" Her eyes searched his as she said that.

Draeger regarded her silently. Niklas was as unhinged as they came but Elena was as cold and calculating as he was mad. *Was or still is? Do wolves ever shed their skins?*

She lifted her hand to stroke his face. "Perhaps it's not too late to start over," she said softly. "We can start over, can't we? This time, it can be different. It *will* be different because we will have control over things." She leant closer to him but he withdrew.

"Elena—" Draeger began, but she raised her hand to stop him.

"Whatever your answer is," she said a little unevenly, "I do not want to hear it... yet." She sat back down at her desk and gestured for him to sit across her. "There are issues that need solving," she said, her calm returning to her. "Issues that are bigger than the two of us." She regarded him with a thoughtful look.

"Now," she said, getting down to business, "let's say we provide your Senate with Ellagrin's assurances on the settlement treaties, shall we? Old and new. That should help alleviate your current predicament at least. Get the Exodus back on track. What do you say?" She looked at him and waited.

"But can you do that?" asked Draeger.

"At a price of course," she added bluntly.

"That's fine," said Draeger, "but what I meant was, will the Doges agree to this?"

"Pah!" replied Elena disdainfully. "Old *fools*, all of them," she said. "Have you seen the state of our finances lately? Resettlement of Ageronians in exchange for much needed *ore* is the only way to plug the current shortfall. I will get them to agree to this. You can come see them agree this for yourself at the Doge Council meeting tomorrow." She smiled at him, her vivid, blue eyes shining confidently. "*Come!*" she said. "Incognito. So that you can see it for yourself." Her lips curled with amusement. "You can tag along with Varg. You remember Varg, don't you?"

Draeger assented.

"Well then, it is settled," said Elena and waved him off in dismissal.

THE DOGE COUNCIL

SUMMER PALACE,
PLANET SKANSGARDEN, ELLAGRIN

*E*lena surveyed the line of Doges filing into the chamber, her expression placid, giving away nothing of her true feelings towards them.

What a sorry lot of senile dotards...

One by one they shuffled past her, to seat themselves at the long table, members of the Doge Council—governors appointed by the emperor to rule the Ellagrin empire. On what grounds Niklas chose some of them was beyond her comprehension.

Lord Agnarr, well past his third century, walked past eyeing her desirously.

He certainly tried it on with me at dinner last week, recalled Elena. *At three hundred and ninety-two, he's no spring chicken even though he thinks he is.* She returned his look with a sweet smile. *Next time, make sure you can outdrink me if you intend to get into my undergarments...*

Behind, entered Lord Alarik, appointed Master of the Mynt and responsible for the empire's finances. Elena scoffed inwardly at the irony. *Niklas appointed you solely on the basis that you couldn't count and so wouldn't miss the odd 'loan' my dearly departed brother partook every so often.*

Lady Josefin, the only female Doge in the court, doddered along. The dowager duchess had taken over her husband's seat almost half a century ago when he passed.

Woman-hater, thought Elena eyeing her warily. The only reason the other Doges supported her appointment was because, like her husband, Lady Josefin deplored change. *After all, what could be better than a dogged old bitch who'd champion the status quo?*

Lady Josefin held onto Lord Borys' arm as she entered, the old man acting the part of the gallant gentleman despite his age, for Lord Borys was the oldest Doge of them all.

Tottering old fool, smiled Elena as he shuffled past her, smelling faintly of perfume and piss.

Elena had chosen the highest chamber in the tallest tower of the Summer Palace for this meeting, partly in hope that at least one of these old coots would die of exhaustion in walking up all seventy-three steps. *Perhaps next month I shall move this to the roof garden,* she mused looking at the two of them, *and maybe take out some handrails too.*

As her gaze moved from one aged Doge to the next, she was glad she had decreed their monthly administrative meetings be held here at the Summer Palace instead. Elena had always preferred this place to the cold, austere surroundings of the Royal Palace on Dalr where Niklas and indeed all Emperors before him traditionally held their meetings. *If I have to listen to their tedious ramblings, at least it will be in pleasanter surroundings.* Her decision however, had not been received without objection.

The Royal Palace on Dalr was in the heart of the capital where most of these Doges were conveniently based, comfortably ensconced in nearby expensive neighbourhoods. So when the monthly meetings were moved to the Summer Palace on Skansgarden, neighbouring *planet* to Dalr, there were rumblings of discontent from many. 'They'll all have to make the trek here if they wish to keep the privileges of running the empire,' was Elena's response as she added to the decree that anyone who refused to abide would be stripped of their title and holdings with immediate effect.

She waited impatiently until the last few Doges had shuffled to their seats, then cleared her throat to gather their attention. "My Lords," she began, "and Lady...," she added, eyeing Lady Josefin.

Lady Josefin nodded grandly in acknowledgement.

"I have been looking at our finances of late," said Elena turning her gaze to Lord Alarik, "and it appears our coffers have been exceptionally low these last two months. As master of the Mynt, Lord Alarik, what do you think is the cause of this shortfall? Have there been crop failures?"

Lord Alarik cleared his throat delicately. "No, empress. There have been no major crop failures in any of the planets nor any natural weather occurrences to blame —"

"Then why is it we've not recouped as much tax this time round?"

Lord Alarik looked a trifle uncomfortable. "Our farmers are producing but only enough for our own consumption with a little leftover for export. Mass production, from which most of our taxation is derived from, has ah... dwindled. There is, after all, no need for export now that trade with Ageron has ceased since, well..." He trailed off uncertainly.

"Since the *invasion*," snapped Elena, finishing his sentence. "There is no need to skirt round the issue, Lord Alarik. We are all here to run the empire, not make polite conversation." She looked around. "Which is why I propose we reinstate the settlement treaties with Ageron."

A murmur of dissent rose like a swell amongst some of the Doges. Lord Borys was first to speak up.

"Your Majesty," he began, "We cannot possibly reinstate settlement treaties with House Ageron. Especially in light of ah… recent events. Now this may be my personal opinion but there is no doubt many of us here bear the same apprehension towards Ageron. These Ageronians cannot be trusted…"

"These Ageronians, Lord Borys, have *ore*. Lots of it. Enough wealth leftover from the Age of Prosperity for several generations to come. Wealth we would like them to spend here in Ellagrin," said Elena. "*Ore* in return for settlement treaties which will address our immediate shortfall. And crucially, the Ageronians are entrepreneurs. When their first few settlements put down roots here in Ellagrin soil, we will see the difference. They have the experience and knowledge to drive our farms into efficiency. Our coffers Lord Alarik, will replenish as they have done so in the days when trading between the two Houses resumed after the War. Much needed *ore* to build, *ore* for social care and other urgent necessities— things our people will thank us for."

There was murmuring amongst the Doges. Lord Magnvar spoke up this time.

"Your Majesty, you are asking us to resume relations with the ones responsible for the first War and more recently, the murder of our emperor. Not to mention the deaths of at least half our military as a result of the failed invasion of Ageron. These are not things that should be forgotten so easily or swept aside. Ageronians cannot be trusted and we should have nothing to do with them. Leave them be. Their binary suns are dying and in a few centuries, they will be no more. I say leave them to die. If we really want to increase our exports, let us export to House Tilkoen."

Fools, berated Elena silently. She stood up and said, "Ageronians are by far the richest in the galaxy and the ones that need our exports the most. The Tilkoens may be our nearest neighbour but their use of advanced technology has meant minimal reliance on Ellagrin produce. They have little need for our crops. We have supply and Ageron has the demand for it. We need revenue to fund our social care, our healthcare, education, and research."

"I don't believe we need Ageronian *ore* to do that," Lady Josefin spoke up. "We are Ellagrins. We have our own traditions and our own values. We don't want things to change around here with the arrival of the Ageronians and we certainly do not take kindly to some rich Ageronian waving their *ore* in our faces much as they did during the Age of Prosperity." She gave a delicate sniff and looked round at the others, suitably gratified at their nods of their endorsement.

Elena seethed. *You would if you realise how many more vineyards that would buy you, old crone.*

"I have to say I agree with Lady Josefin, Your Majesty," piped up Lord Borys in his whiney old voice. "We don't want Ageronians bringing their *ore* here and lording over us—"

"Not even a few *trillion ore*?" questioned Elena. Lord Borys stopped short and suppressed a half-choke whilst Lady Josefin sat up ever so slightly. *Now we shall see just how much your national pride is worth*, thought Elena eyeing the Doges keenly.

She pretended not to notice their interest had suddenly piqued. "There are multiple advantages to the settlement treaties on top of the obvious immediate filling of our coffers," she said. "Ageronians for one, will need residences to stay when they eventually reach Ellagrin and I would imagine them paying a premium for these." She looked at Lord Borys. "Your developments near Lake Tikjvar for example, with suitable endorsement, could no doubt sell at several times more than the average Ellagrin can possibly afford." Elena's lips curled in wry amusement as Lord Borys dabbed his mouth delicately with his handkerchief. *Salivating now at the prospect no doubt...*

"Perhaps I have been too quick to judge," voiced Lord Magnvar, suddenly warming to the prospect. "I dare say the influx of Ageronians to some of the neighbourhoods under *my* tenure would do wonders for the rejuvenation of those areas…"

"The first few Exodus ships are all anticipated to arrive within the next decade," said Elena. *Very soon indeed,* she noted, *which is why Draeger needs this as much as we do.*

"Indeed," interposed Lord Odo, his watery eyes inexplicably brighter and interested all of a sudden, "in fact, Your Majesty, I ah, happen to have several upcoming developments in flight which ah, if Your Serenity permits, I would like to offer for consideration—"

"I suppose I could assist with a few choice residences," cut in Lady Josefin, "for the more *discerning* aristocrats perhaps…"

Elena nodded. She beckoned Tadeusz, the court secretary, bidding him bring up the settlement treaties on the projected console in front of the Doges. "In which case," she said looking around the table, "let us not dally then. If my lords and ladies have no further concerns, I propose we close this meeting on a high with the consensus to reinstate the settlement treaties."

"Indeed!" exclaimed Lady Josefin greedily.

"Quite so, quite so," came the eager susurrations of consent from around the table as the Doges nodded and murmured, each punching in their approval onto the voting pad at the table, all in high spirits at the unexpected windfall in this meeting.

Elena eyed them critically and as they rose to leave the chamber, she added, "Oh, and one more thing my lords… Perhaps I should have mentioned this earlier but no matter. In order to prevent geographical segregation of our peoples and of our neighbourhoods, I had instructed Secretary Tadeusz to include in the agreement you've just signed, a quota to limit the number of properties that can be sold privately to Ageronian settlers."

She looked at Lord Borys whose earlier unbridled glee at the thought of his prized windfall seemed very much dampened at her last comment. He moved to say something but then thought better of it and bit his lip, remaining silent.

"A q... quota?" queried Lord Magnvar nervously.

"Indeed. A quota." confirmed Elena.

"Of how much?" Lord Borys' voice quavered slightly.

Elena smiled. "You need not worry yourselves over minor details," she said. "It won't be significant and any transactions over that limit will be controlled via permits."

"*Permits*?" Lord Borys sounded rather faint.

"Yes. Permits," replied Elena. "Permits authorised solely by myself."

A cough escaped Lord Borys.

"After all," finished Elena, "as Lady Josefin said, we wouldn't want things to change around here with the arrival of the Ageronians."

There was an almost imperceptible choke from Lady Josefin as the Doges filed out of the chamber.

Standing on either side of the double doors, stood Elena's two bodyguards, their faces concealed behind standard army vizards. The smaller of the two chuckled quietly in the background.

THAT EVENING, seated on her golden chaise, Elena breathed deeply as she replayed the day's events in her mind. The windows in the Sun Room had been thrown open to let the

THE DOGE COUNCIL

fresh night breeze in and the sweet scent of roses hung delicately in the air.

She looked at Draeger seated across her and something within brought back an image from the past. She realised with a pang—it was over a century ago when they first danced here, in this room, under the glass dome, beneath the stars. *We were so young then...*

"So," she said with a smile, "what did you think of the Doge meeting just now?"

"It was well played," said Draeger with an approving nod, "and your settlement policies will lay the much needed foundations for the integration of Ageronians with Ellagrins. My people will have to make an effort to integrate and not indulge in a landgrab. You were wise to think of the social effects of the Exodus, empress."

Elena's smile diminished a little. "You don't have to call me empress in private," she said, wincing inwardly. *Does he no longer see me as Elena?* Then she let out a sardonic laugh. "Niklas would have sold all prime land to the highest bidder and let his favourite Doges do the same."

"But you didn't." He was staring at her.

"No, I didn't," replied Elena holding his gaze. She leant forward, closing the gap between them and smiled impishly. "Perhaps like you, I do care what happens to my people after all."

"That is *not* like you," Draeger said.

Elena threw her head back and laughed out loud. "Perhaps not," she said, acknowledging his scepticism," but I do know how aristocrats think. Imagine if all of Ageron's privileged were allowed to buy up Ellagrin land without control—our land, our farms, our businesses. I guarantee you that Lord Borys' state, for one, would become one of the richest 'settler' states in all of Ellagrin and yet barely any of its residents will be Ellagrins. Geographical segregation for one, will become widespread—rich Ageronians in one community and poor Ellagrins in another."

She gave Draeger a measured look. "A segregated society breeds discontent and with discontent comes political upheaval. My survival as head of House Ellagrin needs as little of that as possible." She let out a chuckle. "Like Lady Josefin, I'd like to keep the status quo."

Elena's eyes stayed on Draeger, heavy with scrutiny. The familiar, slightly disdainful line of his mouth, his dark hawkish figure and the standoffish way in which he carried himself... In the soft glow of the chamber, something tugged at her heartstrings.

I want you back, she realised. *And I am tired of having to rely on other men—Tadeusz, Alarik, and so on. Men who will always want something from me in return.* She felt a movement in her belly. *Soon, even that power I hold over them, I may no longer have.* She looked at him. *I need you. I want you back—you and your unconditional support. Your strength.*

She stood up and moved to sit next to him. Then, she took his hand in hers. "Come back to me, my love," she said earnestly. "There is so much we could do, *together*. With both our Houses combined, nothing, no one, will stand in our way." Her eyes glittered at the thought. "We will be stronger than our respective parts. I will give your people safe passage here and who knows, someday in the near future, a combined House of Ageron and Ellagrin could end up buying up half of Tilkoen."

Draeger looked at her sharply.

"When have my views ever shocked or offended you?" she asked daringly. Elena looked at him. *Will he balk at what I'm about to say next, I wonder?* "You must realise also," she said lowering her gaze, "that that lone expedition team you sent out may never find Sansari in time."

Draeger stiffened but remained silent.

Encouraged, she continued, "You do know that mission is a gamble whose outcome *no one* has any guarantee of. Which means you must make do with what other options you have available to you. Make those work. Which we can. *Together.*" She looked earnestly at him. "I want you," she said, squeezing his hand. There was a quaver of vulnerability in her voice. "I *need* you Draeger, more than ever…"

Draeger said nothing but Elena noticed to her satisfaction that his hand was still in hers, and this time, he had not withdrawn it.

ALIN VISITS

"They failed! How in Ysgarh's name could they have *failed?*" Elena threw the goblet with force at Mari who had the misfortune to stand in front of her at that moment. The heavy glass hit the handmaid squarely in her face with a painful *thunk* and amarinthe splashed all over her. The empress dismissed the crying servant girl with an angry flick of her wrist.

"You shouldn't be drinking in your condition my dear," murmured Queen Alin.

"I don't need your advice," hissed Elena, "and I couldn't care less about my condition. I abhor it!" Her slender hand curled around her tiny bump and folded into a clench. "In fact, if I should be free of this abomination inside me, I'd be elated." She laughed bitterly. "Even from his *grave* he torments me…"

The old queen looked up. "I meant to ask," she said, "Have you spoken with Lord Draeger about your pregnancy?"

Elena eyed her suspiciously. "Why do you ask?"

"Because I told him you were with child," replied Queen Alin. She hesitated a moment. *"His."*

Elena spluttered. "Are you out of your mind?" she exclaimed. "Everyone here knows I am pregnant with Niklas' child. It will only be a matter of time before Draeger finds out."

Queen Alin leant close and lowered her voice. "Do not be a fool Elena. Think about it. Nobody knows for sure who the father of your child is, other than you. No one dares bring the subject up, never mind question it. Let the Doges think what they think and let Draeger think what he thinks." She eyed her niece intently and continued, "You have much to gain in this and whilst Draeger thinks this child is his, therein lies a window of opportunity. You have something he needs and he has something you want in return."

"You don't need to tell me what he's after, aunt, I can see that plainly enough for myself," said Elena dismissively. "He just wants me to honour past settlement treaties for his people currently on route to Ellagrin and sign up to new ones for the rest."

"That is correct," agreed Queen Alin, seemingly oblivious to Elena's irritation. "Lord Draeger is under pressure from the Senate at the moment. The deterioration of the Realm is accelerating faster than they've expected. Ageronians on the inner planets are practically being roasted alive. They need to evacuate and they can't because the Exodus programme is at a standstill with both our Houses on enemy terms. The Ageronians have no recourse if their little quest to find Sansari and reopen the Arnemetiaen Gateway fails. They cannot launch their spacecarriers towards the Tilkoen system either, not without knowing if the Tilkoens will take them in. After all, one cannot throw a few billion evacuees out into space for fifty years and hope for the best."

Elena remained silent, letting Queen Alin carry on. *And what's your angle of play in all this?* she wondered, *Because you and I know, full well, that you have no interest whatsoever in the fate of these Ageronians.*

"In the absence of any success in reopening the Arnemetiaen Gateway," continued Queen Alin, "and with no word yet from the emissaries we sent to Tilkoen a century ago for help, the Exodus *needs* to continue evacuating Ageronians before the suns destroy the entire Realm. And where can Draeger evacuate them to, except to Ellagrin?"

"All this newfound concern of yours for the Ageronians is most touching, dear aunt," said Elena, "but I find myself wondering how my supporting Draeger is going to help Akseli?" She eyed the old woman cynically. "Let's face it, none of this would be of any interest to you if it didn't benefit your son in some way."

Queen Alin grasped Elena's hand. "Akseli is facing impeachment," she said, her voice deadly serious. "I am trying to save my son from the *gallows*, Elena. And do not underestimate the power a woman holds over a man, even more so if he thinks she carries his flesh and blood. Lord Draeger has, after all, allowed me to use the private portal to visit you today, which seems to suggest he is not entirely unfavourable to resuming ties with you once more."

Elena raised an eyebrow. "You want me to persuade him to drop the impeachment trial?" she asked.

"If possible, yes of course," said Queen Alin, "although I should think that unlikely. However, resuming ties with Ellagrin will weaken the case against Akseli from many useful aspects." She pondered a moment, then continued. "The power of doubt, perception, the reputations of accuser and of the accused. There is more than one way to sway the beliefs of people to win a trial. You of all people should understand that." She regarded Elena shrewdly. "A fact is only a fact when there is consensus agreeing to it being one," she said. "Now why would House Ageron resume diplomatic relations with an empire that tried to invade them?"

"*Doubt*," nodded Elena, leaning back. She tapped her fingers speculatively. "So you mean to cast doubt on the accusation of the invasion in the first place…"

Queen Alin nodded and went on, "Exactly. I want the Senate to question—did the alleged invasion of Lagentia *really* happen?"

Elena regarded her aunt with grudging approbation. "Perception," she said, agreeing. "Not impossible to influence. After all, the invasion had occurred within the sealed city of Lagentia, hidden from the eyes of the public."

"Would it not be more plausible that perhaps all this was a subversive attempt to sieze the throne from Akseli in the first place?"

Elena considered Queen Alin's last sentence. She had to admit, it was convincing enough. To add to that, her relationship with Draeger in the past, was well known whereas there had been no evidence of any links between her and Akseli other than in the invasion.

"Fine," she agreed grudgingly. "But there is no guarantee that the Nehisi woman won't find Sansari and reopen the Gateway before Ageron becomes completely reliant on Ellagrin. In case you hadn't heard me the first time, they did in fact find their way to one of the natural endpoints where the ambush failed." Elena let out an exasperated sigh. It was a regrettable outcome as there were few chances to locate Tors and her group outside the Ether.

"Which coterie failed?" asked Queen Alin. "The one in Toftir? Kaldr? Sansari? And how exactly did they fail?"

"Kaldr," answered Elena.

"Ah, so one of Ellagrin's natural endpoints," said Queen Alin, thinking.

"Yes, yes," replied Elena impatiently, "You're old enough to remember it yourself surely. We knew there was a chance they would encounter this old endpoint whilst looking for Sansari, but the fools positioned there..." Elena poured herself a new glass of amarinthe and emptied it in a single glug. Queen Alin looked on distastefully.

"She had protection," continued Elena, displeasure clouding her face. "They killed Alber and his men, and escaped back into the Ether. Whilst they journey within it, I have no way of tracking them. Kaldr was one of the remaining natural endpoints on our records inside the Ellagrin system. Within my grasp."

Queen Alin paused to consider a moment. "If they have passed Kaldr, then it will be at Sansari itself where we must stop them," she said. "My Tilkoen friends there will not fail us."

Elena looked at her incredulously. "Tilkoen is light years away from the Ageron system and even from Ellagrin. There is no way to reach them. How will your friends even know about the Nehisi and the search?"

"They are loyalists and they won't forget," said Queen Alin. "Trust me."

Ah, the loyalists and their coterie, recalled Elena. *Friends of hers and Father's. Father installed them all over the galaxy during the War when he destroyed the Gateways.* These secret loyalist groups were to eliminate any remaining Nehisi who chanced to come through known natural endpoints of the Ether either to escape or open up new Gateways for the Ageronians. *Father was adamant no Gateway would come into being ever again. And now, years later, it will be down to this same handful of Ellagrin loyalists to stop Tors and her companions.*

"You know," Elena said quietly, "I have trusted and and listened to you more times than I have my own mother."

Queen Alin nodded.

"I hope for your sake this trust is not misplaced, dear aunt," said Elena.

"I assure you it is not," replied Queen Alin. "When have I ever not watched out for you, my dear?"

Elena begrudged her a nod. Queen Alin had always been the dominant force in her life from her formative years where her own mother was pushed to the background. *Poor Mother, so meek and quiet. And I, rebellious and wilful.* It was no surprise then that Alin, then a young, effervescent aunt offering clandestine jaunts of freedom from a world of drudging duty, quickly became her influencer and confidante.

Mother had tried so hard. Elena recalled the look of helplessness in her mother's eyes when countless times Elena went to her father's sister, Alin, for help and advice instead.

*Mother never understood me. No one did except for you, aunt. But even then, you weren't here to protect me from Niklas...*When the War erupted, her ties with Alin, then consort to Lord Ageron III, were severed and that continued long after her brother, Niklas, ascended the throne.

"So, assuming the loyalists prevent Tors and her companions from reopening the Arnemetiaen Gateway, all I need to do is extend House Ellagrin's support to Ageron," summarised Elena not taking her eyes off her aunt.

Queen Alin nodded.

"But what if I don't want to," toyed Elena. There was a hint of petulance in her tone. "I'm not afraid of the Doges," she said. "When my son is born, he will be emperor of Ellagrin and until he comes of age, I am Queen Regent. My position is secure. I don't need House Ageron's support. It is they that are on the cusp of destruction. They need Ellagrin more than Ellagrin needs them."

Queen Alin's eyes bore into her, cool and sharp as swords.

"I suspect your situation as ruler of Ellagrin cannot be a comfortable one," she said. "If the Doges here are anything like I remember, they will not sit around like docile lambs to see you, a *female*, on Niklas' seat for long. Your position is precarious. You need to resume trade between our two Houses, bring in much needed *ore* into the Mynt and rebuild Ellagrin. You need to be seen in power, in *control* and for that you need Lord Draeger's support. I have helped sow the seeds of interest in Lord Draeger. Now make *use* of it!"

"I wouldn't be so sure, dear aunt," said Elena. "His interest lies in Ellagrin, but not necessarily in its empress. He still thinks of that Nehisi woman, I can tell. And what about my unborn child? I don't see how this lie can work. How will I, when the time comes, explain when my son enters this world golden as the sun and not a creature of night? What then?"

"There will be no need for explanations or anything by that time," stated Queen Alin confidently. "Akseli will be back on the throne and if you play your cards right, House Ageron will support House Ellagrin."

A chill went through Elena. "You have this all planned out, don't you?" she said.

Queen Alin rose to leave. She squeezed Elena's hand. "Do as I suggest," she reiterated, "Get Draeger on your side and help me save my son. Do that and I will make sure the Nehisi woman does not live to return to him."

AN ATTEMPT

*E*lena stood at the balcony of the roof garden and stared at the lush rolling hills that stretched beyond the grounds of the Summer Palace all the way to the coastal mountains, hazy blue-green and majestic in the distance. On the other side of the mountains, deep shimmering fjords carved out by glaciers over millennia, gleamed like mirrors between the mountains and the coastline.

A delicious breeze caressed Elena's face. *This would be perfect,* she thought to herself, breathing in deeply, *if only you were here with me.* She cast her mind back to her conversation with Draeger the other night. *I have made my feelings for him known.* She frowned, noting that he, on the other hand, hadn't. *Still,* she told herself, *he has not turned me down and we will, regardless, have to work together on the resettlement treaties.*

She gave a sigh and switched to more practical matters at hand. Turning around to survey the garden, she wondered if indeed it should be the venue for the next Doge Council.

A small movement behind the shrubs caught her attention.

"Who's there?" she called out, stepping forwards towards

the sound. "Varg?" she said, thinking it was probably Varg whom she knew was stationed at the entrance of the garden. She wasn't worried as Varg was never far.

There was another rustle and as she parted the fronds of the silver palm, she caught sight of a figure in a vizard and cloak. Her heart gave a little leap. "Draeger?" she called out and then instantly felt embarrassed at her own eagerness. The figure turned on his heel and strode briskly towards the entrance. The build and gait was unmistakeable.

"Wait!" Elena called out but he had turned to leave and was making his way to the entrance to do so.

Perhaps he is as reticent as I am to admit we need each other.

Elena hoped Varg was still at the entrance to detain him. She began to run and took a left to take the small path she knew was a shortcut to the entrance where the stairs were.

She did reach the top of the stairs moments before he did. Varg was nowhere to be seen so she stood between him and the stairs. "Stop," she ordered, standing at the top of the stairs, barring his escape.

He stood still, facing her, a silent and hawkish outline under the shade of a spinal ash tree, expressionless behind his vizard.

A smile crept to Elena's lips. "I knew you would come," she said opening her arms to him.

He hesitated a moment before approaching her.

"I've missed you," she continued, and took his arms, draping them around her waist. Then pulling him closer, she pressed her body against his and reached up for the release clasp at the back of his vizard. He jerked back and withdrew from her. Elena tilted her head to one side, flexing an eyebrow. "Draeger?" she said uncertainly.

It happened so fast she barely realised he had pushed her.

Elena screamed as she fell backwards down the steep steps,

its well-worn stone treads a blur of grey as she tumbled down. First, she tried to grab the handrails but failing to reach them, she tucked herself into a ball as best she could in order to protect herself and her baby as she bounced down the steps. Her downward spiral only slowed where the stairs curved round, preventing her from rolling on unimpeded. With a desperate scream, Elena extended both arms out, reaching for the walls, in attempt to stop herself from rolling. It worked. Her chin struck cold stone and the metallic taste of blood filled her mouth. The next instant, she found herself sprawled forward on her belly, looking down at the remaining flight of steps below her. She tried to sit up but couldn't find the strength to move.

Then as if by a miracle, her body slid upwards, lifted up by a pair of gargantuan arms.

Varg!

He picked her up and gingerly set her down on the step, so that she could lean back against the railing. He moved ponderously slow. Despite her own pain, Elena realised Varg was moving much slower than normal. She looked up at him. There was a deep gash at the side of his head where someone had hit him with something heavy, probably to either knock him out or finish him off but Varg being the size he was, she figured, had just succumbed to being concussed.

Elena pointed up the steps, gesturing for him to look for the perpetrator. Varg hesitated, flashing her a concerned look in response but Elena motioned him to hurry on. "Before he gets away," she managed to say. But as Varg turned to go, an excruciating pain filled her so much she screamed again. Varg lumbered back down the steps in panic. "My baby...," cried Elena, clutching her abdomen as Varg carried her and ran down the stairs for help.

* * *

THE CURTAINS WERE DRAWN tight and where both drapes met, a sliver of daylight slipped through, slashing across the dark wooden floor of Elena's bedroom, sharp and thin.

Elena was sitting in bed, propped up against a mound of pillows, resting. There was a small knock on the door and Lady Berit's head popped through.

"Your Majesty," she said, "Queen Alin has come to visit. Would you be willing to see her?"

Elena considered briefly and then nodded. "Send her in," she said.

Moments later, Queen Alin bustled in carrying a small tiffin carrier which she placed on the bedside table with a flourish. A faint scent of fragrant soup wafted across and as Lady Berit politely exited the room, Queen Alin immediately sat herself on the edge of Elena's bed.

"What happened?" she asked, concerned. "I heard you fell down the stairs of the roof garden! By Ysgarh those stairs are at least three storeys high. You're lucky to be alive!"

Elena looked at her with her cold cobalt eyes. "I didn't fall, dear aunt," she said. "I was pushed."

Queen Alin gave her a sharp look. "*Pushed* you say?"

"Pushed," reiterated Elena.

"By whom?" asked Queen Alin.

Elena let out a harsh derisive laugh. "That's the million-*ore* question, my dear aunt. Something *I'd* certainly like to know."

Queen Alin lowered her voice even though there was no one else in the room. "Was it the Doges?"

"*Doges?* You think more than one could be responsible?" she said. Resentment flashed in her eyes. "And here I was thinking maybe one of them—someone I've slighted perhaps—could be the culprit." It rankled Elena to think that the majority of the Doges now despised her. *And I'm the only one that's taking steps to save the empire from financial ruin!*

"Well, they do have motive," said Queen Alin. "Having you and your son out of the picture would open up numerous possibilities for them."

"You think so, do you?"

Queen Alin nodded. "You did after all trick them into handing control of any sale of their land holdings, to you. If that doesn't make one upset, I don't know what will."

"Well," began Elena and stopped for a split second. Her eyes narrowed. *And how did you find that out, you old coot? No one else was in the Council meeting. No one but the Doges, Varg and Draeger.* "Well," she continued hastily, "I merely did what I did for the good of Ellagrin."

Queen Alin nodded. "I'm sure that's why you did that, my dear."

"And what if it wasn't the Doges?" challenged Elena.

"What do you mean?" asked Queen Alin. "Who do you think it was then?"

Elena's mouth turned dry even as she contemplated it. "The perpetrator looked a lot like Draeger," she said.

"Lord Draeger?" Queen Alin turned to stare at her. "Are you sure?"

Elena's brows knitted into a tremulous frown. "I... can't be sure," she said. "I thought it was him at first, which is why I let my guard down. He wore a vizard but everything else—his build, his manner, his gait—I thought it was him." She shook her head. "I don't know," she continued, "but on the other hand, if whoever it was wanted me killed, they wouldn't have resorted to pushing me down the stairs. They would've finished me off in a more... fail-safe manner, using a gun or a sword."

Elena felt wound up, the tension inside her tight enough to

snap. "Or perhaps," she said, "whoever it was just wanted me to lose the baby." She paled at the thought. *Would he go so far as to kill our child?* She touched her bump and as if by instinct, felt a dogged kick in reply. She rubbed it tenderly; the doctors had reassured her the baby was unharmed in the fall. *I won't let anyone harm you,* she said to it silently.

"I hardly think Lord Draeger would stoop to that," said Queen Alin. "The man is far too principled," she added sardonically.

"Regardless," said Elena, "this was a premeditated attack as Varg had made his usual sweep of the roof garden before I entered. Which means the perpetrator either sneaked in or had been lying in wait for me somewhere in the garden beforehand."

"Well, until you find evidence, this is all conjecture," said Queen Alin. She reached for the tiffin carrier. "Now have some soup," she said decanting its fragrant contents. "I had my cook make this specially for you." She lifted the dainty container and handed it to Elena.

Elena inhaled the familiar aroma of spices and herbs before taking in a deep draught of the soup. It brought back memories of her younger years when Queen Alin still lived with her and Mother in Ellagrin. *Before she left to marry Ageron III.* Those were simpler, happier times, before the War, during the golden Age of Prosperity.

Elena felt a stab of pain shoot through her stomach. She gasped in agony and she called out, "Lady Berit!"

The door to the bedroom flew opened as Lady Berit rushed in.

"The soup...," Elena stammered, clutching her abdomen in pain. She looked at her aunt. "What did you put in the soup?"

Queen Alin stood up and tried to help her. "I didn't put anything in the soup, Elena," she managed to say before Lady

Berit pushed her out of the way. The next few minutes were a blur of activity as Lady Berit yelled frantically for a physician and Queen Alin strode quickly out of the room.

Elena struggled to her feet, pushed Lady Berit aside and ran after Queen Alin. Finally, when they both reached the Sun Room, Queen Alin stopped in front of the French armoire to face her niece. "I did not put anything in that soup, Elena," she said firmly rebutting Elena's earlier accusations. However, Elena was past caring.

"Get away from me, all of you!" she shrieked and pressed the hidden clasp for the receptacle at the side of the closet. *I can trust no one! No one! Not the Doges, not Draeger, not you! No one!*

A look of panic crossed Queen Alin's face as she saw the beacon revealed. Turning quickly, she fled through the private portal.

"I will not have anyone harm my baby, you hear?" Elena screamed after her. "*No one!*"

With that, she ripped the beacon out from the receptacle, disconnecting the private portal once more. Then, she turned to lock the door of the Sun Room and activated its shutters, sealing the room and closing out all light from outside.

"No one will get to me or my baby," she whispered as she sat down on the floor and hugged her knees.

PART V

THE SEARCH

PIHLA

Pihla hopped hurriedly out of the endpoint, after Marcus. The winds in the Ether this time were the worst she had ever experienced and she was keen to be out no matter where this endpoint led to.

"Where do you think this—" she began but her words were drowned by deafening shouts. In moments, a massive crowd descended on them, marching and shouting. Pihla teetered on her toes and tried to look around, over their heads, to get her bearings. It was night-time but the place appeared well-lit. They were in some sort of open-air concourse, and there was a utilitarian feel about it, reminding her of a large train station.

"Marcuuus!!" she yelled, waving madly to attract Marcus' attention as the crowd enveloped her like a tidal wave, sweeping her down the concourse. In the distance, not too far from Marcus' fair head, she spotted Niko and Tors' faces amongst the crowd. *Who by Dyaeus are these people?* thought Pihla, bewildered. *Are we in Sansari?*

What unsettled her was the fact that apart from Marcus,

Tors and Niko, everyone else in the crowd were wearing balaclavas. *Why are they masked? Are they protesters?*

There were slogans and bright holos projected into the air above their heads and people were chanting and shouting something in unison. Like their shouts, it was mostly in a language Pihla did not recognise. However, one or two holos did display their words in Standard Lang, proudly declaring: **A GENDER JUST WORLD!** and **EQUALITY FOR MEN!**

Pihla struggled to join the others, but found herself unwittingly pushed along by the crowd. At length, she found herself at the end of the concourse and at the top of a wide flight of steps, cut into the grassy slope and leading to an open area.

However, it was the view that surprised her and for a moment, she forgot all about Marcus and the others.

The concourse had been on top of a mound, an artificial hill of sorts, and from its raised vantage point, an entire city opened up in front of her. Against the night sky, bright lurid skyscrapers rose before her—sleek metal structures gleaming psychedelically, reflecting thousands of winking lights, flashing neon signs and illuminated holographic displays.

The crowd poured down the mound and into the city centre itself, sweeping her with it.

"Get *orfff!*" yelled Pihla, elbowing someone away from her. But it was no use. The moving mass of protesters was unstoppable and she found herself swept in the morass and moved along, slowly but surely, into the city itself.

Here, gleaming tower blocks loomed like a dense forest of shimmering steel and fluorescent lights. Intertwined amongst them, like a lattice of neon undergrowth, were moving sidewalks—an intricate network of pedestrian belts.

Pihla looked up and gaped.

A little higher and weaving their way in between these buildings were transparent chutes containing passenger and cargo pods. Brightly lit from within, they resembled fluorescent capsules and far faster than the moving sidewalks, they hurtled through their cylindrical columns, humming and whizzing like fat gleaming bees of steel, criss-crossing the city.

"Pihla!" Marcus' voice boomed over the chaos.

Pihla turned and found, to her relief, the others huddled nearby. They were standing on a raised block on the pavement, just off the main street, looking as vulnerable as a small herd trapped by flood waters all around in a nature documentary. She hurried over to them, weaving her way through the crowd.

"Where by Dyaeus are we?" she asked, breathlessly. "Do you think this is Sansari?"

"I'm not sure," replied Tors. "But I think, at worst, we are close. We're in the vicinity the Empress showed me but exiting the Ether is not a science…"

"If we could identify the locals, we could give a guess," said Marcus, looking on at the throngs of people marching past, "…except they're all wearing balaclavas!"

"We should approach someone to ask," said Pihla and tried to stop a passer-by. She was brusquely waved off as he marched on, shouting and gesticulating fervently. "Maybe someone in less of a hurry," she added hastily, and went back to stand awkwardly with the rest.

Niko gave a little start.

"What is it?" asked Pihla, distracted by his jerk.

Niko had been standing beside her, sandwiched between her and a small tree. He pointed at the tree. "It's the tree," he said. "It's winking at me."

"What?" said Pihla. "Don't be ridiculous."

"I'm not being funny," said Niko. "It winked. Blinked at me. *Look*! There it is again! Did you see the dots of light?" He plucked off a small branch and held it under her nose.

She noticed its stem did indeed blink with speckles of light before dying down.

"See? I wasn't making it up."

Pihla gave an irritable grunt and turned back to looking at the marching crowd. "That's all really nice and fascinating Niko, but can we please try and focus on getting hold of someone in this place instead?"

"Well, what about these things?" called out Niko. He had bounded over to the other side of the street. "Maybe we can tell it to take us somewhere?" he called out. "To the High Council?"

Pihla turned to see what he was talking about.

Niko was standing on a small patch of green and in its centre, jutting out at various angles like some fantastical art installation, stood a cluster of tall rectangular prisms. The group walked over to have a closer look.

The transparent prisms were, in fact, glass entrances to chutes leading underground.

"These must be linked to those up there!" Niko pointed excitedly at the transparent tubes winding their way around the skyscrapers. "Let's try them out!" he continued enthusiastically. "Although... how do we get into one of them in the first place?" He examined the structure, plastering his hands all over the glass door in attempt to somehow pry it open.

Pihla rolled her eyes and pointed to a thin display panel on the side. "Try the panel?" she suggested.

"Ah! Good idea!" Niko went round and stood in front of it. The display flickered to life with a rather generic face rendered on it.

"Good evening citizen, how may I help you?" it asked good-naturedly.

"How do I enter one of these things?" asked Niko.

"That's easy," the face replied. "Make sure your identification band is within range of the booth and the door should open. If you are experiencing an issue with your identification band, try scanning it here. For assistance or to obtain a replacement for lost or faulty bands, simply look straight into panel for facial identification, then follow the instructions."

Niko positioned his face in full view of panel and gave a tentative smile.

Pihla raised her hand in protest. "It won't have a record of you—" she started to say.

"Thank you citizen. Please can I ask you to repeat the procedure one more time."

"Niko, it won't recognise you," reiterated Pihla but Niko shrugged and turned to face the panel once more, making sure his face pointed directly at it. For good measure, he waved the branch in front of the display after.

"Thank you citizen," the face answered. "I notice you're holding a Dimaga branch. Citizen, are you responsible for breaking off that branch?"

Niko grinned at Pihla. "See? I got its attention. This might just work!" He turned back to the display and answered, "Yes, I am! I certainly did that. Now can you help me?"

"Thank you, citizen." A pod approached and stopped in full alignment with the entrance of the glass box. The doors of the pod parted, swiftly followed by the door of the glassbox which irised open.

Niko flashed the smuggest grin of grins at Pihla and stepped through firstly the doors of the glass box, then into the pod.

"Ask it if it can take us to the High Council," prompted Pihla as she moved in behind him, to get in next.

Niko cleared his throat. "Can you take us to the High Council. We have important bus—" but before he could finish, the pod doors suddenly closed between them, followed by the glass doors of the chute entrance.

"Waii—" Niko's voice cut off when the doors shut.

"What? Wait! *Stop!*" yelled Pihla.

Marcus and Tors jumped forward and they all tried to prise open the glass door. They could see Niko banging against the transparent wall of his pod, trying to get out but the pod began to accelerate. In an instant, it had shot off through the chute, into the distance.

"Stop the capsule!" Pihla shouted at the panel, banging at it repeatedly.

"Good evening citizen, how may I help you?" the face said good-naturedly.

"You have to stop that pod!" Pihla yelled.

"The next pod will be here shortly," replied the face, still smiling. "Please remember! Destruction of Dimaga trees is a public offence! Citizens are advised to take care of all flora, in and outside the city."

"Wait, you stupid system!" shouted Pihla. "Bring the previous pod back! *Bring it back!* Where have you taken him?"

Bing!

Another pod arrived and swished to a halt. The doors parted to let its single passenger out.

Stocky and sporting the biggest pair of dark glasses imaginable, he stepped through. An oversized pair of black trousers, layered over with an asymmetric leatherette skirt, a fluorescent green hoodie and a metallic shoulder bag completed the bizarre look, stopping Pihla's tirade in its tracks.

Those big, black opaque glasses loomed and paused before her face. "Are you okay?" he asked.

"You speak *Standard!*" blurted Pihla, so surprised she temporarily forgot about Niko.

"And you're not wearing a balaclava!" Marcus added.

"Of course not," the man replied, affectionately patting his shiny ultra-tall cowlick, "not with *this* hair!" He pulled down his dark glasses a little and a set of eyes painted in dramatic eyeliner peered at them. "Are you *sure* you're okay?" he said, looking at Pihla again.

"Yes," replied Pihla, staring at him. *Were those Tilkoen features under all that makeup?* "I mean no," she said and pointed at the chute exasperatedly. "Our friend broke off a tree branch and the pod just left with him in it!"

The man sucked in his breath through his teeth at the last sentence. "Ssssssstthh," he said, shaking his head disapprovingly. "Your friend broke a Dimaga branch?"

Pihla nodded. "Yes, but that's because we're new here," she said. "But before we go into that, I was wondering, could you tell us if this place is—"

The man interrupted her with a series of tutts. "That's no excuse," he said. "What your friend did there just now...man, that's veee-ry bad. Protesting is one thing but *vandalism*..." He tutted some more and shook his head reproachfully.

"Can we park the tree debate for a minute?" interrupted Tors. "Our friend just went into one of those pods and it took off. Do you know where it's taken him?"

"Oh yes, of course." The man took his glasses off with an airy swish. "He's probably on his way to the Detention Centre."

"Detention Centre?" Tors arched an eyebrow. "For breaking a tree branch? What's going to happen to him?"

"Oh don't worry," said the man, "he'll be alright. You can get him tomorrow."

"Could we perhaps get him now?" asked Pihla.

The man shook his head vigorously. "At this hour? Oh, no. They're closed now. Don't bother, you'll never get in." He caught her look of concern and added, "Don't worry. The Detention Centre is comfortable enough. There's hot food, vacuum showers, clean beds. They'll escort him over to City Hall tomorrow to be processed."

A large crowd of protesters rushed past, nearly knocking them over. Their presence seemed to jolt the man back into action.

"Where's your Holla holo, man?" he asked, as if realising something was amiss for the first time.

"A... holla *what?*" asked Marcus.

The man tutted again. "Your *H-o-lla ho-lo*," he said, drawing the words out and giving them yet another reproachful look.

"What's a Holla holo?" asked Pihla.

The man tutted and reached into his shoulder bag. "*This*," he said, taking out some small torch-like devices. He considered their blank looks and gave a resigned sigh. "Here," he said, "take mine and make sure you wave it where they can see it." He gave another disapproving tutt, and added, "You're definitely new here, like you said. I'm Ourry by the way."

"Nice to meet you Ourry," said Marcus, "but before we do anything further, can you tell us if this is—"

But Ourry raised a strict bejewelled finger to silence him. Then, he reached over and pressed the button at the bottom of their torch devices. Instantly the following flashed before them, projected mid-air, in the big bright neon letters:

EQUAL OPPORTUNITIES FOR MEN!
   AI JOBS NOT JUST FOR WOMEN!
   DIFFERENT   SEXES,   DIFFERENT   STRENGTHS,
EQUAL PAY!

"*There*! Much better," said Ourry, giving Marcus a friendly slap on the back.

"You're protesting for equal rights?" asked Pihla, astonished. "Against *women?*" Then, momentary distraction over, she shook herself and continued, "Never mind, but as Marcus was saying, can you tell us if this place is—"

Ourry cut in. "You're *kidding* me right?" he exclaimed. "You don't know? We're fighting for *equality* of course! We must protect and exercise our rights as *male* citizens! We can't let the women take all our jobs, or we'll be left with the unskilled stuff and with bringing up our children!"

Pihla flashed Marcus a look. "And to think Niko is missing all *this*," she said drily.

"Oooh!" exclaimed Ourry, glancing at his watch. "Come! We mustn't miss the rally speech!" He propelled them purposefully into the thick of the crowd ahead. "SAMANATA! SAMANATA!" he shouted in unison with the people around them and gestured energetically at Pihla and the others to do the same. "SAMANATA!" he said pumping the air animatedly. *"Equality!"*

Before any of them could react, Ourry marched them in with the crowd. Periodically, he would fuss at them to hold up their Holla holos properly so that the slogans projected well above their heads in full view. As the crowd around them heaved and jostled and moved, Marcus flashed Pihla and Tors an exaggerated shrug of resignation, meaning *just go with the flow for now.*

Pihla sighed and was about to give him a thumbs-up sign when a loud buzz emanated from above. She looked up.

A small drone hovered overhead. It stopped above her and a red laser-thin line scanned over her face before she realised what it was doing.

Then it blared: "UNAUTHORISED PROTESTER! UNAUTHORISED PROTESTER!" and proceeded to emit an ear-shattering klaxon.

Pihla covered her ears. "What, by Dyaeus, is that?" she yelled.

Marcus pointed above them. In seconds, several more drones had appeared and soon Marcus, Tors and Pihla each had at least a couple hovering over them, broadcasting their deafening sirens and announcements.

"Oh my goodness!" shrieked Ourry, grabbing Pihla by the hand and leading them away from the drones. He pulled them through the crowd, pushing their heads down low and bolted into a covered side alley.

Thankfully, the drones lost them and couldn't give chase.

"You don't have a protest permit?" Ourry's eyes bulged with disbelief.

"You need a permit to protest?" asked Pihla.

Ourry gave an incredulous tutt. "Of *course* you do! We're not uncivilised you know!" He shook his head. "And now, you're going have to keep away from the protest area if you want to avoid getting locked up like your friend." He peered cautiously out of the alley to check for drones and then paused to survey them with a critical eye. His look softened when he saw that they were tired, especially Tors who had sat down on the pavement. "Well," Ourry said, sounding a little less stern this time, "you won't be able to get a hotel for tonight, that's for sure. If you don't mind downtown, you can stay at mine tonight if you want."

Marcus took his hand and shook it. "Thank you," he said, keeping his palms firmly clamped over Ourry's, "but before we do anything else, could you *please* tell us where this is?"

"What do you mean?" asked Ourry. "You want to know what district this is?"

Pihla shook her head. "What we've been trying to ask all night," she said, "...is what *city* is this?"

Ourry gave her an odd look and then pointed back towards where they had marched from.

The station atop the hill was just about visible from where they stood in the alley, but it was the structure that towered over it that left Pihla speechless.

*We must have come through **beneath** it, in order to have not seen it earlier.*

It was a structure of impossible proportions, dizzyingly tall and so different to the conventional shape of their Arnemetian Gate. This one was more elegant, more daring in its construction and instead of being arch-shaped like the other gates in Ageron, it was a continuous elliptical ring, so impossibly sleek yet colossal it appeared to defy gravity. It rose in the distance, pivoted on two lofty supports on either side, each subtly curved so as to be pleasing to the eye. A shape resembling a gigantic cheval mirror.

Ourry waved his hand at the Gate in the distance, his ultra-bling rings glinting under the street lights. "That's the Sansari Gate," he declared with a flourish. "Welcome, my friends, to the megacity of Sansari."

And Pihla fell to her knees.

PACHINKO PARADISE

⚜

SANSARI CITY,
PLANET DHARAN, TILKOEN SYSTEM

"This way," said Ourry, leading them through yet another narrow alleyway. "Not far now," he added reassuringly.

"He said that over an hour ago," grumbled Pihla.

"He's taking us through the scenic route," explained Marcus with a grin. In order to avoid detection, Ourry had led them through the backstreets and side alleys, most of them deserted and virtually all of them covered or partially covered by awnings or roof coverings overhead.

"You can't really tell from where we are at the moment," said Ourry as he led them through the alleyways, all paved and surprisingly clean, "but we're in the vibrant downtown district of Juwang East."

Despite that, every now and again, there would be an opening or gap between the buildings where they would catch glimpses of the district with its the bright lights and lively sounds of people and traffic. Sansari, it seemed, was a city that didn't sleep.

* * *

"We're here!" declared Ourry, stopping outside a faded pink door on a back alley. "My home," he said and opened it for them. "You'll have to excuse the mess. I don't usually let people in from the back." He led them through a small, dark corridor, stacked with boxes on both sides…

And into a busy pachinko parlour.

"You live *here?*" asked Marcus, raising his voice above the hubbub.

Ourry nodded cheerfully as they walked past rows of retro gameslot machines, each energetically contributing to the constant cacophony of dings, pings and chiptune chimes threatening to engulf them.

Emblazoned high on the wall overlooking this pinball heaven of old-school hunks of hardware, with their analogue transducers, exuberant tunes and quaint 2D animations, were the words PACHINKO PARADISE in flashing, lurid neon.

"Pachinko Paradise!" yelled Ourry, pointing at it and beaming with pride. He gestured towards the floor with a dramatic flourish as if to present Pachinko Paradise to them.

And it certainly seemed a paradise to its clientele. The place was packed with gamers from all walks of life. Young, old, working professionals still in worksuits, all crouched over their favourite games, absorbed and totally hooked.

Ourry swaggered down the aisle to the beat of the pulsating music and strobes, completely in his element, exchanging daps and fist bumps along the way with his customers. When they finally reached the front entrance, Ourry turned left and up a flight of stairs to the next floor.

They followed behind and found themselves on a small landing, lined with rows of card key dispensers. Here, techno music pumped out, drowning the chaotic pings and dings from downstairs and replacing them with a bass so loud each beat seemed to ricochet off the walls.

Marcus felt his entire body vibrate in response.

"WE HAVE GOOD OLD-FASHIONED *COIN* PAYMENT SYSTEMS HERE!" Ourry shouted, pointing at the card key dispenser units, "...FOR THOSE WHO DON'T WANT TO USE SCANPAY." He waggled his eyebrows as if to explain: "*UNTRACEABLE!*"

Marcus stared, not at the card key machines but above them where a haphazard mountain of items were stored. Pihla broke into a wry smile and Tors raised an eyebrow.

Stacked above the dispensers and nearly touching the ceiling were shelves full of Ourry's stock of merchandise—life-sized Affection Dolls.

"EVERYBODY LOVES A CUDDLY TOY!" Ourry's face split into a wide grin as he punched in a code to get a couple of card keys from the dispenser. He beckoned them to follow him. "THIS WAYYY!" he shouted, cheerfully walking down the sparsely lit corridor lined with closed doors on each side. He stopped somewhere in the middle, six or seven doors down, glanced at the room number to check and then scanned it open. He ushered them in.

It was a room. Small, dark but oddly cosy with a single reclining chair in the middle. The moment Ourry closed the door behind them, silence reigned.

Soundproof doors, thought Marcus, breathing a sigh of relief. The techno music was getting to him.

"Behold!" exclaimed Ourry dramatically, "The Pachinko Paradise *player cubicle*!" He beckoned them to huddle round, then patted the chair and pushed Marcus into it.

"Comfy?" he asked, making Marcus lie down. He fussed Marcus about a bit, tucking his arms into the sides and making sure his legs were stretched out. "Reactive foam support!" he said, sounding like a doctor. "Moulds around your body. *Very* comfortable." He beamed. "So comfortable in fact, I often sleep in this instead of my bed upstairs."

Marcus nodded and sank in further with a sigh. The room was softly lit and the chair was certainly spacious and comfortable enough to beat even the best of beds that he had ever tried.

Ourry beamed proudly. "Our player cubicles are *diamond-grade,* OFREC-registered with top notch immersive entertainment and games. Look!" He whipped out a scancard from his pocket and waved it mid-air. In an instant, a 3D holo of a voluptuous female appeared and stood beside Marcus, eyeing him expectantly.

"Oh hello…," blurted Marcus, looking up at the scantily-clad vision.

Ourry waved his scancard again, this time making a few movements with circular flicks of his wrist in mid-air. "Now," he said to Marcus, "tell me this doesn't feel real..."

The 'lady' bent over, her lips curling suggestively, and stroked Marcus' arm up and down. He stiffened noticeably.

"Oooh…very realistic indeed ," Marcus said as the directed forcefield swept back and forth, caressing his arm. He could see why this could be a completely immersive experience and also why some clients would want untraceable coin payment systems at this establishment.

"What did I tell you, aeh?" replied Ourry triumphantly, "The sensitivity levels of the equipment…*A-mazing,* aeh? That's diamond-grade for you!" He looked round and beamed at them. Then he slapped his forehead. "What am I like? Here I am babbling on and on. You guys must be tired and hungry!"

Ourry waved the holo lady away and gave them each a card key. "You can each take a cubicle and leave your bag inside. You can sleep here tonight. Just lock up and keep the

PLANET DHARAN, TILKOEN SYSTEM

card with you." He pointed at the backlit rectangular outline of a closet, set flush against the wall, and added, "I wouldn't bother with the freshener showers if I were you. They're free for clients to freshen up, and I can tell you some of them *really* need it after spending days here, but in my opinion they don't really clean. These things just remove traces of smoke and sweat, that's all." He continued, pointing at the inbuilt food dispensers on the opposite wall next. "Er, I wouldn't touch those either," he said. "You could get ill eating those things." He rubbed his hands together. "Why don't you leave your stuff here and I'll take you somewhere to eat outside."

"But what if the drones spot us?" asked Marcus.

Ourry looked at his watch and waved his concern away. "The protests should be over by now, so the drones will have stopped patrolling." He chuckled and added, "Besides, the authorities will just wait until you pop up in their recognition detectors when you're out and about in town and locate you that way."

And so, with that reassurance of sorts, they exited the Pachinko parlour and followed Ourry down the next street into a small back alley.

Much like everywhere else in Sansari, the back alley was clean and well lit. Colourful lights hung overhead, strung across in zigzag fashion, providing a convivial canopy under which people gathered around a few tables and a couple of stalls.

They took a table nearest a noodle stall. A cheerful drone, resembling a miniature dirigible flipped on its side, hovered over to take their orders.

"Don't worry," said Ourry noting Marcus' wary glance, "these aren't hooked up to the central system. They won't report you. Now, their *gundruk* noodles are pretty good, as are their fried *kukhura*…"

"We'll go with what you decide then," said Marcus as Ourry enthusiastically rattled off a number of dishes to the drone. The sizzling smells and sounds around were making him hungry.

Their orders arrived several minutes later.

"They're very quick," commented Pihla, as a service bot served them their order. She nodded approvingly as it handed her a spoon for the soup. "We don't have many of these full-bodied models at home. I've often thought these are much better than our servicehands."

"You don't like androids?" asked Ourry, slurping his soupy noodles.

Pihla shrugged. "I don't mind them but generally, where we come from, people prefer their bots to look like machines, not androids. I mean, don't get me wrong, we have partials like AI servicehands or mechanised porters, but hardly ever full-bodied androids."

"How strange," said Ourry, "Why do you think that is?"

"We're just old-fashioned I guess," quipped Marcus. "Preferring to be served by a couple of disembodied prosthetics than a humanoid service bot."

Ourry shook his head and chuckled. "Cultural differences, eh? And where did you say you were from? Pindeshor? Dankali?" He grinned and wagged a bemused finger at them. "I *bet* you're from Pindeshor," he said, "I met someone from there once and he didn't like androids either. Ha ha! You're Pindeshorians aren't you?"

The three of them exchanged glances for a minute and then Marcus spoke up. "Ageron actually," he said, giving in to his instincts to trust Ourry. "We're from Ageron, the Red Realm."

Ourry blinked, confused. "*What?*"

PLANET DHARAN, TILKOEN SYSTEM

Marcus nodded. "We're Ageronians, Ourry," he said. "From Ageron," he added, in case it wasn't clear enough.

Ourry stopped to swallow his noodles and guffawed. "Okay, okay, that was funny. I think." He looked at them, chortled some more and added, "I suppose you're gonna say you came from the Sansari Gate. Haha! Good one! Good one! You Pindeshorians are such jokers!"

"Actually," said Tors, speaking up, "we did technically come through the Gate..."

Ourry stopped short and looked at her.

Marcus chuckled inwardly. Only Tors could conjure up an expression that no one would question.

Ourry's eyes widened. "You can't be serious!" He looked at them, then at Tors again and said, "You *are* serious." He gulped. "But *how?*"

They told him.

"So you came from the *Gate?*" Ourry said after taking a while to absorb their explanation. He shook his head in disbelief. "Well, that's... highly irregular. The Sansari Gate has not worked for centuries." He looked at them a little doubtfully. "Are you sure you *really* came through that?"

Marcus nodded.

"Well," continued Ourry slowly, "I guess that explains your protest permits. And the fact the drones didn't issue you a fine on the spot."

"Oh, they can do that?" Pihla said.

"Well, I did think it was a little odd they didn't announce your name when they were screaming 'Unauthorised Protester'," said Ourry.

"You mean they would've recognised me?"

Ourry nodded. "Oh yeah of course. Just like they recognised everyone else in the crowd. All of whom *had permits.*"

"But they were wearing balaclavas," said Pihla. "Wouldn't that have stopped them being recognised?"

"Ppppft! Oh no!" said Ourry, grinning. "Our systems are far more advanced. It's not just facial recognition anymore. Your voice, your gait, your handprints, even your secretions—pheromones, sweat—all that will give you away between the time it takes you to walk from here to buy your kukhuras from the teashop down the roa—"

"Ooooh by Dyaeus, this is *good*!" Pihla burst out as she had her first bite of kukhura.

Ourry grinned at her.

"By Dyaeus, you're right," joined in Marcus, agreeing, technical facial recognition discussion promptly forgotten. "What *is* this?" The kukhura, crisp on the outside, sweet and spicy, was delicious. He examined his half-bitten morsel. "Is this meat?" he asked.

"*Vitro-pullus*," said Ourry diving in for more. He looked at Marcus and explained, "Cultured poultry."

"Cultured?"

"Uh huh—all meat in Tilkoen is grown in-vitro."

"You don't raise livestock?" asked Marcus.

Ourry shook his head and pulled a face. "Goodness no, of course not! How *barbaric*! This is cultured meat. No animal husbandry. Haven't done so for centuries now, since the Gateways fell and food imports from Ellagrin ceased. All our meat's cultured and our vegetables grown indoors within the city itself." He smiled at them. "It's better this way. For the environment. And we get to preserve our forests."

"Very commendable," nodded Marcus.

"So how did you come to be the owner of Pachinko Paradise?" asked Tors, changing the subject.

Ourry gave a shrug. "Couldn't get a good job I guess. I was never good at languages…"

"Languages?" queried Pihla.

Ourry nodded, then slapped his forehead. "Of course!" he said, "you don't know the history behind all this and the protests you've just seen, do you?" He stopped munching for a bit and turned to face them. "I meant languages as in programming languages," he said, explaining. "For centuries, language has been the main driver behind Tilkoen's technological advancement: language to create our AIs, language to extend them, language upon which everything you see around you has been built—instructional, derivative, neural, modelling languages. Languages for programming bots, languages for designing systems, AI algorithms, everything! *Languages*! To get a good job these days, you need to be good at languages." He winked at Pihla, "Which is what most women tend to be better at."

"How interesting," said Pihla.

"Well, from where I sit, I have to agree with you *completely*, Ourry," said Marcus. "I mean Pihla practically tells the guys in Engineering what to do anyway."

"I'm not surprised," replied Ourry candidly. "She appears a lot smarter than you."

"Er, well, yes," admitted Marcus, not quite expecting Ourry to be *that* frank.

"Anyway," continued Ourry, "we have algorithms to discern the individual's aptitude for specific skillsets, traits and natural talent. And women really tend to fare much better in languages and organisational skills compared to men. Men can, of course, get better over time and with experience, but job selection tests rarely take this into account. So, over time, the best-paid jobs and highest positions in Tilkoen society became dominated by women." He shrugged good-naturedly at Pihla and Tors. "You guys are just better at it than we are, I guess."

"Well, *I'm* all for a female dominated society," said Marcus, "and Ageron and Ellagrin should follow suit. We might have avoided several wars too if we did. In our group, Tors here leads us."

Ourry arched an immaculate but quizzical eyebrow at him.

Marcus nodded seriously and indicated at Tors. "Yup, Ourry my man—she leads, I obey. No questions asked."

Tors stared at him.

"Huh," said Ourry, looking at Tors in fresh light. Then, he pointed at Marcus' pecks. "I'm afraid here, physical prowess is also pretty much obsolete these days."

"Well, muscles are overrated anyway," said Marcus easily, "and besides, they make no difference. I still get bossed around by women."

Tors stared at him for a good few moments before speaking. "There's something very wrong with you."

Marcus gave her a roguish smile. "What can I say," he said, "I'm a thoroughly modern man."

"Anyway," continued Ourry cheerfully, "I wasn't smart enough to get into higher learning so I decided to open a pachinko parlour." His face split into the widest of grins. "It was the best move I ever made!"

"Here, here!" cheered Marcus and they all saluted Ourry with a glass.

* * *

It was nearly dawn before they returned to Pachinko Paradise to sleep.

"I'll take you to City Hall in the morning," Ourry promised. "We'll get your friend back, don't worry. Before you know it, you'll have the Sansari Gate working again too, and complete your mission."

PLANET DHARAN, TILKOEN SYSTEM

"Thank you Ourry," said Tors as they made their way to their rooms, "let's hope so." She gazed at Marcus, perturbed. "Do you think the Sansari Gate will work?" she asked. "It's been so long, even Ourry's never seen it working. More importantly, will the Tilkoens *want* to see it working, after all this time?"

Marcus nodded. "This is why we need to speak to their High Council. Let's hope they view all this positively. We're the last thing they'd be expecting after all this time."

CITY HALL

SANSARI CITY, TILKOEN

"*A*ch!" exclaimed the Councillor. "We have been expecting you."

"You have?" Pihla had blurted out, surprised.

Tall, lanky and with her slate-grey hair slicked back into a bun at the back, Councillor Divya-Hamish Emblazoned Courage did not look like a typical Tilkoen. "And I do not mean your emissaries," she continued in her rolling accent. Her mouth twitched slightly with amusement as she eyed them one by one. "Your emissaries came and returned to Ageron nearly a century ago, but *you*, *all* of you…, through the *Sansari Gate*…"—the Councillor smiled as if she had just won a wager—"We have been expecting you to come through that for some time now."

Ourry, true to his word had taken them to City Hall and when they enquired about Niko, they were escorted to the Administration Wing, where a Councillor Divya-Hamish Emblazoned Courage received them in her extraordinary office.

Situated on the topmost floor, natural light poured down

from a ceiling so transparent it looked invisible. Sunlight filtered through unfettered, as if there was nothing between them and the sky above. However, it was the glass floor-to-ceiling windows that completed the effect, for apart from the side of the room they had entered through earlier, the rest of Councillor Divya-Hamish's office had no other solid-looking walls.

Look at us all huddled together, thought Pihla with hilarity. Apart from Tors who had walked around the office to look out the window, she and Marcus had remained paralysed, rooted in its centre.

Marcus looked faintly green in the face, trying to ignore the effects of vertigo. City Hall appeared to be the tallest building for miles around and with the Councillor's transparent office on its topmost floor, it felt as if they were standing on an exposed roof several hundred storeys high, with the surrounding city unnervingly all around and below them.

"The walls are there, I assure you," said Councillor Hamish amusedly as she walked around the room. She moved easily like the tall gliding mast of a ship. "They are very solid, too," she continued as Marcus followed her tentatively to the edge of the room to peer cautiously over the side. "They are also one-way, so we can see out but people cannot see in."

In the bright light of day, the true scale of the city was revealed. Like a futuristic forest of trees, skyscrapers of every discernible shape and size stretched out on all sides. Towards the east, seen through the imposing ellipse of the Sansari Gate, tall thin towers, glazed in malachite glass, gleamed in the sunlight, slender and graceful. To the west, the sprawl of majestic looking high-rise blocks, prismatic and multi-sided, glinted like jewel boxes amidst clusters of cigar-shaped buildings clad in dark viridian. All across the city, buildings, individualistic and in jarring shades of aquamarine and neon green, sprouted amongst more conventionally-shaped ones, clad in sleek blue-green glass. Winding their way around these marvellous structures were the shuttle-chutes, filled with zipping pods, twisting their way around the city like translucent ribbons, and in the air, urbangliders and smaller shuttles flitted amongst the chaotic tangle of skyscrapers and chutes. To Pihla, the megacity of Sansari looked like a swarming, teeming intricate hive at a colossal scale.

"We have much to discuss," said the Councillor, getting down to business, "but first, I think we should get you reunited with your friend." She looked up and spoke into the air, "Dexa, please bring the gentleman in."

Dexa? Pihla looked around. There was no one else besides them and the Councillor.

The door opened to let in none other than Niko, accompanied by a man in uniform.

"Niko!" Pihla and Tors called out in unison.

"Good to see you too," Niko said. A foolish grin spread across his face. "Turns out breaking off branches from Dimaga trees is a rather serious act of vandalism in these parts," he said, surveying the far reaches of the room a little cautiously. "Fortunately they have been expecting us. Apparently the words 'I've come through the Sansari Gate' invoke some pre-existing protocol, leading them to know exactly what to do and who to bring me to." He turned to the tall Councillor and queried, "I was informed you were the person who kindly got me released early, Councillor Hamish er, Diva, er…Blazing Courage?"

Councillor Hamish smiled. "Councillor Divya-Hamish Emblazoned Courage at your service," she said and bowed.

"Ah… yes," stumbled Niko apologetically, "that's what I

meant. Nice to meet you, ah Councillor Divya-Hamish Blazon Courage."

"Close enough," said the Councillor with a twinkle in her eye, "but you can just call me Councillor Hamish."

"So you say that you've been *expecting* us?" Tors asked.

The Councillor nodded. "Aye, give or take a deviance of fifty years. We have been expecting you. Well, someone from the Ageron system anyway."

"I don't understand," said Pihla, "How?"

The Councillor nodded smilingly. "Ach! Our AIs anticipated that. We utilise predictive technologies here. Please…" She gestured towards some comfortable pod chairs hovering above the floor, "Do have a seat. I will summon the others and all will become clear in due course."

Councillor Hamish herself settled down in one of the chairs and then called out, "Dexa, call councillors Navi Enduring Kindness and Ram Victorious Light. Category 613, Gateway visitors."

A composed voice replied: *Yes, Councillor Hamish. Calling councillors Navi and Ram…*

"Thank you Dexa." Councillor Hamish smiled at them and explained, "Dexa helps facilitate the activities in this building. She also happens to be one of our nation's AIs."

"AI?" ventured Niko.

"Artificial Intelligence," explained Councillor Hamish. "Dexa is one of our artificial intelligence entities. One of four actually, which is why we often refer to them as The Four. Our AIs help in the administration of all of the Tilkoen empire, performing an advisory role to our Congress."

"So Dexa is a programme?" asked Pihla, intrigued.

Councillor Hamish smiled. "Not quite," she said. "We've gone past that for centuries now. Our AIs are entities in their own right. Not quite hardware-based—we went hybrid ages ago. They now reside within our distributed networks across our planets, surfing and tapping into our datastreams. We..." The Councillor paused as a Tilkoen lady appeared and walked towards them. Like Councillor Hamish, she was dressed in a crisp suit.

"Good morning, Councillor Hamish," she said. Well-muscled and big-boned as the majority of Tilkoens were, she walked with firm, heavy strokes.

It took Pihla a moment before she realised why Councillor Navi's ponderous steps made no sound and why she hadn't noticed her enter the room in the first place—Councillor Navi was no more than a hologram.

"Ach, Councillor Navi," greeted Councillor Hamish, "so good to see you. How are the sundews doing this time of year?"

Councillor Navi chuckled and the slight flab beneath her chin wobbled slightly. "Very well indeed," she said. "We had a most abundant flowering this spring, surpassing last year's. In fact, they've started catching prey on their own now. A most welcome development seeing as this summer has brought a lot more secreeda bugs than usual."

Councillor Hamish nodded amiably.

Presently, another holo flickered into existence. This time, it was a squat, broad-shouldered male sitting at his breakfast table and like Councillor Navi, looked deceptively real in the room.

"Thank you both for calling in so promptly," said Councillor Hamish.

"Not at all," replied the man, chomping hard on what appeared to be a hunk of dried fish, dorsal fins and all. "So let's have it Hamish—you mentioned the Gate. Has it finally happened?"

Councillor Hamish nodded. "Yes it has, Councillor Ram,"

she said. "As The Four predicted. May I introduce you to our visitors from the Ageron system: Marcus, Tors, Niko and Pihla."

Councillor Navi walked right up to Pihla, stopping a mere inch in front of her, nose-to-nose. With her hands clasped together at the back, she teetered on her toes and smiled broadly at Pihla.

Tilkoen directness, thought Pihla as she met Councillor Navi's gaze with an equally confident smile.

"Welcome Ageronians," Councillor Ram boomed heartily. "Right on time too, give or take a couple of years."

"I don't understand," said Tors, "How could you have predicted our arrival?"

Councillor Ram grinned at her. "To be fair, our AIs didn't predict your arrival exactly, but they did predict the arrival of some Ageronians through the Gate."

"But how?" asked Pihla. "Our planetary systems have been cut off from each other for centuries, ever since the fall of the Gateways. Any news you would've received would have been via starships and decades out-of-date at the very least."

Councillor Hamish smiled. "Aye! Looking for the logical explanation eh? Your heritage precedes you, Tilkoen. So how did our AIs do it, you ask?" She let out a hearty guffaw. "Well, by taking a crackin' good guess!"

"Our AIs predicted the failure of your binary suns ages ago," said Councillor Ram, "even before you detected it. And thus, it would have been likely that someone from Ageron would be sent here to seek help. We guessed you would send your emissaries over but The Four somehow predicted an arrival via the Sansari Gate, which truth be told, we never thought possible as the Gateways were destroyed in the War."

"We came via the Ether," Tors spoke up, "not quite via the Gateway."

There was a subtle glance from Councillor Ram in Tors' direction, but if the Tilkoens recognised her as a Nehisi, they were certainly too polite to let that show.

"Yes," said Councillor Ram, "that's what we were told to expect, yes. The last Nehisi to make it through the Ether, and you have the beacon with you?"

"We do," said Marcus.

"Excellent," said Councillor Ram. "There will need to be some modifications done to it as we have added tamper-proof tech to our Gate here, but nothing too difficult. You will have to bring it here to our secured unit in Chatadharam and I will get our engineers on it."

"I shall inform the Council of your arrival," said Councillor Navi. "We will need them to formally agree and pass the motion to reopen the Sansari Gate."

Councillor Hamish nodded. She turned to Marcus and the others to explain. "Don't worry," she said, "it should just be a formality to obtain the confirmation from the Council. The motion to assist House Ageron in the evacuation and resettlement of its inhabitants had already been passed decades ago when your emissaries arrived." She smiled. "The only question that remains for us is who will reach Ageron first to give the good news—your emissaries or you?"

Councillor Navi's intense gaze settled on Pihla once more. "Fifty years ago, we sent a small team to accompany your emissaries back to Ageron," she said. "Your uncle, I believe, heads that team."

"Uncle?" repeated Pihla.

Councillor Navi nodded. "Yes, General Batsa Blazing Light," she said and broke into a wide smile. "Your uncle, and a good friend of mine."

"Ah, I see," said Pihla. General Batsa was known to her— her father had spoken of him to her, even though she had never seen him in person. *So that was why she was looking at me closely all this time!*

"Now," said Councillor Hamish getting back to business, "it is settled then. We must get the beacon to Engineering and present motion 613 to the Council. Councillor Ram, may I remind you, this is of the highest security and utmost secrecy. I shall escort our friends and we shall see you at Chatadharam in five hours."

"I shall be waiting, Councillor Hamish," nodded Councillor Ram and he and his breakfast table blurred out.

"See you at the Chatadharam," beamed Councillor Navi and with a wave, signed out.

"What's in Chatadharam?" asked Pihla.

"Oh, the Engineering Institute and Congress," replied Councillor Hamish.

"Congress?" repeated Pihla.

"Yes," replied Councillor Hamish with a grin. "Our version of your Senate, except a wee bit more democratic."

CHATADHARAM

CHATADHARAM CITY, TILKOEN

They were flown in a private shuttle from Sansari to Chatadharam, courtesy of Councillor Hamish. Pihla looked out the window as their urbanglider sped over the heaving, humming, haphazard sprawl of metal and glass that was the megacity of Sansari. Gradually, at the outskirts, the buildings began to thin out until finally wilderness took over.

Pihla found herself strangely relieved to have left the frenetic bustle of Sansari behind. She cast one last look behind. As big as it was, the megacity had diminished into a small shiny blob in the middle of a sea of dense, dark-green forest stretching for thousands of miles in all directions.

"Ourry was right," Marcus said. "Look at the forest. Small settlements, towns, even conventional farming here is non-existent."

Councillor Hamish nodded. "That is correct," she said. "It is the same on all planets in the Tilkoen system. Ninety percent of our terrain remains virgin forest and mostly Dimaga at that."

"What about your population?" asked Niko. "Where do Tilkoens live?"

"In our megacities of course," answered Councillor Hamish. "With food produced within our cities, we have no need to clear land for cultivation like the Ellagrins and we don't spread out like Ageronians. We prefer to live close to each other."

"Packed close and piled up high," commented Niko, voicing his thoughts without censure as usual.

Pihla gave him a disparaging shake of the head in response. Fortunately, Councillor Hamish did not seem to mind.

"Ach!" she announced brightly, "We are approaching Chatadharam! Also affectionately referred to as the Garden City." She looked at Pihla and added with a grin, "You will find it slightly less hectic than commercial Sansari."

The group looked out the window as the urbanglider began its descent. Standing out like a white pearl in the middle of a dark green sea, loomed Chatadharam. It was indeed a garden city and with so many trees in its neighbourhoods and parks, it was as if the surrounding forest flowed into the city, merely thinning out in order to give its buildings just enough space to co-exist.

The urbanglider swooped downwards and soon they were flying over high-rise tower blocks. Unlike the sleek and slender towers of Sansari, these were chunky, white and shaped like massive angular ski slopes. Pihla observed that each tower block was cleverly positioned at different angles to its neighbours and this as a consequence, provided residents with unobstructed views of the city around them whilst ensuring maximum exposure to sunlight during the day. Like Sansari, winding walkways and transparent chutes linked the city's buildings and outside spaces, weaving their way around the city, like a clutch of ribbons carelessly dropped between a pile of hefty gift boxes.

Soon, their aircraft approached a transparent building which Councillor Hamish called the Forum. A tower of about forty storeys high, it was cuboid-shaped with a curved, sucked-in middle section from which a series of landing pads jutted out like silvery bracket fungus on a glass tree. It was on one of these landing pads that the urbanglider settled.

"Welcome to the Forum," said Councillor Hamish, as the airy glass doors whispered open, admitting them into the transparent building.

Pihla looked around in amazement. Judging from where their landing pad was and from where she stood, they were about a third of the way up the building. Councillor Hamish led them towards the centre which was balconied and overlooked a central atrium. From here, they could see the floors below and above.

The Forum looked like an assemblage of crystalline blocks stacked on top of one another like a transparent jigsaw puzzle. Sunlight streamed through the entire building, and with people walking about on each of the floors, the light cast downwards seemed to shimmer and dance.

In the middle of the atrium, extending from the ground up was a massive tree— tall, majestic and with dark green leaves that scintillated in the light. Its twinkling speckles appeared to echo the rhythm of activity in the building.

"By Dyaeus, this is one tall tree," said Pihla. It towered above them, past their floor, up to the level above theirs.

"This is a Dimaga tree," smiled Councillor Hamish. "One of the oldest on this planet and one of the finest specimens of Dimaga, if I may say so."

"Dimaga," repeated Niko, flushing a little, no doubt recollecting his 'tree branch' incident.

"Indeed," nodded Councillor Hamish with a faint smile. "Our national symbol and a protected species, as you found out."

Niko nodded.

"Right," said Councillor Hamish leading them towards the lifts. "This way if you will, please. We'll go to the Congressional Hall as we need to present our case to all of Congress, meaning the Twelve in the High Council and the Lower Council—all one thousand and five of them."

"And then?" Pihla asked.

"And then," said Councillor Hamish, "unless predictions and supporting facts have changed since the last time we debated this issue, we should get a consensus to activate the Sansari Gate and reopen the Arnemetian Gateway."

"Just like that?" said Pihla, slightly surprised at the simplicity of it.

"Just like that,"nodded Councillor Hamish, smiling.

"Huh," said Pihla. Something like this would have likely taken a few days in Ageron. Emperor Akseli's vote for impeachment alone took weeks. Here it seemed, communications were rational, rapid and unencumbered.

* * *

THE CONGRESSIONAL HALL was an immense auditorium spanning the entire second floor of the Forum.

Its doors slid open as they approached and as they entered, the giant space yawned in front of them like a great canyon, falling away into the distance. The walls at the far end, curved and clad in some pitch-coloured padded material, lent the chamber the muted feel of a concert hall.

One by one, small holos flickered to life, each the image of a person's face against the dark, matt surface.

Pihla looked around in wonder. *So this is how they get everyone together at such short notice.*

"This is Congress," said Councillor Hamish as they took their seats in a cubicle overlooking the space, "and you'll soon see how House Tilkoen governs."

A low, continuous murmur of voices from the audience, coming from those physically present in the hall, carried on in the background. A melodic chime echoed in the auditorium, halting the burble of voices and bringing the audience to attention.

Councillor Hamish rose to address the Congress. A larger-than-life holographic image of her projected into the centre of the hall and the air hushed as everyone turned their attention to her.

Councillor Divya-Hamish, member of the High Twelve and Minister of External Affairs, announced a smooth mellow voice. *You may begin...*

"Thank you, Forum," said Councillor Hamish, her voice ringing calm and clear in the expanse. "Fellow councillors, we are gathered here today to discuss motion 613, triggered by the recent arrival of an Ageronian delegation to Tilkoen. We seek authorisation for the reactivation of the Sansari Gate, in order to reinstate the Arnemetian Gateway, linking our city of Sansari to the Ageronian city of Arnemetiae."

Councillor Hamish paused a moment to collect her thoughts. "We have, on previous occasions, discussed the case for the opening of the Gateway and our nation's stance on the resettlement of Ageronians here in our planetary system, the final discussion being tabled, agreed and recorded three years and five months ago," she said. "You will remember, Congress was in agreement that we, House Tilkoen, remain receptive and complaisant to providing assistance to House Ageron in its time of need, and I quote Ideology Principle 2146:

extending help to external civilisations under Force Majeure provisions and assistance."

There was a collective murmur from the audience as images of Marcus, Tors, Niko and Pihla were projected onto centre stage for all to see.

A second chime sounded and the face of another member of Congress was projected alongside Councillor Hamish's.

Councillor Hari Sacred Light from the Magri sector, announced the reposeful voice of the Forum as the plump bearded face of Councillor Hari appeared before them.

"Arrhemm," Councillor Hari began. "Thank you, Forum. I arrr, propose that we run through the likely scenarios for and against the motion for the benefit of the entire Congress before we get to the voting."

"An eminently sensible proposal Councillor Hari," responded Councillor Hamish. "Forum, please invite AIs Aamrutha, Addarsh, Dexa and Maya to Congress."

We are present as requested, came the answer almost instantaneously. Several voices spoke in unison but Pihla could make out Dexa's smooth voice from the mix.

Councillor Hamish's face dimmed out from the central projection as Councillor Hari opened the debate to Congress.

Whilst the proceedings carried on in front, Councillor Hamish turned towards them and said, "You may have recognised Dexa's voice amongst them. Those voices—they are the Four. Our AIs."

"Why four and not one?" asked Niko.

Pihla glared at him but Councillor Hamish nodded and grinned.

"Ach! That's actually a good question," she said. "When we first delved into artificial intelligence centuries ago, we didn't really know what we were doing. As it happened, four teams from different agencies—two universities, one government research project and one private enterprise—embarked on our very first AI Initiative. Developed separately, using different approaches to self-aware learning, we ended up with four separate entities." She chuckled. "They all have different personalities and inclinations too, as you may well notice after a while. Coincidentally enough, their names seem to reflect this too."

"Dexa means 'to teach' in Tilkoen," Pihla mused.

Councillor Hamish's smile widened. "That is correct, " she said, "that's an old Tilkoen word. I'm surprised you know it! Aamrutha means one who cannot be destroyed and Aadarsh means one with principles. Aamrutha was developed by our Defence ministry, Dexa by Dharan university and Aadarsh by the Omni-Bio conglomerate."

"And Maya?" asked Niko.

"Maya means love and compassion. Maya was the fruitful outcome of a grassroots community project in Dankali." Councillor Hamish shrugged. "Perhaps the ones who first created our AIs subconsciously created them with their meanings in mind."

The Councillor turned back to the debate in progress. "Ach! You will see next what I meant by the AIs providing an advisory role," she said.

The group turned their attention back to the discussion on the floor. Councillor Hari was asking, "...and how will we know that if we open the Gateway, the Ageronians will not invade?"

Dexa countered calmly, its tranquil voice soothing by contrast. "Our simulations show that if the Arnemetiaen Gateway is reopened, trade between Houses Ageron and Tilkoen will flourish," it said. A second voice continued, this time a deeper, male voice—Aamrutha, according to Councillor Hamish.

Alternative simulations that myself and Dexa have run indicate a very low probability of invasion, Aamrutha said, its voice like a gentle rumble of thunder. *With Emperor Akseli being deposed, there is a low risk of invasion. For completeness however, we should point out that a small risk to the home security of Tilkoen exists due to the fact that majority of our troops have been sent to the Ellagrin system under the passed Edict 5382—annexation of House Ellagrin— triggered approximately seven years ago, to counteract the predicted invasion of Tilkoen by House Ellagrin. However, as debated and agreed previously, the probability of this is extremely low.*

"Thank you Aamrutha," said Councillor Hari. "Might I point out to Congress as well that Edict 5382 was taken to demilitarise Ellagrin in response to our earlier predictions that an invasion from them was likely. We remain aligned and in support of that decision made." There were nods of agreement from the majority of screens in the auditorium.

Additionally Councillors, chimed in Dexa, *General Batsa Blazing Light and his delegation are expected to reach the Ageron system within this decade. They will warn the Ageronians of our predictions, in that invasion from Ellagrin is imminent. We do not predict any reason nor motive for Ageronians to invade Tilkoen in return.*

Councillor Batista Calm Serenity, announced the cool electronic voice of the Forum next.

Councillor Batista appeared in the central projection. He wore the robes of one of the High Twelve and asked, "The Ageronians, wealthy as they might be, are in desperate need to vacate Ageron before their binary suns fail completely. They need land to occupy. *Our* land. Are we *sure* they will not invade us should we open the Arnemetiaen Gateway?"

A valid question Councillor Batista, replied the AI, Aadarsh. *Analysis show that Tilkoen is so mechanised the Ageronians will not be able to thrive here without our assistance. Additionally, historical records indicate Ageronians are used to investing in Tilkoen technology and profiting through this arrangement, a symbiotic model of interaction between the Houses that has been the norm for centuries. A major step away from this mindset by Ageronians is highly unlikely.*

Remember also, that Ageronians have not exhibited any previous tendencies to usurp, said Maya. Of the four, it sounded the youngest, with a voice that was calm and knowing but childlike at the same time. *With their amassed wealth from the Age of Prosperity, Ageronians are unlikely to take this aggressive route of behaviour. Invasion would not be practical nor preferable—far easier for them to buy their way out of difficulty rather than use force.*

The debate drew to a close as points put forth were satisfactorily answered and no further issues raised.

With that, Councillor Hamish stepped forward to press the motion. "I move to request Congress to vote on the reactivation of the Sansari Gate and consequently the opening of the Arnemetiaen Gateway," she said. "Any objections?"

A momentary pause and then, *No objections received for submission of motion*, chimed the voice of the Forum. *Motion 9773 is therefore tabled. Voting is open and will close by zero four hundred hours today. Thank you Councillors*, it announced. Then one by one, the virtual attendees blinked out and the rest began to file out of the Forum.

* * *

"Now what?" asked Niko as they emerged from the darkened hall into the bright foyer.

"Now we get the beacon securely to the Engineering Institute and wait," said Councillor Hamish, guiding them towards the lifts again.

When it next opened, they were at a much higher floor than before and facing a set of double doors leading to the landing pads again. There, a tall Tilkoen, dressed in military uniform stood waiting.

Pihla felt her legs tremble. *This can't be real,* she told herself, drawing her breath sharply.

It was *him*, the Tilkoen from the Empress' vision to her.

"Ach! Captain Shankar," greeted Councillor Hamish, beaming. "How nice to see you again."

Captain Shankar extended a strong, muscly arm towards the Councillor who shook it heartily. "Councillor Hamish," he greeted with smiling eyes.

Pihla's eyes flicked over his rugged frame. Captain Shankar was as athletic, broad-shouldered and good-looking as she remembered in her visions.

He glanced round the group before resting his eyes on her. They were amber like hers, and intelligent and kindly. "Pleased to meet you," he said, smiling broadly. To her surprise and dismay, Pihla found herself blushing.

"Captain Shankar will be in charge of your security whilst you're here," said Councillor Hamish. "Chatadharam may be relatively safe and I doubt anyone will even realise who you are, nevertheless we cannot take chances with your security and that of your mission due to what's at stake."

"Indeed," said the Captain, nodding. "And in the first instance, I have orders to escort you to the Engineering Institute to get the beacon looked at and adapted," he said.

Councillor Hamish nodded. "Good," she said approvingly. "We anticipate the congressional vote to go ahead unchallenged but the beacon of course, will need to stay in Engineering until the outcome of the vote is known."

"Well," said Captain Shankar, a smile forming on his face as he looked at them, "let's get that beacon over to Engineering, shall we? Then I can show you around Chatadharam."

"That would be great!" replied Pihla, enthusiastically, then turned to glance at the others, half afraid she had come across as overly keen. Thankfully, Marcus and Tors appeared equally excited at the prospect, apart from Niko whose face looked black as a thundercloud.

And so with enthusiasm from almost everyone, they followed Captain Shankar to the Institute of Engineering.

ENGINEERING

CHATADHARAM CITY, TILKOEN

The Engineering Institute was a building unlike anything Niko had ever seen. Situated opposite the Forum and though not quite as tall as its neighbour, it stood out, proud, curvy, blonde and bulbous.

"A beehive," said Captain Shankar, in answer to Pihla's baffled look at the building as they approached it. He led her gently by the elbow and outlined the curve of the building with his finger. "See? The building is modelled after the structure of a beehive."

"Oh, how amazing!" said Pihla.

Niko glowered from behind. *How amazing,* he mouthed in silent mockery as the captain led the way into the building.

"So, does Dexa control this building as well?" asked Marcus.

Captain Shankar nodded. "Yes, you could say that, although strictly speaking, all our AIs operate everywhere. All of Tilkoen is connected so the reach of the Four extend across our distributed networks. Dexa generally manages the servicing of our main government buildings such as City Hall, The Forum and the Engineering Institute."

"How interesting," murmured Pihla.

Tors and Marcus asked further questions but to Niko's annoyance, the captain's answers always seemed directed at Pihla rather than to the group as a whole.

Niko trailed behind in sullen silence whilst in front, Pihla, more talkative than usual, asked more questions. It was clear she was oblivious to the particular attentions of the tall captain, but each time she laughed at his suave prattling, Niko felt yet another pang of annoyance.

The group entered the building, crossed its expansive foyer and headed straight for the lifts.

"No security?" Marcus asked, surprised, as the doors of the lift opened for them.

Captain Shankar grinned. "Embracive bio-scans," he explained. "We already know you from your face, voice and body scans. You'll find these doors will not open if you weren't authorised in the first place."

"Hmm, very clever," remarked Pihla, impressed (again), and Niko rolled his eyes.

There was a slight feel of weightlessness as the lift took them downwards, below ground.

"Oh," remarked Niko, surprised. "I thought we were going up."

"We will, afterwards," said Captain Shankar, "but for now, we're headed to the secure labs underground."

* * *

THE LAB WAS A WELL-LIT and calm space. Several technicians, positioned at various stations, worked quietly, aided by two drones that glided soundlessly around the room. Captain

Shankar led them towards a diminutive woman standing in the middle discussing something animatedly with an assistant.

"Dr Shanoli," said Captain Shankar.

The Doctor looked up and murmured some instructions to her departing assistant. "Captain Shankar," she said with a hint of amusement. "*Finally*, something genuinely important this time!" Her bright eyes shone with intelligence and good humour. "You have something for me, I believe," she said holding out her hand.

As Marcus handed her the beacon, she turned her gaze towards them. "My word," she said holding the beacon reverently, "you have no idea how exciting this is for me. Do you know, there has never been a beacon brought through the Ether in living memory?"

"Dr Shanoli is Head of Engineering here at the Institute," introduced Captain Shankar with a bemused smile.

Dr Shanoli gave a brief perfunctory nod. "We have known since the time House Tilkoen helped build the Gateways that the Ether can't be mapped," she said, examining the beacon keenly, "which is why there was no way to reopen the Gateway without this device having made the journey from Ageron, through the Ether, all the way here in Tilkoen." Her gaze shifted to Tors and she continued, "Now you're probably wondering why we didn't make copies of the beacon in those days, when we could. Well, we tried but that didn't work. The beacons simply can't be copied. Do you know why?"

Tors shook her head.

"Because there is no known way to describe or even transcribe the journey you've just taken," said Dr Shanoli. "Since the construction days of the Gateways, we have been trying to describe it somehow—mathematically perhaps, or even in some form of hybrid descriptor with our newer languages. Maybe this time, we may be luckier. I cannot wait to see what this beacon's memory construct holds in terms of the journey within the Ether!"

"However, first and foremost," reminded Captain Shankar, "we need the beacon configured to fit the Sansari Gate's tamper-proof protocols."

"Yes, of course," grinned Dr Shanoli, "We should be able to fit an adaptor around it, leaving the beacon itself intact. That should enable it to fit our current Gate receptacle. I'll do that first before I take any readouts for analysis."

"Thank you doctor," replied Captain Shankar. "By the way, Level 1 security protocols have been invoked, so you and your team here are pretty much locked in until we call for you. Just so you know what you're in for today," he added slightly apologetically.

Dr Shanoli waved his concern off. "It's fine," she said, "my team and I camped here for weeks when we had to deliver the Community Scoring upgrades. Besides, I can appreciate the secrecy of this—"

"Ah! Here they are!" A deep voice boomed, interrupting the conversation and shattering the calm of the lab.

Dr Shanoli rolled her eyes in irritation as Councillor Ram bulldozed his way through the hushed lab towards them.

"Councillor Ram," greeted Dr Shanoli coldly, "I don't believe you have an appointment with us."

"Level 1 security protocol!" said the Councillor jovially. "I thought I'd come in to check on the team and see if there's anything you need."

"We are quite all right for now," replied Dr Shanoli.

Councillor Ram looked interestedly at the beacon in her hand. "Is that what I think it is?" he inquired, eyes gleaming.

"It *is* what you think it is," said Captain Shankar and proceeded to stand between Dr Shanoli and the Councillor. "Councillor Ram," he said, "you need not have come all the way to the lab. Dr Shanoli and her team have been briefed and they have much to get on with. We will bring the finished article upstairs to you and Councillor Hamish when they are done. Until then, I think we should leave the Dr Shanoli and her team to it."

"Yes, yes, of course," said Councillor Ram placatingly. He turned to Niko and Marcus. "I have a stake in most engineering contracts here, you know," he said, rubbing his hands oleaginously. "A lot of the good work here is done under my name you see., so I thought I should personally make sure this takes top priority."

"I assure you Councillor, a matter such as this cannot *possibly* be any higher in terms of priority, nor in secrecy," said Captain Shankar drily.

"Gentlemen and ladies, if you don't mind, my team and I have work to do," said Dr Shanoli firmly.

Captain Shankar nodded. "We shall leave you in peace, Dr Shanoli," he said and ushered Councillor Ram and the others towards the door.

Dr Shanoli nodded gratefully. "We should be done in about three hours' time," she said. "Perhaps if you come back then..."

"Very good," said Captain Shankar and they all made their way out the door.

SNAKE IN THE BUSHES

*B*ack in the lift, after letting Councillor Ram out at ground level, Captain Shankar selected Level Thirty-Six.

"Where are we going?"asked Pihla. The lift sped upwards so quickly her ears popped.

"Out," replied Captain Shankar as the doors slid open at the thirty-sixth floor. "We have a few hours before Congress finishes voting and Dr Shanoli gets the beacon adapted. Just enough for a whistle-stop tour of Chatadharam." He tilted his head to one side and flexed an eyebrow. "Preferable I think, to waiting in some secure facility staring at the walls, no?" He pointed ahead, "We can grab a belt from here."

The entire thirty-sixth floor was open plan with clusters of seating, dining pods and a couple of kiosks dotted around selling refreshments. The space flowed out seamlessly onto a balcony of almost the same size, area-wise, as internal floor itself. Tors guessed they must be on the broadest level of the Institute, at the bit where its girth was largest. Here, on the balcony, paved walkways meandered through a patchwork of manicured grass and colourful shrubs, smooth and gleaming like golden streams in the late afternoon sun. Office workers strolled along them whilst others sat on the neat squares of grass chatting or working on their handhelds.

"Very nice," murmured Pihla, admiringly. "If only Alandia's business district looked half as nice as this!"

"When have you ever wanted to spend time in Alandia's business district anyway?" Niko piped up.

Pihla pretended not to hear. "Everything here seems so smart and orderly," she said, turning to Captain Shankar. "And so efficient too…"

"You haven't seen anything yet," said Captain Shankar leading her gallantly through a series of verdant arches bursting with tiny lemon blossoms. The natural makeshift tunnel led to a glass chute opening.

Niko examined it nervously as they stepped into it. "No pods?" he asked.

Pihla snickered—the chute looked remarkably similar to the one with the pod that Niko had encountered previously in Sansari, except this was smaller and certainly not large enough to accommodate a pod within it.

"No," said Captain Shankar, slightly puzzled. "These are pedestrian belts."

"Whoooaaaa!" Niko wobbled as something invisible moved him forward in a smooth sliding motion.

"This will take us to the Sky Garden," said Captain Shankar, grasping his arm to steady him. Niko wrenched himself away, slightly miffed at being assisted.

"How does this work?" asked Pihla as she stepped onto the belt, intrigued. "Maglev technology?" The absence of anything physical underfoot felt odd.

Captain Shankar nodded at her, impressed. "Yes, it's very similar," he said and held her hand to steady her. Pihla detected an involuntary *hmmph* coming from Niko. For some strange reason, Niko did not seem to find anything the captain had to say or do agreeable in the slightest.

The non-existent yet solid-feeling 'surface' underfoot began to move them along, gradually getting faster and faster, like a river current sweeping them along. It also appeared to keep them upright, even when going round a bend.

"Don't be afraid to walk along it if you want," said Captain Shankar and showed them how.

By now, the belt had whisked them away from the Engineering Institute and was winding its way between buildings. Pihla looked down. The transparent chute enabled her to see all the way down to street level, which at that moment was about over thirty storeys down. It was spectacular and surreal at the same time.

"Yeaahhh!" exclaimed Marcus enthusiastically as the belt took them between the buildings and zipped past two more skyscrapers at exhilarating speed. A few fellow pedestrians glanced up momentarily from their wrist consoles, amused at the reaction, before turning back to their reading. The belt then wound its way around a tall glass tower, shaped like a prism in gleaming rose-gold glass. It glinted and shone in the light.

"That's beautiful," said Pihla admiringly.

Captain Shankar leant over and said, "That's a hospital, actually."

"Well, that's got to be the most beautiful hospital I have ever seen," replied Pihla.

"Indeed," murmured Captain Shankar absently, his gaze fixed on Pihla, "most beautiful."

Pihla felt a flush rise in her cheeks and turned away, unable to speak. But she made the mistake of turning towards where Niko stood. He shot her a nauseated look.

The belt began to slow down as they approached the next building. It was shaped like a large pebble, wide with a flat top covered almost entirely in turf. They stepped off the belt and onto the elevated sea of green.

It was beautiful—open-air and so expansive Pihla almost forgot they were on top of a high rise building. It stretched in front of them, undulating gently in the wind.

"It's like the sea," breathed Tors. Elegant trees and tall reed grasses swayed and swished gently in the breeze, like the gentle rushing sound of ocean waves.

"This is Kendriya Park," said Captain Shankar taking them across the grass towards a small outdoor cafe complete with babbling brook beside it. "You can drink from that, you know," he said, pointing at the stream. "It's filtered water. Goes through to the building below and is used by everyone who works inside."

They took a table nearby and a waiter came over to take their orders.

"What, no servicebots?" remarked Pihla, as the young Tilkoen whipped out his handheld and punched in their table number.

"Here at Bezzie's we like to keep the service personal," he said chirpily, his bowtie bobbing up and down as he spoke. "Although if you prefer, we can summon a boooring ol' servicebot for you?" He rolled his eyes melodramatically at the suggestion.

"Oh no, no. This is fine," replied Pihla hastily and ordered her drink based on Captain Shankar's recommendation.

"So, did you always live in Ageron?" asked the captain politely when the waiter flitted off with their orders.

"Mostly," replied Pihla. She was beginning to feel a little conscious of the attention coming from the captain. "I was born in Tilkoen, in Sansari actually, where my mother's family is from."

"Oh, so you do have ties here," said Captain Shankar interestedly.

Pihla nodded. "My mother's Tilkoen and my father's Ageronian," she said. She paused and bit her lip. "We—my father and I—got separated from my mother when the Gateway fell. I have not seen her since." Pihla hesitated a moment and gave him a searching look. "Actually, I was hoping to trace her."

Captain Shankar patted her hand. "I can help you with that," he said, genuinely moved. "That was a long time ago and I can only imagine the pain of separation you must have endured all this time." The gravity of Pihla's personal situation was not lost on him.

She nodded gratefully at him, words failing her. The past few days had been a whirlwind of events but despite that, the urge to look for her mother had never been far from her mind. Where was she? What did she look like now? Did she even remember Pihla?

"So do you know Councillor Ram well then, Captain?" asked Marcus casually.

Pihla suppressed a wry smile. Marcus was always on the job digging for nuggets of information. He never could help himself.

"That old antique?" scoffed Captain Shankar. "Goodness no. He's probably as old your emperor."

"Emperor Ageron III?" said Marcus.

Captain Shankar nodded. "Yes. Not the son, which I believe you mentioned is currently standing trial." He paused as thee same waiter minced over with their drinks.

He set Pihla's drink in front of her with one hand, and with the other placed a raised salver covered in a glass cloche next to it with a flourish. "This one's on the house, honey," he said with a wink.

"Oh," said Pihla and peered at the cloched salver. A thick veil of smoke obscured its contents inside.

"You eat it," the waiter added helpfully, and lifted the cloche to reveal some artistically stacked sugared fronds inside before flitting away to the next table.

"Ooooh... me first!" said Niko and popped one in his mouth. He pulled a face. "Blurrgh! Eww...it's rank!"

Pihla shot him a disparaging look and withdrew to sip her drink.

"As old as our previous emperor huh?" said Marcus, turning back to his conversation with Captain Shankar.

"Doesn't look it I know, but Councillor Ram has had a lot of rejuvenation," said the captain. "And I mean a *lot*. He was already a junior in the Lower Council when the War broke out and after the Gateways were destroyed, they elected him to the High Council. He's so old he remembers Ageron *before* it was called the Red Realm. Apparently Councillor Ram was a diplomat there in the old days."

"Is that so?" said Marcus. He rubbed his chin thoughtfully. "I did wonder why he was so interested in the beacon. Sentimental reasons perhaps?"

Captain Shankar shrugged. "Who knows," he said, "...it's so long ago. Because of his old connections perhaps? Councillor Ram likes to reminisce about the old days and his royal connections with House Ageron. In fact he boasted once that he knew your Queen personally."

"Which one?" Niko sniggered. "Ageron III had so many wives." He stopped for a moment as a different waiter approached the table to set down another salver of the smoked stuff. "Ah, sir, we don't really want another one of these...," he said but the man didn't seem to hear him.

"The fair one, he always used to say," continued Captain Shankar, "you know, the one they called Alayne? Eileen?"

Pihla tapped the waiter's arm to get his attention. "Er, sir, he just told you, we don't need another one—"

Marcus glanced sharply at Captain Shankar. "*Alin?*" he ventured.

"Yes!" said Captain Shankar, nodding vigorously. "*That's* the one!"

"Sir, we don't need another one of these," insisted Pihla but the waiter had turned on his heel and fled.

"Alin…" repeated Marcus uneasily, "Councillor Ram knows our Queen Alin…" He looked at Captain Shankar. "Why do I have a bad feeling about this?"

"I think we should go back to the Institute," said Tors, standing up, "like *now*."

Captain Shankar nodded and got to his feet. "I think so too," he said gravely.

"*Excuse me,* sir!" Pihla called after the waiter. "I said we don't need—"

And then the entire place flashed white with an almighty *BOOM*.

* * *

When Pihla opened her eyes, she was sprawled on the floor facing bits of broken glass, the air thick with acrid smoke. Her ears were ringing but she could just make out that people around her were shouting. She struggled to her feet and looked around, covering her nose and mouth with the back of her hand in attempt to breathe easier.

Someone grabbed her shoulder. "You okay?" It was Captain Shankar, sounding extremely muted. Pihla nodded numbly. Ahead, Marcus could be seen crouching next to Tors who was sitting up.

Pihla looked around for Niko and spotted him sitting dazedly a few feet away.

The bomb, she realised, *it was in that cloched salver.* And Niko had been sitting right in front of it.

The force of the blast must've thrown him across, she thought to herself as she stumbled over to help him to his feet. "By Dyaeus, Niko, you were next to the blast! Are you okay? Any bits missing?"

Niko coughed. "Told you that stuff was rank," he said, dusting bits of broken glass and debris off. She let out a sigh of relief, glad he was alive and unhurt.

"We have to get back to the Engineering Institute immediately," said Captain Shankar, gathering them around. "I think this bomb was meant to keep us away. Permanently."

Marcus nodded and they ran for the belt.

PART VI

AGERON

THE NOOSE TIGHTENS

COMITIUM
ALANDIA CITY, AGERON

From Lord Marius' office on the fifteenth floor of the Comitium, Queen Alin looked out the window, her eyes tracing the hot, dusty streets of the city below.

"Ageron himself named it Alandia," she said, "meaning 'river land', to signify the fact that all roads of our empire flow through it."

Alandia, the capital, had been built to replace Lagentia after the LON became sentient and the former capital had to be sealed and destroyed as a result. Alandia had been rebuilt to purposely look different to the former capital. Where Lagentia was a grand old dame with her hefty square stone buildings, Alandia was more refined, vibrant. It was a city of spires—old and new, ancient and modern—beautiful, opulent structures of polished stone and jewel-like colours. Tall, slender and sleek, these cut a fine outline against the horizon, now a vivid blend of scarlets and pinks in the dramatic light of the setting suns.

In the middle, where the three main neighbourhoods of

ALANDIA CITY, AGERON

Storico, Esquilino and Prati intersected, was Otia Park, Alandia's largest urban parkland. For a brief moment, Queen Alin saw it as it used to be—with meandering paths and varied planting, verdant, lush and exotic. Then, her eyes flicked back to the present. Today, the park no longer gleamed like the emerald it once was. Bathed in the ubiquitous crimson hues of the dying suns, its trees and plants had been replaced over the last century and a half with hardier varieties in order to withstand the planet's drier, harsher climes.

Lord Marius stood behind her, looking out at the same view, his hands clasped behind his back.

"How much longer do you think, before Alandia too, becomes uninhabitable?" Queen Alin asked.

"Not as long as we would like," replied Lord Marius. "Heatstorms decimated three cities in the southern hemisphere here last month. It won't be long before Alandia starts experiencing some of these." He turned away from the window and gazed at the live feed projected above his desk. The day's Senate meeting was being streamed directly from the Ecclesia downstairs into his office.

Queen Alin looked on abstractedly. Ever since the surprise announcement of Akseli's impeachment, she had decided to keep abreast of events in the Senate by watching their meetings herself, instead of relying on her spies to report to her. This was within the privacy of Lord Marius' office of course. But with Elena suddenly cutting off all connections via the private portal, Queen Alin was worried. Her initial plan to get Elena to renew relations with House Ageron was now thwarted. With the Senate having voted to impeach Akseli, it was now down to the impending trial itself.

What other levers can I pull to get the trial dropped? Or at the very least, weaken Draeger's case against Akseli? Her options were becoming painfully limited. She had hoped Elena would mend relations between the two Houses, thus making it difficult for Draeger to criticise House Ellagrin for its part in the failed invasion. In fact, she had hoped the relationship between Elena and Draeger would allow the defence to cast doubt on the invasion itself, suggesting Draeger falsified the event to seize the throne from Akseli. None of that mattered now. None of that could be used to help Akseli now. She pursed her lips in frustration. *Oh Elena... what, by Ysgarh, made you paranoid enough to cut all ties and disconnect the portal?* Alin shuddered inwardly. She herself had only just made it back through the portal in time. *I could have been marooned in the Ether if she had disconnected it before I reached the other end.* Gloomily, she turned her attention back towards the ongoing meeting.

Lord Albertus was at it again, voicing his concern at the destruction caused by heatstorms on his three cities. There was panic in his voice as he spoke.

"*There,*" said Lord Marius, slapping the side of his thigh. He pointed at the old Praetor, "He's bringing up the same issue of the heatstorms we just talked about."

"Yes," said Queen Alin and took a seat by Lord Marius for a closer look, "but people *are* being moved to planets farther away from the epicentre of the suns already. What more is Albertus after?"

Lord Marius let out a grunt. "Yes, we have moved the people to Ceos, Deva, and even as far as Vasa—planets with sufficient land for the displaced but land that is unsuitable for cultivation." He paused as Lord Velius interrupted Lord Albertus in the floor.

"...finances are not the problem, my lords. Our coffers will see us out several generations over—the wealth our empire has amassed through the Age of Prosperity has ensured that— but our people cannot eat *ore*..."

ALANDIA CITY, AGERON

"It is all very well to move people to the outer planets," voiced Lord Augusta, "but the displaced require food and jobs. Food which the outer planets are unable to cultivate and jobs which do not exist!"

"If these climate disasters ravage more crops, we will have to impose rationing across the Realm," said Senator Mamercus. "Food imports from outside the Ageron system are but an inbound trickle and with House Ellagrin no longer an ally, shortages will become a reality soon."

"The suns only need take out one of our planets and food shortages will become apparent," cried Lord Augusta. He raised his arms in exasperation. "My lords, this discussion is going round in circles. We *have* to do something. The Exodus *has* to happen, with or without a Gateway."

"And what do you propose we do, my lord?" piped up Lord Velius irritably. "We *cannot* evacuate our people anywhere else but to our outer planets, and that as a temporary measure. Look, we can no longer evacuate to the Ellagrin system because House Ellagrin is now the enemy. There has been *no news* of the Sansari Gate so we may never be able to reopen the Arnemetiaen Gateway, and we cannot evacuate to the Tilkoen system until our *damned* contingent returns from there with confirmation that the Tilkoens will take us in! So, *what else* by Dyaeus, do you suggest we *do,* Lord Augusta?"

"Looks like the Senate is panicking," said Queen Alin, watching carefully.

Lord Marius nodded. "Until Akseli's impeachment is concluded one way or another, we are in a power limbo of sorts," he said. "The Senate is running like a headless chicken whilst Lord Draeger tries to provide direction via his supporters in the background but—"

Queen Alin's lips curled into a wry smile. "But until Akseli is deposed, Draeger cannot impose his will. And without a clear ruler…"

Lord Marius assented. "*Hah!*" he exclaimed, jumping to his feet. "They are fighting!"

Half the Senate had descended onto the floor in what looked like a massive disagreement.

Queen Alin could see Lord Reku shouting, Lord Albertus gesturing lividly and Lord Patrin trying to maintain order. "What's happening?" she asked, not quite believing the scene in front of them.

Lord Marius let out a wicked cackle. "*Mayhem!* No one can agree on a way forward. The Senate's breaking into factions." He looked at her and continued, his eyes gleaming, "You, my lady, may get your wish after all. With all this infighting, Lord Draeger's position will be considerably weakened."

Queen Alin arched an eyebrow. "Weakened and chaotic enough perhaps for us to reverse the motion and drop Akseli's impeachment trial?"

Lord Marius gave a crafty smile. "Oh yes, quite likely," he said with relish. "At this rate, I should think there is *every* possibility of that happening."

Queen Alin leant back. The prospect of overturning Akseli's impeachment gave her hope. *After that, it will be a far simpler plan to obfuscate the facts of the invasion attempt and then reinstate Akseli as Emperor.* But as the Queen Mother rose to put her plans into action, the doors of the Ecclesia flew open. Lord Metavius had burst into the debate chamber. Queen Alin stopped and watched intently.

"My Lords!" Lord Metavius shouted at the top of his voice, stilling the fighting crowd. "Our Emissaries to Tilkoen"—he paused for a quick breath—"They have *returned.*"

EMISSARIES

COMITIUM
ALANDIA CITY, AGERON

"For the record," mentioned Chancellor Rasmus as they made their way to the third floor of the Comitium, "we are about to meet with the social team to discuss the *Istria* settlement in Ceos."

Lord Draeger nodded as the Chancellor led the way to the secured wing of the building, away from prying eyes. "They will be here shortly," the Chancellor explained as they entered the private meeting room. He sat down, slightly breathless from the long walk up the stairs. "So, after this initial meeting, there will be a formal one with the Senate," he said, "and hopefully with good news to share with everyone."

Draeger rubbed the back of his neck and grunted. It was not an easy feat staying calm when one was about to discover the fate of the empire in the next few minutes. "So our emissaries to Tilkoen have returned with a contingent of Tilkoens with them?"

"They have, yes," said Chancellor Rasmus.

"Hmmm," pondered Draeger, "that's a promising indication, I suppose." He glanced at the Chancellor. "These Tilkoens, do they speak Standard Lang? I understand some Tilkoen, however to speak it…." He spread his hands in a gesture of helplessness.

Chancellor Rasmus nodded understandingly. "I have taken the liberty of sending for a translator, just in case," he said.

Draeger raised an eyebrow. "Is that wise?" he asked. "We cannot have any of this meeting leak out uncontrolled, especially if turns out to be the outcome we don't want."

"Courage, my lord. At any rate, the translator I've obtained is someone whom we can trust implicitly," said the Chancellor. He dropped his voice slightly in modesty but there was a hint of pride in it as he spoke: "My daughter, Lianne."

"*Daughter?*" Draeger shot him a surprised look. "I didn't know you had family."

"I don't," replied Chancellor Rasmus. "Not by blood, anyway. Lianne is my adopted child. I have always kept her existence secret. As you know, having no ties, family or alliances has simplified matters in how I operate as Chancellor. It has been my key strength in serving you and your father before you."

Lord Draeger looked at the old man and smiled. "He who has no attachments cannot be bought."

The Chancellor nodded. "Indeed," he said. "I adopted her during the war. She was a Tilkoen child, orphaned when the LON attacked Lagentia. You'll meet her shortly…"

As if on cue, the doors opened and five Ageronians entered. Draeger recognised them as the emissaries he had sent out a century ago. They were followed by another four—two men and two women—visibly shorter and stockier in appearance.

Tilkoens.

ALANDIA CITY, AGERON

They were dressed alike, in neat uniforms of sage, bearing the sigil of House Tilkoen on their right-hand cuff. Last to enter the room was also a Tilkoen, but one dressed in Ageronian garb. An elderly woman, she wore her gray hair in a loosely coiled braid at the nape of her neck.

Lianne.

Draeger's eyes followed her as she walked past at the end of the entourage. *Of course,* he thought to himself as the initial surprise faded, *she would be in her twilight years by now if she was a child when Lagentia was destroyed.* He marvelled at the revelation. The Chancellor and his secrets. And what an unlikely secret indeed! One would be hard pressed to suspect this old woman was in fact the daughter of the relatively youthful-looking Chancellor.

The delegation stood around the table and Draeger turned his attention to matters at hand. Ambassador Alba, tall, formidable and as composed as the day he named her chief negotiator, began the introductions with Lianne translating from the side.

First to be introduced was the Tilkoen councillor, Daxa Serene Light, a tanned, wiry lady with bright eyes and a broad smile on a rather expansive face, features typical of a Tilkoen. Next to her stood councillors Chimini Calm Reflection—a compact, muscular woman with dark, long lashes, Soumy Bright Insight—a brawny but scholarly-looking young man and finally their leader, General Batsa Blazing Light—a retired soldier whose warrior-like moustache gleamed a robust red against his tawny, angular face.

General Batsa extended his hand to Lord Draeger as Ambassador Alba introduced him. He was a large man and the neckline of his tunic, slightly open, revealed a mountainous chest entirely covered with coarse red hair. As they shook hands, his fingers, each adorned with a jewelled ring, winked and glinted cheerily. Lord Draeger found himself liking the hearty and rather pugnacious general.

"Chancellor Rasmus informs me my niece is in your service, Lord Draeger," said the General.

Draeger glanced questioningly at Chancellor Rasmus who gave a nod back. "General Batsa Blazing Light," the Chancellor explained with a smile, "is no other than Pihla's uncle."

"One of two uncles actually," replied General Batsa beaming widely. "I have a younger brother, Chief Air Marshal Batsa Blazing Calm, who serves back in Tilkoen." He paused briefly as Lianne translated his words.

"Ah," replied Lord Draeger nodding, "A thousand pities she cannot meet you at the moment, General—your niece is on a mission."

"We can discuss my niece at a later time but for now, I believe we have more urgent matters to discuss." General Batsa removed his helmet and sat down heavily at the table. The rest of his delegation followed suit.

Tilkoen directness, noted Draeger, glad for once to get straight to the point. He sat down next to Lianne and clasped his hands together attentively.

"Ambassador Alba and her team had shared with us some data on the state of your planetary system," said General Batsa, launching directly into business. "We fed them through our AIs and your estimations are in line with our initial modelling, in that we expect things to escalate exponentially in the next few decades, in particular Anavio, Bellun and Trimon, the planets closest to your suns."

Draeger nodded. "Your estimations are correct. Evacuations have already been in progress for some time now. Until recently, our people have been evacuated to settlements in the Ellagrin system, under our Exodus programme, for over a century now and we continue, at present, to relocate entire cities to the outer planets within the Ageron system itself."

General Batsa nodded. "Your situation is very grave as the data shows. We are here therefore, on behalf of House Tilkoen, to extend our help to Ageron. You may extend your Exodus programme to the Tilkoen system." The General gestured at his colleagues. "My councillors and I are here to work out the details of what will be a mass migration effort between both Houses. We will need to agree the where and how. Expatriation and integration. Your people will be integrated with ours in cities all over Tilkoen. Work has already begun back home on our planets in order to accomodate the anticipated influx into our cities."

"Your cities?" enquired Chancellor Rasmus. "Would it not be easier to open up new areas for development?"

General Batsa shook his head firmly. "We observe strict policies on any clearing of our Dimaga forests." He looked round the table. "Which by the way, applies to *all*, our own people included." He beamed proudly. "In fact over eighty percent of the Tilkoen system is primeval forest, accounting for the balanced wellbeing of every planet."

Lord Draeger nodded as Lianne translated for him. "You have our wholehearted gratitude and thanks, General Batsa," he said. "House Tilkoen has once again come to Ageron's aid. This is a debt we will not forget and one we will repay with interest."

The General waved away his thanks warmly. "Our two Houses have always worked well together," he said matter-of-factly. "The pragmatic commercial sensitivities of House Ageron and House Tilkoen's interest in technology have naturally tended to align with each other."

Lord Draeger nodded. Indeed, it was this commonality

that led to the successful building of the Gateways all those centuries ago.

"Unlike the Ellagrins of course." The General scowled. "Flighty *aesthetics*, pah!" He leant closer. "I must warn you," he said, his voice tremulous, "we have highly developed AIs back on Tilkoen and their prediction models suggest very strongly that Ellagrin will invade Ageron at some point soon, in the event the binary suns begin to fail and the balance of political power shifts."

Chancellor Rasmus let out a loud cackle much to the General and the delegation's surprise. "My apologies," he hastened to say. "Your predictions are impressive and if I might add, *entirely correct*! However, I'm afraid what you've kindly warned us of has already happened. Not too long ago in fact."

"Ah-*hah*!" bellowed the General in response. "The Four, our AIs, are never wrong!" He eyed Chancellor Rasmus keenly. "I'm guessing the invasion was successfully thwarted? Otherwise we wouldn't be here having this meeting…"

"Yes," replied Chancellor Rasmus. "Fortunately so. Although as a consequence of that, we find ourselves at an impasse with House Ellagrin at the moment."

"*Harrumph*!" The General brought his fist down on the table with a bang. "Sly, conniving, cretinous nation of frothy overdressed landlords!" he bellowed. "I'll tell you what we'd do to those double-crossers before they come trampling their peasant feet on our soil!" He paused and drew himself up, his tone suddenly sombre. "Lord Draeger and Chancellor Rasmus, if you permit," he said seriously, "…a word, in *private*?"

Lord Draeger gave Chancellor Rasmus a nod and soon the room was emptied leaving only him, the Chancellor and

ALANDIA CITY, AGERON

General Batsa, with Lianne to translate. The old Chancellor closed the doors softly behind the delegates.

"It is a pity we had not arrived early enough to have warned you of the impending invasion attempt," said General Batsa as they all returned to their seats.

Lord Draeger nodded. "That would have been useful to know," he said a little ruefully, "but how did you come about that prediction?"

"We Tilkoens have come a long way since the early days of predictive tech," continued the general. "Our AIs are highly cognisant and we have for the past five hundred years governed our nation, our way of life, based on guidance derived from the AIs' predictions."

"Are you saying that you base your governing decisions on predictions from programmes?" The Chancellor was credulous.

General Batsa nodded his head. "Do not be so quick to judge, Chancellor Rasmus," he said. "It is not as simple as that and we certainly do not blindly follow the Four's predictions." He looked at them. "We are fully aware that AIs predictions are not guaranteed in any way. However, they provide us with *possibilities,* likely scenarios, each with a quantifiable probability, and it is based on these scenarios that the Tilkoen Congress makes its decisions." General Batsa sank into his seat with a sigh. "So far our AIs have not been wrong. Not for the last five hundred years in fact. They predicted the re-emergence of Nehisi from detected activity in your region, they predicted the accelerated decline of your suns before the signs were evident, and they predicted House Ageron would reach out to Ellagrin to resettle their people."

"Hardly a surprise though is it?" said Chancellor Rasmus. "The Ellagrin system, after all, is the system closest to ours."

"True, but we know that Ellagrin does not physically have

enough space to resettle all Ageronians," continued the General. "Not for all the *ore* you can throw at them. There just isn't enough space. So somehow, billions of Ageronians *must* go somewhere and this is the issue we must discuss but with *utmost secrecy!*"

General Batsa looked at them and then continued, "With the Tilkoen planetary system adjacent to Ellagrin's, the outcome as it would seem would be inevitable: *Ellagrin will invade Tilkoen.*"

Draeger and the Chancellor looked at him astounded.

"House Ellagrin has never sought to invade Tilkoen. There is no reason to. Besides, the recent failed invasion attempt has weakened Ellagrin," said Lord Draeger. "They are in no position to invade you anyway."

"Lord Draeger is correct," said the Chancellor. "Ellagrin's recent failed hostilities against us have weakened them greatly. It would be impossible for them to mount any form of attack on anyone. Is it entirely possible that your predictions are wrong?"

General Batsa shook his head and ran his thick fingers through his beard several times. "The simulations predicted Ellagrin invading us upon achieving an alliance with Ageron. They also predicted the same outcome even in the event of a failed alliance with Ageron. It is curious yes? In fact, they predicted given the opportunity and time, Ellagrin will invade any damn empire it can lay its hands on. Ageron included." He eyed Lord Draeger and the Chancellor interestedly. "We ran the simulations for months," he said. "Months and months, using different data, completely unrelated data, *random* data. But every single time, the outcome from the AIs was the same: they all predicted that an attack from Ellagrin was inevitable. In fact, our AIs predicted that attacks from Ellagrin on both

ALANDIA CITY, AGERON

House Tilkoen and Ageron were likely to occur given sufficient time."

"Yes, but on what *basis?*" asked the Chancellor. "If anything, I would have thought *we'd* be more likely to invade you than the Ellagrins."

"As if we haven't enough problems of our own..." grumbled Lord Draeger.

General Batsa permitted the Supreme Commander a smile before answering the Chancellor's question. "That unfortunately, the AIs can't tell us," he said. "They can't identify the specific triggers for these predicted scenarios, which leaves us in the dark. For millennia, Houses Tilkoen and Ellagrin have existed peacefully, neither one needing nor coveting anything from the other. Rivalry between Tilkoen and Ellagrin does not exist the way it did between Ageron and Ellagrin during the Age of Prosperity. Our Houses are not in competition with each other—Ellagrins farm and Tilkoens engineer. If anything, these factors promote cooperation between the two Houses resulting in increased benefits for all. Why would Ellagrin, all of a sudden, decide to invade us when they've not had any reason to for millennia, not now and not in the past?"

General Batsa stopped to mop his brow. "Now, *this* is where it gets interesting," he said. "We couldn't understand why the simulations were giving the same results every single time so we looked into the data that was entered. And there is a lot! Our AIs utilise all sorts of data in their predictions: unconnected data, historical data, political events, current news, solar forecasts. In short, *everything*. And there it was..." His eyes gleamed. "The simulations all had one common thread. Two pieces of seemingly unrelated data—a shared bloodline between Ellagrin and Ageron, and the imminent destruction of the Ageron star system. Somehow these two findings are inextricably linked and *somehow* they are the key factors driving our AI's decision trees to the same conclusion."

"How so?" asked the Chancellor, bewildered.

"We don't know," admitted General Batsa. "The AIs merely predict scenarios but as to the triggers behind those scenarios, their underlying causes…there is no way to pinpoint these out of the billions of contributing factors used in their simulations." He paused and looked at Lord Draeger gravely. "Suffice to say, all our simulations indicate Ellagrin as an aggressive force. In time, given the chance, House Ellagrin will attack our Houses."

"Are you certain?"

General Batsa nodded vehemently. "Whatever it is, it's driving the results to the same conclusion. Every. Single. Time."

Lord Draeger and the Chancellor remained silent, deep in thought.

Then General Batsa spoke again. This time his voice was quiet, a guttural whisper almost. "This is why we are moving to demilitarise Ellagrin," he said. "To neutralise them before they become a threat. We will strike them before they strike us."

The Chancellor stared at the General, not quite believing his ears.

"Demilitarisation of Ellagrin? By force?" voiced Lord Draeger.

General Batsa nodded. "It has not been an easy decision for us, nor one we have taken lightly. Plans were drawn up and preparations spanning years were implemented once we were convinced this was the only way forward." He looked at them. "Our destroyers will breach Ellagrin space any day now with their planet Skansgarden first to fall. My brother, Blazing Calm, holds command."

ALANDIA CITY, AGERON

The General stood up to leave the room. As he reached the door, he turned to Lord Draeger and smiled. "Our actions are taken purely on the basis of logic. This demilitarisation and disarmament of Ellagrin will prevent future wars and remove any opportunity for future hostilities or invasion from them. We believe this to be the more civilised approach to the Ellagrin threat." He nodded and added, "And who knows, perhaps in time, it will be both our Houses that carve up the Ellagrin empire between us."

WHISPERS

RED PALACE, AGERON

Queen Alin climbed the steps to the top of the tower. It had taken her the best part of an hour to navigate her way from the main residential area of the palace to the ancient quarters and a further half hour to reach the room at the top of the disused tower. Pausing a moment to regain her breath, she produced an old key from the folds of her robe and slid it into the rather ancient-looking keyhole. The door opened soundlessly, revealing a circular room surrounded by windows cut into the thick, stone walls. Queen Alin closed the door behind her and entered. It was bare, but awash with the blood-red hues of the setting suns streaming through the windows, it echoed the ominous portent she felt within.

The Queen Mother stood before one of the windows and looked out at the harsh, arid landscape beyond as she waited. The Red Mountains stretched before her in all their crimson glory, sharp and craggy, their razor-like ridges dominating the landscape for miles around. The scene, ravaged as it looked, was beautiful in its own perverse way.

Could it be that I have grown accustomed to the Realm? wondered the Queen Mother, comparing the scene before her to the rolling green hills of the Summer Palace from which she had recently fled. By comparison, Ellagrin's lush green landscape and clear blue skies seemed almost garish, a glib contrast even, to the harsh, unforgiving landscape of Ageron. Perhaps this landscape captured her frame of mind better than that of her original home, Ellagrin.

The return of the emissaries from Tilkoen was a harsh blow to her and Akseli. Overnight, this news had stopped the infighting within the Senate and with that, the opportunity to get many of the wavering senators to drop Akseli's trial.

The returning emissaries have brought hope, she thought bitterly, *and hope is the last thing we need at this stage.* Akseli's trial would now go ahead as planned and she had no doubt Lord Draeger would be gunning to have him sentenced and executed as quickly as possible. *So that he can get on with resuming the Exodus and saving his people, that righteous fool.* She frowned as she continued to look out the window.

At last, as the scarlet fingers of the suns dipped below the window sills, the door opened. Queen Alin turned around expectantly. Her visitor had finally arrived.

"My lady..." The woman bowed. A greying lock of hair tumbled out from the cowl of her cloak.

Queen Alin nodded and greeted her by name, "Lianne."

"I came as soon as I could get away unnoticed, my lady," said Lianne. "I have news..."

"So I heard in your brief message," replied Queen Alin. "I myself was also at the Comitium not too long ago, but you mentioned this was secret and... *significant?*"

Lianne nodded vigorously, her eyes shining, eager to please as ever. "Our emissaries," she said, "the ones we sent to the Tilkoen system all those years ago... They have returned and with them a few members from the Tilkoen council as well."

Queen Alin let out a dismissive snort. "Everyone knows that," she said. "Did you call me here to tell me that?"

"No, my lady, there is *more*," said Lianne. "You see, everyone else apart from the Supreme Commander, the Chancellor and the Tilkoen General were told to leave the room. And myself of course. You see, I had to translate for them—"

"So?" Queen Alin let slip a hint of impatience in her tone. *For a Tilkoen, this damp flannel of a fool certainly displays none of their renown promptness nor efficiency.*

"The Tilkoens are about to embark on an offensive to demilitarise Ellagrin, my lady," Lianne burst out. "Imminently."

Queen Alin shot her a sharp look. "What do you mean? The Tilkoens are about to attack Ellagrin?"

"Not about to," replied Lianne. "They already have. They sent out destroyers and fightherships to the Ellagrin system a decade ago. Apparently their AIs predicted the threat of invasion from the Ellagrins and they're doing this as a defensive measure."

"I don't understand," said Queen Alin, puzzled. "Ellagrin is in no position to invade anyone, not anymore since the failed invasion at Lagentia. Are you sure of this?"

Lianne nodded vigorously. "The Tilkoens were adamant their predictions were veritable. The Tilkoen General, General Batsa, said their fleet is expected to reach Ellagrin space imminently." She looked at Queen Alin. "What will you do my lady?"

The Queen Mother looked at her. "What do you mean?" she asked.

"I mean, Ellagrin's empress," said Lianne. "Aren't you going to warn her? I mean, you're family after all…"

A look of surprise flickered across Queen Alin's face. "What did you say?" she said sharply.

Lianne flushed and bit her lip.

The Queen Mother leaned forward. "The Ellagrin system is at least two decades' spaceflight away. And if I did choose to warn her, how would I do that exactly? " she asked, her eyes boring into Lianne.

"The… the private portal?" stammered Lianne, "I thought you could reach her that way, perhaps."

For a moment Queen Alin stared at her. Then she reached out for Lianne's face. Lianne flinched, but the Queen only patted her cheek lightly as though she were an adored pet. "And how have you come to know about this private portal?" The Queen asked, lifting Lianne's face so it came into full view. *There is not a single soul on Ageron other than Draeger, Akseli and the Chancellor that know about the private portal. Neither Draeger nor Akseli would have cause to encounter Lianne, which means…*

And then it dawned on her. *Lianne must have learnt this from Rasmus, the only other person who would know.* But how and why would the Chancellor divulge this to an ordinary civil servant like Lianne?

Rasmus, you keeper of secrets, she thought to herself intrigued. *Well, it would seem I am about to uncover a secret of yours too, you old snake. Who is Lianne to you? Friend? Lover?* But to Alin, they did not appear compatible in the way lovers were.

"I… I must have heard it somewhere, my lady," stuttered Lianne. "A rumour… I must be mistaken."

"Mistaken indeed," said the Queen Mother drily. She considered a moment, then continued. "Ellagrin is no longer the concern of the Realm. After all, we are supposedly in conflict with them." *At any rate, Elena has disconnected the portal so I can't warn her even if I wanted to.* Her eyes took on a calculated look and she looked at Lianne. "Well, we do nothing," she said, impassively.

"No, no, of course," agreed Lianne hastily. "My lady, if there's nothing else you require of me…"

Queen Alin looked at her and smiled. "You have done well, my dear," she said, "and I appreciate your coming all the way here to give me this information."

Lianne blushed and looked like a pleased puppy.

"You must have had a long, tiring journey," said the Queen Mother. "Why don't you stay and rest first. You're not expected at the Comitium yet are you?"

"No, not immediately, my Lady," replied Lianne, "but I should really go home—" She sounded a little uncertain.

"Nonsense." Queen Alin waved her protestation off. "As you can see, there is plenty of space here at the Palace,"—she leant forward—"so much that *no one* will even know you are here." The Queen Mother grasped Lianne's shoulders in a taloned grip. "My dear," she said sweetly, "I think I should like to get to know you better."

"But, but my lady…," faltered Lianne.

"You will stay with me and we shall get to know each other better." The Queen Mother's eyes glimmered a steelier blue than ever. "After all this fine work, did you really think you would be leaving so soon?"

AKSELI

⚜

Later that evening, in his luxurious quarters in a secured wing of the Red Palace, a servant girl served Akseli sweetmeats, dried bloodfruit soaked in amarinthe and some bread with honey. The surroundings were comfortable and lavish, befitting an Emperor, albeit in name only. In truth, they were but a gilded cage and the only key to freedom was Akseli winning the trial.

Akseli reached for the girl, grabbing her buttocks as she walked past him with the tray. She squealed in protest, but not too forcefully for his temper was well known amongst those who served him.

"Come," he said, his voice commanding, "join me." The girl hesitated but in her fear, made no attempt to leave the room. He gestured for her to sit on his lap.

"My lord," she protested weakly as he reached out to pull her in. His hands were in the midst of undoing her corset when the doors swung opened.

"Leave us," commanded Queen Alin. The girl hurried away,

arms clutched tight in attempt to hide her exposed breasts. Akseli leaned back eyeing his mother coldly.

"To what do I owe the pleasure of your visit, Mother?"

"How are you relaxed at a time like this? Draeger has brought forward the impeachment trial. Do you realise you could be facing execution this time next week?"

"I am well aware, Mother," said Akseli. "As I am aware too of the setback to my public campaign by the untimely return of our emissaries." He pushed his plate away with a clatter and reached out for the amarinthe instead. "I can only do so much with popular rhetoric. The *Let's Make Ageron Great Again* campaign doesn't quite have the same ring of urgency it had before, no thanks to the joyful optimism cast by the successful return of our emissaries."

"The bloodthirsty son of a bitch," said Queen Alin venomously. "Bringing forward the trial like this. He knows the Senate won't care if you hang or not, now that they can evacuate everyone to Tilkoen." Her eyes narrowed. "Still, it's the voting at the end of the trial that counts. He needs a two-thirds majority vote in order to convict you and we must stop that at all cost."

"We need to ensure we have enough supporters in my favour for the Senate vote at the end of the trial," said Akseli. His voice was strained, reflecting his uncertainty on that front. "And as for the trial itself, I have done what I can in terms of witnesses—there should be enough to cast doubt on the events that occurred in Lagentia."

The Queen Mother nodded. "If we could cast doubt as to whether the invasion attempt even occurred, that will put our defence in a stronger position." She sighed bitterly. "If only Elena hadn't cut off ties so suddenly. We could have cast Draeger's motives into doubt by citing her involvement with him."

"At the end of the day, everything hinges on the two-thirds majority vote," voiced Akseli. "We need the Praetors on our side if we are to swing this my way." He downed another nervous draught of amarinthe.

"I know, I know," said Queen Alin, frowning. "I have been working on Lord Patrin…"

Akseli almost choked. "Patrin? That straight-laced canid? He's almost as bad as Rasmus—you won't sway him even if you threatened to bed him Mother," scoffed Akseli.

"I went to see his wife actually," said Queen Alin tolerantly, "although I did meet him as well."

"Well, what did you do there? Ask him to corral the other Praetors for my release?"

"No,"said Alin, becoming annoyed at her son's petulance, "I already tried that months earlier when the motion for impeachment was first tabled, but he declined. Anyway, his wife, Lady Ursule is expecting soon."

"What do I *care*, Mother?" spat Akseli.

His mother continued unperturbed. "Lady Ursule was most grateful for my little gift to her in her time of need."

Akseli eyed his mother suspiciously. "What gift?"

"Anneliese, my handmaid," replied Queen Alin. "Lady Ursule has no competent servants in the house."

Akseli clenched his fists in exasperation. "I have no interest in your resolving other people's domestic issues, Mother," he retorted. "How is all this going to help us with Patrin himself?"

Queen Alin gave him a sharp look. Akseli stopped and eyed his mother warily.

"We know we need Patrin to support us because he can influence the others," said Queen Alin. "The Praetors like him. They look to him for guidance because he is impartial, non-extremist and he supports no faction. He is the *safe* choice."

"Yes, yes, we know that," said Akseli, getting impatient

again, "but that also makes him impervious to our attempts to influence him. He is another Rasmus. And that is useless to us."

Queen Alin eyed him cunningly. "Ah, but everyone has a weakness, son. A secret. Even Patrin and you'll find the impartial Praetor far more amenable to our plight than you think, once he knows that we know his."

Akseli looked at his Mother. He had no doubt she had set in motion a trap of some sort for Patrin. *Beware the one bearing gifts.*

"That may be, Mother," he said calculatingly, "but speaking of secrets, the Chancellor Rasmus still holds sway over you with yours. You may find your hands tied if you try to do anything to sway the votes. In fact, you may find you can't even make your move on Lord Patrin for that matter."

Queen Alin's eyes glittered. "Ah," she said, "but at last, I have found the old man's weakness. A *secret*."

Akseli lifted an eyebrow. "Oh?"

Queen Alin took his hands into hers and gripped them tightly. "It has been a long time coming but we have had a stroke of luck, my son," she said. She leant forward to whisper in his ear. "Rasmus has a *daughter*."

Akseli was taken aback. "You *are* full of surprises today, Mother."

"Mmm-hmmm," nodded Queen Alin. "With that, we finally have a way to control Rasmus."

"So, with Rasmus out of the way, we need Lord Patrin to convince the other Praetors and their senators to vote appropriately at the end of the trial," Akseli said.

The Queen Mother nodded. "That is the plan, yes," she said, her mouth drawn into a thin, apprehensive line. Then, she sat up straight. "Speaking of the unexpected," she said, "you'll never believe this, but according to the contingent from Tilkoen, it appears House Tilkoen are about to demilitarise Ellagrin!"

Akseli arched an eyebrow, intrigued. "Oh? On what basis? And does Elena know this?"

"No, she doesn't. The Tilkoens say they are doing this to save both their people and the people of Ellagrin, by preventing future acts of aggression from Ellagrin."

Akseli paused for a moment, then looked at his mother, noting the expression on her face. "And you are not going to tell her?"

"No," she replied. "I can't anyway. No one can. She disconnected the private portal after the Doges' attempt on her life."

Her son eyed her cannily. "I see," he said slowly, "but even if you could, you weren't going to warn her anyway, were you?"

Queen Alin returned his gaze levelly. "No," she said as she rose to leave. "No, I wasn't. Now let's get to work. We have a trial to stop."

LORD MARIUS COLLECTS

ALANDIA CITY, AGERON

*L*ord Marius was on his way out when Metella, his servant, caught him just in time to deliver a message.

"What, *tonight?*" asked Lord Marius, "but I'm on my way out…"

"Forgive me, my lord," pressed Metella. "She says it cannot wait. It is tonight. At the agreed time."

Lord Marius sighed and shook his head. "Very well," he said as he adjusted his cloak and hat. Marius glanced at the time and decided he could afford to walk there. "I shall make my way there now," he told Metella who nodded dutifully before closing the door.

The route Lord Marius took was a scenic one: past the communal gardens next door, then across the piazza and down a cobbled lane flanked by neat stucco townhouses. The leisurely walk took him slightly over half an hour, enough he surmised, to make anyone following him think he was out for fresh air.

At length he arrived at a rather conservative-looking apartment block in the middle class neighbourhood of Regola.

He glanced up at the second floor, satisfied to see the window he was after glowing softly from behind closed curtains, a sign it was occupied.

Lord Marius produced a key and let himself into the building. He walked up the stairs with the quiet ease of a cat and stopped outside the apartment at the end of the corridor. The door, as promised, had been left slightly ajar. Taking out his recording device, he discreetly flicked the switch on and entered.

The apartment was compact and a little shabby—a single room large enough to fit an area for cooking and eating, and a corner for sleeping partitioned out with a floor-to-ceiling length curtain drawn across the width of the room.

Lord Marius strode across noiselessly and pushed the curtain back to ensure his recording device took in the full view of what lay behind. And what lay behind, in perfect pose, was a very naked Lord Patrin thrusting rather enthusiastically into the rear of a very accommodating young lad on all fours, equally busy servicing the needs of a naked female at the same time.

"Lord Patrin!" bellowed Lord Marius jubilantly.

Lord Patrin gave a shriek of surprise, pulled out and fumbled about helplessly for something to cover himself up. At the interruption, the lad straightened up, and despite Patrin's emphatic gestures for him to clear off, leant back to relax in full-frontal nudity. The girl too, remained on the bed, her nakedness unashamedly in full view of Lord Marius and his recorder. She appeared unperturbed in the slightest.

"Why young Annius!" exclaimed Lord Marius, clearly enjoying himself. "Applying yourself beyond your duties in the Admin department I see."

"My lord," the young man acknowledged with a lazy smile and stretched himself out even more, leaving nothing of his slender, well-toned figure left to the imagination, much to Lord Patrin's agitation.

By now, Lord Patrin had managed to pull his pants on. "Get out of here!" he yelled, frustratedly waving at Annius and the girl. They both got off the bed, taking their time.

Lord Marius laughed. "Working late tonight eh, Patrin? Is this your idea of an office get-together?"

"Mind your own business, Marius," hissed Lord Patrin, "and turn that damn thing off!"

"Now, now, Patrin," said Lord Marius cheerfully, "there is no need for such harsh words between friends." He sat down on the bed in front of Patrin, camera still recording. "Now who would have guessed that a respected Praetor such as yourself would be indulging in such infidelity?" he said reproachfully. "And with Lady Ursule having just given you your first child too." He clucked his tongue disapprovingly. "And what's all this?" Lord Marius moved nearer for a close-up view of the empty Stim syringes lying carelessly on the bed. "Our virtuous, principled Praetor getting high in a depraved orgy with clerk and nanny? Your good lady wife not enough for you?"

"Turn… that… thing *off*!" screamed Lord Patrin, his eyes ablaze with anger and desperation. If this ever got out…

And then it clicked.

"What the fuck do you want Marius?" he said, red with rage.

Lord Marius clicked the recorder off and smiled at him. "Ah," he said amiably, "we finally cut to the chase. Excellent! I never liked foreplay, even in conversation."

Lord Patrin glanced at him nervously. "Don't… you can't… you can't tell my wife," he said. "Please…"

Lord Marius burst out laughing uncontrollably. When he finally stopped, he said, tears in his eyes and in danger of starting off again, "My dear Lord Patrin, of all the things I expected to hear, this was the last! Here I am thinking you were more afraid of your reputation in tatters, yet here you are, terrified of Lady Ursule finding out. By Dyaeus, the things that never cease to surprise me!"

"So you're not going to tell her?" stammered Lord Patrin, a glimmer of hope in his eyes.

"Well that all depends on you," replied Lord Marius. He dangled the recorder to focus the man's attention. "I need your help."

"M… my help?"

Lord Marius nodded at Lord Patrin, his look deadly serious. "Yes. The time to shine is upon you, Lord Patrin. And this is what I need you to do…"

PART VII

TILKOEN

ENGINEERING INSTITUTE

CHATADHARAM CITY, TILKOEN

They caught the belt back to the Institute, even running on it in order to get there faster.

"Dr Shanoli?" called out Captain Shankar as they burst into the lab. A few technicians stopped work to stare at him. "Where is the beacon?" demanded the captain.

A youngish technician looked up from his bench and stammered, "With Dr Shanoli, sir."

"And where is Dr Shanoli?" asked the Captain. The technician stared back at him blankly. With one hand, the captain lifted him bodily from his chair and looked him in the eye. *Where did Dr Shanoli go?*

"Up... upstairs," the young man stammered. "We had finished adapting the beacon and Councillor Ram came in to tell us you had called for the debrief. So, Dr Shanoli took the beacon and followed him upstairs."

"I did *not* call for a debrief," said Captain Shankar. "Now, upstairs *where?*"

"I... I'm not sure. Meeting rooms?" replied the technician.

Captain Shankar let him go and spoke into his wristband,

"Dexa, confirm Protocol Level 1 lockdown status. Have either Dr Shanoli or Councillor Ram been detected?"

Captain, lockdown was initiated immediately, upon your instructions received twenty minutes ago, came the familiar composed voice of Dexa, sounding perhaps a little tinier, coming from his wristband. *Unfortunately, neither individuals have been detected on any of the floors. However, I can also confirm no persons have exited the building as per lockdown protocol.*

The captain turned to the others. "The lockdown secures all exits on each floor as well as that of the entire building. They are still here as no one can exit their floor nor the building itself. I have teams searching each floor as we speak. We'll take the twenty-fifth floor where the meeting rooms are."

The lift took them there in minutes.

"Just as well your Level 1 Protocol rights allow you use of these lifts," said Niko. "Imagine walking all the way up from the basement to the twenty-fifth."

They split up at the twenty-fifth, flinging open the door of every meeting room to search. They ended up in the last room at the end of the corridor, empty-handed.

"They're not here," Marcus panted.

Captain Shankar glanced at his wristband for the latest updates. "The security teams have just completed their search on the floors below ours—no joy. *Where* can they be?"

"Don't you have cameras in the building?" asked Niko. "Wouldn't they have spotted Dr Shanoli or Councillor Ram?"

Captain Shankar frowned. "We do and they *should* have been seen but they haven't. Not by the cameras, not the bio-scans, not the detectors."

"So you have all these detection systems yet no trace of either person?" asked Pihla. "I thought you even detect people by their pheromones."

"But we do," said Captain Shankar. "As with most places, there are cameras, motion sensors, heat sensors, body scanners, pheromone gauges and voice scanners in this building. Having said that, there are ways to bypass the bio-scans but not easily." He looked really worried. "Councillor Ram obviously planned this in advance. This was premeditated."

"So here's a thought," Tors spoke up. "Your scans may not be working but as a fugitive or thief, I'd still need to decamp somewhere if I were still here in the building, before I make my escape somehow. Somewhere where no one's watching. Somewhere where there are no cameras or bio detectors or anything like that." She looked at Captain Shankar. "Is there anywhere in this building like that besides the secure labs underground?"

The captain straightened up. "There is actually," he said. "The only other place we don't watch in this building would be Dr Shanoli's office due to the nature of her work. It's just on the thirtieth. *Hurry!*"

They ran for the lifts.

* * *

THE DOOR to the doctor's office was slightly ajar.

Captain Shankar pushed it open some more. A bare ankle, at an unnatural angle, lay on the floor, visible from the doorway. A sharp draft of air breezed past.

"The window!" yelled the captain, charging in as fast as he could. He sprinted past Dr Shanoli's body and headed straight for the balcony, just in time to see Councillor Ram heaving himself clumsily over the glass railings, ready to jump into an urbanglider hovering mid-air beside it.

Captain Shankar launched himself at the councillor with a belligerent bellow. Wrapping his arms around the Councillor's wide midriff, he grabbed him tight to prevent him from leaving the building.

Councillor Ram kicked at the captain, wriggling his fat body violently, in attempt to extricate himself. The urban-glider floated next to the balcony, tantalisingly close by, as the two men tussled with each other, one trying to get off the balcony, the other attempting to keep him on. The councillor eyed his glider desperately as he tried to push Captain Shankar away, his face red and puffy, his breath laboured from the exertion of wrestling with the formidable captain. The top of the beacon peeped precariously out of his shirt pocket, pushed out by all that struggling.

"Get *oooffff!*" he screamed in exasperation as his fat fingers fumbled to push the beacon back into the pocket. Captain Shankar spotted it and made a grab for it. In the heat of the moment, with all the councillor's writhing, the beacon slipped out!

Councillor Ram snatched at it frantically, managed to catch it but squeezed too tightly. With a slip, the beacon launched upwards into the air.

"No! *No!*"

In desperation, the councillor kicked himself free and leapt for it. He missed, fell forward and lurched over the railing.

From behind, Marcus and Niko rushed forward to help but Captain Shankar had already launched himself off the balcony to catch the beacon. Niko lunged forward and made a wild grab for him, catching him by his ankle, just in time. For Councillor Ram, it was too late. As Niko yanked Captain Shankar onto the balcony to safety, the councillor hit ground.

"Good catch," Captain Shankar wheezed, still hanging onto the beacon for dear life as the two men collapsed on the balcony floor.

Niko waved his thanks off. "You're crazy," he said, gasping for breath. "You were going to go down with the beacon!"

Captain Shankar tried to catch his breath. "My orders were to protect the beacon at all costs," he rasped, "especially when billions of lives depend on it."

Niko stared at him for a minute then nodded soberly, agreeing. "But still crazy," he said.

* * *

THE OTHERS RUSHED IN, crowding around them.

"It's here," said the captain, still lying on the ground. He held up the beacon for Councillor Hamish to see, "Undamaged."

There was a collective sigh of relief.

"I didn't realise Tilkoen loyalty included sacrificing oneself in the process," added Pihla, helping the captain up. She turned to extend her hand to Niko but he was already on his feet and busy dusting himself off.

"Ach! Dexa alerted us to Councillor Ram's suspicious movements on the balcony a few moments ago," said Councillor Hamish as the security team swept into the room. She shook her head as they covered up Dr Shanoli's body, "Tragically, it appears we are too late."

"Well, fortunately, Captain Shankar saved the day," said Niko with a look of admiration for the captain.

Pihla glanced at him, noting the hint of discomfit beneath those words as well. She elbowed him. "*Fool*," she said. "The captain saved the beacon but you saved his bacon. I'd say it was *you* that saved the day."

For once, Niko couldn't think of a snarky comeback to that.

As Dr Shanoli's body was taken away, Councillor Hamish gave Captain Shankar a sympathetic pat on the arm.

"We think Councillor Ram had ties with House Ageron's Queen Mother, Akseli's mother," he told her, "and both do not want the Gateway reopened."

"Well, I'm afraid the emperor and the Queen Mother are going to be disappointed," said Councillor Hamish, barely able to contain her excitement. "We have a Go from Congress to activate the Sansari Gate. You, my friends, are going home via the Arnemetiaen Gateway!"

ARNEMETIAEN GATEWAY

The large concourse of Sansari station looked eerily empty as they gathered under the towering presence of its monumental Gate. The station and its immediate surroundings had been sealed off by perimeter forcefields. It couldn't feel more different to the day they first found themselves here, where the entire area swarmed with protesters.

"This way," said Captain Shankar, leading them into the station building itself.

They're certainly keeping this lowkey, noted Tors. Which made sense of course. As Councillor Hamish explained, until the necessary preparations and logistics had been agreed between Houses Ageron and Tilkoen, news of the Sansari Gate being functional once again had been muted, although from what Tors observed, it appeared Tilkoens in general were rather unexcited with the news. *Perhaps also because the debate and ultimately the decision to resettle Ageronians in Tilkoen had been decided decades ago.* This was something the Tilkoens had been expecting to happen for some time now.

Despite the general disinterest from the public, security,

though purposefully inconspicuous, was tight with the military posted both inside and outside the seal forcefield to prevent any unauthorised or accidental incursions into the area.

Inside the station were the others, waiting. Tors could see Councillors Navi and Hamish chatting with the rest of the High Twelve, all dressed in their distinctive robes, minus of course, the recently departed Councillor Ram. A few of the councillors shimmered like ghostly apparitions.

Holos, realised Tors. *Of course! Not everyone would be witnessing this momentous occasion in person.*

"Ach!" beamed Councillor Hamish and waved them over excitedly. "Are you ready?" she asked.

"As ready as we'll ever be," replied Marcus, flashing Tors a slightly conflicted smile.

At that moment, it dawned on her that their search was finally over and that realisation hit her with a feeling of apprehension. The prospect of returning to Ageron suddenly felt very real and with it, the one person she had avoided thinking about all this time: Draeger.

Pihla gazed at the Sansari Gate, its towering vertex gradually disappearing in the burgeoning darkness of the evening. She turned to Councillor Hamish and asked, "How by Dyaeus will you be able to hide the Gateway once it's activated? It will be visible for miles around."

"Ach!" said the councillor. "That's easy. The surrounding forcefield emits an accompanying holographic cloaking projection. No one outside will see anything different to what the Gate looks like on any other normal night."

"I see," said Pihla, nodding appreciatively.

Then, with typical Tilkoen promptness, Councillor Hamish gave a nod to the engineer to power up the Gate.

After checking the diagnostics on the control panel, he gave them all the thumbs up.

"Aye, we are *ready*!" announced Councillor Hamish. There was an expectant hush all around.

There was a hum as the Sansari Gate started up.

Tors flinched at the sound and Marcus shot her a sideways glance. He extended his hand out to her, a touch of concern in his face.

He knows it reminds me of the time at the Lagentian Gate...

Tors reached for the offered hand gratefully and together, they held hands as the familiar white ribbon of light flickered to life.

Gradually the glaring whiteness lengthened and spiralled inwards, incomprehensibly and unfathomably so. The hum intensified and the Gateway began to take shape until finally, a gleaming white tunnel radiated into existence.

"Well, I'll be damned…," murmured Councillor Hamish as they all stared at the Arnemetiaen Gateway before them.

"Look!" Tors called out, pointing at the other end. "There's someone on the other side!"

A lone figure sat at the other end. Startled, he jumped to his feet. The familiar red of his cloak flashed into view.

"Bet he wasn't expecting today to be an eventful day at work," said Marcus under his breath.

Moments later, after much gesticulation, several more Reds appeared behind the first soldier.

"Those are our Reds, all right," said Marcus and waved at them. One or two waved tentatively back.

Councillor Hamish looked at them and smiled. "Well," she said, still marvelling at the Gateway tunnel, "that there on the other end must be…"

Marcus nodded. "The Ageron city of Arnemetiae…where we first started out all those months ago."

"Arnemetiae," repeated Niko, with a mixture of awe and disbelief.

The Reds formed two straight lines flanking each side of the tunnel and stood in attention. The first of them gave a wave across the tunnel.

Tors looked at Marcus. "Now what do we do?" she asked uncertainly.

Marcus held her gaze and squeezed her hand. "Now," he said with a deep breath, "we go home."

And together, with Pihla and Niko and Councillor Hamish, they walked slowly down the Arnemetiaen Gateway.

PART VIII

AGERON

REUNITED

COMITIUM,
ALANDIA CITY, AGERON

*I*t was a strange feeling to be back in Ageron again, but more than that, it felt different. The Realm, when they left it, had been despondent and dead, but now, with their triumphant return through the Arnemetiaen Gateway, it seemed all of Ageron had suddenly come alive with purpose and activity. The empire threw itself into preparations for the mass evacuation to Tilkoen in a surge of revived energy. Everywhere, a sense of hope that had not been felt for centuries filled the people's hearts.

Tors gazed out the window from the top floor of the Comitium, half-listening to Pihla's impassioned arguments to Chancellor Rasmus about inoculations and restrictions to biological imports into Tilkoen. They were discussing the ramifications of the Evacuation—the new programme replacing the Exodus.

Evacuation definitely sounds more urgent, Niko had jokingly remarked. But he was right. With climate change spiralling out of control and no longer confined to the inner planets, the urgency to evacuate was now more immediate than ever. But then luckily, so was the solution. With the Arnemetiaen Gateway functional once more, there was no need for the Exodus programme. No need to spend decades building spacecarriers to transport people out of Ageron. Unfortunately, the luxury of decades to spare no longer held true either.

In response to this urgency, Lord Patrin had convinced the Senate to put Akseli's impeachment trial on hold and focus its energies instead on the Evacuation Programme. A programme that would encompass the planning, logistics, settlement, economic and naturalisation initiatives needed to coordinate and deliver the mass migration of their people from one planetary system to another. *One last push,* Lord Patrin had argued. *If planned and orchestrated well, we will be able to escape our dying system relatively unscathed in a matter of years.* It was an ambitious but realisable target. With House Tilkoen an advanced and abiding ally, the Evacuation had kicked off to a solid start in the mere weeks since their return. With Tilkoen technology and organisation, both Houses threw themselves into the mammoth task of planning a steady and orderly migration of Ageronians out of Ageron and into Tilkoen.

Tors continued to stare out of the window, ignoring Pihla's latest attempt to reel her in on the finer details of what an orderly migration programme needed. In front of her, the city with its eclectic mix of spires, traditional palazzos and modern complexes glowed in the sanguine daylight. Alandia was a city of contradictions, where the old jostled side by side with the new and where rich seams of refined beauty nestled amongst gutters of poverty. Now, more than ever, these contradictions echoed the tumult of her feelings inside her.

A flicker of old grief filled her heart. They had returned from their mission less than a month, yet she and Draeger had not spoken. *If I leave, it will be much easier for both of us,* she thought to herself, unable to face the prospect of facing him, but the presence of Empress Yoon dwelled on her mind.

Draeger. I must see him. My Yinha's son...

Tors sighed. It was a promise she had to honour. *I shall have to take him to her. And the sooner the better so we can both move on.*

"Then let's make sure we get that in writing, don't you think, Tors?" Pihla's voice came over determinedly, snapping Tors back to the present.

Tors turned to look at the both of them. Pihla had just about succeeded in getting the Chancellor to agree to banning all plants, foodstuffs, pets and every bio-organism imaginable from being brought through the Arnemetiaen Gateway into Sansari.

"It's *not* a recommendation," Pihla said hotly, "it's got to be a ruling. We have to prevent bringing contamination and disease into our adopted home. I'll get Niko to work out the details with our Senate and the Tilkoen Congress first thing tomorrow."

"Yes, yes," replied Chancellor Rasmus sounding more harassed by the minute.

Pihla, having won her little wrangle with him, turned to Tors. "Did you know that Tilkoens produce all their food artificially?" she said.

Tors looked at her amusedly. "I think so. I seem to remember Ourry mentioning that."

Pihla nodded her head vigorously. "I have seen it with my own eyes," she said. "No animal husbandry and no soil cultivation. Everything is grown under hermetically sealed, artificially controlled environments. Completely sterile, ergo *no diseases*. Even their food supply chain leaves little room for contamination. This is why we have to be careful when our people move over. We Ageronians eat from farm to plate, which, if repeated in Tilkoen, could open them up to viral infections not seen for centuries, not to mention the need to repurpose some of their forests for farming which is totally forbidden under the main terms and conditions of resettlement."

Tors smiled at her friend. *She certainly has talents not confined to engineering, though she can't seem to see that herself.* Pihla's remarkable performance negotiating with the thousand-strong Tilkoen Congress had captured the imagination of the public but all that had done nothing to change her frame of mind. *I'm an engineer, not a politician*, she had protested even though her prowess at Congress suggested otherwise.

"Now, about the issue of homes—" Pihla launched into the next item of discussion, not giving the poor Chancellor any reprieve, when the door opened.

Tors' breath caught as Lord Draeger strode in.

"Chancellor, Pihla," he greeted with a nod and then gestured for them to carry on, "please, continue..." He approached Tors swiftly, barring her way out of the room before she could run.

"You have been... busy," he said, before throwing a brief glance at Pihla and the Chancellor. They rapidly turned away to rattle off something about housing developments. "I have been trying to see you for the past few weeks," he said, visibly as tense as she. "Can we talk somewhere else... in private?" He moved nearer, not releasing his gaze on her and the familiarity of his scent surrounded her. It reminded her of their sparring days at Villa Castra, his warm breath in her ear, his fingers grazing her skin. A lump rose in her throat. Even now, the tug of longing remained, the seduction of his aura and the indescribable closeness between them.

And then, as it'd happened countless times before, the

smart of betrayal and the image of him with Elena would rear its ugly head. When she discovered he, Hostus, was in fact Lord Draeger, who had for years been known to be in intimate liaison with the Ellagrin princess. Tors' resolve hardened. "This is as good a place as any to discuss whatever it is you want to discuss," she said, looking at him squarely in the face.

He flinched, unsure as to how to continue. "What are your plans, Tors?" he asked.

"I don't see what my plans have to do with you," she replied, defensive.

Draeger gave a quiet nod. "I have no wish to intrude," he said, acknowledging her stance, "but we do need to know what your plans are."

"We?" said Tors icily. "Who's we? And after all that has happened, what right do you have to ask what my plans are?"

Draeger shifted uncomfortably, no doubt made worse by the fact that Pihla and Chancellor Rasmus were listening intently despite their pathetic attempts to look as if they weren't. "You are the last Nehisi after all," he said, trying to reason with her. "It's not just I, but all of us. By Dyaeus, if the entire empire knew of you, all of Ageron too would want to know."

Tors bristled. At that moment, the baby inside her kicked. *Not the last Nehisi,* she said to herself with bitter defiance. She turned to face him. "Why?" she challenged. "So I can open new Gateways for the Ageron empire? So that House Ageron can be great once again?" She glared at him coldly. "I have no wish to don the shackles that my ancestors once bore for House Ageron. The Lagentian Gateway is no more, destroyed when the LON attacked. And the Leodis Gateway... well, I can tell you the Yoons have destroyed the Huangshan Gate on their end. Neither House—Ellagrin nor Yoon—wish to have connections with Ageron. Be content you have the Arnemetiaen Gateway to allow your people escape to Tilkoen. That will have to be enough for Ageron. That will have to be enough for *you.*"

Draeger remain silent in response. At length he said, "It will be whatever you wish. I will honour it but we have to consider your safety. You are Nehisi and many know who you are, what you are, and what you look like. By Dyaeus, if just half of the Senate had their rapacious hands on you…" He clenched his hands, leaving the sentence unfinished.

"I don't need your protection," Tors retorted. "I have managed well enough on my own if you remember." Draeger met her gaze and Tors felt her insides lurch with a mix of unspoken resentment and shattered hopes, the longing in his gaze familiar enough to break her heart.

At that moment, there was an indistinct mumble in the background followed by the creak of the door opening. Tors glanced up only to see Pihla and the Chancellor rapidly exiting the room.

Draeger drew closer to her. "Please Tors…," he said.

I cannot bear it, she thought to herself. *I cannot bear getting into this right now.* Her escape barred by him, she turned helplessly to look out the window.

"Tors…," he said, his words stumbling. He trailed off, unable to continue.

Her heart sank. *What hope is there when he cannot even say the words?* The moment for words had long gone, even before she had left him to go into the Ether to search for Sansari. Now, it seemed the chance to say what was not said would never return. Did he ever really love her or was she just the means to save his people? Would it always be him and Elena, with her playing the fool? Not once had he said anything to give her an inkling of what, if anything, she meant to him.

Indeed, the notion of speaking to her, to explain what happened, to seek closure or even severance, may not have occurred to him at all.

It is too late, thought Tors as the evident silence from him sent a wave of grief crashing through her. *Too late for us. I can't stay here. I have to leave and leave soon, before my bump shows.* The attraction of disappearing into the Ether again, to return to her old nomadic life, to disappear somewhere far away, called out to her. She yearned for freedom. *The way things used to be.* Away from attachment. *Freedom.* And freedom from Marcus too, despite his quiet loyalty and unconditional love for her and her yet unborn child.

Marcus never once asked whose baby this is. She softened at the memory of his words to her that day on the mountains of Yoon. Marcus who had stayed with her through thick and thin, who supported her, protected her and who pursued her relentlessly with the use of his terrible jokes. Her resolve wavered but she shook herself. *I must leave before I lose the will to do so.*

"I have a message for you," she blurted. The Empress Yoon's request and her need to get this over and done with pressed upon her. *If I show you the way to Sansari, you must bring him to me,* the Empress had said and Tors could sense considerable weight behind those words. There was something of great significance and importance.

"The Empress Yoon," she told Draeger, "your grandmother. We met her before we found Sansari. In fact, she is the reason I managed to find Sansari." The memory of the ancient dowager came flooding back. "I am to bring you to her," said Tors.

"The Empress Yoon…" said Draeger. There was a far-off look in his eyes.

"With the Evacuation underway, now would be the opportune time to do so," said Tors. She paused and added, "This wasn't a mere request. She's... I don't know... there was something more..."

Draeger assented. "I know," he said. "The Oracle told me many years ago—that I would one day set my eyes upon the Huangshan Mountains of Yoon."

"I would like to, *need* to get this done with as soon as possible," said Tors.

"I understand there are things between us," began Draeger, "... unfinished matters." He was trying, again, to explain, his voice thick with emotion. "I am... unaccustomed to explaining things."

"Then *try*," said Tors. She gazed levelly at him. *Last chance, Draeger.* "Tell me then," she said. "Explain it to me."

"I—" he began and stopped. His deep, dark eyes looked at her unsteadily. This was not a man made for easy discourse. "I had hoped," he said, "that you would... stay, after we return from Yoon."

"Why?" asked Tors. "Why should I stay?"

"I...," he faltered. "I uh... need you. *We* need you... the empire needs you."

"The *empire* needs me?" snapped Tors. Heat rose in her face. *I'm a tool to him. A tool! To him, to Elena, to the empire. That's all I ever was to him and all I shall ever be. He's never loved me. I'm a fool to think he ever could. I'll be opening new Gateways for him whilst he runs off to play happy family with Elena.* Her cheeks burned. *When will I learn that I am but a game to these aristocrats?*

"Tors..."

"It doesn't matter," Tors cut him. *It's too late. For the both of us.* She looked away and said, "All I need now is to finish this so I can go."

He nodded helplessly. "We can go soon if that is what you

want. Perhaps away from all this noise and distractions, I can explain…"

He's agreeing to this so that he has a chance to make amends...

She shook her head firmly. "No," she said, looking at him sadly. "There won't be anymore explaining. After this, I shall be gone. This time, for good. There will be no returning."

A clean break and a fresh start. She thought about the child she carried. *A new life for us*, she decided, as she turned to leave the room.

CELEBRATION

ARNEMETIAE CITY,
PLANET ILIA, AGERON SYSTEM

The streets of Arnemetiae had never seen such fanfare nor such pageantry such as this for over a century. Indeed, celebrations were being held simultaneously across the empire to kick off the Evacuation—the programme to migrate all inhabitants of Ageron and resettle them in the Tilkoen system. Here, at the Arnemetiaen Gate itself, celebrations were about to be beamed across, live, to all twelve planets of the Realm.

The empire has not witnessed a celebration like this since the last time Ageron himself got married, noted Lord Marius wryly. He tried briefly to remember who it was that the late emperor last married but couldn't. Shrugging the idle thought off, he made his way to the security checkpoint at the front of the Arnemetiaen Central Station. All around, forcefield barriers had been erected in a predefined perimeter around the station. These barriers would remain so, barring anyone from accessing the station and its Gateway until the Evacuation Programme progressed to the point where actual migration of citizens were to commence.

In front of the shimmering barriers stood rows and rows of soldiers, Ageronian and Tilkoen, side by side. Their smart uniforms, in alternating shades of sage and red, reflected the partnership between the two Houses.

Once cleared by security, Lord Marius headed for the Grand Marquee at the centre of the station concourse. Behind it loomed the Arnemetiaen Gate, its gleaming arch looking grand and imposing. There was a palpable sense of excitement in the air. The Gateway had of course, been switched on periodically over the past few weeks in order for the teams working on the Evacuation to carry out their tasks. However, for the majority of the empire's citizens, tonight's broadcast would be the first time they would see the Arnemetian Gateway in all its working glory.

Lord Marius cast a disinterested glance at the flamboyant pyrotechnic displays, holographic fireworks and euphoric music in front before proceeding to enter the marquee where fellow Praetors, various senators and Tilkoen dignitaries assembled.

"Tonight will be quite a spectacle…" The familiar voice of Queen Alin stopped him in his tracks. Lord Marius whirled round to see the Queen Mother stroll up beside him. "My dear Queen Alin," he said, offering his arm to her, "May I?"

"You are too kind, Lord Marius," murmured Queen Alin and rested her hand in the crook of his arm as they both entered the marquee.

"What a momentous night this is, my lady," commented Lord Marius as they sauntered towards the glittering congregation of guests.

"Indeed," agreed Queen Alin, "and most entertaining for the masses, no doubt."

Lord Marius snickered. "Not half as entertaining as the things I've seen lately," he said giving her a knowing look.

PLANET ILIA, AGERON SYSTEM

The Queen Mother smiled at him. "I hear you have taken to evening walks of late," she said.

Lord Marius chuckled wickedly. "I have indeed," he replied, "and they have been quite *eye-opening...*"

"You have a gift for persuasion, Lord Marius," the Queen Mother continued, flashing a beatific smile at a passing courtier. Lord Marius waved her praise away.

"I had excellent ah, material to work with, my lady. The rest was merely a case of asking nicely." He turned to face her, becoming serious. "It was a good move getting the Senate to postpone the impeachment," he said. "Far better than to gamble on their support in the trial itself. For now, anyway. At least until we can be sure of their loyalty."

Queen Alin nodded, agreeing. "The early success of the Sansari mission was unexpected," she said. "The timing sooner than we wanted. But Akseli and I thought we could take advantage of that. An operational Gateway coupled with recent disasters across Amorgos have helped our ah... *friend* position the need for evacuation over and above Lord Draeger's petty urgency for an impeachment trial."

"Well, no one seems to be talking about impeachment now that all eyes are focussed on the Evacuation," Marius said, "but what of the Emperor's position in the interim?"

"The trial is on hold for now," Queen Alin said. "Akseli is back under house arrest again and cannot interfere with the Senate or matters of government, not until the trial resumes and its outcome determined." She shrugged. "Not ideal but at least this buys us some time."

Lord Marius nodded. "Time for opportunities to arise too..."

"Oh?" said Queen Alin, intrigued.

Lord Marius lowered his voice. "Haven't you heard? It

appears our Supreme Commander is planning a short trip away. A mission it seems, to engage with House Yoon."

"House Yoon?" said Queen Alin. Her utterance was sharp but it vanished quickly and her cold, calm exterior returned. "But the Yoon withdrew from civilisation during the War, destroying their own gate and cutting themselves off from the rest of us. Why make contact with them once more?"

"It seems the Empress Yoon herself requested it," said Lord Marius.

"The Empress…" For a second, Marius thought a haunted look crossed her face.

"He plans to travel through the Ether to see her," he continued.

Queen Alin glanced sharply at him. "So, with the aid of the Nehisi woman?"

"That is the plan, I believe. With the Evacuation now underway and progressing at pace, there is talk of Rasmus installed as Dictator in Lord Draeger's absence to keep the Senate in check until his return."

"Hmmm," murmured Queen Alin. She said nothing more as they were nearing the congregation of guests. However, something in her voice suggested that this latest piece of information had presented her with some interesting options.

Spotting Lord Draeger in one corner speaking to his generals, Lord Marius steered Queen Alin to the opposite end where the portly figure of Lord Reku stood. However, the contrived detour failed in its objective when the passers-by in front of them moved on to reveal the familiar grey figure of Chancellor Rasmus right next to Reku. A sideways glance revealed Queen Alin's less than amused reaction at the view that assailed her.

"My dear Queen Mother," Lord Reku bowed, seeing Queen Alin. "You look absolutely divine."

PLANET ILIA, AGERON SYSTEM

"You are too kind, Lord Reku," murmured Queen Alin graciously. "How splendid you look." She regarded his velvet red tunic embellished with its rows of military medals. Marius chuckled inwardly—Reku loved showing off the fact that he was Legatus on top of being a Praetor.

Lord Reku beamed at the compliment, his wobbly jowls stretching up and down as he did so. "What a night, eh my lady? What a *triumph!*" He beamed at her and Lord Marius.

"My Lady," Chancellor Rasmus edged forward and gave a bow.

Queen Alin turned to face him. "Chancellor," she said with a thin smile.

"Chancellor," echoed Lord Marius in greeting the old man. *You sly fox*, he thought, eyeing him steadily. *No doubt you'll be hovering over us all night to curb what we say to the Praetors*. He then realised the Chancellor was accompanied by two others: a man of medium-height and slight build, and an attractive woman with the most startling green eyes. "I don't think we've ever been introduced," Lord Marius said, gazing at her. She cut a striking figure with her raven locks and vivid lapis gown.

"May I present to you, Vittoria and Niko," introduced the Chancellor. "They were part of the team that located Sansari."

"Ah! The last Nehisi," said Lord Marius with unconcealed bluntness. "*Charmed*, my lady," he said, bending down to kiss her hand. "Your talents are legendary of course, although I have to say, no one warned us of your exceptional beauty."

The woman gave him a polite nod but said little else.

"So brave," Queen Alin spoke up, "... and courageous. We are so grateful my dear, for saving us all."

"I had help," came the curt reply.

"Aye, from what I've seen, I would say it was a *team* effort,"

CELEBRATION

chipped in a tall lady who appeared at Vittoria's side. She gave her a quick wink before turning towards them, and Lord Marius found himself under the scrutiny of a pair of intelligent-looking eyes. "Councillor Hamish," the tall woman said in an agreeable, rolling accent and held out her hand. "At your service."

Lord Marius looked at her appraisingly and shook it. "Lord Marius," he said, introducing himself, "Praetor of Ceos and more recently, at Lord Patrin's behest, caretaker Praetor of Ilia." He raised his shoulders diffidently, "At least until Praetor Sebastia recuperates from this terrible illness."

"Ach! The *top* man himself," said Councillor Hamish with admiration. "Now with the Arnemetiaen Gate the centre of importance in the Evacuation, your job here on Ilia is no doubt going to be the most important in the empire!"

Lord Marius' chest puffed up a little. "I am but a servant of House Ageron," he said self-effacingly, "but yes, I bear the responsibility of ensuring preparations at the Arnemetian Gate here stay on track."

"Preparations for the Evacuation have been smooth so far," said Councillor Hamish, "and I'm sure that is without doubt due to you and your teams here."

"Ah," said Lord Marius, "and in no small part due to Tilkoen technology and efficiency as well!" He paused as he spotted Lord Patrin a few feet away. "Lord Patrin!" boomed Marius, making everyone jump. Cornered, Lord Patrin reluctantly walked over.

"Now this fellow here," announced Lord Marius generously, "is the most honourable, upright servant of House Ageron—my dear friend Lord Patrin."

Lord Patrin smiled a little helplessly and gave a courteous bow. Behind him, struggling to keep up, trundled a vision in a frothy marigold ensemble, complete with maid and baby in tow.

"Lady Ursule!" exclaimed Lord Marius. He noticed Lord Patrin shift uncomfortably as his wife approached Marius.

"Queen Alin, Lord Marius, Chancellor..." Lady Ursule smiled shyly, "How lovely to meet you." She gestured to her maid, "Anneliese..." Her handmaid nodded obediently and handed her the baby.

Queen Alin's smile went wide. "Ah... the precious one," she said as Lady Ursule brought the baby closer to her. "How has he been?"

"Very well, my lady," said Lady Ursule. "He is truly the most wonderful, contented babe," she said, "thanks to Anneliese here. I cannot thank you enough my dear Queen Mother. Without Anneliese, I would be lost!"

"I am so glad my girl has been able to help you, my dear," Queen Alin murmured. She shifted her gaze to Lord Patrin. "My Anneliese is a girl of many talents, you know," she said with a smile. Lord Patrin nearly choked but managed to cough out a polite response, "Indeed, indeed, my lady."

Marius observed with immense glee that Patrin didn't once look him in the eye. "My dear Lord Patrin," he said, slapping Lord Patrin heartily on his back, "you seem rather subdued lately. Suffering from the strains of fatherhood perhaps?"

Lady Ursule laughed. "Assuredly not, my dear Lord Marius. Anneliese here has been tending to darling Cyrus night and day. Patrin here on the other hand,"—she patted him affectionately on his chest—"lifts not a finger in that respect. If my husband appears tired, it most certainly is *not* due to the baby I can assure you."

Lord Marius gave a hoot of laughter. "Not the baby you

say," he chortled, eyeing an increasingly red Lord Patrin. "I believe you my dear lady, I believe you."

"We were just saying how well things are progressing with the Evacuation," Councillor Hamish spoke up, smiling.

"Indeed," said Lord Patrin, eager to change the subject. "It is a huge undertaking: the organisation of the Evacuation itself, the logistics involved, programmes to integrate our people, culture, language. Absolutely massive and with the urgency to move our people across before the next great climate disaster strikes, we are all systems go, as the Tilkoens say."

"Indeed, indeed," agreed Councillor Hamish. "With our joint technologies in place, it will be a fairly orderly and efficient process. In fact, I believe the benefits of this are already showing—the use of our lottery broadcast system for example…"

"Oh?" enquired Lady Ursule.

Chancellor Rasmus nodded. "The introduction of this Tilkoen technology has made our evacuation selection process entirely transparent and this has quelled much of the distrust amongst the citizens." He gave a delighted chuckle, "It's also vastly reduced any opportunity for tampering with the selection process as a result."

Lord Reku beamed oleaginously. "How marvellous! Things are indeed looking up! Much better than the previous programme I have to say. The Exodus was rife with rumours of corruption and a rigged selection process."

"Well, we still have the problem of what to do with our people already on route to Ellagrin under the Exodus," voiced Lord Patrin. He frowned. "Relations between our two Houses remain strained. We will have to find a way forward before our first spacecarriers arrive at Ellagrin."

"Perhaps House Tilkoen could help facilitate the mending

PLANET ILIA, AGERON SYSTEM

of relations between Ageron and Ellagrin," suggested Lord Marius. He flashed Councillor Hamish a benign smile. "I believe the Ellagrin system is nearer to Tilkoen than we are. Perhaps if word was sent from Tilkoen to Ellagrin to negotiate some sort of deal?"

Councillor Hamish appeared resistant to the idea. "The Ellagrin system is approximately a decade's flight away by longsleep from Tilkoen," she said, a little reticently, "so if a resolution hasn't presented itself in the near future, then... *possibly.*" She shrugged noncommittally. "I must warn you though, there is still much distrust of the Ellagrins amongst Tilkoens—as a result of the War you see—but I'm sure relations will mend in good time. All in good time."

"Oh, I'm sure relations between House Ageron and Ellagrin will mend eventually," said Queen Alin. "The demise of the Emperor Niklas would have already contributed somewhat to the end of this animosity and with the more compassionate Empress Elena at the helm, well, anything could be possible..."

"Even reconciliation?" Marius piped up innocently.

"Why not? Perhaps she will soften," replied Queen Alin. Marius noticed her eyes were fixed upon Tors, not him. "Apparently she is expecting her first child."

"Really?" enquired Lady Ursule inquisitively. "But she's unmarried..."

Queen Alin nodded, lowering her tone conspiratorially. "Rumour has it, no less than our Commander *Draeger's*."

"*No!*" said Lady Ursule disbelievingly.

"Yes!" said Queen Alin, closing her eyes, nodding.

"Hearsay, hearsay," interjected Chancellor Rasmus, casting a discreet glance at Tors. Her face had grown ashen, rigid.

"Well, if there's one way to persuade a man to calm down, it's a child," Lady Ursule went on, tittering knowledgeably. She looked at her husband and smiled, "Don't you think?" Lord Patrin said nothing but patted her hand.

"Indeed," chimed in Queen Alin, and engaged Tors with an innocent smile. "Anyway, speaking of rumours, is it true the Supreme Commander is about to embark on another mission?"

"Well if anything, a baby will stop all that nonsense," giggled Lady Ursule. She gave her husband's arm a little squeeze. "If there's one way to persuade a man to stop wandering off, it's a child."

"I…," replied Vittoria haltingly, "…lords, ladies, if you will excuse me…" Without a further word, she turned on her heel and left. Her friend Niko blurted his apologies and hurried after her.

"Anyway," said Lord Reku returning to the gossip in hand, "I have to say, that's certainly an innovative form of diplomacy. If I had known a baby was all it takes to end a war, I would have gladly sacrificed myself for the greater good hahaha!"

"Well," said Queen Alin, "at any rate, it would be a propitious outcome for us indeed. The new empress appears more sympathetic compared with her brother."

Lord Patrin nodded. "Indeed, indeed. Unhinged he was, Emperor Niklas. And don't forget, their father Mikael was mad too."

"Oh yes," said his wife nodding vigorously, "slaughtering the entire Nehisi tribe and all that." She squeezed Queen Alin's arm genially, "Don't you agree, my lady? In my opinion, the man was utterly insane! A *lunatic*!"

Lord Marius studied Queen Alin covertly. She had bristled at the comment although the others appeared not to have noticed. *Do these fools not know the mad Emperor Mikael was Alin's brother?*

PLANET ILIA, AGERON SYSTEM

Queen Alin looked on coldly as they continued to gossip.

"Perhaps it runs in the family," continued Lady Ursule, oblivious to Queen Mother's sudden frosty demeanour. "Madness in the male genes!"

And they all laughed, Marius noticed, all except the Queen Mother and the old Chancellor.

PIHLA

"So, I was thinking maybe we could join Team Alpha Two to have a look at this Tilkoen registration system of theirs," said Niko, trying to get Pihla's attention. He took the stack of old Exodus tickets from her and rifled through them like an oversized pack of clacking metal cards. "We need to work out how to migrate Exodus passenger data into their system if we want to start using their embracive bio-scans to register evacuees instead of these antiquated tokens."

Pihla gave a non-committal grunt in reply and continued reviewing the diagnostics on her handheld.

They were on the concourse of Arnemetiae Central Station, overseeing the installation of a dynamic forcefield system which would be used to manage the entry flow on the approach to the station itself. One of many Tilkoen innovations adopted in the Evacuation, the forcefield system would negate the need to erect physical structures or modify the old station's Departure Hall.

A few army groundcars cut across the platform, beeping

curtly and deftly avoiding the engineers and workmen, all hard at work installing, testing and surveying. Overlooking this hive of activity, in quiet grandeur, was the Arnemetiaen Gate itself, her vast arc gleaming in the afternoon sun.

Niko cleared his throat and tried again. "I was also thinking we could go across the Gateway today to have a look at their concert crowd-flow systems in person. You know, like the one in that downtown Sansari venue Councillor Hamish mentioned the other day. Maybe we could introduce something similar in the station itself as an added layer. What do you say?"

Pihla looked up from her handheld and tapped it impatiently. "Hmmm," she said, her eyes narrowing.

"Hmmm what?" asked Niko.

"Why don't you just come out with it. You're just trying to find an excuse to cross over to Sansari, aren't you?"

Niko spread his hands out, nearly dropping the wad of tickets at the same time. "You got me," he said and grinned.

Pihla rolled her eyes at him.

"We never have time to properly look around," explained Niko. "It's always Evacuation work and besides, don't you want to explore the city some more? Find out how their pedestrian belts work? See where they lead to?"

Pihla shook her head annoyedly. "Look," she said, "we have such a tight schedule as it is. Besides, the Gateway is controlled and secured *for a reason*. Only authorised personnel, people who need to work to get the Evacuation up and running and those on specific tasks for the Evacuation that use it."

"But that's *us*," protested Niko. "We're one of those personnel, so let's just go!"

Pihla sighed exasperated. "Not for a jaunt, Niko. Look, not

anyone can go through the Gateway at the moment. Not without authorisation. We have to follow process."

"Yes, but you have authorisation. You're even *wearing* it!" He pointed at the access wristband just visible under her sleeve, issued to specific personnel which had to be scanned in at both ends of the Gateway in addition to the usual checks by the border teams. But Pihla seemed to be in no mood to accommodate anything at the moment.

"I'm not taking you through unless it's for legitimate reasons, Niko. This is no different to any other border control. Imagine if people decided to ignore that and take a field trip over to Sansari just to 'have-a-look'? We'd have chaos on our hands. Look, just leave me alone alright? I have things to get on with here."

Niko started to object but she shut him up with an irritable "*Go!*"

He backed off and made his way back towards the station's main entrance. *What's gotten into her?* Something was off. He glanced back but she had already disappeared behind the ticketing offices, towards Departure.

A tall familiar figure strode towards the same direction.
Shankar!

Niko froze. *Was that why she wanted to get rid of me? What by Dyaeus is that devil up to?* He turned and stopped, trying to resist the urge to go back there to find out. *I can't go back there,* he agonised, imagining Pihla having a go at him if he did just that. *What would my excuse be? Besides she told me to go. She'll bite my head off if I go back.*

He paused uncertain of what to do next. *What is Shankar doing back there?* He tried to imagine Pihla telling Captain Shankar to shove off. *I hope she's biting his head off this very minute.*

A few minutes passed and then some, but no emergence of Captain Shankar.

What is that no-good captain playing at? Niko rapped his hand against his thigh in annoyance. *No, I can't go back there. What would I say anyway?* The stack of tickets in his palm clacked noisily.

The tickets! He was still clutching the tickets. *Well*, thought Niko quickly, *I'd better give these back to her in case she needs them.*

He hurried through the ticketing offices, trying to not look as furtive as he felt and walked past a couple of military groundcars parked on the massive foyer, their army personnel standing in groups chatting. One of them, Luca, waved at him. Niko smiled and gave a wave back, taking care to maintain an easy going stride as he made his way towards Departure.

Then he stopped short.

Ahead, standing in front of the Departure gate was Captain Shankar talking earnestly to Pihla. Both had their backs to him so it was difficult to make out their facial expressions, especially Pihla's. Conscious of Luca's eye on him and unable to backtrack without looking suspicious, Niko continued walking towards Pihla and Captain Shankar.

The Captain had stopped talking and was now taking Pihla's hand in his, leading her through the Gateway itself. Niko felt the heat rising at the back of his neck.

She lied to me! She lied to me to go with him.

He was now almost at the Gate himself, almost catching up with them. Captain Shankar was speaking with the guards at the pass. They talked and laughed a bit with the Captain slapping the guard's back as they both shared a joke. The man then scanned both the Captain and Pihla's wristbands before disabling the forcefield barriers to let them pass.

"Wait!" Niko yelled out after them. He saw Pihla stop before the start of the bright white tunnel.

"What are you doing here?" she asked.

"I… I… I came to give you back this," Niko said waving the tickets at her. He walked up to them, but stopped just before the barrier.

Pihla walked back towards him and stood facing him. The pale translucent barrier shimmered between them. "What are you doing?" she asked, her voice tight. Captain Shankar came up behind her, straight faced, inscrutable.

Niko glared at him. "What by Dyaeus are *you* playing at?" he asked angrily. He turned to Pihla next and said, "You just told me a minute ago that no one was allowed to go across. Yet you're doing just that…" He edged closer towards the barrier.

"Sir," began the sentry, moving towards Niko. However Captain Shankar waved the soldier down. "It's okay. We forgot to take those with us," he said, pointing at the wad of tickets in Niko's hand. "Could you lower the barrier for a moment soldier?"

The sentry gave Niko a slightly wary look before nodding. The barrier between them shimmered briefly before disappearing.

"Here," said Niko hotly, holding the tickets in his outstretched hand.

Pihla reached out to take it from him.

He looked at her, glanced at Captain Shankar, and then back at her again. "So first you lie about going across to Sansari and now you're going there with him?"

"It's not what you think Niko—"

"Well, what is it then?" pressed Niko. "You telling me you're not going across and then doing just that behind my back with the important captain here. Am I not important enough for you?"

"That's not it..." voiced Pihla uncomfortably.

"You've changed Pihla," blurted Niko. "I thought we were friends. Best mates. There were never any secrets between us before."

"It's not that—"

"Well, what is it then? Why the secrecy?" Niko glared at Captain Shankar. "Why all this *skulking*?"

"That's not—" Pihla began weakly.

"Batsa," Shankar cut in, "I'm taking her to see General Batsa."

"General Batsa?"

"Yes," nodded Pihla, "He's my uncle and we're going to see my mother..."

"Your *mother*?" repeated Niko, suddenly feeling rather foolish. "Oh by Dyaeus! You mean to say you've finally found your mother? That's *great* news!"

But Pihla didn't look him in the eye.

"What's wrong?" Niko noticed neither of them smiled back. Then Pihla glanced at Shankar, and gave a weary nod.

"Why don't you come with us," said Shankar and went back to the pass gate to submit the authorisation for Niko.

* * *

THEY WERE GIVEN a lift in a patrol car across the half-kilometre or so of the Arnemetiaen Gateway tunnel, all the way to the other end where General Batsa Blazing Light waited for them. From there, they boarded his urbanglider out of Sansari and into its sister city of Chatadharam.

Throughout the flight, Niko sat at the back with Captain Shankar whilst Pihla sat in front with the General. She looked out the window most of the time and none of them exchanged so much as a word throughout the entire journey.

Eventually, the urbanglider descended on a well-kept patch of parkland within Chatadharam, several blocks away from the instantly recognisable hunk of a building that was the Forum. Here, amidst the manicured planting stood a large marble folly.

"This way," said General Batsa solemnly as they alighted. He led them inside the structure.

It was circular with a tall domed ceiling and deceptively larger inside than it appeared from the outside. A round skylight at the top let in natural light. The curved walls inside were covered in panels of onyx, each a gleaming square tile no more than the width of a person's palm. As they walked past, names, in beautiful calligraphy, appeared across each tile in a subtle gleam of gold, before disappearing again.

General Batsa walked halfway round the hall and stopped in front of a specific section of panels. Directly in front of him, on a square just above head height, flashed a name in gleaming gold: Nayana Laceria.

Her mother's name was Nayana, Niko recalled from past conversations. He covered his mouth with his hands. *Oh by Dyaeus, this is a mausoleum.* "Pihla...," he stuttered, "I am *so* sorry. I had no idea."

Pihla managed a weak smile and said, "I know. Captain Shankar put me in touch with General... Uncle Batsa. I've known for some time but it is only now that I've well... decided to come. To finally see her." She turned away to face the beautiful lettering and to hide her tears from him.

General Batsa took Pihla's hand gruffly and placed a small earpiece in it. It was smooth and shaped like a small pebble. "Her last message to you," he said. "Put it to your ear to listen."

As Pihla placed the pebble gently against her ear, Nayana's

name on the tile shimmered out and in its place emanated a faint holographic projection. A woman's face floated in front of her.

"Mamma…" Pihla called out softly, and reached out into the empty holo in front of her, trying to touch it.

Meanwhile, Niko followed General Batsa and the captain to wait outside the mausoleum and give her some privacy.

* * *

"She was elected to the High Council you know," said General Batsa as they stood outside in the sun, waiting.

"She was one of the Twelve?" asked Niko.

General Batsa nodded his head. "Yes and after the War, she stood up against the likes of Councillor Ram to preserve the Sansari Gate so that one day Pihla would be able to walk through it again and come home." He wiped a tear from his cheek gruffly.

"May I ask, how did she die?" asked Captain Shankar.

"It was shortly after the War had ended," said General Batsa. "There was an explosion at a rally—the Objectors wanted to destroy the Sansari Gate for good."

"Objectors?" asked Niko.

General Batsa nodded. "Tilkoens who did not want the Gateways reinstated. As you found out when you first came, Objectors still exist to this day and like Councillor Ram, some are Ellagrin sympathisers. After the War, we tried to find a way of reconnecting the Arnemetiaen Gateway without needing Nehisi assistance but the Objectors formed to movement against this. People who wanted to prevent the resurgence of Bridged Travel." The General shook his head. "It was a time when many Tilkoens were looking inwards, tending towards isolationism. Most were fed up of the War between

House Ageron and Ellagrin, which had spilled over into Tilkoen. Many deemed that war was based on petty reasons. The rally was meant to be a peaceful one, until someone detonated a bomb by the main plaza. Nayana was at the wrong place at the wrong time."

Niko bowed his head in silence. *Pihla's father didn't mind her being in the Rebellion because he had hoped that would bring her here, one day, to her mother. But it's too late…*

"She wanted so much for Pihla to grow up here. To experience our way of life. Unlike Ageron, everyone here has a voice. An equal one. A say in how we wish to be run and how we wish to run things. And Nayana wanted that for her, maybe even for her to be a councillor like her."

She'd make a great councillor too, thought Niko. The Evacuation work going on at the moment meant the both of them dealing constantly with the Ageronian Senate and the Tilkoen Congress. *We make a great team,* he noted with pride, *if only this captain will stop trying to lure her away into the military side of things.* He eyed the captain with a surreptitious look of resentment. Ever since they had successfully completed their mission, things were settling down nicely, and he and Pihla were making a real difference to the Evacuation. Niko could see them working closely together in this bright new future. *It'll be like the old days in the Rebellion, but better.* He had hoped to take things further with Pihla now that life had begun to settle into normality. If only a certain captain wasn't in the picture…

General Batsa sighed and went on, "Sadly, this was not to be. I will always remember the day the Ellagrins pushed through the Arnemetiaen Gateway with their Hauks and destroyers. And then they destroyed our beacon at Sansari, disconnecting the Gateway."

"That must have been the day Pihla and her father were

travelling through the Gateway to Sansari," Niko said. "She said they barely made it back to Arnemetiae before it disconnected."

General Batsa nodded and blew his nose loudly. "The Ellagrins had swarmed through the Gateway that day, trying to flee the Ageronians. They were being pursued, so they destroyed our beacon at the Sansari end to prevent the Ageronians from reaching them. There was no time to warn anyone." His head bowed at the weight of the recollection. "We lost a lot of people that day—innocent citizens trying to get home."

General Batsa stopped and looked up. Pihla had emerged from the mausoleum.

Before Niko could think to approach her, Captain Shankar loped across the green to her side. She collapsed into his arms, sobbing.

"Let's go home," said General Batsa and they all walked back slowly to the urbanglider.

MARCUS

"She is going to *what?*" Marcus was almost shouting in disbelief. "She can't go back there again! She's only just returned!"

"It was her decision, not mine," replied Draeger quietly.

"This is madness!" said Marcus. He looked at the Chancellor. "And you are letting her do this?"

"Tors is to take me to see the Empress Yoon," explained Lord Draeger to Chancellor Rasmus.

"The Empress Yoon...," said the old Chancellor.

Lord Draeger nodded. "It would seem," he said, closing his eyes in recollection, "that the Oracle was right after all."

"What Oracle?" snapped Marcus. "Is this one of your religious beliefs?"

The Chancellor shook his head gravely. "I'm afraid not," he answered. "The Oracle is not a myth. The last empress of Yoon brought it to Ageron centuries ago. The Oracle told our emperor of our dying suns long before it began. It also foretold that Lord Draeger would one day see the Huangshan mountains of Yoon."

Lord Draeger looked at Chancellor Rasmus. "I shan't be away very long," he said. "However, in my absence, we will have to confer the title of Dictator to you to run things." The old man raised an eyebrow.

"I don't imagine the Senate to balk at this," continued Draeger. "Akseli remains under house arrest until the trial resumes. With you as Dictator, you can keep the Senate in check under the capacity of emperor in a time of emergency. And this *is* a time of emergency, with the urgent need to push forward with Evacuation preparations and get our people ready to evacuate as early as possible. I've discussed this with Lords Conor and Metavius. Dictatorship will also give you the necessary powers to keep the Queen Mother and other troublemakers in check."

"I don't anticipate the Senate to object," the Chancellor said, thinking it over, "seeing as my role will be to keep the status quo." He let out a chuckle. "Which is something none of them with their current benefits, the Praetors especially, will have any desire to change. But are you sure about this 'trip', my lord?"

"Yes," said Lord Draeger. "Now would be a good time, whilst our people are preoccupied with the task of Evacuation. Morale throughout the Realm has never been higher and with an end in sight, our people have hope and a goal to work towards."

"How long will you be away?" questioned Marcus.

"A month, we think, perhaps less," replied Draeger. "You see, do you not, that now is the only time to do this? Whilst the focus is on the Evacuation?"

"Yes," Marcus admitted. "But to take her out back there again… " He shook his head, concerned.

"What if we delayed this until the first phase of the Evacuation has commenced?" suggested the Chancellor.

Yes, thought Marcus. *After she has had the baby...*

"Akseli is under house arrest," said Draeger, "and for now at least, what remaining interest on the subject of impeachment has faded with everyone's focus on the Evacuation. Now is the opportune time, the *only* time I should think." He grimaced and added, "Besides, Tors herself is keen to do this as soon as possible." He turned to the Chancellor. "Dictatorship will enable you to keep Evacuation preparations running without having to wrangle with the Senate. Don't forget, you also have General Basta's support and with the Tilkoens behind you, team Alin and her troublemakers will be quite well-behaved, I should think."

The Chancellor agreed and chuckled. "Yes, I noticed our partnership with the Tilkoens seems to have killed off much of the grumblings and protests coming from Akseli's camp of supporters. In fact, General Batsa's comment last week about his troops making an example of any slackers in the Evacuation seems to have whipped our senators into a spirit of industriousness. All the same, my lord, this conferred post has to be but a temporary measure…"

Draeger reached out and grasped the Chancellor's hand in a grateful shake. "I understand, old friend. I look to you once again, as my father did before me, to keep us on the path."

The Chancellor's grey eyes twinkled. "Just don't make a habit of it, my lord," he said, "for I think after this, I should like to retire."

"It is settled then," said Draeger. "I shall run this past Tors to decide the date we leave."

"Very well, my lord. Let me get her on my way out," said the Chancellor and left the room.

* * *

"I still don't see why the hurry to go back into the Ether," started Marcus again as soon as the Chancellor left.

"Now would be just as good a time as any," Draeger replied. He tried to reason with Marcus. "We will be careful. There is no other way to get to the Yoon system, you know that yourself. They destroyed their Gate when they withdrew from the rest of the galaxy centuries ago."

"You can't go!" blurted Marcus, "Not with her." He was adamant.

Draeger faced up to him, straightening up. "I assure you, she wants nothing to do with me—"

"She can't go into the Ether again. She just can't!"

"It's her decision."

"No! Absolutely not! I forbid it!"

"Why?"

"Because she's *pregnant*!"

Draeger stopped short. "What do you mean?" he asked and the door opened.

Tors walked in and stopped when she saw their faces. "What?" she said, conscious of the wall of tension between the two.

At length, Draeger spoke up. "Is it true?"

"What's true?"

"You are... with child?"

Tors slammed the door shut and glared angrily at Marcus. "You *told* him?"

"I had to," said Marcus. "You can't go back out there in your... condition!"

Draeger reached towards her. "Is it...?" He hesitated to finish the sentence.

She flinched at his touch. "I could ask you the same question too," she replied icily. "The other night, at the Gateway opening celebration... they were talking." She looked at him, stony-faced. "It appears Empress Elena is with child too," she said. "*Yours.*"

Draeger remained silent.

"Is *that* true?"

"I did not mean to hurt you," he ventured softly. "I never have."

Tors flashed him a scornful look. "Well you *haven't*," she said and strode over to Marcus who was standing awkwardly by the side trying his best to appear detached from the entire exchange.

"You needn't worry," she said, her gaze still directed at Draeger. "Besides, this baby isn't yours." She did not wait to see his facial expression but turned to face Marcus instead.

Marcus took her hand into his. "You don't have to do this," he said, his eyes pleading. "You don't have to go."

"I have to," Tors replied. "That was the deal. I made a bargain with Empress Yoon. In exchange for the location of Sansari." She looked at him earnestly. "I don't know what you saw in your visions with the Empress, but this was mine. My task and mine alone. I have to do it. I have to take him to her."

She turned to look at Draeger. "And when I've fulfilled my end of the bargain," she said with a tone of finality, "we are done. Do you hear me? *Done.*"

PARTING WAYS

ARNEMETIAE GATE, AGERON

A gust of wind blew through the airy concourse of Arnemetiae's Central Station, whipping Chancellor Rasmus' cloak about as he stood at the Departure area. Dressed in grey from top to bottom, he cut a distinctive figure amidst the milling teams of red and green—Ageronian and Tilkoen military and crew—all hard at work preparing the area and testing the high-tech crowdflow system for what would be for several continuous years ahead, a steady stream of citizens departing the Realm to settle in Tilkoen.

As he surveyed all this, Chancellor Rasmus reflected with a sigh. There was a sense of deja vu in the air. He had felt it before, when the group first left to search for Sansari, except this time it was different. Calmer.

The calm before a storm? wondered the old man. But, he noted, this time it *was* different. *There are no riots,* he realised. *In fact, there is no more Rebellion.* Rebels who hadn't dispersed were now part of the Ageronian army, mostly under Marcus, now a prominent Centurion. His heart lifted and he chuckled to himself. *Could this be,* wondered the old Chancellor, *what peace feels like?* Certainly there was work to be done on the Evacuation but they were all striving towards a common goal and its end was now tantalisingly close to being realised. *The optimism in our people echo this too.* Chancellor Rasmus sighed again. *Then why do I feel a certain sentimental melancholy?*

Standing several feet nearby were Pihla, Marcus, Tors and Captain Shankar. Niko was late as usual and hadn't showed up yet.

Captain Shankar aside, this was the original team, he mused. It seemed like only yesterday when this group had assembled here, in this very spot, to embark on the search for Sansari. *And now, they are about to go their separate ways...*

To his left stood Pihla with a small backpack. *That would be all of her worldly possessions to take with her to Sansari,* the Chancellor guessed. Beside her towered Captain Shankar, talking to her earnestly. He had apparently offered Pihla an attractive post in the Tilkoen military where she could use her engineering skills and lead their teams. Chancellor Rasmus wondered if she had made a decision yet.

"Pihla!" someone called out. They all turned to see Niko approaching at speed from behind. "Pihla, *wait!*"

Pihla had picked up her backpack and was hoisting it onto her shoulder. "What?" she hollered. Captain Shankar visibly annoyed at the interruption, remained standing close to Pihla. He seemed keen to finish their discussion.

"*Pihla!*" Niko called out breathlessly, putting an end to any hope of finishing *that* discussion.

"Well, I'll see you on the other end," Captain Shankar said to Pihla as Niko bounded over.

"What do you want?" asked Pihla. Her eyes followed the captain as he sauntered off towards checkpoint security at the Gateway entrance.

Niko put his hand on his chest and paused to catch his breath. "So... so you're leaving for Sansari?"

"Yup," said Pihla, jacking up her backpack in attempt to find a more comfortable spot for the straps on her shoulders.

Niko glanced at the departure gate where Captain Shankar was standing, waiting for the border guards to clear him to pass. "You... you're leaving to join *him?*"

Pihla turned to face Niko. "Nope," she replied flatly.

"But you're going to Sansari, aren't you?"

"Yes," replied Pihla, "but not to join their armed forces." She cocked an eyebrow at him. "I'm going to try my luck working for Congress. Just like my mother."

"The Tilkoen Congress?" repeated Niko, surprised. "You mean the... the same one we've been liaising with on behalf of the Senate all day every day, until you quit last week?"

"As far as I know, there is only one Congress," replied Pihla drily, "so yes. I've moved over to the Tilkoen side of things. So, if you can tolerate working with me all day, everyday, until the Evacuation is complete, negotiating immigration and resettlement policies on behalf of Ageron..." She trailed off, her mouth sardonic but her eyes twinkling.

Niko went rather red for some strange reason. "I uh,... well that's um... unexpected," he said.

"Well, the Tilkoens needed someone to represent them in negotiations between our two Houses. Someone who can understand both Ageronian and Tilkoen viewpoints. So I thought I'd ask, since I'm technically a Tilkoen citizen as well as an Ageronian one, and what do you know... they accepted." Pihla's face split into a grin. "Besides, I'd rather work with a known quantity like you than the likes of some of our senators." She gave him a friendly jab on his arm and winked, "So I'll see you at City Hall next week?"

Niko nodded awkwardly. "Sure," he said coolly, "just don't think you can be bossing me around."

Chancellor Rasmus permitted himself a discreet smile as the two dispersed. *A happy ending for one pair at least.* He looked over to the other side where Marcus waited with Tors and shook his head. *On the other hand...*

"I've made him Centurion," voiced Draeger. He had approached the Chancellor in his usual noiseless manner.

The Chancellor gave the Supreme Commander a small bow in acknowledgement. "You chose well," he said nodding at Marcus' direction. "Lord Conor is most impressed by him."

Draeger nodded. "He is a good leader and a trustworthy one." He gave the Chancellor a weary smile. "I'm afraid I have left you on 'caretaker duty' to watch over things whilst I'm away."

The Chancellor nodded. "You needn't worry," he said. "Evacuation plans are in full flow now and progressing well. The Dictatorship conferred to me will give me the powers to keep the Praetors in check and with Lords Conor, Metavius and Patrin behind me, we'll keep the Senate in under control until you return."

Draeger nodded. "Don't forget, you have General Batsa as well and with that, Tilkoen support."

"Yes, General Batsa is a good ally, " the Chancellor said. He lowered his voice and continued, "The Tilkoens are however, going ahead with the demilitarisation of Ellagrin. Nothing it seems, will persuade them otherwise."

Draeger pondered. "There is nothing we can do from here. Elena has disconnected the private portal and there's no way to get a message across even if we wanted to." He rubbed his chin thoughtfully. "The Tilkoens will have reached the Ellagrin system by now, according to General Batsa. It's too late."

Chancellor Rasmus nodded his head gravely. "So the

Empress Elena won't know until they're on her doorstep," he said.

Draeger nodded. "General Batsa had insisted this was to be a peaceful operation designed to prevent the future acts of aggression predicted by their AIs, not an invasion involving force."

"But what if, despite the show of military superiority, the empress decides not to back down?" asked the Chancellor.

"Let us hope then that she doesn't take the foolhardy option," replied Draeger.

"Indeed," said the Chancellor. He shook his head again. "What do you think of all this, my lord? I mean, to base so much on a *prediction*. Do you think there is basis behind the Tilkoens' decision or is it purely speculation on their behalf?"

Draeger paused awhile before answering. "AI predictions aside, I know Elena well enough to know that she will invade Tilkoen if and when the opportunity arises. After all, she and Akseli had planned to do so if their invasion attempt at Lagentia had succeeded. Akseli would have utilised our military and Ellagrin's to take over and carve out Tilkoen between our two Houses. So perhaps a peaceful disarmament of Ellagrin is the solution to that problem." His dark, fathomless eyes turned towards the Chancellor. "House Ageron has no part in House Tilkoen's policies, nor any say for that matter. Especially now when we are reliant on the Tilkoens for the Evacuation. We made our choice, Rasmus, as did she…"

The Chancellor nodded sombrely. "On a different note," he said, changing the topic, "what will you do when you meet the Empress Yoon?"

"I don't know," replied Draeger, reflecting. "The Oracle foretold of this meeting but nothing more. Perhaps it is something to do with my mother's legacy, perhaps not. I simply do not know."

"And after that?"

Draeger's head remained bowed in deep thought. "After that, I come back to Ageron and we see the Evacuation to its completion," he said, conscious of all the other things concerning he and Tors that he had left out in that sentence. He gave a ponderous shake of the head. "At that point Rasmus, we will have an emigre population on our hands. Do we call Tilkoen our new home or do we remain emigres until we find new home planets?"

"Are you suggesting Tors help us search for new worlds? To open up new Gateways?"

"Perhaps," Draeger answered slowly, "…perhaps not. We have yet to think about the consequences of this. After all, it didn't work out so well for all of us the last time. " He looked at the Chancellor. "Also, she wishes to get away from all this when we get back from Yoon…"

"Understandably so," said the Chancellor. "There is still time to figure all this out," he said kindly, "and perhaps the Empress Yoon may be of help in that respect. She did after all, give us the Oracle to help guide us through the centuries."

"Yes she did," said Draeger, *although perhaps not so with matters of the heart,* he told himself ruefully.

The Chancellor looked away and in the direction of the others who were now hovering by the Departure gates. *The time has come for them to go their separate ways,* he noted with a tinge of sadness as they made their way towards the waiting group.

* * *

DRAEGER APPROACHED Niko and Pihla first.

"Good luck, the both of you," he said, first shaking Pihla's hand and then Niko's. "Keep up the good work on communications between our Senate and their Congress."

"We will," Niko said, answering for the both of them.

Turning to Marcus, Draeger held out his hand. Marcus shook it. "I trust you to support our Chancellor," said Draeger, "and to keep him safe."

"I shall," promised Marcus. "Just as I trust *you* to keep her safe," he said, glancing at Tors. Draeger raised his eyebrow slightly before acknowledging with a curt nod.

Then, it was Chancellor Rasmus' turn. "A speedy and safe return, my lord," he said to Draeger before turning to Tors. He gave her a brief affectionate hug. "Take care of yourself," he said, welling up.

"You take care of yourself too, Chancellor," Tors replied with a smile. "Until we return…"

Then, they all watched as Pihla and Niko cleared security to join Captain Shankar through the Arnemetiaen Gateway and into Sansari. When the trio had disappeared out of sight, Draeger turned to Tors.

"Ready?" he asked.

She nodded. It was very quick, no more than a subtle wave of the hand to draw a wide arc, so quick no one else would have noticed if they hadn't been paying attention and looking carefully. Tors cleaved the opening into the Ether and Draeger followed her into its engulfing darkness.

RASMUS

COMITIUM,
ALANDIA CITY, AGERON

It was late at night and Praetor Maximus Rasmus could hear the distinctive footsteps of Phocis, his secretary, shuffling down the corridor of the Comitium towards his office.

What in Dyaeus' name does he want at this hour? Rasmus closed his eyes and leant back in his chair as he waited for the inevitable knock on the door. "Enter," he said when the anticipated tap came.

"Your Excellency," said a breathless Phocis, handing him the canistrum.

Rasmus gave a perfunctory nod. Try as he might, he just could not get used to his new title as dictator of Ageron whilst Lord Draeger was away.

As was customary with private messages, the small cylindrical canister was sealed. Rasmus twisted the top open, crumbling its resin seal in the process, and tilted the canistrum. A flowered hairpin tumbled out onto the palm of his hand, followed by a small silver cross.

The old man sat forward. "Who gave you this?" he demanded.

"I... I don't know," replied Phocis, slightly taken aback. "It was on my desk when I returned from my comfort break." He glanced at the rather unremarkable object. It was a child's hairpin, a little rusty but apart from a few small enamel flowers on it, nothing but an old trinket.

Rasmus looked at the items in the palm of his hand. First, the hairpin: *Lianne*. This was their signal to meet. Then, the silver cross: *the meeting location*. Rasmus fretted inside. *Something has come up.* He placed the pin carefully inside his desk and looked up at Phocis. "That will be all Phocis," he said, dismissing him.

"Yes, Your Excellency," answered Phocis and turned to go.

Rasmus stood up to put his cloak on after him.

"Oh," said Phocis, noticing, "Would you like me to get your urbanglider ready, Your Excellency?"

Rasmus shook his head. "No, that won't be necessary," he said. "I'm not leaving yet. Just going to get some air. You go ahead Phocis, and go home. It's late."

"Yes, Your Excellency," answered Phocis gratefully. As he shuffled off down the corridor, Rasmus turned to close the door behind him.

"Your Excellency?"

Rasmus almost jumped. He'd forgotten about Lucius, his bodyguard.

"Yes, yes Lucius," he replied slightly irritably. "I'm just going out for some air."

"I'll come with you, Your Excellency, " said Lucius. "It's late—"

"No," snapped Rasmus, "that won't be necessary. I'm not going out— just round the corner to the balcony. I need a smoke... *alone*." Lucius began to protest but Rasmus waved him off impatiently. "I'm not leaving the building," he said pretending to get really annoyed. "I'll be in the balcony smoking. I'll come back after I've cleared my head."

Lucius nodded and withdrew to his position by the door.

Despite the flutter of disquietude he felt inside, Rasmus forced himself to walk down the corridor normally whilst he was still within Lucius' sights. *Lianne,* he worried, *are you in trouble?* Once he turned the corner and was out of Lucius' line of sight, he hurried past the balcony, down the stairs and out onto the street. At this time of night, the area around the government building was thankfully empty of people. Rasmus hailed a passing autocab.

"Ecclesia Sansovino," he instructed, tapping his docket on the payment pad.

"Ecclesia Sansovino, sir," confirmed the autocab in its gender-neutral voice before whirring around and entering the main road to join the traffic. For once, Rasmus was glad for these 'automated tin cans' for this was the one time he didn't want anyone asking about where he was going.

* * *

Ecclesia Sansovino was one of the oldest churches in Alandia. Tall, ornate and cavernous, it was a place of worship for the public, to whichever Gods or deities they chose to pray to—all three hundred and twenty five of them and mostly from Old Earthian religions.

Rasmus stepped out of the autocab, walked past the church's row of large Ionic columns and into the building itself. Inside, the cool quiet space was dimly lit by electrical sconces which cast realistic flickers into the shadows of the vast oval-shaped nave. The church was empty.

It's nearly one in the morning after all, noted Rasmus as he made his way down the nave, past the altar and into the left sacristy. The door to the sacristy had been left slightly ajar. Rasmus pushed it gently to enter. He blinked as his eyes adjusted to the brighter lighting here.

It was a fairly modest-sized room, five by five metres and lined with a bank of panelled cupboards almost reaching the sills of the tripartite windows. An armoire, an old dressing screen and a few sacramental robes hanging on a rack filled the rest of the space.

Lianne stepped out from behind the screen. "Are you alone?" she whispered.

"Lianne!" said Rasmus, relieved to see her. "Yes, I'm alone. Of course. Are you alright? What's the matter? "

Lianne didn't answer him directly. "I need to see it…" she said instead.

"See what?" asked Rasmus, bewildered. "What by Dyaeus are you talking about?"

Lianne looked at him nervously. "The secret," she pressed, "the one you mentioned to me before. The evidence that has kept Lord Draeger safe all these years. You said to me once that it's here. Hidden. Somewhere."

"What are you talking about child? There is no such thing," said Rasmus, dismissively. *Lady Yinha's secret has nothing to do with you. It is not something you, or anyone, need know about.*

"But father—"

"Go *home* Lianne," Rasmus cut in irritably. "All this conspiracy gossip going around the Senate has gotten to your head. Calling me out for this as an urgent matter? Utter nonsense!" He turned to leave.

"I wouldn't leave just yet, Your Excellency." A familiar voice rang out, sharp as blades.

Rasmus whirled around. *Queen Alin.*

The Queen Mother stepped out from behind the armoire.

Standing next to Lianne, she looked almost younger and most certainly stronger than Lianne, bent with her arthritis and her dull grey locks.

"Well?" enquired Queen Alin, "Where is it old man?"

Rasmus eyed her steadily. "I don't know what you are talking about, my lady. If you will excuse me, it is rather late." He turned to leave but found his way barred by the hulking figure of Queen Alin's guard-attendant.

"What is the meaning of this?" snapped Rasmus, irate. "Call off your guard at once or—"

"Or what?" Queen Alin replied calmly. Her lips curled into a self-satisfied smile. "Justus here is going to keep us right here for a bit longer so we can talk," she continued, placing one hand on Lianne's shoulder.

"Please father," pleaded Lianne, her voice tremulous, "just show her where it is. Please…"

Father, noted Rasmus, his heart sinking. *So Alin knows she is my daughter.* "Oh child, you are being played and you don't realise it," he said.

"Why do you keep defending the Supreme Commander?" voiced Lianne. Her tone, petulant and defiant hurt Rasmus even more.

I had taken pains to keep you out of all this. Shield you in order to protect you, and yet you walk right into this... "You don't understand Lianne," Rasmus said.

"No I *don't*," Lianne retorted, "because you don't tell me. You don't tell me anything. But I learnt from working with the Senate, with Lord Reku, and by listening at the Comitium. People talk, father, and they all say the same thing—that Lord Draeger is the one who had liaisons with the Ellagrin empress, not our Emperor and it is most likely that it was he who planned the invasion with her. To take the throne. Why do you keep protecting him?"

ALANDIA CITY, AGERON

"Do not talk about things you do not know, child."

"I'm not a child anymore, father," Lianne said bitterly. "Besides, you've never acknowledged me as yours anyway. I'm your secret. As if I am something to be ashamed of. Well, most of the Praetors think as I do about Lord Draeger. So *why* are you helping him seize power?"

I'm not, thought Rasmus, *Fools! You're all being hoodwinked, by her.* He regarded the Queen Mother with contempt. "You planned all this, didn't you," he said. "You've been scheming and undermining Draeger's position all this time. We should have gone ahead with Akseli's trial and finished it."

Queen Alin smiled. "Ah, but you didn't, old man."

"Draeger spared your son, my lady."

The Queen laughed harshly. "He postponed the trial, not put it off. And let's not pretend that he's going to spare Akseli. If Yinha's spawn is anything like its mother, Draeger will not let Akseli live. The only sentimental person is you, Rasmus and sentimentality we know, is a weakness that can be exploited to great effect." She pulled Lianne closer to her, holding Lianne's arm in an iron grip. Rasmus noted the subtle sheen of her flesh-coloured gloves.

"It took me awhile," continued Queen Alin, "but I figured it out eventually." She looked at Lianne with disdain. "Love can be both a powerful tool and a great weakness," she said, "and you just *love* to talk don't you Lianne? You just *love* to be helpful." The Queen Mother looked back at Rasmus with a cold, cold look that only made Rasmus' heart sink to his stomach. In her other hand, a small gun was pressed firmly against Lianne's side.

"What do you think you are doing?" Rasmus reached forward but Justus, Alin's guard-attendant, grabbed him roughly and held him back. Rasmus winced as the man's massive hand clamped firmly on his shoulder.

Queen Alin gave a disparaging smile. "A test of fatherly love," she sneered. "Take him back out to the nave Justus, so he can show us. My patience runs thin. Now *where* is it?"

They moved out of the sacristy and back into the enormous nave, Justus shoving Rasmus on like a rag doll and Lianne shuffling helplessly in front of Queen Alin.

Rasmus looked around. The expansive chamber was deserted.

"No use looking for someone to help you, old fool," said Queen Alin. "The doors have been locked."

All around, the solemn figurines of all three hundred and twenty five saints surrounded them, each staring silently from their niches in the shadows, the flickers of light from the sconces illuminating their faces intermittently before being swallowed up by the darkness again.

The Queen Mother shoved Lianne in front of her to face Rasmus. "Where is it?"

"You know I can't ever tell you that," said Rasmus. He could feel Justus standing behind him, his grip tightening on his shoulder. The pain was crushing. *But I cannot relinquish it. It is the only thing that stands in her way, the only thing that has prevented her from attacking Lord Draeger all these years. I have to protect it in order to protect Draeger. I promised Lady Yinha this all those years ago...*

The Queen held Lianne's right hand up. It was so rapid Rasmus did not register what had happened until Lianne's scream of pain filled the air.

He looked on in helpless horror as Justus held him back.

Her hand!

Lianne's cries, incoherent, like a wounded animal's, continued. She would have crumpled to the floor if Alin wasn't still holding onto her arm. On the marble floor, her

ALANDIA CITY, AGERON

hand, cleanly severed from her wrist down, lay in a dark pool of blood. Alin had sliced it off with the plasma gun.

"Stop snivelling, Lianne," snapped Alin. "You're not going to miss it," she said. "You were never that good at transcribing anyway." She turned to Rasmus, her eyes glittered like ice. "I shan't be as magnanimous in my next shot, old man," she said. "And I suggest you hurry before she bleeds to death."

Rasmus grew cold. *Lianne! Lianne...*

"*Where is it you old fool??*" screamed Alin. Her eyes clocked Rasmus' flick from one saint to the next. "Is it behind one of these statues?" she demanded. "Which one old man? *Which saint?*"

I cannot, thought Rasmus. *I must not. Oh Lianne...*

"Father..." choked Lianne, clutching her arm in agony. "Please father... just give her what she wants."

Rasmus looked around desperately. Through the ancient tripartite windows that encircled the entire church, a pale crimson glow had begun to sweep through the nave—it was nearly sunrise. He hoped Lucius would have sounded the alarm for his absence by now.

But where would they look for me? They wouldn't know where to find me. His heart sank. *They wouldn't find us here in time.* He looked at Lianne, barely standing. *She will bleed to death the longer I delay.* He recalled her, eleven or twelve years of age, a small Tilkoen slip of a girl orphaned by the LON attack in Lagentia. Now, an old woman, within retirement age, she was still his daughter. Still that little girl he had adopted.

Oh, how I have failed you, my daughter...

The Queen Mother raised her gun and placed it against Lianne's temple. "I *will* kill her if you don't show it to me, you know it, Rasmus," she warned. She paused and then continued, her tone a touch softer. "But equally, I will spare her if you do. Like you, I am a parent simply trying to save my child."

Rasmus shot her a look. *Does she mean it?*

"Now *walk*, Rasmus," she said with steely determination.

Despite his reluctance, Rasmus found himself stumbling in front of them and soon halted in front of a particular statue.

Queen Alin gave a snort of derision. "Saint Michael," she scoffed, "the saint for protection against evil. I should have guessed."

Rasmus stood before the saint and hesitated.

"*Now!*" barked Queen Alin, jolting him back into action.

Rasmus knelt down before the figure.

The Queen Mother snickered. "Come now Rasmus, now is not the time for prayer."

The old man bent and placed his thumb on the second toe of the Saint's foot. A discreet blip sounded as his thumbprint was scanned and authenticated. Beneath the Saint's feet, a small door to the secret compartment irised open with barely a whisper. Rasmus reached into its inky depths to take it out.

A glint of gold.

Queen Alin let out a small gasp as Rasmus drew the exquisite piece out into the light. It was a golden bracelet. A token of love.

"A... a bracelet?" Lianne said weakly.

Justus who was standing behind Rasmus, reached over to relieve it from Rasmus and handed it to Queen Alin.

The bangle gleamed as she turned it over to inspect it. Etched around its side amidst the intertwined leaf and flowery motifs was the unmistakeable imperial insignia of Ellagrin.

"Genomic apostil," corrected Rasmus, looking at Lianne. Alin had loosened her grip on her and was scrutinising the bracelet. He leant weakly against the foot of Saint Michael pretending to catch his breath. He remembered keeping a commemorative dagger in the same compartment. *If I could just reach for it, perhaps I can also salvage this situation.* His heart began to beat faster, but he continued talking. "Favoured by Agerons and Ellagrins alike as a love token, they're usually gifted from husband to wife after the birth of the child. The apostil registers the genetic identities of both parents, along with the child's. It is often used by the wealthy to prove lineage or inheritance claims due to its tamper-proof Tilkoen cryptography, although"—he glanced at Alin—"for some reason this fell out of favour during Emperor Ageron III's time."

Queen Alin ignored him and continued to turn the bracelet slowly in her hand, her fingers methodically searching for something. She found it: a small outdent in the centre of one of the intricate flowers. She pressed it and a stream of holographic calligraphy sprang from the bracelet, casting an eerie glow about.

The golden letters swirled upwards in a double helix formation, strange and beautiful, the ancient glyphs floating upwards like haunting spirals of smoke. Even Rasmus himself stood still and stared as the symbols swirled, then morphed into modern letters to form a word. No, a *name*: Mikael. The elegant swirls twined with the second part of the helix. A second set of letters: *Alin*. Once coupled together, the stream of golden letters burst into a shower of golden discs forming a third name: *Akseli Mikael Aleksander*.

With everyone looking at the hologram in rapt attention, Rasmus lurched for the dagger in the compartment. He fumbled, searching wildly and found it.

It was as if time froze. A single decision compressed into one split second of reaction. But before he even had the chance to stab Justus, BAM! A blinding light surged in his vision, exploding out of the darkness before he went down under the crushing blow of the guard.

The cold stone floor came up to meet him.

It took some time before he was conscious again. Justus had hoisted him up to lean against the base of the statue and Rasmus' head throbbed like a dozen juddering hammers. Lianne was sat on the ground beside him. She stopped sobbing when she saw him open his eyes.

Rasmus looked up at the Queen Mother. "Let her go," he uttered weakly. "You said you would. You have what you want now. Just let her go…"

Alin studied him with detached interest. "Did you know," she said indifferently, "how I've watched over your precious Draeger in his younger days?" She gave a harsh, derisive laugh. "That witch mother of his, Yinha—she made sure of it." Hatred raged in her eyes. "I prayed for his health every day of his life, Rasmus. Every single cursed day. And that was the worst part, not my having to make sure the other consorts didn't murder him, but praying for his health. Praying for the longevity of the sorry little lord's life, when my son, *my* own son had to be content with the leftovers. But no more. You have nothing on me anymore and Akseli will now take back the throne that is rightfully his."

"But it's n… not his to claim," stammered Lianne. "The bracelet shows Akseli is Emperor Mikael's son. He's not Ageron's son—not the rightful heir to the throne."

Alin looked at her scornfully. "Even now your analytical skills astound me." She laughed, this time almost hysterically. "Oh the irony! Akseli is in fact second in line to the throne. *Just not this one.*" Then she turned her gaze onto Rasmus. "But I have plans for him to sit in *both*. A pity you won't live to see it, old man."

The shot came searingly hot at first then cold all at once.

ALANDIA CITY, AGERON

Rasmus looked down at himself. A dark red stain began to bloom and spread against his grey tunic. The room seemed to grow colder and a chill unlike anything he'd felt before seeped into him.

Lianne... Dyaeus almighty, please let my child live...

It was too painful to speak. His eyes searched Alin's for a glimmer of mercy as Alin turned to the sobbing Lianne. His hopes lifted for a second as she considered a moment. Then, with callous disdain she said, "You're not even worth it," and gave Justus the nod. The guard turned and stabbed Lianne in the neck.

Rasmus looked on helplessly as his daughter's aged body crumpled to the floor. As the darkness of death gradually engulfed his last vision of her lying in front of him, Rasmus saw Alin calmly place the gun in his daughter's remaining hand and walk away.

BODEN'S MATE

Boden's mate: Chess term. Boden's Mate, named for Samuel Boden, is a checkmate pattern in which the king, usually having castled queenside, is checkmated by *two* crisscrossing *bishops*. Immediately prior to delivering the mate, the winning side typically plays a *queen sacrifice* to set up the mating position.

The night felt unusually warm, even for Olicana whose distance from the suns should have meant slightly cooler temperatures compared with the other planets closer to the suns. The Queen Mother sat at her veranda, regal and reposeful under the soft glow of the hanging lanterns, engrossed in a game of chess with Lord Marius. She appeared to be in good spirits and the cheerful chirr of wetabugs in the evening seemed to echo her buoyant mood.

"I hear the Senate's vote was unanimous in transferring the Dictatorship to Lord Patrin," she said. Her eyes gleamed with intent as she moved her pawn.

Lord Marius rubbed his chin thoughtfully and considered his next move. He noted, rather smugly, that her queen was exposed. *Always too impatient, and always too eager to go on the offensive.* With a triumphant grunt, he reached out and took her queen with his knight.

Queen Alin let out a snort of reproof.

"Yes," replied Marius seemingly oblivious to her outburst of annoyance, "in light of Rasmus' mysterious death, Patrin is being sworn in as we speak. Tomorrow's official ceremony crowning him Dictator of Ageron will be broadcast live across the empire."

"Well," said Queen Alin perhaps a little too brightly, "I suppose the show must go on."

Marius shot her a sharp glance. *What does she know about his death and does she have anything to do with it?* He wondered how much of her elation was to do with her deep-seated hatred for the Chancellor and how much of it was because she knew something Marius didn't.

The Queen continued, "There is after all, lots to do: the much anticipated Evacuation and all that." She permitted herself a small giggle. "Can't have a power vacuum, can we? People don't like that sort of thing. Now with Patrin at the helm, everybody can get back to work."

Marius glanced at her interestedly.

But Queen Alin kept her head bowed as she mulled her next move, her eyebrows knitted in deep thought. At length, she decided to move her bishop back in retreat.

"Isn't it tragic?" Lord Marius said airily and moved his bishop to open up. He was pleased with his move and having lost her queen, Alin's position was very much weakened. *Now would be the time to capitalise on this weakness,* Marius told himself, relishing the prospect of threatening her rook next.

"Isn't what tragic?" enquired Alin casually. Without hesitation moved her pawn to threaten his King.

"The Chancellor's death," replied Marius. He looked at her intently. *Hmmm...* there was no discernible reaction from her when he mentioned the Chancellor. He turned back to the game and pondered her audacious move before deciding it wasn't that threatening after all.

"Ah…" said Alin noncommittally after a while.

"Very mysterious too," continued Marius conversationally before picking up his King and castling. "They say they found him next to the murderer's body. A woman. And Tilkoen! Do you think there is some conspiracy in all this?"

Queen Alin laughed. Far too knowingly, Marius felt.

"You men and your conspiracies," said Queen Alin. "The woman was reported to be an Ageronian citizen, orphaned in the War. Nothing to do with our newfound Tilkoen friends and certainly no conspiracy theory." She looked at Marius, her eyes sparkling with mirth and mischief. "Perhaps she was Rasmus' bit on the side…"

Marius nearly choked. "Bit too old for him wouldn't you say?" he sputtered.

"In relative years, hardly," said Queen Alin. "Tilkoens only live to about two hundred. They say she was about a hundred and ninety. Practically middle-aged if compared to us."

"But without rejuvenation…" Marius shuddered, revulsed. "She looked far too old for my liking."

"Well, I wouldn't put that past Rasmus," Queen Alin cackled wickedly. "I always did suspect his tastes in women bordered on gerontophilia." She pondered her next move. "Now, what about the state of events at the Senate. How are the Praetors taking Patrin's promotion?"

Marius shrugged. "It has certainly calmed everybody down, including the Tilkoens as everyone is keen to keep Evacuation efforts going without hitch. And I will say this, the Senate like Patrin. Patrin is like Rasmus. He's their conservative choice." He gave an emphatic sigh and rubbed his chin, fingers rasping meditatively against his grey beard. "It's such a shame no one sees me that way. Even when Rasmus was alive, Patrin was always the favoured one." Marius gave her a wry grin. "He gets the support of the Senate by virtue of his non-extremist views. Nothing too radical to rock the gravy boat of our distinguished Praetors, heh? Patrin the safe choice…"

Queen Alin chuckled. "If only they knew."

"Mmmm," agreed Marius, "but what about the Tilkoens? Rasmus's death may spook them."

"Not if Patrin stays in power," replied Queen Alin simply. "Of course, Patrin will have to make you Chancellor as well," she added, "…as promised."

As promised. Marius smiled at her. "If that is what you wish. I am, as ever, merely at the service of the empire. But what about General Batsa? Have you considered the potential come back from him? He's always been a staunch supporter of Lord Draeger and Chancellor Rasmus, and the Tilkoens are suspicious of you and Akseli. Don't forget, they have a military that equals ours, perhaps stronger if their technological advances are to be believed."

Queen Alin shook her head. "As long as Akseli remains under house arrest and Patrin is Dictator, the Tilkoens will not interfere. They have no reason to. Besides," she leant forward lowering her voice, "a little bird told me that most of their troops are on the other side of the galaxy anyway, in what appears to be an exercise to demilitarise Ellagrin…"

Marius' eyes widened with interest. "Really?"

"*Really,*" Alin said without divulging anything further, much to Marius' annoyance. "Worry not. The Tilkoens have enough to keep them busy. Draeger's allies, Pihla and the human Niko, are in Sansari working diligently on preparations. Here in Ageron, even Rasmus' staunchest supporters Praetors Conor and Metavius won't have anything to protest against as long as Patrin is Dictator."

"What about that Marcus, the ex-rebellion leader?" asked Marius.

Queen Alin dismissed that with a casual wave of the hand. "Marcus Thaddeus is but a Centurion under Lord Conor. Hardly high ranking enough to do anything other than follow orders." She leant back and smiled self-satisfiedly. "You see, everything is as it should be."

"Hmmm," pondered Marius. *And what of your next move then?* He glanced at Queen Alin and then back at the chessboard. "I hear that General Batsa is returning to Sansari in a fortnight's time," he said. "For the foreseeable future too, seeing as the Evacuation is running so smoothly. Which will further ensure little or no interference from the Tilkoens going forward."

"Indeed," nodded Alin self-assuredly.

"But what of Akseli?" asked Marius. "Lord Draeger could return anytime. Akseli will have to claim the throne before that happens. Aren't you planning to orchestrate that?"

Yes, yes," answered Queen Alin impatiently, "it will happen, don't you worry. But first,"—she looked at him, her face creased in smugness—"*checkmate*!" She clapped her hands gleefully.

A groan escaped Marius. He studied the pin carefully. "Boden's mate," he said, looking at the criss-crossing bishops.

"Indeed," smiled Alin. She looked at him, her pale blue eyes glinting like icicles caught in the light, and pointed at the bishops. "My two bishops—you and Lord Reku," she said with deadly intent. "And like Boden's Mate, you will both help Akseli reclaim the throne."

Marius smiled as it dawned on him the parallels between the chessboard and Alin's setup with the Senate. "Very clever!" he said, although deep down the realisation disquieted him slightly. *So, myself and Lord Reku.* Amongst the twelve Praetors that led the Senate, only he and Lord Reku were also Legati. Where the other Praetors could only concern themselves with matters of administrating their respective planets, as Legati, Lord Marius and Lord Reku commanded their planets' armies too.

Reku and I—our armies answer to us directly and together we make up more than half of the empire's military, Marius realised, *and Alin knows this. She intends to use the military to pressure the Senate to reinstate Akseli as emperor. If Reku and I back this, the other legions will follow. With Draeger away, they are at the moment without leadership . With the pressure of our armies, and with Patrin's blessing, the Senate's vote to reinstate Akseli will be virtually unchallenged.*

Marius smiled at her. *You were always good at this game...* Then he asked, "And when would you like your bishops to make their move, my lady?"

Alin looked at him and smiled. "Imminently, Lord Marius. Imminently. But before that, I have one more move to make..."

Marius' eyes darkened. " Something tells me getting Akseli back on the throne isn't all you have in mind," he said quietly.

"Well," Alin replied with an intensity in her voice that made him go cold, "as the Old Earthian chessmasters used to say, to win the game, sacrifices must be made. And I intend to win."

"And what are you intending to sacrifice in order to win?" Marius asked.

Queen Alin reached out and picked up the Queen he'd taken earlier. "A queen," she answered.

Marius felt a chill run down his back.

"Or in this case," said Alin, placing the piece in his hand,"an *empress.*"

ENEMY AT THE HORIZON

SUMMER PALACE,

PLANET SKANSGARDEN, ELLAGRIN

*E*mpress Elena awoke with a jolt at the banging on the door.

"Who is it?" she demanded as Grete, her handmaid, bleary-eyed in the antechamber stumbled to check the door. "It's Tadeusz, your Majesty," she called out.

"By Ysgarh, at this hour?" Elena struggled to sit up. *This bump,* she thought to herself irritably, *even a pig could sit up more easily than this!* "Let him in, Grete," she snapped, thoroughly awake now.

Tadeusz, the young court secretary entered hurriedly and knelt at the foot of her bed.

"What is it Tadeusz?" asked Elena, pulling her robe over her nightgown.

"Forgive me, Your Majesty," said Tadeusz, fumbling over his words, "but an... an emergency. The Generals bade me get you. Our scanners have p... p... picked up..."

"Picked up *what* Tadeusz?" urged Elena.

Tadeusz looked up at her. His eyes were wide with fear,

"You'd b... better see it for yourself, Your Majesty," he said haltingly, "...in the conference room."

Elena dressed hurriedly and made her way to the conference room, accompanied by Tadeusz. Converted from one of the Summer Palace's reading rooms, its panelled walls evoked a feeling of studious contemplation. That feeling now jarred against the air of tension emanating from the dozen or so Generals and Doges packed into the workspace, talking and looking anxiously at the multiple rectangular holos that encircled them.

Like cattle trapped in a pen, observed Elena as she entered. "What's happening?" she demanded, looking round the room. The sight worried her. *It's not just the Doges present, all the Generals are here too...*

General Asbjorn stepped forward. "Your Majesty," he addressed her with a clipped bow and led her to the centre holograph. "Our scanners picked this up an hour ago," he said.

Elena looked at the projection: a large dot flanked by a handful of smaller ones next to the schematic of their outermost planet, Kaldr.

"Tilkoen fighterships," continued the General and pointed at the larger dot, "and that one's a destroyer." Several more smaller dots entered the projection as the General spoke and Elena could feel a ripple of concern swell up amongst the herd behind her.

"What are Tilkoen ships doing in Ellagrin space?" she asked.

" We... we don't know, Your Majesty," Lord Magnvar answered.

"Have they tried to hail us?"

"No, your Majesty," he said.

"Have *we* tried hailing them?" snapped Elena, getting impatient.

"Yes, your Majesty," spoke up General Dag. "Numerous times, but no response so far."

"There are more approaching our space," Lord Borys added anxiously as yet another large dot appeared.

General Dag almost choked at the sight and Elena glanced at him. The man, dishevelled and slightly the worse for wear, had paled to a chalky white. *Another destroyer*, she thought apprehensively, *and many more fighters besides.* Further smaller dots appeared, flanking the larger one.

"What about our own fighter ships?" she asked, turning to General Asbjorn. "Our Hauks. Have we dispatched them?" she asked, her eyes searching his for any spark of initiative, purposefulness, motivation. *Anything. This lot are useless!* General Dag shuffled aside as she strode forcefully into the centre of the holographic workspace. "Well?" pressed Elena.

General Asbjorn nodded across at General Einar who switched the holo to display their fighters in formation. "Here they are," pointed the General, "in position, just outside Kaldr. Weapons on both of Kaldr's satellites are also ready and facing the approaching threat."

"And what then if they breach our space? *When* they breach our space?" Elena demanded to know.

"Well," began General Dag, "we will advance our fighters forward and cut them off there."

"If they intend to invade, they will try and bypass Kaldr to take Skansgarden first," said General Asbjorn, "to take control of our main administration hubs."

Elena drew a sharp breath.

Invade, the general had said. His words resonated.

Why are the Tilkoens invading us? Part of her wondered if they were somehow aware of her and Akseli's plan to invade them. *But that's impossible—that would have been the next phase had the invasion of Lagentia succeeded and no one else knew what we were plotting. Besides, the first phase had failed anyway.* She turned to General Einar. "Are we equipped to defend, General?"

The General looked doubtful. "We are in position, Your Majesty," he said haltingly, "but there is not a lot we can do."

"What do you mean there's not a lot we can do?" she questioned sharply.

General Einar cleared his throat nervously. "We are in formation and ready to defend, Your Majesty, but we cannot possibly match the Tilkoens in numbers or military might. They are far more advanced…"

"Do you mean to say—" Elena began before a series of chimes interrupted her. The main holo in the centre began to flash.

"Incoming message," said General Asbjorn. "It's coming from the first Destroyer. They're hailing us!"

The other Generals turned to look uncertainly at each other.

"Connect us then!" Elena snapped. *Ysgarh help us, I'm surrounded by fools!*

The holo fizzled out of focus for a split second before sharpening back into a visual of a Tilkoen commander, complete in sage military uniform and wearing at least half a dozen war medals on his left breast.

"I am Air Chief Marshal Batsa Blazing Calm from the GR4 Conciliator fleet, representative of House Tilkoen," the General's deep voice boomed over the speakers. His tanned face with its typical broad cheekbones, accompanied by an even broader set of shoulders, seemed to fill up the space of the projection.

Batsa? noted Elena. The name sounded familiar. She glared at him. "What is the meaning of this Air Chief Marshal? You are about to encroach on Ellagrin space. This is a *hostile* act."

The General gave a curt nod. "We are not here in a hostile capacity, Your Majesty," he said. "Our presence here is not as an act of aggression. House Tilkoen hereby gives you, House Ellagrin, notice. We are here as part of Motion 7285 of the Tilkoen Congress, to secure the demilitarisation of Ellagrin. If you abide, there will be no cause for a military offensive. You are to surrender to our fleet and allow us entry into Skansgarden to sequester administrative powers from the Ellagrin royal court in order to begin forced disarmament."

"On what grounds?" Elena demanded. She moved closer, her voice angry as a viper's. "How *dare* you! We have not engaged in any hostile act against House Tilkoen, yet you have the audacity to invade us?"

"This is not an invasion, Your Majesty," replied the Air Chief Marshal calmly. "Our information sources indicate an active invasion from yourselves is imminent. It *will* happen. Perhaps not today, nor even this decade, but with utmost certainty, *it will happen*. Our predictive intelligence have never been wrong."

Elena threw her head back and laughed. "What *nonsense!*" she said, her tone caustic. "And you call yourselves technologically advanced! Even the priests here have less propensity to spew religious foretelling than this! This... this *incursion*," she hissed with contempt at the word, "constitutes a flagrant breach to galactic laws and a breach of the right of the Ellagrin people to self-rule."

However, Chief Marshal Batsa Blazing Calm remained as unflappable as his name. "This move will negate a future offensive from yourselves," he continued unruffled, "and will result in a smaller cost to all, House Ellagrin included. A conflict-free demilitarisation of Ellagrin constitutes a far more peaceable approach. House Ellagrin will continue to operate, its sovereignty undiminished, if it co-operates with us in the process of disarmament."

Elena gave a derisive snort. "And if we don't?"

"If it comes to it, you cannot beat us in battle," said the Chief Marshal matter-of-factly.

Elena bit her lip in silent fury.

Air Chief Marshal Batsa Blazing Calm pressed on. This time, his words seemed to be directed at her personally. "We believe that plans were afoot for Ageron and Ellagrin to mount a joint invasion on Tilkoen. This pre-emptive strike ordered by Tilkoen's Congress will extinguish any future... *tendencies* towards hostile actions and preserve peace in the region. Please Empress, consider this. For the good of your people and ours."

Elena looked at the Doges and Generals around her for their assessment or response, but none were forthcoming. *Spineless fools.*

Lord Borys pretended to cough delicately into his hanky and General Dag who stood nearby averted his eyes, not daring to meet her gaze. *I am surrounded by gutless imbeciles.*

She turned back to face Air Chief Marshal Batsa Blazing Calm. "I shall need time to consider the terms," she said coldly.

The Air Chief Marshal bowed. "Of course, Your Majesty" he said. "I shall transmit our terms over for your review. You have three days to provide your answer, before we take action." With that the message cut off, returning the holo to its previous display of outer planet Kaldr's space.

A sudden rumble of dissension swelled up like a wave around Elena. She eyed them with incredulity. *Now you have an opinion?*

"He has effectively demanded our surrender," protested Lord Alarik, "what cheek!"

"They mean to invade us, Your Majesty," added General Dag, looking nervously at the dots on the holos.

Elena eyed them all critically and said to General Dag, "Well General, I didn't hear even a peep of a response just now, nor anything remotely resembling an action from you. What do *you* suggest we do then?"

The General bit his lip and remained silent. A few stray hairs lay pasted slick with sweat against his pasty forehead. Elena glared at him with a look of revulsion and contempt in equal measure.

"Perhaps we could try to renegotiate terms with them, Your Majesty?" ventured Lord Magnvar.

"Now wait a minute, Lord Magnvar," voiced General Asbjorn, "We are no match for the Tilkoens. We should consider this offer seriously."

"What? Surrender?"

"We will do *no such thing*!" screamed Elena. There was a stony silence as she eyed each of them with displeasure. "Have you lost your heads or your manhood? You would give our empire up without so much as a fight?"

Lord Borys ventured in a small voice, "But Your Majesty, the Tilkoens are too strong for u—"

"*Useless*!" Elena shouted at them. "All of you …are useless! *Must* I be the one that digs us out of this? There will be *no surrender*!"

She turned on her heel and left the room.

I have to see him. I need him to help me find a way out of this. Her mind whirled, evaluating their options. Any option. *The Lagentian Gateway is no more. Destroyed.* She grimaced. *There will be no cavalry this time.* She sensed her woeful lack of alternatives closing in on her, compressing and constricting like a deadly python's embrace. *But there MUST be a way. A way to exert some influence over the Tilkoens somehow, a way to get them to back down.* She hastened down the corridor, almost running now, towards the Sun Room. Towards the private portal.

ELENA SEEKS HELP

RED PALACE, AGERON

It was late morning and in the bright glare of day, Draeger's personal quarters looked completely different. Newly decorated right up to its gilded cornicing, swathes of red velvet sheathing now replaced the priceless wood panelled walls.

"I had decided my new solar needed quite a bit of remodelling," came the dangerous drawl from the other end of the room.

Elena whirled round, startled.

In the middle of this newly claimed space lounged Akseli, his left leg draped idly over the arm of a chair of rather regal proportions. He eyed her with laid-back insouciance.

"My lord," she greeted indifferently.

"I see you have not lost your grasp of decorum and title," he replied drily. "Not 'Your Excellency' anymore is it, *empress*?"

Elena gave him a cool look in return. "I was under the impression these were your brother's quarters."

"Well, I've decided he doesn't need them anymore," Akseli said airily.

Elena gave him a questioning look.

"Why, haven't you heard?" Akseli continued, regarding her with thinly veiled amusement, "The Supreme Commander has left Ageron to go on quest."

"A quest?" Elena shot him a wary glance.

Akseli nodded. "With that Nehisi woman of his, no less," he answered with relish.

Elena smiled thinly. "So, you've decided to do some remodelling," she said, putting him in his place. "My congratulations."

Akseli gave a harsh, derisive laugh. "Don't worry Elena, Draeger will be back soon. Unless of course the two lovebirds make up and decide to stay away on honeymoon."

Elena felt the heat rise in her face.

"So what brings you here, empress?" asked Akseli. "Is there anything I can do to help? Or is it only my brother you want?" He leant forward, studying her with predatory interest.

Elena swallowed down her pride. "Ellagrin is under siege," she blurted. There was no subtle way to say it. *I am running out of options.*

"Really?" Akseli said, unperturbed, "I had no idea. By whom?"

Elena eyed him suspiciously. "House Tilkoen," she said grimly. "They are in Ellagrin space as we speak, threatening us."

"Threatening you?" said Akseli, sounding unconvinced. "The Tilkoen system is about a decade's spaceflight from Ellagrin which means they had to have launched their spaceships a decade ago. So they had decided this a decade ago." He looked at her. "That sounds highly improbable, don't you think?"

"I am not imagining this, my lord," said Elena. "It appears the Tilkoens decided years ago that Ellagrin's a security threat to them and thus decided on a plan to force us into demilitarisation. Their AIs predicted that Ellagrin would eventually invade them so to pre-empt this, they've turned round to disarm us instead."

Akseli gave a disbelieving snort.

"I know," agreed Elena, shaking her head. "Even I think they're almost as mad as Niklas was."

Akseli considered a moment. "Maybe not," he said with a careless shrug. "Their predictive technology's not as far-fetched as it sounds."

Elena eyed him suspiciously. "Do you know about this? Don't lie to me. Did you know this would happen?"

Akseli raised his hands up in a helpless gesture. "How could I?" he said drawing a cynical smile. "In case you haven't noticed, I have been under house arrest all this time. He moved his leg off the arm of the chair and sat back properly. "Ah, empress," he said, his mouth widening into a glittering smile, "you have missed much since throwing your tantrum and cutting yourself off from the rest of us." He looked at her with an expression on his face that she was unable to read. "Did you know, that in the time since you disconnected the private portal, our emissaries to the Tilkoen system have returned?" He continued to look at Elena with that cold, reptilian gaze. "And with them, a small contingent of Tilkoen representatives. But that's not all you've missed."

Elena glanced at him, feeling increasingly uncomfortable.

"On top of Ageron now having confirmation from the Tilkoens that they will take us in, the mission to Sansari…"—he paused to observe her reaction—"they returned victorious." He gave a smug smile. "The Arnemetiaen Gateway now links Ageron with Tilkoen."

Elena felt a constriction in her throat. *None of this news helps me, nor Ellagrin. If Ageronians now have the ability to evac-*

uate and resettle in Tilkoen, there is no need to depend on Ellagrin anymore. There is no need for them to help us either. Her heart sank. Before, Ellagrin was Ageron's only destination for resettlement and therefore a need that Elena could leverage. Now, it would seem, there was nothing to be traded with House Ageron that Elena could make use of in order to rid Ellagrin of the Tilkoens. *And on top of everything, Draeger isn't even here. What's more, he's with that woman. Think, Elena. Think.*

She brought herself confidently closer to Akseli, leaning in so her eyes met his. "I don't know what to do," she said simply. It was the truth. "Will you help me?" It was a simple appeal, without flirtation or pretence, but for that, it was a powerful one.

He stilled in the power of her gaze. "What is the situation at the moment?" he asked, forcing himself to meet her scrutiny. "Have the Tilkoens begun attack?"

Elena shook her head. "No," she replied, "not yet. They have demanded we sign up to their demand for demilitarisation and surrender Ellagrin to disarmament. I have three days to give my answer, before…"

"Before they 'negotiate by force'?"

Elena nodded grimly. "They will take Skansgarden first I think: the Summer Palace, the seat of power. The Doges and majority of members of the royal court are based there now." Elena grimaced. "I had moved most, if not all of our administration from Namsos to Skansgarden." She kicked herself for this. *I was a fool to have done that. Father based the court at the Royal Palace in Namsos for a reason—that dark, dank fortress was simply much better protected. We could have held out in its bunkers far longer. But that's too late now.* She shook it off. *I have to focus and solve what I can.*

"Well," said Akseli, "as much as I'd like to, I'm afraid with the Lagentian Gateway destroyed in our last ah… joint-venture, there is no way for House Ageron to send any troops to you to withstand this Tilkoen threat currently at your doorstep. Have you tried to engage with the Tilkoens?"

Elena chewed her lip. "Yes," she said, "They're led by a certain Air Chief Marshal," she said, her tone filled with contempt at the recollection of how calmly he rejected her arguments. "A Chief Marshal Batsa Blazing Calm."

"Batsa you say?" Akseli mused. "You know," he said, "there is also a General Batsa here in the Tilkoen contingent that returned with our emissaries. And he did mention a brother in the military…"

Elena studied him carefully. "You know," she said, "for someone who's under house arrest, you seem to know quite a lot about what's going on. So you think your General Batsa in Ageron may be related to this Chief Marshal Batsa?" She pondered further. "Possible relations aside, with the Arnemetiaen Gateway active, you can now contact their Congress in Tilkoen itself, can't you?" She took Akseli's hand in hers. "Help me broker talks between Ellagrin and the Tilkoen Congress," she said. "Help me persuade them to call off this attack, this demand for demilitarisation."

Akseli withdrew his hand from hers. "You want me to help you," he said, "the same way you 'helped' me when my brother was pushing for my impeachment?"

"Your mother and I," said Elena, "we tried to convince Draeger. *I* tried to convince him and it was not for the lack of trying I can tell you." She slid closer to Akseli, almost pressing her body against his. "Do not forget, my support for you has cost me dearly. Does that alone not prove to you where I stand in all this?" She held his gaze. "We have always been allies, Akseli," she whispered. "There is much we can still do together to benefit each other…"

But Akseli made her wait a moment longer before giving

his answer, his eyes flicking all over her face in close proximity. He reached out and fingered her hair lightly. "We may be able to come to an arrangement..." he said. A smile crept to his lips. "I shall help you," he said and stood up. "After all, we are family."

"But how?" asked Elena. "Will you take me to see the Tilkoen Congress?"

"No," said Akseli, "but I will talk to Lord Patrin to engage with Congress."

Elena sat up. "Patrin?" She eyed him suspiciously. *Lord Patrin has your ear?*

Akseli smiled at her, his expression dagger sharp. "Like I said, you've missed much in the last few months, empress. Lord Patrin is Dictator of the Realm whilst my brother is away, and let's just say, fatherhood has made Patrin a much more reasonable man these days." He continued, "Just agree to that Chief Air Marshal's demand for demilitarisation and sit tight. Disarmament takes time, even with all their Tilkoen efficiency. It won't happen overnight. Stall them, delay them whilst I get Patrin to sort this out."

"How exactly—" asked Elena but Akseli dismissed her with a wave of the hand.

"I will take care of it, Elena," he said with an air of finality.

She bit her lip and nodded. "Very well," she said and turned to leave the room.

* * *

AKSELI SAT DOWN and leant back, tossing his feet carelessly on the seat of the chair in front where Elena had sat down earlier. He closed his eyes, hummed to himself and waited.

"What did you mean exactly by 'take care of it'?" came the

anticipated enquiry as the cleverly camouflaged door to the adjoining compartment opened.

Akseli opened an eye and looked at his mother. "I merely agreed to help her," he said.

"You have?" repeated Queen Alin. The disapproval in her voice was evident. "How? Persuade Batsa and the entire Tilkoen Congress to just forget about the whole demilitarisation thing? How clever! Now why didn't anyone think of that?"

Akseli opened both eyes and sighed. "No, Mother. I merely told Elena I would take care of it." He slumped back into his chair and closed both eyes, relishing the annoyance building up within her.

"What do you mean exactly?" pressed the Queen Mother.

Akseli ignored her and leant further back into his chair. "With the majority of the Tilkoen troops in Ellagrin space, their capital planet lies unprotected."

"Yes," said Queen Alin, "but you said a few moments ago that you'd help Elena."

"Oh I'll help her alright," laughed Akseli. He sat up slowly. "By sending our troops through the Arnemetiaen Gateway. By taking the Tilkoens' capital, Sansari."

WAR

CITY HALL,
SANSARI CITY, TILKOEN

Attention. Fire. Fire in the building, came the announcement. *Please begin evacuation procedures. Attention. Fire...*

On the top floor of City Hall, Pihla, in the middle of a meeting with the city planners, stopped mid-sentence. The hair on her neck stood on end. *Something's not right,* she thought. *This is not a routine fire drill.* She looked across the table at Niko, but before she could say anything...

BANG!

As she clamped both ears with her hands, a shock wave followed, knocking her off her feet. The entire building shook. From the ceiling, alarms started blaring, piercing enough to jolt anyone into action.

"Dexa, switch glass to clear," instructed Councillor Divya-Hamish from the other end of the table, raising her voice over the clamour. The walls instantly transitioned from opaque to clear, giving them an uninterrupted view of the city outside. Smoke in thick black clumps arose from the building across the road. A corner section of it had been blown off and shards of glass and metal struts jutted out like torn ligaments.

Niko walked up to the glass and looked out. The building opposite was not the only one in flames. Smoke arose like ominous spires across Sansari, forming a rough trail all the way from the Gate, through the city centre, to their building. In the distance, casting shadows over the cityscape below, a dark cloud headed their way at great speed.

"By Dyaeus, that's not a thunder cloud," said Niko as the nebulous mass moved like a swarm of bees towards their building. He backed away from the view.

"They're not urbangliders either," said Pihla uneasily. She recognised their sleek outlines, engineered for maximum manoeuvrability and the unmistakable red slash across the cockpit and nose-cone.

"Avems!" she yelled. "*Get down!*"

Through the transparent wall came a blazing stream of white, shattering it and continuing upwards, cutting through the ceiling.

"Get down! Get—" yelled Pihla as the deafening roar of the Avems overhead swallowed up the rest of her sentence. The others ducked under the table for cover as Pihla glanced upwards. Through the punctured ceiling, the vivid blue sky shone through as bits of mortar fell on them like showers of hail. As the wind howled through the breached walls, Pihla ushered the others towards the exit. *Before we get blown off or blown up,* she thought, looking furtively at the skyline for the return of the Avems.

Attention. Fire, repeated the announcement. *Fire in the—*

Excuse me, Councillor Hamish... Dexa's calm, clear voice cut over the building's fire announcement.

"Dexa!" responded the Councillor, struggling to her feet. "Who is attacking us?"

SANSARI CITY, TILKOEN

We are under attack from the Ageronians, Councillor, replied Dexa briefly and efficiently. *You are all in danger. It is highly likely their fighterships will circle back to attack the building once more.* Dexa paused a moment as the building announced:

Attention. Bomb-proof cladding initiated. Please keep away from the windows. Please keep away from the windows.

"Don't be alarmed," said Councillor Hamish as the room darkened considerably and the building started to seal itself in a grey metal covering. "They're sealing us in, in case those Avems circle back for another go." The room, briefly plunged in darkness, lit up again as secondary floor lights came on.

Pihla peered through the slits in the grey metal cladding that had enveloped the walls and ceiling.

Across the city, other buildings seemed to morph into a matt grey as each too, donned its bomb-proof armour cladding. Shuttle-chutes with capsules carrying passengers were being emptied as quickly as possible, their capsules zipping downwards into underground stations.

"Dexa," urged Councillor Hamish, "we must get to Chatadharam, the three of us: myself, Pihla and Niko. Can you get us there?"

Yes Councillor, replied Dexa. *I have already taken the liberty of contacting Captain Shankar. He will take you to Chatadharam where the rest of the High Council have regrouped in order to coordinate defensive actions. You may wish to know also, that defensive protocols have been initiated across all major cities on our capital planet.*

"Ach, excellent! Thank you Dexa," replied Councillor Hamish and hurried the others to the lifts outside. "Take the lifts to basement two," she instructed, "then get yourselves into the underground network as fast as you can." She glanced at Pihla and Niko. "You two stay here with me," she said, "until Captain Shankar arrives."

Initiating Protocol 313 Switchover in case of primary node failure. Commencing draining of Cluster A, continued Dexa. Right on cue, the building shook again, this time from another impact several floors below.

Councillor, our scanners indicate the Avems are intent on bombarding this building, said Dexa. *I'm afraid I shall have to disconnect soon and withdraw AI control of this building, leaving it to its auto functions only.*

"Understood, Dexa," said Councillor Hamish and lurched to one side as the building shook once more.

"What does she mean?" asked Pihla reaching out to steady the tall woman. "What is Dexa doing?"

"Dexa's core is in this building," explained the Councillor. "In fact, all our AIs' cores are. They're housed underground, beneath this building. If your Emperor knows this, then he means to raze City Hall. To the ground and below."

"So he means to destroy the AIs," said Pihla.

"Yes," said Councillor Hamish, "but he doesn't know doing that won't wipe them out." She paused until the spate of loud booms died down. "Our AIs run on an active-passive redundancy, here and in Chatadharam, linked via private networks. The cores of Dexa and the others co-exist as identical copies on both sites. Protocol 313 will effectively offline this site and bring their instances in Chatadharam online instead."

Although, may I add Councillor, that if our underground Vault is breached, interjected Dexa, *protocol 399 Expunge will run automatically.*

"Protocol 399? *Expunge?*" Pihla cocked an eyebrow at Councillor Hamish.

"Ach, yes," nodded the Councillor. "If there is a risk of the enemy getting access to The Four's cores here, they will be automatically destroyed."

Excuse me Councillor, interrupted Dexa, *Captain Shankar has*

SANSARI CITY, TILKOEN

just landed. You may make your way to the helipad, exit point level thirty-five. Please hurry...

The building juddered, emanating a deep rumble that seemed to come from its centre. Pihla felt herself sway as the pounding from outside added to further unsteadiness. *Are the lifts safe?* she wondered as they ran towards one. It brought them swiftly down to level thirty-five.

Have a safe flight, Councillor, said Dexa from inside the lift. *I shall see you on the other side...*

"Thank you Dexa. See you in Chatadharam," said Councillor Hamish as the three of them ran to the helipad. Through the doors, Pihla could see Captain Shankar's urbanglider just setting down, dainty as a dragonfly.

"Let's *go!*" yelled Captain Shankar, waving madly. They raced towards him, conscious of the crescendoing hum of the Avems in the distance like an angry swarm.

As they sped away from the city, Councillor Hamish spoke over the drone of the urbanglider, and asked the captain, "Do you have details of what's happened?"

"We are being attacked by the Ageronians," answered Captain Shankar. "They have seized control of the Sansari Gate and now with both ends—Sansari and Arnemetiae—controlled by them, the Arnemetiaen Gateway is theirs." He turned to look at Niko and Pihla. "It would seem your Emperor Akseli has been planning this for a while. And now, he's sent his ground troops and Avems across the Gateway."

"*Akseli?*"

Captain Shankar nodded. "Dictator Patrin conceded his Dictatorship today—to Akseli. Your Senate has reinstated Akseli as Emperor."

"Emperor!" exclaimed Pihla. "Why would the Senate reinstate him?"

"That's Ageronian politics for you," said Niko glumly as he

looked out of the window. "So councillor, why didn't Dexa or your other AIs predict this?"

"They didn't," admitted Councillor Hamish. "The AIs' predictions have always pointed towards the threat coming from Ellagrin, not Ageron. And Lord Patrin's actions to relinquish his post is *most* unusual. As the saying goes, the whole thing smells of scomber..."

"Well, this Akseli is a sly one, alright," said Captain Shankar. "He already had ground troops in place at our Sansari Gate. They've been there for months working under the guise of Evacuation personnel. Now we can't get near the Gate to disable it even if we wanted to."

"But what about the forcefield barriers in place?" asked Niko. "They're network controlled. Akseli can't easily disable them."

Captain Shankar nodded. "Those barriers are designed to prevent pedestrian shuttles from getting through," he said, "and yes, they did keep the Avems out for a bit. However, in the face of a destroyer's firepower..."

Pihla grimaced. "Yeah, a Destroyer would blast its way through that."

"Yes," continued Captain Shankar, "which it did. The Avems were through within seconds." He glanced at the shrinking view of the destruction behind them.

Pihla turned to look too and then wished she hadn't. Entire neighbourhoods of Sansari lay smouldering and overhead, the dark outline of a destroyer hovered as the smaller fighters swarmed round it like a cloud of locusts.

* * *

THEY HAD NOW LEFT Sansari behind and the urbanglider was skimming over the tree tops of the forest below. All around

SANSARI CITY, TILKOEN

below, swathes of forest, wild and untouched stretched for miles and miles like an endless sea of green. As they flew on, Pihla wondered at the tall cylindrical forms of the Dimaga trees which dominated the landscape, their swollen, speckled trunks winking rapidly in the waning sunlight.

"Why do they blink so?" she wondered aloud. Like the small tree branch Niko broke off the other day, they were emitting flashes of light and with the gradual onset of evening, the forest had burst into a beautiful sparkling light show.

Councillor Hamish who was sat next to her, peered over her shoulder. "Ach," she said, her face turning serious, "this is why we don't allow clearing of our forests for farming or settlement under the terms of the Evacuation programme."

Pihla tilted her head at her. "Why is that?" she asked. "Is there a reason why the terms of our resettlement stresses the prohibition of cutting down these forests?"

"Aye!" nodded Councillor Hamish, eyeing her keenly. "Do you wonder why we Tilkoens live packed tightly together in our cities? And why one of the prime criteria for resettlement of your peoples is that they do so in our cities?"

Pihla shook her head.

"It is not by choice," said Councillor Hamish, "although it so happens we Tilkoens tend to prefer more socially dense living arrangements anyway. We do so because we *have* to." She pointed at the Dimaga trees outside. "Did you know Dimaga means 'mind'?" She looked at Niko and continued, "And yes, as you've observed, the surface of their trunks and their branches seem to wink in and out all the time."

"Yes," said Niko, "there's some mottling on its surface that keeps flickering on and off. It's like a light show."

"Cellular automata," explained the councillor. "We found out early on, that their cambium cells respond to simulation in a boolean fashion. They emit a flash of luminescence in the process, a process which mirrors digital computation—"

"Biological computers, " said Pihla in wonderment.

The councillor nodded. "It was in the early days of our AI development when we realised we couldn't possibly build enough hardware to deliver the computing power needed for machine learning with what little mined resources we had on our planets. But we realised we didn't need that. We could harness the Dimaga to perform computer-like operations."

"So you were effectively using them as a biological equivalent of a processor," said Pihla.

"Yup," said Councillor Hamish. "And we didn't even need to build a network. You see, the roots of the Dimaga spread far and wide. They are in fact an underground hyphal fungal network." Her eyes gleamed as she nodded. "Yup," she said acknowledging Pihla's surprised look, "these aren't even trees. So you see, the Dimaga not only augments our processing power, it provides us with connectivity. The millions and millions of linked Dimaga all over our planets—they, combined with our wired and wireless connections to our AI Cores, form one massive distributed network."

"So that's why you've never terraformed any of your planets," said Pihla.

"Yes," replied Councillor Hamish, "What you see down there is not just a forest. You're looking at one colossal biological networked computer system."

"You know, no one knows this," voiced Niko. "We just thought Tilkoens were eccentric tree-huggers, that's all."

Councillor Hamish gave a small chuckle. "State secret. Telecommunications in all of Tilkoen takes one of three forms: wired, wireless and organic. Occasionally, the Dimaga introduce minute errors into the transmission of the data that they receive and output, but nothing our error correction algorithms can't handle."

"So the Dimaga provide processing power and relay the massive amounts of data across the planet," said Pihla. "Genius!"

"Indeed," smiled Councillor Hamish. "The flora itself poses no threat of course, as they have no concept of what these streams of data they're handling are, but they are an abundant and ready resource. So there you have it... now you know."

Pihla gave a low whistle and sat back. *So that's why most of Tilkoen is left in its natural state. That's why they like to keep as much forest as they can—their technology runs on Dimaga. The symbiosis between nature and machine...*

"Tower 1, Cara Sparrow 36 requesting entry into airspace. Sending authorisation code through," Captain Shankar broadcast to the control tower.

Pihla looked out and saw the familiar buildings and parks of Chatadharam ahead. The garden city looked as it always had, except for an almost imperceptible shimmer around it. *A forcefield dome,* she realised and wondered if it would hold under fire from a destroyer.

Cara Sparrow 36, you are authorised to enter, responded the Tower. *Please proceed through designated coordinates 230519 intersection 5 ortho 667.*

"Thank you, Tower 1," responded Captain Shankar, guiding the aircraft downwards through what Pihla guessed was an invisible segment of the forcefield that had been disabled. She held her breath as they descended and let out a sigh of relief as they passed through unscathed. Either that or they'd have crashed against an invisible wall.

The transparent form of the Forum loomed ahead, its organic-looking landing pads jutting out of its midsection greeting Pihla with comforting familiarity. Around the building, the city with its numerous parks and open spaces looked the quiet and peaceful. However, the bright of their greenery was marred with large shadows—shadows of a Tilkoen battlecruiser and fighter ships hovering, just outside the forcefield dome.

"We should hurry," said Captain Shankar as they landed. "It won't be long before the Avems from Sansari reach here." He looked at Pihla's worried face. "But don't worry. Chatadharam will be better protected than Sansari. We are smaller and we have underground bunkers."

No sooner had they disembarked, the bombing began. First, came muted thunks from above as a few Avems breached the frontline Tilkoen fighters to bombard the domed forcefield.

"We'd better get inside," urged Councillor Hamish. Pihla could feel the thumps and whumps becoming more and more frequent. They were powerful too, each one reverberating with residual shockwaves that coursed through her body. She glanced upwards and saw Tilkoen fighters deep in action, fending off the Avems. Further away, the battlecruiser, solid and squat, was firing in all directions, picking the Avems off as they attempted to breach the dome into the city.

But there are so many of them. She squinted into the distance, observing their manoeuvres. The Tilkoen fighters were too hooked up on formations. *They don't seem to know how to handle these dogfights. Our Avems, by contrast, are like an unpredictable swarm. It will only be a matter of time before they break through the formation...*

Captain Shankar stopped just before the entrance into the building. "This is where I leave you," he said.

Pihla turned around to look at him. He paused a moment to face her and stretched his hand out. "Come with me?" he asked, "We could use a fighter."

SANSARI CITY, TILKOEN

Pihla felt a shiver run down the back of her neck. *I've been here before—in the vision the Empress showed me...*

Captain Shankar looked up and indicated at the sky above. "As you can probably tell, we're not doing very well up there. You know how these Avems move, how they attack. We could really use your help right now."

She looked at him, momentarily frozen. *A choice*, the Empress had said.

"Pihla..."

It was Niko. He had stepped forward. She could see the look on his face. *He doesn't want me to go...*

"I have to go," she found herself saying to him. "I can't stay here to watch our friends die. I know our military tactics and how to counteract them—I've had enough experience of that during the Rebellion. I can help our Tilkoen friends."

"But—" said Niko.

BOOM!

The next hit from above punched down like a ton of bricks. They all cowered as the next bombardment of shells pierced through the forcefield, hitting the deck, spraying debris everywhere.

"See if you can get in contact with Marcus!" Pihla yelled to Niko. "See if there's a way he can stop this from Ageron!"

BOOM!

Another shelling, this time nearer, causing the helipad to shake and shudder.

"Get inside!" shouted the Captain, waving them into the building. He turned to Pihla. She nodded and together they ran back to the urbanglider. The dome had been breached and the deafening sounds of firing and the constant scream of fighter ships above filled her ears.

"Pihla, wai—!"

Pihla heard Niko call out over the clamour. She ran to the

back of the urbanglider as it lifted off, grabbed the side to hang on and looked out of the open door.

Niko was standing at the helipad looking up as the aircraft rose. He reached out for her and tried to grab her hand. He missed and grasped empty air instead. The heavy pounding of artillery overhead engulfed all sense of hearing.

Goodbye, Pihla mouthed and blew him a kiss as the urbanglider lifted away.

ZUGZWANG

HUANGSHAN MOUNTAINS, PLANET YOON

Zugzwang: Chess term, meaning 'compulsion to move' in the Old Earthian language of German. When a player is put at a disadvantage by having to make a move and where any legal move weakens the position. Zugzwang usually occurs in the endgame.

It was snowing this time on the top of the mountain when they emerged from the Ether. The dusky evening sky was awash with streaks of pink and marred by gentle snow flurries cascading down like soft feathers in the fading light.

The mountains of Yoon!

Draeger's eyes, perfectly adjusted to the fading light, took in the magnificent vista: majestic mountain ranges stretching as far as the eye could see, interspersed with ridges and rivers below, like toy models.

"Keep the breathing-strips on until we get to the village," said Tors, checking hers before bending down to release her skates. "Oxygen levels up here are too thin to sustain us."

Draeger nodded as he rapped the back of his heels against

the rock. Like Tors', inbuilt skates flicked out from underneath the soles. *An excellent piece of customisation from Pihla, I bet,* he mused. He glanced at Tors. "All set?"

She nodded and pointed at the start of a long and winding sliddery, gleaming subtly in the fading light. "We head that way," she said.

Draeger eyed the path with slight trepidation. "It's quite steep," he began. "Be careful. You shouldn't be speeding down that in your con—"

But Tors was already tearing down the slope with wild abandon.

"…dition," finished Draeger, shaking his head. *Reckless as ever.* He pushed himself off and skated down the sliddery after her.

Their path down the sliddery was steep and swift. At times, its silvery path criss-crossed others. Much as roads would, Draeger guessed but he had little time to contemplate. Ahead, Tors was flying down the slope at breakneck speed. Draeger swore, then tucked in, crouched down low and tried to keep up.

Eventually, his perseverance was rewarded. Ahead, the twinkling lights of a small village greeted them. *Here at last,* thought Draeger and bent to accelerate further only to have Tors swerve round and yank him to an abrupt stop.

Ah, realised Draeger. Thirty feet ahead, where he was headed, was a sheer drop off the edge of the mountain. Had she not stopped him, he would plunged into an abyss.

Tors tore off her breathing-strip. "We're going up that way," she said, pointing at some steep steps cut into the rock face, on their left. They led up the mountainside where the warm glow of a building perched on top, its jutting roof ridges faintly visible, beckoned.

With a thousand steps, I walk in peace. His mother's words came to him, remnants of a childhood memory. *This was how she described the ascent to the monasterial palace, her home.*

"Here, let me take that," he said, taking the backpack off Tors as they began their ascent up the narrow steps in the dimming evening light. She hadn't protested—that was a good sign.

The trek was fairly straightforward but not without risk due to the narrowness of the steps, some treacherously camouflaged by thick snow.

"It helps not to look down," advised Tors as she led the way.

Draeger looked down and staggered, immediately assailed by a sense of vertigo.

"Told you not to look down," remarked Tors, not even casting so much as a glance behind her. Draeger grunted in reply but kept his eyes ahead of him from then on.

At last, they reached the top where a monastery of stone sat.

Akasa.

He recognised the monastery from childhood holos. It was dark now, the sun having long disappeared behind the mountains, but Akasa's pale walls shimmered softly in the glow of its lanterns draped along the walls.

* * *

"Tors!" A rather buxom nun bounded down the entrance path to give Tors a big bearhug.

"Sister Chun-Hei!" Tors exclaimed, pleased to see her.

The nun beamed at Draeger and turned to hug him. "The Empress is expecting you," she said.

"Thank you, sister," Draeger replied. *Her eyes,* he noted

with surprise as he drew back. They were dark like his, like unseeing black sockets.

Sister Chun-Hei led them through the ornate gates and down a cloister. They passed several other nuns along the way.

They all have eyes like mine, thought Draeger and for the first time in his entire life, didn't feel self-conscious of his own strange eyes.

The melodious sound of chanting of evening pujas filled the air as they walked down the covered walkway with its hanging jasmine, white and glowing in the evening light. For a brief moment, their scent transported Draeger back to his childhood. *Perhaps mother planted all that jasmine at the Red Palace to remind her of home.*

The walkway ended at a set of heavy doors. Here, Sister Chun-Hei stopped to pull a thin red thread hanging on the side. A faint chime sounded. Then, with a bow, the nun retreated, leaving the two of them there.

The doors open soundlessly. Tors led the way, taking them down same cavernous passageway, past its many statues and into a circular room.

Draeger blinked in wonder. Before him, stood an open-air atrium with a mirrored floor, littered with thousands of small butter lamps. They lit the place up, their flickering flames reflected and amplified by the floor, and in the middle of this dazzling lake of molten gold, sat the Empress. Draeger approached her and knelt.

"*Avia…,*" he called her. *Grandmother.* He looked up at her ancient face and her eyes, black and infinite, met his.

"*Nepos,*" she answered. *Grandson.* Then for a brief instant, her face shifted. Draeger blinked in disbelief.

Mother? For an instant, it was his mother's face that looked upon him. Then, in a flash, it was gone and once more the wizened face of the Empress gazed upon him.

"Son of Yinha," she continued, her voice, ancient and distant, "I feel her spirit in you." She looked frail but beneath that diminutive body, strength flowed from her, a formidable presence. "Come," she beckoned, gesturing at the cushions on the floor beside her, "Sit."

She smiled and turned to Tors, gently cupping her face in her hand before letting go. *I see you,* she greeted Tors. Something exchanged between the two women.

Draeger glanced sharply at the Empress. *Her voice...* It was much clearer and younger, with a melodic lilt to it, and it rang clearly in his head. *How is this possible?*

The Empress turned to face him, her face serene. *Yes,* she said directly into his mind. A ripple of amusement. *I am talking to both of you...*

Draeger sat down on a cushion.

Events have been taking place since your departure from Ageron, continued the Empress. She showed them images of swarming Avems and their bombing of a city.

Draeger sat up, dismayed. "Those are our Avems!" he exclaimed. "Is that Sansari? Is this currently happening?"

Sansari, Tors spoke up, her voice ringing as clearly as the Empress' in his head. *Is it... under attack?*

The Empress nodded gravely. *House Ageron has launched an attack on Sansari. Akseli has taken control of the Sansari Gate.*

Draeger jumped to his feet. "I must go back!"

The Empress lifted her hand in gentle remonstration. *Not yet, nepos—*

"I have to stop this," protested Draeger.

Zuqzwang, said the Empress. A hint of reproach. *In chess, it is the compulsion to move.* She touched his hand. *There will be time enough to do what needs to be done. But first...*

But first? asked Tors.

First, said the Empress brightly, *we have some tea.*

A nun came forth, bearing food and hot butter tea. Draeger sat back down.

"We were working in partnership with the Tilkoens to evacuate the Realm," Tors said, out loud this time. "What happened, Your Reverence?"

"Alin," muttered Draeger. "I should never have left."

The Empress sipped her tea. *Akseli is now Emperor.*

Draeger's heart sank. "And Rasmus…?"

The Empress stared at him, the depths of her eyes pitch black and indistinguishable. *A coup,* she answered. A tinge of sadness. *The Chancellor is dead. Murdered.*

"Murdered!" repeated Tors, shocked. "But is the Senate not doing anything about this? The Tilkoens? General Batsa… he would have done something about this."

The Empress shared more with them. Draeger shook his head as he saw it.

"So they voted Lord Patrin to replace Rasmus as Dictator." The cleverness of that move was not lost on him. "And they chose Patrin so no one, including the Tilkoens, would balk at the choice or suspect any foul play." He frowned. "But if Akseli had Patrin under his influence, there was a good chance he could have controlled the Senate anyway from behind the scenes. Why murder old Rasmus?"

He held your mother's secret. A wave of anguish. Another image, this time of a golden bracelet. Holding it was a young Emperor Mikael and Queen Alin in ceremony with a baby in her arms.

The naming ceremony, said the Empress, *of Akseli.*

Draeger drew in a sharp breath. "Akseli is Mikael and Alin's son? He is *Ellagrin*?"

The Empress nodded. *Your mother Yinha knew this* and *she*

used that knowledge to protect you. It has kept you alive growing up. Before she died, she left the bracelet with Rasmus. If Ageronians found this out, Akseli could lose all claim to the throne. She sighed. *Now that Alin has it back, her secret is safe. There is nothing left to hold her or her son back.*

Draeger rotated his tea cup in the palm of his hand, thinking. He was a soldier after all and strategy was often not far from his thoughts. "The Tilkoens have left their planetary system undefended," he said. "By concentrating on the demilitarisation of Ellagrin, most of their military is now in Ellagrin space, too far to get back to Tilkoen to defend it." He grimaced. "This was an opportunity too good to miss."

The Empress assented. *Akseli has sent troops through the Arnemetiaen Gateway to take Sansari. Sansari, the capital of Tilkoen.* The Empress considered a moment. *If Sansari falls...*

"House Tilkoen will fall," finished Tors.

The Empress nodded gravely. *Akseli will soon rule House Tilkoen.* Her ancient eyes regarded Draeger impassively. *And once Ellagrin is sufficiently weakened by the Tilkoen forces sent to demilitarise it, he will turn on Ellagrin.* She looked up into the night sky, her eyes equally black and fathomless, and told them: *Akseli is poised to rule the three most powerful Houses in the galaxy: Ageron, Tilkoen, Ellagrin.*

"Can't we stop him?" asked Tors.

The Empress paused. *Perhaps,* she said, *perhaps not. But that is not what matters most. Empires rise and fall. Civilisations merge and evolve. We foresaw all this... the different possibilities, different possible outcomes. For centuries, we have moved to influence them as best we can. However, the only thing that truly matters is not the survival of our dynasties. It is the survival of the billions of lives still in the Ageron system. We have to act despite Akseli's advantage. You have less time than you think—the binary suns will fail suddenly and spectacularly. We have foreseen that.*

The Empress's gaze flicked over to Tors. *Nehisi,* she said to her and only her, *I have not forgotten, Nehisi. You have brought him to me as promised and as promised, the debt is paid. You are free to go your way.* She sighed. *After all, it is only right—your people have served his for far too long.* The Empress smiled at her. It was like a warm kiss of sunshine. *But he needs you, Nehisi,* she said. *As capable as my grandson is, he cannot do this alone. But it is your choice, not his, not mine.*

I cannot promise anything, said Tors truthfully. *Only that I shall decide when we return to Ageron.*

The Empress nodded and sat back, regarding them serenely.

"I should have removed Akseli when I had the chance," said Draeger bitterly.

It is not Akseli that is behind all this, said the Empress. *This game started long before either of you were born. This started with the Queen Mother and must end with her. Now, it is time...*

"Time?" asked Draeger.

Time to finish what was started, said the Empress rising slowly. *The end game is nigh.*

ENJOYED THE BOOK?

If you've enjoyed *The Search for Sansari*, **please leave me a review**—I'd love to know what you think! And if you've loved reading this as much as I did writing it, spread the word!

Get the exciting finale *House of Yoon* today on Amazon.com!

The prologue of *House of Yoon*, the long awaited finale to this epic trilogy follows. Please note, the final version of the initial chapter may differ slightly from this version.

Join me online for release news, freebies and other exclusives at warwickeden.com

For limited time only, you can also get the prequel novella 'Emergence' (for free) from the website which tells about the origins of the Nehisi and how the very first Gateway came to be built!

HOUSE OF YOON

PROLOGUE

A soft chime sounded in the distance, indicating the hour of dawn had arrived. In the circular atrium of the throne room, the Empress Yoon, pregnant with her thirteenth child, looked up at the sky above and sighed.

Yin shi. The hour of the Tiger.

Dawn. The first few hints of pink had begun to appear.

Lightening streaks of day softly chase the receding dark of night...

The Empress paused to contemplate her next verse.

"Your Reverence..." The gentle singsong voice of Biyu, her eldest, brought the Empress's attention back to the discussion at hand. All around them on the mirrored floor where they sat, flickered a thousand butter lamps, their light gradually waning in the face of the encroaching daylight streaming in from above.

Empress Yoon looked around her. Her daughters were all sat at her feet in a circular fashion, around an empty space in the middle where their collective visions had been shared and discussed throughout the night. It looked the perfect picture of an intimate family gathering if not for the fact that each and everyone of them were identical, albeit at different stages of life.

"Yes, Biyu," said the Empress. Her eyes, dark and fathomless, looked into her daughter's, one pair the mirror image of the other. She turned to address her daughters, "To summarise what we have seen so far, it would appear that the suns Remus and Romulus will undoubtedly fail within this millennia."

Biyu nodded, agreeing. "Within the next five centuries, if we go by my vision of Emperor Ageron dying of old age as an indicator of the timeline."

"The dying of the twin suns, we agree, is inevitable," said Empress Yoon, looking at her daughters, "but the genocide and the war..." She trailed off with a heavy sigh. "What of your alternative vision, Yintai? The one you shared earlier, just before the hour of the Ox..."

Yintai, slightly younger than Biyu, spoke up. "Perhaps it could be avoided, your Reverence," she said. "Perhaps, if the Nehisi were very lucky and that possibility comes to fruition, then the massacre could be avoided. But even then, the plant... that plague." Her brows drew into a tremulous frown. "They may not survive it."

The Empress leant back in her seat. "Then, we must start to put our plans in place now. We must try to prevent the genocide or the war, or both if we can. Without the Nehisi and without the Gateways, billions will be trapped in Ageron when the suns fail."

"Mother, can *I* help save these people?" said a little voice. Niu, the youngest was but four.

The Empress smiled and patted her cheek affectionately. "We shall see, youngest daughter," she said, "but paradoxically, you are too old for this particular task I have in mind."

She turned to her other daughters and said, "We know

roughly when the war will begin, which means we need to introduce one of our own within the Houses now, in order to influence what is to come."

"Get our pieces in place," said Niu, tugging at the folds of her mother's robe, "just like that Old Earthian game we like to play, Mother…"

The Empress's smile widened. "Yes, Niu," she answered, impressed, "just like chess."

"It will be difficult with House Ellagrin," voiced Yanyu. Still within her twenties, Yanyu was as calm and analytically dispassionate as her older sisters Biyu and Yintai. "The Ellagrins prefer to breed amongst their own kind."

Yintai nodded. "That is true," she said. "Ellagrins are obsessed with preserving the purity of their lineage. It will be difficult to marry into their House."

"There is little opportunity to effect the future within the Ellagrin bloodlines," admitted the Empress. "We have to look to the Ageronians instead."

"Emperor Ageron II will sire a son a year from now," said Yintai. "It is almost certain—myself and Biyu foresaw the same thing."

"Yes," said the Empress, "That son will succeed him, not the others. It will be by marriage to this child then, if we are to act in time."

"A betrothal, your Reverence," said Biyu.

The Empress nodded.

"But with which one of us?" asked Yintai.

"Niu is the youngest…" suggested Yanyu.

"Me?" Niu perked up. "I can help now?"

The Empress bent to kiss her on the forehead. "No," she said, looking at Yanyu. "It may not be received favourably as Niu is fairly grown. And they may view her precocity with suspicious sentiment."

"Then...?" Yanyu looked at her mother's belly.

The Empress smiled and nodded. "Lady Arnemetiae is a good friend. We shall ask Emperor Ageron to be your sister's ward until she is old enough to marry their son."

Her daughters nodded.

"Very well," said the Empress, visibly tiring, "have we thought of everything?"

Biyu looked at her mother, then at her bump. "Our sister will no doubt face opposition within House Ageron. Ageron emperors have many consorts. There will be threats..."

The Empress Yoon nodded, agreeing. "That cannot be helped. However, I have every faith she will rise to meet these challenges." She caressed her belly. "She will know what to do, as would you if it were you in her place."

Her daughters assented. Their unborn sibling would think as they thought, do as they did. After all, they were all of the same.

"Now, have we thought of everything?" asked the Empress.

"Perhaps if we could see a little further," suggested Yintai, "just in case there is something we've missed..."

"Very well," said the Empress indulgently and beckoned Niu to come closer. Then, she placed her hands gently on either side of Niu's head. "Your turn, little one. Let's see what *you* see a little further down the timelines than your sisters," she said.

"You mean I can help now?" said Niu, wriggling excitedly.

The Empress nodded and laughed. "Yes, you can help," she said. "Your sisters and I are too old to see any further ahead than what we have, but perhaps you can..." She closed her eyes for a moment, then opened them again and looked towards the floor at the centre of where they sat. The mirrored surface began to cloud over again, and all twelve women turned their black, unseeing eyes towards the unfolding vision.

"The death of a green planet," pointed out Yintai, "…no, several green planets. All alike. They must belong to the same planetary system."

The vision continued, image after image, one blurring into the next, faster and faster with Niu not mature enough to control the torrent of them: disease on the green planets. A solitary dying tree, its trunk and branches winking out of existence. An elliptical Gate.

"The death of another planetary system after Ageron?" said Biyu in dismay.

"There are several possibilities to this one, daughters, none of which are dominant," the Empress said, looking intently. "Their course can be changed. That Gate…" She paused, recognising its distinctive shape. "That it is the Sansari Gate, which means the planetary system in question is Tilkoen."

Niu's vision morphed again.

"The maturing of a fourth species, your Reverence," continued Biyu. "A non-organic specie…"

The image faded and several more appeared, this time more clouded and even more incomprehensible. The Empress let her hands fall from Niu's temples.

"It is unclear," she said. "Too far ahead, too many possibilities clouding each vision." She sighed. "Never mind," she said. "We can't tell at this point what it is that may trigger that particular future for the Tilkoens, but whatever that threat is, I'm sure the Tilkoens will disconnect their Gate to prevent it from reaching them… as will we with ours. For now, it is the Ageronians who are at risk. We will act on the probable futures we have seen and hope that our actions to influence them will preserve those billions of lives."

She looked round at her daughters gathered around her. "It

is settled then.," said the Empress with finality. She hugged her pregnant belly. "Your sister goes to Ageron." There was a tinge of sadness in her words and Niu looked up at her mother, hands wrapped around her mother's belly with affection.

"Mother, what's her name?" she asked.

"Yinha," replied the Empress, looking down at her. "Your sister's name is Yinha."

GLOSSARY

A (ANNO AGERON): Old Earthian for 'Ageron year', abbreviated as AA. Used to refer to the years after the founding of the Ageron empire. For example, year 3424 AA was the year of the Great Massacre.

AGERONIANS: Of or relating to the indigenous peoples of the planetary system of Ageron. Tall, dark-haired, brown-eyed. Industrialists, merchants, entrepreneurs. Dynastic rule. God of worship: Dyaeus. Average lifespan: 300-400 years.

AGERON SYSTEM: Planetary system comprising twelve planets: Anavio, Bellun, Trimon, Amorgos, Segontia, Ilia, Olicana, Othon, Ceos, Deva, Vasa and Casar. Binary suns: Remus and Romulus. Ruled by House Ageron. Capital planet: Amorgos. Capital city: Alandia (former capital city: Lagentia)

. . .

ASGHARIANS: Of or relating to peoples of the Asghar tribe. Tall, dark, muscular, aggressive. Nomadic slave-traders. Average lifespan: 200-300 years. Believed to be indirectly responsible for the movement of Nchisi out of the Peregrinus sector and into the Ageron planetary system.

AVEMS: Ageronian starfighter ship. Extremely agile and manoeuvrable. Built to deliver massive firepower from the nose and wingtips, it is also equipped with hyperdrive, allowing for medium-range space travel as well as on-planet aerial combat.

BRIDGED TRAVEL: Method of travel through the Ether via gateways, negating need for interstellar travel. Founded by Emperor Ageron II, House Ageron. Prevalent throughout the known galaxy and catalyst to the golden Age of Prosperity.

CITY HALL: Government administration building for House Tilkoen. Located in the city of Sansari on planet Dharan, Tilkoen system.

ELLAGRINS: Of or relating to the indigenous peoples of the planetary system of Ellagrin. Tall, fair-skinned and fair-haired, Ellagrins generally have distinctive blue eyes. Agriculturists, biotechnologists. Dynastic rule. God of worship: Ysgarh. Average lifespan: 300-400 years.

. . .

ELLAGRIN SYSTEM: Planetary system comprising five planets: Toftir, Brekky, Dalr, Skansgarden, Kaldr. Ruled by House Ellagrin. Capital planet: Dalr. Capital city: Namsos (later moved to Summer Palace on planet Skansgarden)

ELDUR: Rare crystalline mineral, naturally occurring. Greatly sought after as an energy source for powering space-carriers.

ETHER: Transdimensional subspace between planets and interstellar systems, enabling transition from one place to another. Ability to manipulate the Ether by Nehisi tribe was a key factor in driving interstellar travel via gateways without resorting to interstellar flight.

GATE: Superstructure. Built by Tilkoens to maintain an endpoint of the Ether in its open state. Tilkoen technology. Primary material: solenite. Forms part of a Gateway: two Gates, one on each end, combine to make up a Gateway. Gates are named after the city they reside in. Main gates include:

- Lagentia Gate [location: planet Amorgos, Ageron system]
- Namsos Gate [location: planet Dalr, Ellagrin system]
- Arnemetiae Gate [location: planet Ilia, Ageron system]
- Sansari Gate [location: planet Dharan, Tilkoen system]
- Leodis Gate [location: planet Vasa, Ageron system]
- Huangshan Gate [location: planet Yoon]

GATEWAY: Superstructure. Transient passage or tunnel constructed across the Ether, connecting two endpoints (natural or effected). Based on Tilkoen technology and founded by the Ageron empire (circa 2980 AA), gateways are powered by natural Eldur to persist a physical tunnel comprising two endpoints opened up by Nehisi pathfinders, punctured through the Ether substrate. Main gateways connecting major planetary systems include:

- *Lagentian Gateway* [connects the Lagentia Gate to the Namsos Gate] ;
- *Arnemetiaen Gateway* [connects the Arnemetiae Gate to the Sansari Gate] ;
- *Leodis Gateway* [connects the Leodis Gate to Huangshan Gate]

Gateways are always named after their constituent gate on the Ageronian side.

HAUKS: Ellagrin starfighter ship. Built to counter the agile Avems, it is also equipped with hyperdrive, allowing for medium-range space travel as well as on-planet aerial combat.

NATURAL ENDPOINT: Thinner points within the Ether substrate. Naturally occurring apertures in the Ether leading to various locations. Gates were installed at natural endpoints to form the main gateways of the galaxy.

. . .

NEHISI: Of or relating to peoples of the Nehisi tribe. Origin unconfirmed but it is widely believed that the Taors displacement crisis may have led them to flee their home planet somewhere in the Peregrinus sector. The tribe was given sanctuary by House Ageron and later accepted and integrated into Ageronian society. Olive-skinned, dark-haired with green or blue eyes. Nehisi are the only peoples who have the ability to manipulate the Ether. Average lifespan: 300-400 years.

ORE: Standard currency used across known galaxy.

RED PALACE: Seat of power of House Ageron. Palace built into the Red Mountains of planet Amorgos, Ageron system. Accessible only by air.

ROYAL PALACE: Seat of power of House Ellagrin. Fortress in the capital city of Namsos, on planet Dalr, Ellagrin system.

SUMMER PALACE: Summer palace on planet Skansgarden, Ellagrin system. Favoured residence of empress Elena.

THE COMITIUM: Administration building and hub for House Ageron. Its main assembly hall where the Senate debates and votes is called The Ecclesia. Located in the capital city of Alandia, on planet Amorgos, Ageron system.

. . .

THE FORUM: Government building for House Tilkoen where the Tilkoen Congress debates and votes in its Congressional Hall. Located in the garden city of Chatadharam, on planet Dharan, Tilkoen system.

TILKOENS: Of or relating to the indigenous peoples of the planetary system of Tilkoen. Stocky, brawny, tanned and muscular, Tilkoens generally have angular features and brown or amber eyes. Technologists. Democratic and AI-led rule. Average lifespan: 200 years.

TILKOEN SYSTEM: Planetary system comprising six planets: Birgunj, Dharan, Itahari, Dankali, Pindeshor, Telkuwa. Ruled by House Tilkoen. Capital planet: Dharan. Capital city: Sansari.

YOON: Of or relating to the indigenous peoples of the planet Yoon. Little is known about the Yoons. Dark-eyed with features adapted to life in the snow-covered, high altitude mountains of the planet. Philosophers. Matriarchal society. Average lifespan: unconfirmed/unknown.

Printed in Great Britain
by Amazon